When I Was His

MJ Masucci

This book is a work of fiction. Any resemblance to actual persons, living or dead, or actual events is entirely coincidental. Although every precaution has been taken to verify the accuracy of the information contained herein, the author and publisher assume no responsibility for any errors or omissions. No liability is assumed for damages that may result from the use of information contained within.

ISBN 978-1-950175-59-8

Chapter 1

I can see the glint of the cold steel in the streetlights as the figure approaches. My father tells me to stay in my seat and steps from our SUV. No words are exchanged, and all I can process is a bang and a flash of fire as my father crumples to the ground. I'm left alone as the assailant retreats. A scream erupts from me.

"Ryleigh, wake the hell up."

My eyes shoot open and I'm staring up at my roommate of the past four years, Sadie Fulbright. She has her hand on my shoulder, and I can see the look of concern on her face.

"Shit, I'm sorry."

"You haven't had these this bad since your freshman year."

I sit up and wipe the sweat from my face with the collar of my t-shirt.

“I know. I don’t know why they came back.”

Sadie went back to her bed and plopped down, “Probably because of stress. You have a lot going on. We have a lot going on.”

She was right, we did. In a few days, we will graduate from Columbia University with degrees in business administration. We’d recently secured a small apartment in Chelsea and put the deposit down. It was all coming down at the same time. I had interviewed and was hired for a position in public relations.

Sadie would be working in the same building but for a marketing company. Our lives were changing. No more late nights staying up studying to maintain our B+ averages.

My mother and stepfather wanted me to come back home to Hudson Brook in Northern Westchester to live for a couple of years. I said no. Both my brothers moved out of the house when they graduated. I wanted to follow suit.

My mother had been married to Anders Stewart for almost fourteen years. She started dating him a year after my father was murdered. I was, in a few words, fucked up after I saw him get shot. My six-year-old brain couldn’t process what I’d seen, especially when I huddled near his bloody body on the deserted street. A car finally came by and stopped to call the police. It didn't matter, it was too late. My father was dead the minute the bullet entered his heart.

I didn't talk for almost eight months after the incident, and when I did, it was in the form of a scream. I went to therapy and was out of school for almost a year until I could deal with the trauma. I had nightmares for a while and was okay unless the stress was too much for me to handle. My subconscious usually manifested that stress by dragging up the most horrible memories of my life.

The first couple of weeks I lived with Sadie, I thought she would tell me she wanted to move out. The first night it happened, she freaked out and ran to get the RA. By the second week, she was used to my nocturnal disruptions. I calmed and rarely had them until I was stressed again.

"Why do you want to live with me?"

Sadie tucked her blonde behind her ears and fixed her smoke gray eyes on me.

"Because I love you. I don't want to live with anyone else and I need a roommate. I can't afford the rent in Manhattan. If we don't room together, I have to move back home."

I laughed because Sadie had younger brothers who were triplets. They were sixteen and drove her nuts.

"This should stop once we get settled. Graduation will be over soon enough," I said.

"Will your entire family be there?"

"My parents will, but Finley has some meeting with a venture capitalist and Matthew is not sure he can get out of work."

"Seriously? He freaking lives in the city. His boss can't give him a stinking couple of hours off?"

"He has a new job. His boss is an ass."

"Fucking traders. Greedy bastards is what they are."

"He's making good money."

"He doesn't need it."

It was true. Matt, Finley and I all had trust funds. My father started them when we were babies. When he died, we gained control of them on our twenty first birthdays. I could afford to live in a better apartment, but Sadie couldn't. She was proud and I didn't want to damage her pride by telling her I would pay seventy five percent of the rent. She wouldn't allow it and I didn't bother to ask.

"No, he doesn't but he wants to save it for his retirement."

Sadie snorted. "He's all of twenty-four. Why the hell does he need to worry about retirement now?"

Financial stability was important to not just my brother but all of us. Though my mother was secure after my father died, we all felt insecure without him. He handled most of the financials and investments.

I shrugged. "Anders is proud of him. It's what he's been preaching to us all these years."

"What about you? Are you splurging on anything?" she asked.

"Maybe some furniture."

Sadie bit her lip which I'd come to recognize as a coping mechanism.

I caught her gaze. "What?"

"You said we would wait until I had a couple of paychecks under my belt."

"Why can't you just allow me to buy the furniture?"

"Because it's our place and I want to split the cost."

I chuckled. "You're a pain in the ass."

"But you love me. Let's go back to sleep."

She slid under the covers and turned out the light above her head, leaving me in darkness. I leaned back against my pillows and looked at the ceiling. I couldn't sleep after the nightmare. It was just after 4 am and we had nothing going on for the day. I decided to grab my phone and text Ty.

Tyler Barnes was my next-door neighbor when I was growing up. He was twenty-five and a detective for the NYPD. He'd been with the department for almost five years. It was obvious Ty still had a crush on me, but I wasn't interested, at least that's what I told him. We were only three years apart, discussed it and decided it was better to be friends.

He often visited me at my dorm on his days off, and we'd go to the park or have lunch. He usually worked the night shift, and I texted him to see what he was up to.

What are you doing tonight?

Working on some paperwork. What's up? You're awake early.

Had a nightmare.

Ty was well aware of my nightmares. We shared a tent several times when our parents took us camping and I woke everyone up with my screams. It was probably because Ty told me bears came around at night and I was scared. My phone vibrated with his call, and I went out into the hallway, answering just as I got to the lounge.

"You had a nightmare? I thought you were over those?" he said with concern in his voice.

"I still have them occasionally."

"I wanted to talk to you about something."

Ty's voice sounded serious, and I braced myself for what he had to say.

"Tell me."

"I pulled your father's file."

My chest felt heavy at his words. My father's murder was never solved and had become a cold case, and I wasn't able to provide much information since I didn't remember anything. What I'd never told anyone was that I had seen the man's face.

In my nightmares, I always try to see it again, but his image never crosses my vision. It's frustrating but after all these years, it probably wouldn't make a difference.

"Why are you dredging up the past?" I squeaked.

The last thing I wanted was to bring this to the forefront. My mother and brothers were settled and pulling it back to the surface could cause problems.

"Because it's an open case. A lot of detectives work on cold cases in their spare time."

"But why my father's?"

He lowered his voice, trying to soothe me. "Because I knew him, and I want to see justice done. Don't you?"

Tension was tight in my neck. "I do, but it hits so close to home."

"Ryleigh, I would never hurt you or your family, you know that."

"I know. It just hurts."

"I would be surprised if you said it didn't any longer. Your father deserves justice. He was a good man."

Tears threatened. I had to agree that he was a good man. He took care of all of us and didn't deserve what happened to him.

"I miss him," I sniffled.

"I know. You can always talk to me if you need a friend."

"Thank you."

Ty had been one of the few people I could talk to about how I felt. I knew how sensitive the issue of my father's murder was to my family, and I kept my feelings to myself. After sixteen years, I still had many questions.

"Did you discover anything?" I asked eagerly.

"I just pulled the file a couple of days ago. There's a lot of paperwork to go through."

"Would you tell me if you did?"

"Of course. You're an adult now."

"Can you tell that to my parents?"

Ty chuckled, "What now?"

"They want me to return to Hudson Brook after I graduate."

"But you already secured an apartment."

"I know. I did it without telling them because if I didn't, they would work on me until I gave in. Finley and Matthew moved out after they graduated. I want to do the same."

"How are they, by the way? I haven't talked to either one of them in a few weeks."

"Matthew is busy with his new job. He's making gobs of money in his new position. Sadie's calling him a greedy bastard."

"He's not greedy, he's smart. What about Finley?"

"Still begging the VCs for money. He's missing my graduation to hold out his bowl for more porridge."

Finley had been chugging along for the past year and a half, working on his software start-up. Now, it had several employees and a small office in midtown; as his applications gained traction and more seed money came in, so did the limitations of his time. He was a classic workaholic, just like my father.

"Sounds like Finley. He could always be found in the computer lab in high school on his off hours and after school. I guess it worked out. Why did he bother to go to college?"

"I have no idea. Probably to find employees. It's like a nerd factory over there." I sighed, remembering the last time I went to his office. "I hate visiting—they all look at me like they've never seen a woman before."

Ty laughed, "It's not that. It's because you're gorgeous."

I ground my teeth because even though Ty and I had decided to be friends, it bothered me when he said things like this. I knew he wanted more, but I couldn't give myself to him.

It wasn't his looks that turned me off; he was very handsome, with his thick chestnut hair and cornflower blue eyes. It was his career. I never wanted to face what I did when I was six. If we got involved, I would always worry that two officers would show up at my door telling me Ty was dead. I couldn't take it again.

"Stop embarrassing me. I'm sure it's not that at all."

"You don't give yourself enough credit. Are you dating?"

"Not really. I haven't found anyone I want to get involved with."

I did, but after my last boyfriend got the word out that I occasionally suffered from nightmares, guys stopped approaching me. It was ridiculous, but soon I would be out of college, and a whole new pool of men would open up. I yawned into the receiver.

He laughed. "Oh? Am I keeping you awake?"

I yawned again. "I only got four hours of sleep so far."

"Then what the hell are you calling me for? Go back to sleep," he chastised.

"How do you stay awake all night?"

"After three years, I'm used to it. It doesn't bother me."

I couldn't stay up all night. I didn't know how Ty got used to those crazy hours.

"But you sleep the day away. Doesn't that get to you? Everyone is awake while you're slumbering?"

"First off, I get out of here at seven. I'm in bed by eight and up by one. I have several hours to go before I have to be on shift again. It gives me plenty of time to enjoy the day."

I changed my voice to sound like Dracula. "Still, you're like a vampire."

He mimicked me. "Then I'll be sure to latch onto your lovely neck with my fangs next time I see you."

Again, I felt the warm heat of embarrassment on my face. I yawned again and segued into telling him goodbye.

"I'll see you sometime this week."

"I'll see you at graduation," he said.

"How?"

Tickets were limited per student, and Ty didn't know anyone else who was graduating.

"I'm running plainclothes security. Can't be too careful these days."

"Oh. Well, I'll see you on Wednesday then."

"Can't wait. Talk to you later."

"Goodbye."

We hung up the phone at the same time, and I put my head down on the arm of the rust-colored couch I was sitting on.

"Ryleigh, wake up."

My eyes fluttered open, and I picked my head up to see my next-door neighbor, Laura, standing next to the couch. She was wearing a short pink satin robe and carrying a white shower caddy with all her bath products inside.

I winced as I sat up. "Shit, I fell asleep here. My neck is killing me."

"When?"

I yawned. "Maybe 4:30."

"Did you have a fight with Sadie?" she asked.

"No, just a nightmare. I'm surprised you didn't hear it. I came out here to talk to Ty."

She quirked an eyebrow. "Ty. How is Mr. Hottie?"

Laura had a crush on my childhood friend, but Tyler wasn't interested. She came on to him several times, but he rebuffed her advances.

I scowled, "He's fine."

"He - is - fine. You're out of your mind. The man practically throws himself at you, and you still don't want to date him."

I could hear longing in her voice. She wanted him even though he didn't want her.

"Dating Ty would be like dating my brother."

"Send him my way."

"He'll be at graduation. He has security detail."

"I'll be sure to look for him."

"What about David?"

She shrugged. "It fizzled. He has to move back to Delaware after graduation. Long distance relationships aren't my thing."

Laura's family lived in Manhattan,, and she would be moving back with her parents, who had an apartment in Midtown. I was glad because I considered her a good friend. It was nice to have people you know living in the same city as you.

"I know what you mean."

She turned to leave. "I must get in the shower. My parents are meeting me for lunch at The Wyatt today. You want to come?"

I yawned again. "I'm wiped. I think I'll spend another couple of hours in bed."

Laura walked away as I rose from the couch, pulling my t-shirt over my panties. This was a coed dorm, and though some of the women and men felt comfortable strolling around in their underwear, I did not. I hurried down the hall to my room. Sadie was still sleeping as I locked the door and slid into bed.

Two hours later, I was awakened by my phone. It was nearing 10 a.m., and I grabbed it from the small shelf next to the bed, where I had dropped it when I came back to the room.

I wiped sleep from my heavy eyes as I answered. “Hi, Mom.”

“How are you?”

I turned onto my back. “Good. Just waiting for graduation.”

“Are you packed?”

“Most of my stuff is at the apartment already.”

My mother sighed loudly. The apartment and living in Manhattan remained a point of contention between us.

“Are you sure I can’t talk you into moving home?” she whined.

I frowned. “Why are you so intent on me moving back home?”

“It’s lonely here. Anders has been working late the past few weeks.”

I turned to my side. “But he won’t forever. You know him.”

“I do, but I would love to have at least one of my children home.”

“Have another baby,” I mumbled.

My mother could since she was in her forties. She tried with Anders, but it never happened. He adopted me and my brothers a few months after they married.

Her voice grew harsh. “Excuse me?”

“Nothing,” I said quickly. “I want to live in Manhattan. You don’t get on Finley or Matthew’s asses about coming home. Why me?”

“You’re my only daughter. Don’t you want to share some girl time?” she reasoned.

“You have tons of friends. You can have girl time with them.”

“They’re not my daughter.”

Sadie muttered something in her sleep, and I pulled the quilt over my head and lowered my voice.

I grunted. “No, Mom. I’m not having this conversation again. I want to stay in the city, and that’s final.”

She exhaled loudly into the receiver. “Don’t fault me for wanting to spend time with you.”

I knew what she was doing. She was trying to guilt me

into coming home and living, but that wouldn't happen. Four years of freedom, and I wasn't willing to give it up.

"Then come to the city to have lunch with me," I compromised.

"I can't. I have tennis lessons at the club at noon, then lunch with Lila Van Pelton."

"See, you're busy. You don't need me."

Sadie pulled her pillow over her head and groaned.

"Mom, I have to go. Sadie and I have a thing."

She snorted. "Jesus, Ryleigh, you can't even make up a good lie?"

"We do!" I protested.

"Fine. Go do your *thing,* and I'll talk to you later. I love you."

"Love you, too."

I swiped the end button before she thought of something else to say, shoving off the quilt. Sadie peeked out from under her pillow.

"What did she want now?"

My best friend was well aware of my mother's manipulations to get me to move home.

"Same old shit. I don't know how many more times we have to go through this. I'm staying in Manhattan. Sorry, I woke you up."

Sadie sat up. “We should get up anyway. Where were you this morning?”

“I couldn’t sleep, so I called Ty. Laura woke me up in the lounge.”

She wrinkled her nose. “Eww, you fell asleep on the make-out couch?”

I threw my stuffed tiger at her, “Big deal. It’s no worse than falling asleep on the carpet in there.”

I was referring to a few weeks ago when Sadie drank a few too many and passed out in the lounge. She was too heavy for me to drag down the hall, so I gave up, leaving her there.

She smirked, “If you were a good roommate, you would have rounded up the masses and had them carry me to our room.”

I chuckled. “I know, I suck as a roommate. Still want to live with me?”

“We signed a lease. I have no choice now.”

“I hate you.”

“I love you.”

She threw the tiger back at me and slung her legs over the side of the bed. I couldn’t believe we would be out of here for good in a few days. Four years had passed so quickly. In two weeks, I would start my new job, and I was damn nervous but excited for the future.

Chapter 2

“When is this going to be over?” I whispered to Sadie.

“We have the guest speaker, then receive our diplomas. What’s your problem?” she hissed.

“I’m tired. We shouldn’t have gone out last night.”

For the past hour, we'd been seated, enduring the class speakers' presentations. Personally, I was eager for it to end. Last night's indulgence in too many beers left me with a nagging headache behind my eyes. I regretted not taking an aspirin before leaving the dorm.

Shifting in my chair, I attempted to find a more comfortable position, crossing my legs to alleviate some discomfort. Sadie nudged me as I stifled a yawn, the grogginess setting in. I gazed down at the floor until Sadie's soft curse caught my attention as they announced the guest speaker.

“Oh, my fucking God,” she muttered.

As my eyes lifted, they locked onto the captivating figure striding confidently towards the lectern, commanding the stage with an effortless grace. A soft gasp escaped my lips, caught in a trance by his magnetic presence. His allure was undeniable, a symphony of rugged charm and refinement.

In a heartbeat, my mind wandered to forbidden fantasies, imagining the sensation of his touch and the whispered promises that lingered in the air. His sandy brown hair, meticulously styled fade, beckoned my fingers to trace their path through its thick strands.

Clad in a charcoal suit that accentuated every sinew of his sculpted physique, he stood as a vision of masculine perfection. The fabric hugged his form, hinting at the power and strength concealed beneath its tailored lines. Around me, I sensed a collective awe, as if time itself had paused to admire Oliver Fox.

His words wove a spell as he began to speak, casting us all under hypnotic sway. His voice, smooth as honey, enveloped the room with each syllable, stirring a longing within me. My pulse quickened, my skin tingling with a feverish heat as I hung on to every intoxicating inflection. As his tongue darted out to moisten his inviting lips, I felt a surge of desire, a primal urge to surrender to the irresistible allure of this enigmatic man.

In the presence of Oliver Fox, my imagination danced with tantalizing possibilities, each moment a whispered invitation into a world I knew I might never enter. His reputation preceded him, a man of influence whose ventures spanned the breadth of the city, country, and beyond. His trajectory was impressive from a real estate tycoon to a diverse portfolio.

I hung on to his every syllable, drawn into a realm where the boundaries between aspiration and reality blurred. As the time arrived to claim our hard-earned diplomas, I found myself on the brink of encountering the elusive Mr. Fox himself, poised to hand us our tickets to the future.

With each step toward the stage, anticipation swirled within me, mingling with a fluttering of nerves. His proximity ignited a symphony of sensations, making each movement toward the platform an act of delicate balance.

As I drew closer, I couldn't help but be captivated by the depths of his gaze, pools of blue reminiscent of precious sapphires. Even his lashes seemed to hold a secret allure, framing eyes that spoke volumes without uttering a word.

Oliver's smile, a beacon of warmth and charm, welcomed me as I approached, a gesture that bridged the divide between admiration and reality. In that fleeting moment, as our hands met in a handshake, his hand soft and warm, gently closing over my cool and clammy one.

“Miss Stewart, congratulations.”

“Tha - thank you, Mr. Fox,” I stuttered.

“I wish you good luck.”

As Oliver Fox released my hand with a nod, I found myself drifting back to my seat in a haze, my mind swirling with lingering impressions of his presence. I was grappling with a sense of bewilderment as if I had just glimpsed a deity walking amongst mortals.

After graduation, refreshments were served, and we found ourselves surrounded by family and friends, sipping sparkling cider amidst a flurry of photographs. Among the familiar faces, Laura Layton and several other classmates joined our group.

"Congratulations," Ty's voice broke through the chatter, and I turned to find him behind me, dressed sharply in a black suit and white shirt. His discomfort with the formal attire was evident, a departure from his usual slacks and sports jacket. I embraced him, feeling the warmth of his affection as he pressed a gentle kiss to my cheek.

"Thank you," I replied softly, meeting his gaze.

"You look wonderful," he murmured.

I smirked. "As do you. Going all out with the full suit?"

"Only the best for special occasions," he quipped, releasing me and exchanging pleasantries with my family before slipping away into the crowd.

"He's so in love with you," Sadie whispered into my ear as Ty disappeared from view.

"Stop it. He's just a good friend," I protested, though a flicker of uncertainty danced in my mind.

"He wants to be more than friends," Sadie insisted, her tone tinged with conviction.

“He does not,” I shot back.

But he did. Ty made it clear several times that he wanted to be more than friends, but I felt no chemistry with him.

“What are you two talking about,” my mother asked.

I quickly segued from our conversation about Ty. “How my lame brothers didn’t bother to come to my graduation.”

“Matthew was here to see you get your diploma, and Finley saw you via Facetime.”

I raised my eyebrows, “Really?” I almost squealed.

“Yes. Matthew had a client meeting so he couldn’t stay, and you know Finley is in California.”

I felt warmth in my chest that my brothers took the time to see me graduate. They were both wrapped up in their own careers, Finley especially since he was building his tech company.

“At least they took the time.”

“Make sure you call to thank them,” my mother said.

I raised my eyebrows. "For what?"

"You'll see."

I frowned and was about to question my mother until she turned to talk to Laura's mother.

"What was that supposed to mean?" Sadie asked.

I shrugged. "I have no idea."

After pictures and the reception, we went out to lunch with our parents. By the time we got back to our apartment, it was well after 3 p.m., and we were exhausted. All I wanted to do was plop down on my bed and take a nap. Our apartment was in a door-manned building with sunny exposure, and my parents insisted we lived in a good area.

I knew the rent would be tight with Sadie's budget, but her parents agreed they would feel more comfortable if we lived there. The Fulbright family didn't have much money, but they gave Sadie whatever they could to help her out. They wouldn't have to if she would stop being so stubborn and let me pay a bigger portion of the rent.

We took the elevator to the fifteenth floor, and I waited for Sadie to open the door. She halted, stopping short, which caused me to bump into her and almost knock her down.

"What gives?" I asked.

"What the fuck!"

I looked over her shoulder and saw that our living room had been fully furnished with a large beige sectional, two dark wood end tables with white ceramic lamps, a matching coffee table, and a large multicolored area rug. On the wall hung a big flatscreen television, and below it was a console made of the same type of wood as the coffee and end tables.

"Holy shit, this must be what my mother meant. My brothers bought us living room furniture for a graduation gift."

Sadie narrowed her eyes. "Are you sure you didn't have something to do with this?"

I shook my head. "Absolutely not. I knew you wanted to help pay for the furniture."

"I didn't want to *help* pay for it; I wanted to pay half."

"Well, we don't need to worry about it. I wonder how they orchestrated this?"

Sadie wandered over to the coffee table and scooped up the thick white envelope that sat there. She slipped her finger under and pulled out the card. Inside were two five-hundred-dollar visa gift cards and a note from my brothers. The handwriting looked like Matthew's.

Ryleigh and Sadie,

. . .

Congratulations on your graduation. Please accept this gift for your first new home; you both deserve it. We're very proud of you. The gift cards are for art or whatever you need for your apartment. The world is waiting for you. Good luck.

Love,

Matthew and Finley

Sadie sniffled and wiped her eyes as she read the card.

"Are you crying?" I asked with a smile.

"It's sweet. My brothers couldn't even bother to come."

"That's because we only got four tickets apiece. It wouldn't be fair to take two brothers and not the other. Your parents were there, and that's all that counts."

"I guess."

"Did you really want your brothers there?"

She giggled, "Maybe for a second. They're already fighting over who will get my room. I'm not even out of the house for two seconds yet."

"Be glad you didn't have to move back there."

"I am. We should call your brothers."

I agreed. I never would've expected my brothers to give us such an expensive gift. Matthew could more than afford it, but Finley was pouring his profits back into his business and needed every penny.

"I'll send Finley a text. There's no way of knowing where he is right now. He might be in a meeting."

I typed out a heartfelt text to Finley and called Matthew as Sadie headed to her bedroom to change her clothes.

"There's the graduate. How does it feel?" Matthew asked as soon as he picked up.

"Great. Thank you for coming to my graduation. I knew you were busy."

"Cut the crap. You knew I would be there. Anything else you want to say?"

"Smug bastard. Thank you for the furniture and gift cards. You didn't need to do that."

"I think we did. We had this discussion."

Matthew and I had lunch a few weeks ago and I told him Sadie wanted to wait for her first few paychecks before we got living room furniture. He knew how I felt about having a big, empty room with nowhere to sit but our bedrooms.

"I love you, Matthew."

"I know you do. Remember that when I need a home-cooked meal or someone to watch Blackie."

Blackie was Matthew's French bulldog. I loved the little guy and had no qualms about babysitting if my brother had to go out of town. His apartment was on the Upper West Side, facing Central Park. Sadie and I stayed there several times, enjoying the terrace, rooftop deck, and building gym.

"I'll take him right now if you want to give him up."

He chuckled. "Hell, no. That's my buddy. I have a meeting with my boss in six minutes. We should get together for lunch this week."

"I'd like that. You're buying?"

"As always."

"Talk to you later."

He ended the call, and I went to my bedroom to change into shorts and a t-shirt. When I was down to my lavender lace underwear, I looked in the mirror over my dresser. My body was lean and slightly muscular, thanks to hours in the gym.

I pushed my mahogany hair over my shoulders and leaned in to look at my bloodshot hazel eyes. My headache had faded some, probably because I drank a gallon of water at lunch.

"You have abs."

I looked up to see Sadie leaning against the doorjamb. She had changed into tiny powder blue shorts and a matching tank top.

"Now I just need to keep it up. I have to figure out a schedule."

"Workout in the morning or evening?" Sadie asked.

I flexed my stomach in the mirror, seeing how my abs popped. They were nowhere near bodybuilder status but still respectable.

"I'm not sure. Maybe morning. My gym is only a few blocks away, but winter will be hard."

"So, you bundle up, and you're good to go."

I pulled on my shorts and t-shirt while Sadie plopped down on the new couch, stretching out.

She put her leg on top of the couch. "This is very comfortable."

"I hope so. I bet it cost enough."

I was willing to guess that Matthew picked out the design. He decorated his apartment on his own and had great taste. Without him, Finley's place would have wood boards on concrete blocks like a poor college student.

"Your brothers were very generous."

"Yes, they were. They just want us to be secure. What should we spend the gift cards on?"

I sat down next to her and grabbed the cards from the table.

"We need some linens and stuff for the kitchen."

"We have time until we start our new jobs. I guess we could go tomorrow and pick up some stuff from Macy's."

"Sounds good to me. Right now, I just want to relax."

"Want something to drink? We have champagne in the refrigerator."

Sadie stared at me and burst out laughing. "How could you possibly want to drink after last night?"

I shrugged. "We graduated. One glass of champagne isn't going to hurt."

"You had two glasses at lunch."

"My parents insisted."

That's not what happened. I thought a little hair of the dog would help the pounding headache that was still nagging by the time we got to lunch.

"They didn't have to pay," she protested.

"They wanted to. You need to stop thinking every time someone offers to pay for something, it's because they feel sorry for you," I huffed.

Sadie bolted up. "Why would you say something like that? You have no idea how it feels. I worked my ass off to get my scholarship to Columbia. No one handed me anything."

I glared at her. "Does that mean that I did get handed something? I didn't ask for my father to get murdered. I would gladly return my trust fund if I could have him back."

I stalked off to my bedroom and slammed the door. I wanted to start off living in our new home on a good note, but this wasn't it. I crawled onto my bed and buried my head in my pillow. A minute later, I heard my door open and the mattress dip with the weight of Sadie.

She put her hand on my arm. "I'm sorry. I didn't mean to upset you."

I turned over to look at her. "Neither did I. I don't want to fight with you. We're roommates and best friends."

She smiled. "I know. I don't know why I'm so sensitive about the money thing."

I caught her gaze. "You've always been. It doesn't mean anything."

She looked away. I felt horrible that she had to struggle, but her father didn't make as much money as Anders. Throughout college, I always tried to buy things for our room and pay for meals while being sensitive to her feelings.

"When you don't have it, it does."

"Let's stop talking about this before we have another argument."

"Deal. Let's have some champagne and take it easy."

She got off my bed, and I followed her to the living room. I was already in love with the couch. It was comfortable and I arranged myself on the chaise while Sadie opened the bottle of champagne. We toasted to our graduation and the good times ahead. We talked briefly until we both dozed off, waking up when the sun started sinking in the sky.

"Do you want to share a pizza with me?" I asked.

"Sounds good. Can we get mushrooms on it?"

I wrinkled my nose since mushrooms weren't my favorite, but I compromised.

"Only half."

"I'll call it into Lou's down the street. They deliver. I'm paying," she said.

I frowned but let it go. After security, rent, and filling the refrigerator with food, I knew Sadie had little left of her contingency fund.

"Fine with me."

"Do you want to get a Caesar salad with it?"

"Nope, just the pizza. I'll go back to eating better tomorrow."

Sadie chuckled. "You mean after you eat leftover pizza for breakfast?"

I laughed. "Yeah, after that."

"Dammit, Ryleigh, wake up."

Sadie shook me out of another horrible nightmare. I was disoriented and sat up, squinting at the light from the hallway.

I exhaled loudly. "Fuck. I'm sorry."

"I guess I should've expected it."

It was stress. So many changes in such a short time. I should've expected it. When I was in sixth grade, our class went to some nature preserve for the weekend, and I woke up screaming. It was the change. I never went on a school trip again.

"I don't know how to stop," I said apologetically.

"You're like having a baby."

I bit my lip. "Was I screaming at the top of my lungs this time?"

"No. You were calling for your father. I waited to see if you would stop, but you got louder."

"I'm sorry," I said again.

She squeezed my shoulder. "Stop apologizing. I'm used to it. I understand."

"But you shouldn't have to deal with my nightmares. Maybe I should've moved home."

"Bullshit. This will pass like it always does. Another week or two, and you'll be fine."

She rose from my bed, and I looked at her retreating figure.

"Sadie, can you sleep with me?"

"Boy, that must have been a bad one."

At the beginning of freshman year, after Sadie discovered my nightmares and I told her the story of my father, she pushed her bed next to mine. Within a couple of weeks, the nightmares passed, and I was fine. Now, I needed her comfort again.

"Yeah. If it'll stop you from giving me a heart attack, I'll do it."

I smiled weakly and flipped the covers back on my bed so she could slip in on the other side.

~

Sadie and I spent the next few days getting our apartment into shape. We spent the gift cards on art for the walls, kitchen, and bathroom items. We roamed the neighborhood to familiarize ourselves with the s and shops. Luckily, our apartment had a washer-dryer combo, so we didn't need to use the laundromat around the corner.

The night before we started work, I had no appetite, even though we got my favorite sweet and sour chicken from the Chinese place on the corner. I picked at the food with my chopsticks.

“What’s the matter?” Sadie asked as she spooned up some pork fried rice onto her plate.

“I’m nervous.”

“Just picture them in their underwear.”

“How would that help? You’ve been watching too many Brady Bunch reruns.”

“It’ll help calm you.”

“No, it won’t. I just need to get over first-day jitters.”

“Soon enough.” Sadie put her fork down and looked at me. “Does this mean I’m in for another nightmare tonight?”

I chewed on the inside of my cheek. “I hope not.”

After the second day of living in our new apartment, my nightmares had abated. I slept soundly through the night ever since.

“Me either. I don’t want to be exhausted for my first day.”

“You could always sleep in my room,” I said.

“Do you want me to?”

I shrugged. “Would you? I hate to inconvenience you.”

“It’s not an inconvenience. Your bed is comfortable. If it will stop you from having nightmares, I’ll do it.”

“Good, then it’s settled.”

I felt better and dipped a piece of my chicken into the tangy sauce it came with. We spent the rest of the night watching television and munching on popcorn we made with our new air popper.

I managed to avoid any nightmares with Sadie sleeping beside me, at least the kind that woke me with a scream. I had a small one that jarred me from sleep shortly before the alarm on my phone went off at 6 am.

This one had taken me to the point where I almost saw the murderer's face. It was so frustrating, not that it mattered. The trail for my father's killer had long gone cold. I doubted Ty would find any clues. Sadie popped out of bed as soon as the alarm sounded.

"Do you mind if I shower first?"

I yawned. "Go ahead. I'll make a pot of coffee."

"Thanks."

She grabbed her robe and padded out of my bedroom. A minute later, I heard the shower running in the hall bath. I pushed the covers off and went to the kitchen, hitting the button on the coffee maker to brew. I made sure to set it up the night before. By the time Sadie emerged from the steamy bathroom, the aroma of coffee filled the air.

I took my time in the shower, conditioning my hair twice and shaving my legs. I don't know why I bothered since I barely had stubble. I found Sadie sitting on the couch, drinking coffee from one of the large yellow polka-dot ceramic mugs we recently bought. She looked very professional in her black skirt, white blouse and black heels.

"You took a long time in there."

"I shaved."

"Oh. Get a move on. I want to leave for the subway by 7:15."

We both needed to be in the office by 8:30, but the ride on the train was only about fifteen minutes. I think Sadie wanted to familiarize herself with her surroundings before she went up to her office. She was on the tenth and I was on the fourteenth floor of the twenty-three floor building.

I hustled myself into the bedroom, pulling on a pair of light blue lace boy shorts and a matching bra. I decided not to fuss with my hair and put it in a tight ponytail before I put on the sapphire-colored dress I'd selected the night before. The clock was nearing 7 a.m., and I did a fast makeup job with mascara, a little blush, and lip gloss.

"What do you think?" I asked Sadie as I came out of my room.

"I like it. That dress looks good on you."

"Which shoes?"

"My nude heels. I think they would look fine."

"I agree. Get them on, and let's get out of here."

I went to get my purse, sliding on my shoes before leaving the bedroom. We were in the elevator when I groaned.

"What?" Sadie said.

"I forgot my travel mug. I didn't even drink any coffee. Did you remember to shut off the maker?"

Fuck. I was useless without coffee. I hoped I could get some before I went upstairs.

"Yes, as soon as I got a cup."

"Maybe I can get a cup from the small deli next to the office."

"Don't. You know how it makes you more nervous."

"I feel groggy."

She smirked as we exited our building. "That's surprising with the length of time you were in the shower."

"I need the power of caffeine."

"I'm surprised your adrenaline isn't spurring you on. You didn't have any nightmares last night; that's good."

I didn't bother to tell Sadie I had one. I would keep that information to myself.

"Yeah, I was good."

We hurried to the subway station several blocks away. It was a lovely late May morning with clear skies and a slightly warm breeze. I couldn't wait for the summer. I loved the heat and wearing as little clothing as possible. When we arrived, the train platform was crowded, and I knew we would be standing for the ride to midtown. It didn't bother me.

Chapter 3

My first day at Blaze Public Relations Inc. was spent as a get-me girl. Get me this and get me that. I might as well have been called a gopher because that was what I was doing. My boss, a sharp-nosed woman named Beatrice, was a joy with her mousy brown hair so tight in a bun. I wouldn't be surprised if it cut off blood circulation to her brain, was a bitch.

She barked out orders at me like I was a child. I could see that I might have made a mistake by accepting this position. When lunchtime came, I was grateful. My feet hurt, and I was sure a blister was starting on my left heel from running around.

"Rough day?"

I saw Beatrice's assistant, Candice, peering into my cubicle as I rubbed my foot. I'd liked her immediately when we were introduced this morning; she was maybe a few years older than me and had a pleasant demeanor, serving as a buffer to Beatrice's brashness.

"I'm figuring it out."

"It gets better, I promise. Want to get some lunch?"

"Yes. Thank you."

I followed Candice to the elevators as she pulled her golden blonde hair from a black clip at the back of her hair.

"That's so much better. I hate keeping my hair up, but it annoys Beatrice when it's loose."

I smiled. "I'm glad I put mine in a ponytail."

"Keep it that way; it makes life easier."

We stepped onto the elevator, which was almost empty, with just two businessmen looking at paperwork in a folder. They glanced at us as we entered the car.

"How do you like it so far?"

"I think I'd like it more if I actually did something other than make copies and get coffee."

"I was in your position a couple of years ago. Learn fast, and you'll be given more responsibility. I think it will be soon since you seem to be very intelligent."

I felt my face heat and looked down at my shoes, mumbling thanks. Flattery embarrassed me. Candice and I went next door to the crowded little deli. We waited in line while deciding what to get to eat. I wasn't hungry and stuck to a small salad and iced coffee.

"That's it for you?"

"I'm nervous."

She chuckled as she paid for her turkey wrap and iced tea at the cashier. We chatted during lunch until her phone chimed with a request from Beatrice.

"She bothers you during your lunch hour?" I asked.

"Sometimes. She rarely leaves the office for lunch. I have to get her something to eat. I'll see you upstairs."

It was time to go back anyway. I packed up my half-eaten salad and threw the remnants into the garbage. It had gotten warmer since I went inside this morning, and I wished I could stay out longer. If this is what the working world was, I think I'd rather be back in school.

"Ryleigh!" Beatrice bellowed.

I had just sat down at my desk to enter some information into the database when she practically screamed from two doors down. I jumped up to see what she wanted, poking my head into the chaos that was her office. Papers were on every free inch of her desk, a small round conference table in the corner, and stacked on the bookshelves behind her.

"Yes, Beatrice."

“I need lunch. Can you get me a green smoothie from the deli?”

I was surprised since Candice was the only one that got Beatrice lunch. Maybe after three days on the job, she trusted me more.

“Sure. Now?”

“Yes, now. See Aida for petty cash when you come back. And bring a receipt if you want to get reimbursed.”

“Yes, ma’am.”

She rolled her eyes. “Don’t call me ma’am. I’m not much older than you.”

That was a lie—Beatrice was nearing forty, which would make her almost old enough to be my mother. But I just nodded, hurrying from her office and stopping at my desk to grab the last twenty in my wallet. The hallway was empty when I went to the elevator to wait for the car to come down. When it did, and the doors opened, I couldn’t move because of the lone occupant inside. I stood there like a dummy.

“Are you getting on, Miss Stewart?”

Oliver Fox’s voice rolled over me like hot butter. He once again had me mesmerized with his beauty. Today, he wore a black suit, crisp lavender shirt, and purple tie. He looked so well put together. He folded The Wall Street Journal he was reading and stuck it under his arm.

“Well?”

"I—uh...."

The door started to close, and he hit the button on the panel to hold it open. I finally recovered and stepped inside, immediately hit with the scent of his cologne. That clean scent was perfect for him. I moved to the corner of the elevator as the door closed, and as it did, it dawned on me that he addressed me by my last name.

"How did you know my name?"

"I handed you your diploma, did I not?"

His sapphire eyes focused on my hazel ones with such intensity that I had to look away.

"Yes, but you handed many people their diplomas that day. You couldn't possibly remember my name."

He chuckled. "You underestimate my memory. Your name is Ryleigh Stewart, is it not?"

"Yes, but...."

He held his hand up to stop me. "I always remember faces, especially one as pretty as yours."

I could feel my heart pounding as he continued to speak. Why would this man remember someone like me? After graduation, I went on my laptop to search for images of Oliver Fox. I found him in several with gorgeous women in his arms, much prettier than me.

"Thank you for the compliment."

"It's well deserved."

Thankfully, the elevator dinged onto the main floor, the doors opened, and Oliver gestured me out when I didn't move. I moved and felt his hand on my back as we exited. He removed it and said goodbye to me. I stood there like a statue, watching him walk away. It was then that I realized I was aroused. My nipples were straining against my red lace bra, and down below, my panties were damp.

Jesus Christ, he was turning me on just by his very presence. I wondered what would happen if we spent time alone or he touched my bare flesh. Would I explode into flame? I fanned myself as I walked toward the glass doors of the building.

~

At the end of the day, I met Sadie on the sidewalk. We walked to the subway together.

"Guess who I met today?" I asked.

"Who? You're lucky to be working in PR. I bet you'll meet some celebrities."

"Oliver Fox."

Her eyes widened. "That gorgeous guy who spoke at our graduation?"

"Yes. Fox Asset Corporation is in my building. Can you believe that? He remembered me from graduation," I said excitedly.

"What did he say?"

"He called me Miss Stewart and then said my entire name. Why would he remember me at all?"

"You're hot," she said.

A man in front of us turned around and smiled at me. I frowned as if to tell him to mind his own business.

"See," Sadie whispered.

"Shut up. Let's get home. I need a shower."

We moved toward the subway station, hoping the air conditioning was working in the car. I was sweating by the time we got off the train. Even though the A/C was blowing at full force, the amount of people in the car made it feel warm. I was glad we only had one more day to go before the weekend.

When we walked in the door, I ran to the bathroom as Sadie pulled her key from the lock. She cursed at me and banged on the wall a few times as I let the cool spray cascade over my body.

She rushed in when I came out with a fluffy white towel wrapped around me. I could understand her need to rid her body of the clammy sweat that coated her skin. Later, we sat on the floor in the living room, eating day-old Thai food from white containers and talking about our day.

"I still can't believe you met Oliver Fox again."

I sighed. "He smelled so good. The entire elevator was filled with his cologne."

"Sounds like you have a bit of a crush."

I had more than a crush on Oliver Fox. He was like a God to me, untouchable. I couldn't match up to the women he dated, and I was so much younger. It would never happen, but a girl could dream.

"I do, but he's too old for me. I read an article that said he was thirty-six. It doesn't matter. You should see the beautiful women attached to his arm. I looked through dozens of images and didn't see the same woman twice. He must be quite a catch, and obviously, he doesn't want to be caught."

She cocked her head. "He's probably the type that will play the field until he's fifty and then finally get married. He's handsome, rich, and not desperate for companionship."

"Did you meet anyone interesting at your job?" I asked.

"There are a few guys that I might be interested in."

I caught her gaze, giving her my full attention. "Tell me."

"This one guy, Dan, is really nice. He's in the cubicle next to mine. I don't think he's dating anyone. I don't see pictures on his desk like with some of my coworkers."

I snorted. "That doesn't mean shit. Some guys don't display pictures of their significant others."

"Speaking of guys, have you heard from Ty?" she winked.

Everyone tried to push me Ty's way, but it would never happen. We grew up together, but I never felt anything for him other than brotherly love.

"No, why would you bring him up?"

"Because he still has a crush on you. I still think you're a fool for not dating him."

"Ty is like my brother."

"Just because he's a police officer doesn't mean he'll get hurt."

Sadie knew how I felt because of my father's death, but it was true about Ty being like my brother. We used to play together when we were little. He taught me to swim in his pool when I was four. My father was always busy with work and didn't have time. I would always be thankful for Ty.

"But he *could*, and I can't deal with that pain."

"Okay, suppose something happened to him now. Would you feel something?"

The question was ridiculous because I loved Tyler. He held a special place in my heart, and to lose him would be devastating.

I frowned. "Of course, I would. I love Ty. But I'd prefer not to think about it."

My phone rang, and I put down my fork to answer it.

“Speak of the devil,” I said as I swiped the green button on the screen.

“Hello, Ty.”

“Hello, stranger. How is your new job?”

“Okay. I like it.”

Sadie nudged me with her foot and made kissing noises. I gave her the dirtiest looks, but she only laughed.

“Would you like to have lunch this upcoming weekend?” he asked.

I smiled to myself. “Let me check my schedule. You know I’m so busy with all my events.”

Ty chuckled. “How about Saturday? I have the day off.”

“Won’t you be sleeping?”

I had no idea how he functioned, working nights and getting little sleep during the day.

“I get up at 1:00, but I could get up earlier if you want to go out at noon.”

“I could deal with a late lunch. I want you to get some sleep,” I said with concern.

“I’m fine. I almost always get up before one.”

“Where?”

There was a place we always met, so I had no idea why I was asking. It would be the same, and Ty would agree.

“Want to meet me at Iron Horse?”

“Yum, they have the best burgers.”

“Our place. How about 1:30?”

“Hold on a sec.”

I put my hand over the receiver and asked Sadie if she wanted to accompany me. She declined.

“1:30 is great. I’ll see you there.”

“Talk to you later. I have a few errands to run before I go to work.”

“Bye.”

I hung up and saw Sadie smirking at me.

“What?” I squeaked.

Her smirk became a wide smile. “Lunch with Ty?”

I snorted. “As friends. Stop reading into our relationship so much.”

“I think he’s perfect for you.”

I rolled my eyes as I dipped my Hoy Joh in plum sauce.

I was disappointed that I didn’t see Oliver Fox all day Friday until I walked out of the building to go home. He was sliding into a long black sedan driven by a muscular man in a gray uniform. I couldn't see his face behind the dark glass of the window as it pulled away.

That night, I had a wonderful dream of a man with sapphire eyes making love to me. I woke up feeling flustered, with a dull throbbing between my legs. It had been months since I'd dated anyone or had sex—maybe it was time. I stayed in bed until I heard Sadie get up. When I opened my bedroom door, she was banging around in the kitchen making coffee.

"How did you sleep?" she asked as I padded into the kitchen.

I shrugged. "Pretty good. I'm glad I have my first week under my belt. I feel better than I did last weekend."

"Told you it would pass."

"I have lunch today with Ty."

"I know. I still think you should proclaim your love for him."

I splashed her with water from the sink as I washed out a glass from the night before.

"There is no love other than brotherly."

"Are you two going dutch?"

I shrugged again. Tyler was the perfect guy, polite, respectful and decent, but he wasn't for me.

"Ty likes to pay even though I tell him no. He's very

gentlemanly. I think he'll make some woman very happy."

She waggled her eyebrows. "He pays, and he's a gentleman? Maybe I'll snap him up."

"You always pick jerks."

"But they're good in bed, so I can't complain."

Sadie was less picky about the guys she dated, and she didn't have hang-ups about sleeping with her dates by the third outing or earlier. I needed to feel comfortable before I got between the sheets with someone. It was possible if I felt an instant connection, that could change.

"Any prospects?"

"Not yet, though Dan asked me to lunch yesterday."

I wanted to sound excited, but Sadie forever searched for the guy who could care for her. I had a different attitude. I wanted independence.

"And you never said anything?" I screeched.

She shrugged. "There was nothing to tell. We had lunch and went back to work. He told me about his summer soccer games in Central Park. I might head over there to watch one of these Saturdays."

"That's nice."

"I guess. I'm unsure if he's boyfriend material as opposed to a good roll in bed a few times."

She took the words right out of my mouth. She tried too hard, and guys could smell the desperation.

"Be cautious. He's a colleague, and if things go south, it could get messy."

"I'm not planning on getting involved with him unless there's genuine chemistry and he's open to something casual," she replied with a hint of determination.

"Not interested in something more serious?" I probed.

"We're young, and this city is teeming with eligible bachelors. Why tie myself down?" she retorted confidently.

I couldn't help but feel differently. While the allure of freedom was there, I secretly longed for the stability of an exclusive relationship, though I kept that to myself.

"Fair enough," she conceded.

Grabbing a mug as the coffee finished brewing, I craved the caffeine kick despite a restful night's sleep. We lounged in the living room, surfing channels until I drained my cup and headed for a shower. With a lunch date scheduled with Ty at 1:30, punctuality was key.

Emerging from the bathroom, I pondered my wardrobe options, torn between a breezy sundress or a more casual ensemble. The Iron Horse had a laid-back vibe, and I sought Sadie's input.

"How about a summery dress with sandals?" she suggested.

"Really?" I questioned, unsure.

She appeared beside me, effortlessly selecting a floral sundress that grazed mid-thigh.

"Don't spoil it with a bra," she advised with a mischievous grin.

"I'm not sure I feel comfortable without one," I hesitated.

"Are you serious? Why not? This dress isn't see-through, and your figure is stunning," Sadie countered.

"I would feel naked," I confessed.

"This dress has a plunging back. What bra would you wear?" Sadie reasoned.

"I have the one with the cross straps around my waist," I offered.

Sadie shook her head. "Don't be ridiculous. Try this on without one."

I shrugged off her black silk robe, the familiarity between us making nudity a non-issue after years of friendship. Slipping into the dress, I adjusted the spaghetti straps.

"You look great. Check it out in the mirror," Sadie encouraged.

Walking over, I examined herself from different angles. The lack of a bra felt liberating, especially in the warm weather.

"I like it," I admitted, a smile creeping onto my lips.

Testing the fit, I bounced lightly on her heels, pleased with the lack of jiggling.

"I like it too. Wear your white sandals and leave your hair loose. Ty will love it," Sadie suggested.

"I'm not doing it for Ty. I'm doing it to feel comfortable," I clarified.

Sadie rolled her eyes. "Whatever."

"What are you doing today?" I inquired.

"Absolutely nothing. I want to sit around, watch television, and eat junk food. Maybe I'll call my parents," she replied.

"That's it?" I pressed.

"That's all. Enjoy your lunch with Ty. I'm taking a shower," Sadie declared, slipping out of the room.

As I leaned towards the mirror to apply some makeup, I opted for a light touch, given the heat. Leaving my hair cascading around my shoulders, I located my sandals. I paused just before reaching the door, realizing I had forgotten to put on panties. Chuckling to myself, I slipped on a pair of white lace boy shorts before heading out.

~

Arriving at The Iron Horse, I found Ty leaning casually against the building. His grin widened as I approached, enveloping me in a warm hug. I felt the soft press of his lips against my cheek, his nose buried in my hair as he held me close, his fingers tracing lightly over the bare skin of my back before releasing me.

"You look great," he complimented.

"So do you. I haven't seen you look this laid-back in ages," I observed.

He was wearing worn blue jeans with a frayed knee and a BattleAxe t-shirt from their recent tour. His hair seemed to have grown longer, brushing against the collar of his shirt. I ran my fingers through his locks before tugging gently at the back.

"You need a haircut," I remarked.

He smirked. "Haven't had the time."

I smoothed down his wavy hair. "I like it longer."

Ty raised an eyebrow. "Oh?"

"Yeah. You always get it cut so short. It looks better this way," I insisted, wrinkling my nose playfully.

"I'll take that under advisement," he replied with a playful grin.

"I'm starving. Let's head in," I declared, eager to satisfy my hunger.

The Iron Horse's exterior may have appeared nondescript with its darkened windows and weathered brick facade, but stepping inside revealed a cozy interior. Thick, dark wood tables and plush cushioned chairs created an inviting atmosphere adorned with vintage rock posters from Woodstock and Led Zeppelin, among other memorabilia.

Seated at a table against the far wall, the hostess handed us menus. I already knew what I wanted—a cheeseburger with gruyere, sautéed mushrooms, and waffle fries. Despite not typically being a beer drinker, the allure of a sweet microbrew called Sunday Sundae, with hints of chocolate and caramel, was too tempting to resist.

"What are you getting?" Ty inquired as she closed her menu.

"A cheeseburger," I confirmed.

"Let me guess, mushrooms and gruyere?" he teased.

"How did you know?" I chuckled.

"Seriously? I've known you for your entire life," he reminded me.

"What about you?" I prompted.

"Double grilled cheese with fried pickles and shoestring fries. They have a red stout I want to try. Are you getting a beer?" Ty questioned.

"Sunday, Sundae," I replied.

"Too sweet for me," he remarked.

Our conversation was interrupted by the arrival of a platinum blonde waitress, clad in the uniform of a black Iron Horse t-shirt and black jeans, ready to take our order. Once she left, Ty turned back to me with another question.

"How is everything?"

I shrugged. "Good. Work is good, and the apartment is good. I'm adjusting to everything."

He stared at me momentarily as if he was weighing the question he wanted to ask.

"Any nightmares?"

"Not really," I lied.

Ty was well aware of my nightmares. When we were kids, we camped out in my backyard in a big tent. I scared the shit out of him when I woke up screaming. He moved his sleeping bag next to me and held my hand for the rest of the night.

"That's good. I'm happy to hear it."

"How about you?"

"Things are good. I might be able to transition to the daytime."

I chuckled. "And give up your vampire tendencies?"

"I am not a vampire. I like being out at night," I protested.

"Exactly, you're a vampire. I should check you for fangs."

Ty sneered so I could see he didn't have the fangs I accused him of.

His eyes traveled over my clothing. "I like your dress."

"Thanks. It's very comfortable."

"It's cute. You're cute."

I felt my face heat and thanked God that the waitress came with our drinks. I took a long sip, letting the sweetness of the Sunday Sundae roll over my tongue. I had my eyes closed and Ty was staring at me when I opened them.

"I've never seen you enjoy beer so much."

"I hate most of it, but this stuff is delicious."

"Want to taste my stout?"

I wrinkled my nose, knowing his beer would be bitter, and shook my head. We chatted about things going on in our lives. Ty told me about a few of the cases he was working on, then paused. I waited because I knew his next words would be about my father.

"I reviewed our evidence for your father's case."

I raised my eyebrows. "The department still has it?"

"Of course. It's an open case. They wouldn't get rid of anything yet."

I feared him digging into my father's case and what he would ask of me. It took me months to try and put it behind me, but it was still there.

"I still think you're wasting your time. There wasn't much to go on back then."

He took a sip of his stout and licked the foam from his lips. "I wanted to ask you some questions."

I sighed loudly. "Is this why you wanted to take me to lunch?"

He shook his head. "No. Of course not. I would never. You're the only witness. The few cameras in the area didn't catch much because your father's SUV was out of range. Do you remember anything from that night?"

"No. Everything is shadow. I remember hearing the shot and crouching by my father's body."

I sniffled as tears welled in my eyes, picking up my napkin to dab at them. Ty reached across the table and gently stroked my arm.

"I'm sorry. I want justice, but I won't hurt you by doing it."

"I want this case solved. My father deserves it," I said tearfully.

"If you remember anything, will you tell me?" he asked hopefully.

"I'll tell you, but I don't. I want to see his face, but I can't. In my nightmares, it's just a blur."

"Did you ever try hypnosis?"

I shook my head. "No, I don't want to."

"It's your choice. I'm only asking because it might make you remember."

"What if I told you I don't want to remember? It's been sixteen years since it happened, and I'm still not free. Sometimes I feel trapped."

The waitress came to our table with the food, but my appetite had disappeared. Ty dug into his grilled cheese, taking a big bite but stopping in mid-chew as he looked at me.

"What's wrong?"

"I'm not hungry."

He swallowed what was in his mouth and put his grilled cheese back on his plate.

"Don't let it consume you. I won't ask again unless you offer."

I picked up a waffle fry and nibbled one corner until I finished it. Ty smiled as I took my butter knife and quartered my burger, a habit I had for years.

"Good."

We didn't speak about my father's case for the rest of lunch. I enjoyed spending time with Ty. It was like we were kids back in Hudson Brook again. He insisted on paying the bill even though I offered him money, and after that, we went out into the bright sunshine.

"Want to hang out for a while, or do you have something to do?" he asked.

“I can hang out for a bit.”

“Let’s go for a walk, then.”

He put his arm around my shoulders, and I thought nothing of it even though he caressed my bare arm with his fingers. We talked about memories from home and strolled the sidewalks full of those who were enjoying the warm May weather. An hour later, Ty was yawning continuously.

I chuckled. “Go home.”

“I’m fine.”

“You’re yawning like you’re ready to go to sleep.”

“I want to see your new apartment,” he said, ignoring my comment.

“I’m not sure.”

Ty raised his eyebrows. “You’re not sure? What am I, some jerk off the street?”

“NO! Sadie decided to do nothing today. She might not be ready for visitors.”

“Call her. We’re not far from your place.”

I fished my phone from my small purse and hit her contact number.

“What’s up?” Sadie said as she crunched on whatever was in her mouth.

I frowned. “What are you eating?”

“Pretzels.”

I stared at Ty, who shoved a mint in his mouth while I was talking. He gave me a warm smile.

“Ty wants to come by. Are you decent?”

“I’m certainly not naked. What exactly do you think I do when you’re not here?”

I ignored her snide comment. “Can I bring him over?”

“Yes. I’m dressed and sitting around watching some crappy eighties movie. What the hell did people do without cell phones and internet back then?”

“I have no idea. I’ll be home in a little while.”

Sadie took another bite of pretzel and chewed into the receiver.

“Bye,” she mumbled before she hung up.

I looked at Ty. “Let’s go.”

Chapter 4

I kicked off my sandals, the cool hardwood floor a welcome relief against my overheated feet. Depositing them in the closet, I hung my purse on the doorknob before returning to the living room. Ty's eyelids drooped, his breathing slowing as he drifted off to sleep, a soft snore escaping his lips. Sadie's mischievous giggle filled the room, adding a mysterious air to the scene.

We walked several blocks to my apartment building. I loved the heat, but I was uncomfortable and longed for the air conditioning. When I got upstairs, Sadie was lounging on the couch with the bag of pretzels between her legs. She threw them on the coffee table as we walked into the small entryway.

"Hey, Ty," Sadie greeted.

. . .

Ty crossed over to the couch, bending down to embrace Sadie. She shot me a sly glance before releasing him.

"You look like you're making yourself at home," Ty remarked, straightening up.

"Of course. Care to join me?" Sadie invited, patting the cushion beside her. Ty accepted the offer, sinking into the couch with a contented sigh.

I slipped off my sandals, relishing the release from the day's weight as I carried them into the dimly lit bedroom. The closet swallowed them whole, and I hung my purse on the doorknob, a silent sentinel guarding my belongings.

I kicked off my sandals and carried them to my bedroom, where I deposited them into the closet, hanging my purse on the doorknob. When I returned, Ty's eyelids drooped as he laid his head back on the couch. He was asleep in a minute, softly snoring. Sadie giggled.

"That was quick," Sadie remarked, her voice a whisper in the stillness.

"He only got a few hours of sleep before we met for lunch," I replied, my tone hushed, as if afraid to disturb the delicate balance of Ty's repose.

"Should we wake him up?" Sadie questioned, a hint of concern threading through her words.

"Leave him alone. We can hang out in my room," I suggested, my voice barely above a murmur.

Sadie rose from the couch with silent grace, the pretzel bag in hand crinkling as she placed it atop the refrigerator. We left Ty to slumber, retreating to my room.

"What did you talk about at lunch?" Sadie inquired, her voice a gentle prompt, probing but careful.

I toyed with a loose thread on my comforter, my gaze fixed upon it as if it held the answers to all my unspoken fears. "He asked me some questions about my father's murder."

"But you don't remember anything," Sadie stated, her voice a mix of sympathy and understanding.

I winced at the reminder, the ache of loss throbbing beneath the surface. "I know, but it upset me. I know he's trying to solve the case, but I don't want to discuss it. It hurts too much."

Sadie's hand found mine, a silent gesture of comfort. "I'm sorry," she murmured, her words a soothing balm against the raw edges of my grief.

"It's not your fault. It's not anybody's fault but the man that killed him," I replied, meeting her gaze for the first time, the weight of my sorrow heavy in the silence between us.

"Maybe the case will never be solved," Sadie offered, a tentative hope lacing her words.

"I hope not. Someone needs to pay for his death," I declared, the conviction in my voice a testament to the justice I sought.

Sensing my agitation, Sadie changed the subject, a subtle shift in focus to ease the tension that hung between us. "Dan called," she announced, her voice a welcome distraction from the darkness threatening to consume us both.

"From work?" I questioned, my curiosity piqued.

I wanted to shake my head at her. Sadie had a bad habit of jumping into relationships with both feet, and when they didn't work out, I had to pick up the pieces. But I couldn't say anything because I knew I should be a supportive friend.

“He wants to have brunch tomorrow,” she said excitedly.

“Did you say yes?”

“Of course. He's paying, and it's all the mimosas you can drink.”

“Is that the only reason you're going?” I questioned.

Sadie sawed her bottom lip with her teeth, smearing the light lipstick she wore. “That, and I'm curious about him. For all I know, he could be the one.”

I sighed. “You're not even twenty-two yet and want to get chained down? What happened to enjoying yourself?”

“Unless Matt plans to ask me to marry him, I'll have to find someone else.”

I frowned. “You haven’t even dated Matt. He can be a dick when he wants to be.”

“You say that because he’s your brother. I say the same thing about mine.”

I shrugged. “Forget Matt. He’ll break your heart.”

“Newsflash, Stewart, your brother is hot. Both of them are hot, but Matt is more my speed. Finley is sort of a nerd even though he’s a gorgeous nerd.”

“He’s married to his business right now anyway; I doubt he has time for women.”

“I bet he gets plenty to share his bed.”

I narrowed my eyes. “Gross. I don’t want to think about my brother sleeping with women.”

“What about sleeping with me?” Sadie asked.

I put my fingers in my ears and started to sing a song. Sadie loved to push the envelope when it came to sex. She started tickling me, and I had to take my fingers out of my ears to push her hands away.

“So what time is this brunch?”

“11 am at The Wyatt. They serve champagne brunch buffet.”

I arranged my pillows against the headboard and leaned back. Sadie averted her gaze because she knew I might chastise her.

I raised my eyebrows. “The Wyatt? That place is expensive. How much does Dan make?”

“His parents have money. They own a few restaurants and car dealerships in New Jersey.”

I frowned but didn’t comment about money. I know Sadie wanted a better life than she had growing up. She didn’t have what I did, but her parents loved her and tried to give her whatever they could afford.

“Does he drive a new car?”

“It makes no sense to drive in the city, you know that. He told me he has a BMW at his parent’s home.”

I heard Ty grumble and we both looked out the bedroom door to see him repositioning himself, so he was stretched out on the couch. We left him alone and let him sleep. I felt sorry for him with his schedule. I didn’t know how he did it each week.

“Ty seems happy.”

“As far as I know, he is.”

She caught my gaze, a look of knowing. “He would probably be happier if he could date you.”

“How would you know?” I asked.

“Because he loves you.”

“He has a crush on me. He doesn’t love me.”

I knew that wasn’t true because he did love me, and he was in love with me. But his love was unrequited. I would never feel anything more than sisterly love for Ty as much as he wanted it to be different.

"Keep telling yourself that. You never told me if you found any of the guys interesting at your office. Anyone you could see dating?"

"Not really. I don't know many people."

"Have you seen Oliver Fox?"

I thought back to my disappointment when I didn't see him all week. I think I had a case of puppy love or infatuation, but nothing would ever happen between us.

"Yesterday, when I was coming out of the building. He was getting in his car."

"Wouldn't it be crazy if he asked you out?"

I could see the wheels turning in her head. You would think she had a chance to date Oliver Fox.

I scowled. "Are you nuts? What would he want with me?"

She nudged my leg. "Why wouldn't he want you? You're young, smart, and beautiful."

I snorted, feeling uncomfortable. I always did when people talked about my looks. "Says you."

"So you're not young?"

"I'm smart but not beautiful. I guess I'm a little above average."

Sadie chuckled. "You're fucking kidding, right?"

"Not at all."

"Do you know how many guys wanted to date you at school?"

"I can't imagine since I haven't had a date in months."

She continued. "Plenty."

"Then why didn't they ask?"

"You would have to ask them."

I was curious about the droves of men who wanted to ask me out because none seemed interested.

"Like who?"

"Rick Chalian. He had a big case of the likes."

Rick was my lab partner in one of my business classes. Nothing told me that he wanted anything but a platonic relationship.

"He never acted on it. I think you're wrong."

"Believe what you want."

My cell began to ring. I hurried to retrieve it before it woke up Ty and saw it was Matt calling.

"Hi. Not working today?"

"I just got finished. What are you doing?"

"Nothing really. Ty is here with me and Sadie. He's sleeping."

"He should get a job that doesn't keep him out until all hours of the night."

I laughed. "Shut up, Matt. You work fifteen-hour days. You're not one to talk."

"I need you to take care of Blackie."

Blackie was my brother's French Bulldog and I loved that little dog besides, being at Matt's luxury apartment was like a spa day.

"For how long?"

"Until Wednesday. I have a client in Dallas I need to see."

"Can I bring Sadie?"

"Yeah, I expected you to with your nightma..."

Matt stopped talking and I waited for him to continue. When he didn't, I finished his sentence.

"Nightmares. I don't have them as much. Can we order food?" I asked, changing the subject.

"Do whatever you want but make sure to clean up Blackie's mess when you walk him, or you'll get fined."

I wrinkled my nose. I wasn't keen on cleaning up Blackie's poop, but it was a necessary evil.

"I know the drill. When are you leaving?"

"Tomorrow morning."

“I have to work. I won’t be able to walk Blackie during the day.”

“Don’t worry, I’ll ask the concierge to take care of it.”

“I’ll be there by noon.”

“Awesome. Thank you. I’ll bring you back something, Texas.”

“Like what? A steak?”

Matt laughed loudly into the receiver. “How about a whole cow?”

“As long as you keep it in your apartment.”

“I’ll talk to you when I get back. Love you.”

“Love you too. Have a safe trip.”

“Will do.”

I hung up the phone and saw Sadie’s face in the mirror; she was grinning from ear to ear while rubbing her hands together. She’d stayed with me at my brother’s place before. We had more space to move and two bathrooms.

“Matt is going away?” she asked.

I nodded. “Yes. He wants me to watch Blackie.”

She clasped her hands together. “I can’t wait. I’m ordering a black truffle burger for dinner.”

“He said we can order whatever we want.”

“I’m excited. Should I go pack?”

“We’re not going over until noon tomorrow.”

She pursed her lips. “Fuck. I have brunch with Dan. I won’t be home at noon.”

“Just pack your bag, and I’ll bring it over with me.”

“Works for me.”

She bounced up from my bed and went to her room. I could hear her drawers and closet door banging as she packed her clothes. Matt’s apartment was ten times the size of ours. It made me wonder if he got lonely living in such a big place with only Blackie to keep him company.

Matt's apartment was a mansion compared to ours, a sprawling oasis in the heart of the city. With ten times the space and amenities to match, it made me wonder if he ever felt a pang of loneliness in such a grand place, with only Blackie to keep him company.

The lavish residence boasted a large terrace overlooking Central Park, a luxury that seemed unimaginable in our modest surroundings. Three bedrooms ensured that Sadie and I could each have our own space, a rare indulgence in our cramped city living.

The floors gleamed with dark wood and light marble, a testament to Matt's impeccable taste. But the pièce de résistance was the wall of glass that framed the park, offering a breathtaking view of the lush greenery beyond.

Peeking out of my bedroom door, I observed Ty still nestled on the couch, his slumber undisturbed by the flurry of activity around him. It afforded me the opportunity to focus on the task at hand: packing my suitcase for tomorrow. As I folded clothes and gathered essentials, Ty began to stir, his awakening signaled by a resounding yawn that filled the room.

“Did you have a nice nap?” I asked.

“I’m sorry. I was exhausted.”

I exited my bedroom to sit near him, “We didn’t need to have lunch today. It could’ve been dinner, so you could sleep later.”

“I’m fine. Are you going somewhere?” he said as he gestured to my suitcase that I left outside my bedroom door.

“I’m spending a few nights at Matt’s place. I need to watch Blackie.”

“You’re leaving tonight?” Ty asked.

I shook my head. “No, tomorrow afternoon. He has to go to Texas.”

“Will you be all right in that big apartment by yourself?”

“She won’t be by herself,” Sadie said as she came out of her room.

“You’re going?”

“Of course. I’m not passing up the chance to sleep in that place.”

Sadie grabbed a soda from the refrigerator and returned to her room, leaving me alone with Ty. I heard her talking a minute later, which meant she was on the phone.

“What are you doing tonight?” Ty asked.

“Nothing, really. I’ll probably watch some television and order a pizza.”

“Pizza sounds good. You don’t have anything going on tonight?”

He smiled. “You ever feel so lazy that you don’t want to do anything? That’s how I feel right now. I just want to decompress for the rest of the day.”

“You can hang out here. What do you want to do?”

“Nothing. This couch is comfortable.” He moved over to the chaise and kicked off his shoes. “I’m sorry I had my shoes on your couch.”

I flicked my hand. “It’s fine. I’m sure you won’t be the last person to do it. Matt and Finley got us this couch. The whole living room was a graduation gift. They also gave us a couple of gift cards to get other stuff.”

“That was nice of them. How is Finley?”

“As busy as ever. You know him; he’s worse than Matt regarding work.”

“Your brothers are workaholics,” he stated.

I chuckled. “Look who’s talking?”

He bit his lip. “I want to apologize again for the thing at lunch. I didn’t mean to upset you.”

“It’s forgotten. I wish I could help.”

“I’m exploring a few things, but I can tell you about them later if they pan out.”

I sighed loudly and grabbed the remote from the table, switching on the large flatscreen television. I stretched out and had the top of my head against Ty’s thigh. He began to stroke my hair and I closed my eyes. If I had those feelings for him, I would go for it.

As I stirred from sleep, the apartment enveloped in the fading light of dusk, I found Ty still lost in slumber. With a groggy sigh, I sat up, rubbing the remnants of sleep from my eyes, my mind foggy with the remnants of dreams. Where was Sadie? My gaze wandered around the dimly lit room, searching for any sign of her presence.

A flash of yellow caught my eye, and I spotted a sticky note resting on the coffee table. I reached for it with a curious frown, unfolding the message scrawled in Sadie's familiar handwriting.

Hey sleepyhead,

. . .

Didn't want to wake you or Ty. Dan wanted to meet for drinks. I'll be back later. Have fun.

Love ya,

Sadie

It seemed it was just Ty and me for dinner then. Crumpling up the note, I gently shook Ty awake, his form stirring as consciousness slowly returned.

"Shit, did I fall asleep again?" Ty's voice was rough with sleep, his eyes blinking blearily as he took in his surroundings.

“So did I. Sadie isn’t here, so it’s just us for dinner. What do you want on your pizza? I’m starving.”

“Pepperoni and meatball.”

My mouth watered. “Mmm, that sounds good. Let me call Guiseppe’s around the corner. They deliver.”

“Where’s the bathroom?”

I pointed. “Down the hall, the middle door on the left.”

Ty rose from the couch with a lazy stretch, his yawn reverberating through the quiet apartment as he navigated the short hallway toward the bathroom. Seizing the opportunity, I quickly dialed the pizza place, placing an order while Ty was occupied.

By the time he emerged, rubbing the remnants of sleep from his eyes, the order was in. He reached for his wallet, and I intercepted him with a determined stance.

"You paid for lunch. This is my place, so I pay for dinner," I insisted firmly, my tone leaving no room for negotiation.

"I insist," Ty countered, his expression equally resolute.

"Tough. I'm paying," I declared, unwilling to back down.

Ty relented with a resigned sigh, and I slipped to my room to retrieve a twenty from my wallet. He was waiting in the doorway as I returned, his gaze sweeping over the surroundings of my room.

"Cute room. I like the comforter. You always did like blue," he remarked, a hint of nostalgia coloring his words.

My room was a sanctuary of varying shades of blue, a reflection of my lifelong affinity for the calming hue, though the walls remained white per the landlord's decree.

"Thanks. Mom helped me pick out the bedroom stuff," I replied, a fond smile tugging at the corners of my lips.

As I passed through the doorway, Ty followed me into the kitchen, his presence comforting.

"What do you want to drink?" I inquired, turning to face him.

"I don't suppose you have any red stout in there," Ty replied with a playful grin, his eyes dancing with mischief.

I wrinkled my nose. "Absolutely not. If you're a regular visitor, I might consider it," I teased in response.

"I'd like to be," Ty replied, his voice soft with sincerity.

I could feel the warmth of his body beside me as I reached for two water bottles, preparing to set them on the small breakfast bar. But before I could react, I found myself enveloped in Ty's embrace, the drinks slipping from my fingers to thud against the counter. His lips met mine in a tender kiss, igniting a spark of familiarity that danced between us.

For a moment, I hesitated, unsure of how to respond. But then I surrendered to the kiss, allowing myself to be swept away by the familiarity and warmth of Ty's touch. He was a great kisser, a fact I knew all too well from our shared history of adolescent experimentation.

He pulled me against him and stroked my partially bare back with his fingers. I was lost in the moment and ran my hands through his hair before I finally returned to reality and backed away.

Ty was apologetic. “I'm sorry. I really like you Ryleigh.”

I clenched my jaw. “We can't.”

“Tell me, why not?” he demanded.

“Because you’re like my brother. I’ve known you my entire life.”

“Then you just kissed your brother,” he said with a grin.

“That’s not funny.”

He clucked his tongue. “It’s kinda funny.”

“Just don’t do it again. I love you, Ty, but not in that way.”

I snatched one of the water bottles from the counter, opened it, and took a swig. My heart was pounding, and even though I’d just told Ty I didn’t think of him that way, I was aroused. I tried to ignore it as I got plates from the cabinet. The pizza arrived ten minutes later, and before I got off the lobby phone, Ty was out the door. I yelled at him when he got back.

“I wanted to pay. Take this,” I said as I thrust the money at him.

He put his hands up. “Nope. I’ll let you pay the next time we have lunch.”

“You better.”

As Ty set the pizza down on the small dining table, a chuckle escaped his lips, his easygoing demeanor diffusing the tension that had simmered between us moments before. With appetites whetted by anticipation, we dug into the cheesy slices with gusto, the savory flavors momentarily distracting us from our kiss.

Conversation flowed freely as we discussed our plans for the upcoming week, Ty tactfully sidestepping the sensitive topic of my father. His considerate gesture didn't go unnoticed, and a sense of gratitude welled within me, tempered by the lingering unease of our earlier kiss.

As the clock neared 10 p.m., Ty bid his farewell, pressing a chaste kiss to my cheek before disappearing into the night. Alone once more, I found myself grappling with the conflicting emotions that had stirred within me at his touch.

The unsettling realization lingered in the recesses of my mind: perhaps my body knew something that my heart was unwilling to acknowledge. But this was Ty, my steadfast confidant and unwavering support. I couldn't risk jeopardizing our friendship by entertaining romantic notions.

Sadie wasn't home when I went to sleep, and I prayed I wouldn't have a nightmare.

When I woke up, Sadie's door was closed. It was just after 9:30 a.m. and I knew she needed to be up to get ready for her brunch. I knocked on her door and heard mumbling from behind it.

"What?" she asked, her voice thick with sleep.

"Time to get up. Don't you have brunch with Dan at 11?"

"Shit, I forgot to set my alarm."

I opened her door as she sat up in bed. Her hair was a tangled mess, and clothing was strewn on the floor. I knew something happened last night while I slumbered away.

"Did you bring Dan back here?"

"For a while."

I raised an eyebrow. "Did you have sex?"

She gave me a sheepish look. "Not quite."

"What's not quite?"

"We did other things, and then I asked him to leave."

I shook my head. She was getting into the same pattern she always did, but I didn't want to get into an argument, so I let it go.

"I won't even ask. Do you like him?"

"He's really nice."

"Could you see yourself with him?"

She shrugged. "I think so, but I'm not deluding myself yet. He could be a jerk, and I just haven't found that part out yet."

I decided to change the subject. "Do you want coffee?"

"Yeah," she yawned. "What happened with Ty last night?"

My heart skipped a beat. “Happened? Nothing. We ordered pizza and watched television.”

“You’re a fool. That man is in love with you.”

I didn’t want to rehash this conversation. “I’m making coffee. Go shower.”

“Yes, Mom!” she called as I walked to the kitchen.

I was eating an English muffin and sipping coffee when Sadie came down the hall dressed in a cute peach dress with a plunging neckline and short hem.

“How do I look?” she said as she twirled around.

“Dan will want to eat you for brunch,” I teased.

“He already did that last night.”

I held my hand up. “Oh God, I don’t want to hear it.”

She widened her stance and crossed her arms. I waited for her to chastise me.

“Why are you such a prude about this? It’s not like you’re a virgin.”

I gulped my coffee, wincing as it burned my tongue. “It’s private. I don’t tell you about my sexual exploits.”

“I would listen if you did.”

“No. Have a cup of coffee.”

“I think I’ll pass. I’ll probably have one with brunch.”

She kissed me on the cheek, wiping the lip gloss she deposited there.

“I’m leaving at 11:30. Come to Matt’s after you finish,” I said.

“I’ll be there. There’s a black truffle topped burger with my name on it for dinner. I have my suitcase packed.”

I rolled my eyes. “Just the one suitcase?”

“And my small overnight bag.”

I snorted. “Jesus, Sadie, we’re only staying for three nights.”

“I don’t want to return here if I can help it.”

I put my cup down. “I’m taking a shower. I’ll see you at Matt’s. Have a good brunch.”

Chapter 5

Navigating through the bustling city streets with the cumbersome weight of my luggage was no easy feat, but with the doorman's help, I managed to hail a cab, grateful for the assistance as I loaded my belongings into the trunk. The journey to Matthew's apartment passed in a blur of honking horns and flashing lights, the anticipation of seeing his beloved French bulldog, Blackie, fueling my excitement.

As the cab pulled up to the elegant building, the doorman once again came to my aid, helping me unload my suitcases and overnight bag before ushering me inside. The marble foyer greeted me with its familiar opulence, and I couldn't help but smile as Blackie bounded towards me, his stumpy tail wagging furiously in excitement.

"I missed you too, buddy. Daddy's off to Dallas, so you're stuck with me," I chuckled, sinking down to the floor to greet him properly. Blackie's enthusiastic barks filled the air as he nuzzled against me, his affectionate gestures a comforting reminder of the bond we shared.

Rising to my feet, I offered Blackie a treat, knowing full well that Matthew kept a stash of gourmet dog cookies in the closet. With a wag of his tail, Blackie accepted the bone-shaped delicacy, scampering off to enjoy his snack near the refrigerator.

Matthew's apartment was masculine with dark leather furniture and custom beige drapes unchanged since his move two years prior. Stepping out onto the wide terrace, I took in the breathtaking view of Central Park, the city skyline stretching out before me in a mesmerizing panorama.

I had always loved this place, with its spacious rooms and unparalleled views, and there were times when I couldn't help but wish it were mine. Matthew had even offered one of his bedrooms to me when I talked about living in Manhattan after graduation, but I had promised Sadie that we would share an apartment together. As much as I cherished the idea of living in luxury, my loyalty to my friend outweighed any desire for personal indulgence.

I rolled the suitcases to the two guest rooms, depositing Sadie's in the slightly smaller one before I moved to mine. It was cool in the apartment because Matthew kept the thermostat at around sixty-five in the warmer weather. I went to raise it since my skin was breaking out in goosebumps.

Blackie followed me around the apartment, and I scooped him up in my arms, trying to avoid his pink tongue as he tried to lick me.

“Want to go for a walk, boy?”

He barked and I put him down. I wasn’t sure when the last time Matt walked him, so I decided to take him out.

It was a beautiful day out as I crossed the street, walking Blackie into Central Park. It was bustling with people out enjoying the weather; mothers and fathers walked with their children in carriages, teenagers hanging out in groups on the lawns, and people throwing balls back and forth.

Blackie was picky but he finally did his business and I picked it up with one of the bags I had stowed in my pocket then deposited it in one of the wire trash cans in the park. I was walking toward the street to go home when I saw the most beautiful sight, Oliver Fox running.

He was dressed in a pair of thin red runner’s shorts and a white tank top. His body glistened with sweat, and I couldn’t stop looking at him. I wasn’t the only one. Oliver Fox attracted admirers everywhere he went, it seemed.

I put my head down, fiddling with Blackie’s leash as he came near. I didn’t want him to think I was staring at him.

“Miss Stewart, how are you?”

I looked up and Oliver was wiping his face with the hem of his shirt. His abs were exposed and I thought I would cream my panties right there when I saw how defined they were.

"Hello, Mr. Fox."

He grinned. "Oliver, please."

"You can call me Ryleigh then."

He kneeled and scratched Blackie behind his ears. He closed his eyes, liking what Oliver was doing. I didn't know what to say as I gazed down at his muscular body. He stood a minute later after he won over Blackie.

"What's his name?" Oliver asked.

"Blackie."

"Is he yours?"

"No. My brother's. He's out of town and I'm watching Blackie for a few days."

"Lucky dog," he said as he jogged in place.

I couldn't help my eyes from straying to his sweat soaked body. "Isn't it too hot for a run?"

He smirked. "Nah. I do it all the time. I should finish."

I returned his smile. "Have fun."

"The fun part is after. That feeling of euphoria. You should try it."

I wrinkled my nose. "Not my thing."

He chuckled. "I'll see you."

I watched as Oliver ran by me, looking at his muscular legs and taut ass. I wondered what it would be like to grab his ass while he was...I shook the thought out of my head. It would never happen even though I could just imagine how good he was in bed. I'm sure he had plenty of practice. I looked down at Blackie and saw he was panting. It was too warm for him to stay out here for long.

I stopped at one of the vendors and bought a bottle of water, pouring some into the other poop bag I had and making a bowl. Blackie lapped the water and when he was finished, I picked him up and carried him home. He wasn't that heavy, and he seemed to enjoy being in my arms.

~

Sadie got to Matthew's apartment an hour after I did. She was a bit tipsy but all smiles.

"How did it go?" I said as I let her inside.

She slapped her hand to her chest. "Wonderful. I think I'm in love."

"So fast?"

"I'm kidding... but if Dan keeps this up, I will be soon enough."

I grin wickedly. "Suppose he sucks in bed?"

"Not the with way he uses his tongue. What did you do?"

"I took Blackie for a walk and met Oliver Fox in the park."

Sadie raised her eyebrows and sat down next to me. "Doesn't it seem interesting how you keep bumping into him?"

My best friend loved conspiracy theories. I thought nothing of my chance meetings with Oliver Fox. It was just coincidence.

"Not really. He works in the same building as me and he probably lives around here. Look at these apartments. This is an expensive area. He might even own a penthouse. In fact, I'm sure he does."

"Maybe it's karma. You're attracted to each other so you keep meeting up."

"I doubt that. It's more like coincidence."

"Suit yourself. I'm going to change," she said.

Sadie rose from the couch as I paged through the magazine I was reading. We spent the rest of the day hanging out on the terrace and sipping glasses of chilled white wine before we ordered food from the full-service kitchen for residents.

Sadie got the black truffle-topped burger she'd been craving, and I ordered an endive salad with broiled salmon. Blackie slept with me on my bed, and I woke up early so I could take him out and feed him before I left for work.

I didn't see Oliver Fox for the entire week and when I did, I wasn't paying attention. I was texting on my phone and bumped into him as I walked through the lobby for lunch, knocking me off balance. Oliver reached out to grab me before I ended up on my ass. His strong hands remained wrapped around my biceps until I stopped swaying.

"Are you all right?" His voice tinged with concern.

I should ask you that. I'm very sorry." My apology hung in the air, heavy with regret.

"You can make it up to me." His words, laced with a hint of challenge, ignited a spark of curiosity within me.

I frowned, my mind racing to catch up. "How?"

"Have lunch with me." His casual confidence in his proposal caught me off guard.

I stared at him in disbelief, my mind struggling to process his unexpected request. "Excuse me?"

"Lunch, the meal in between breakfast and dinner. Have it with me." His explanation bordered on the absurd, yet his persistence was undeniably charming.

"I'm not sure." Doubt gnawed at the edges of my resolve, uncertainty clouding my thoughts.

Stupid brain, engage already.

"When will you be sure?" Laced with gentle insistence, his question pushed me to confront my hesitations.

"Yes." The word tumbled from my lips before I could stop it, my decision made in a moment of reckless abandon.

"Miss Stewart, you're not making sense. Are you injured?" His concern, palpable in his brow furrow, drew me back to reality.

"I mean, yes, I'll have lunch with you. I only get forty-five minutes, so I can't go far." My clarification came with a rush of embarrassment, my cheeks flushing with color.

"We can eat in my office upstairs. What would you like?" His practicality, starkly contrasting my scattered thoughts, grounded me in the moment.

"I'm not sure." My uncertainty echoed in the space between us, a reminder of the chaos swirling within.

"You're not sure of much today, are you?" His observation, delivered with a wry smile, elicited a reluctant chuckle from me.

"No, I guess not." I conceded, my admission tinged with self-deprecation.

"What were you getting to eat before I asked you to lunch?" His question, a gentle prompt, nudged me back on track.

"A turkey wrap at the deli next door."

"A turkey wrap it is. Anything to drink?"

"Water."

Oliver furiously typed on his phone before he placed his hand firmly on my back and led me to the open elevator. I didn't know what I should say, so I kept silent. He looked up at me and smiled.

"You're not very talkative."

The fact that I was intimidated by his presence had much to do with it. I didn't understand why he was interested in me.

I shrugged. "I don't know what to say. Why do you want to have lunch with me?"

A smile played at the corners of his mouth. "Why not? Don't you think you're worthy of someone asking you to lunch?"

I tried not to squeak when I answered. "Of course, but you're Oliver Fox."

He chuckled. "So I am. What does that have to do with anything?"

"I'm not exactly in your league. You run a corporation. I don't know where I want my career to go."

He held up his finger. "Correction, I own a corporation. What are you doing now?"

I caught his gaze. "I work in public relations. I'm not sure I want to continue for long."

"It's not satisfying?"

“My boss is not the nicest person. I’ve spent the last two weeks as a glorified gopher.”

Oliver stifled a laugh. “A rodent?”

“No. You know, go for this and go for that. I thought I would be doing more.”

“What do you want to do?”

“I’m finding myself. I might want to do something different. My roommate Sadie works in marketing, and she loves it. Maybe I should try it.”

“I have openings at my company if you want to apply. I’m sure we can find a spot for you.”

The elevator dinged on the top floor of the building. Oliver held the door and let me step out into the opulent offices of Fox Asset Corporation. The place was filled with tons of glass and dark marble floors. The front reception desk was curved and made of rich mahogany wood, topped with a slab of granite as dark as the floors.

Oliver led me through the offices until we got to his on the corner of the floor. It was massive and had a wall of bookcases with tons of books. Every square inch of shelves was filled with books. Oliver had a long conference table with high-backed leather chairs on one side of his office. On the other was a sitting area with a contemporary white leather sectional bigger than my apartment's.

Next to that was a smaller round glass table with four white cushioned elegant dining chairs. Oliver’s desk was of carved wood, at least six feet long and four feet wide. On it sat three oversized monitors, stacks of folders, and a lone keyboard and mouse.

To say I was in awe was an understatement. Was this how a billionaire lived, surrounded by expensive and elegant things?

“Your desk is beautiful.”

“Thank you. It’s antique. I need space to work.”

He shut the heavy wooden door behind me and ushered me to the couch.

“This place is bigger than my apartment.”

“I like it.”

I didn’t sit down, instead walking to the windows overlooking the city. You could see everything. From there, I went to the bookshelves, fingering several of the books, mostly about business. Oliver stood behind me.

“You read all these?”

“You don’t think so? I like to read, especially if it helps my business.”

I felt inadequate around this man. “Oliver, why am I here?”

“You like to put your cards on the table right away, don’t you?”

A fit of inferiority hit me, and I looked at the floor.

"I don't understand what you want with me."

"I want you. Is that a good enough answer?"

I met his penetrating gaze. "It sounds a bit irrational. Why? You can have anybody you want."

Oliver touched my shoulder. "But I don't want just anybody."

"We're worlds apart when it comes to life. You're a good fourteen years older than me."

Why the fuck was I talking him out of dating me? This man wanted me.

He smirked, "You've been doing your homework on me?"

I felt my face heat as embarrassment took hold. "No, I haven't. It's obvious you're older than me."

"Why? Do I have wrinkles? Is my paunchy belly and arthritis giving me away?"

Paunchy belly? Not from what I saw the other day.

"No. I doubt you have either. How old are you?"

I knew exactly how old Oliver was from the information I found on the internet. He was thirty-six years old.

"You tell me. I'm sure the numerous articles you read stated my age."

I bit my lip. "I didn't read many."

"So you do admit to reading up on me?"

If we were going to start a relationship, the best solution was the truth.

"Yes, I have. I was curious after our meeting at graduation," I said softly.

He raised his eyebrows. "You never heard of me before then?"

I stared out the window. "I did, but I never looked you up."

"I'm not sure if I should be flattered or offended. Which is it?"

"Neither. Did you look me up after graduation?"

"I did. I have contacts at Columbia. I know you graduated with a 3.5 GPA, pretty respectable."

"Is that all you inquired about? Or do you know every little detail of my life?"

"No. I'm not a stalker."

"Are you sure?" Now it was my turn to smirk.

As we continued our banter, we were interrupted by a knock on the door.

"Come," Oliver said. I don't know why, but the way he said it made my belly clench. His voice was smooth and seductive. In walked a man dressed in a navy blue business suit with brown hair that had silver at the temples. He was carrying a silver tray with a cover. He nodded at Oliver and placed it on the dining table.

“Thank you, Henri.”

The man stood at attention, his hands behind his back.

“Do you require anything else, sir?”

“No. We’ll speak after lunch.”

“Yes, sir.”

Henri backed out of the room, closing the door as he exited.

“Who was that?”

“One of my assistants.”

“One?”

He stepped closer, and his cologne enveloped me like a hug. I wondered what it would be like to be in his arms or to feel his weight on top of me. I blushed at the thought.

“I have three. My business is very complicated and too much work for one person to assist me with.”

“Then how do you handle it all?”

His tone was authoritative. “Because it’s my responsibility to know all aspects of my company. You’re quite inquisitive.”

“It’s part of my nature.”

“I like it. Please sit down.”

I took my seat at the table, and Oliver remained standing.

“What kind of water would you like?”

“Excuse me?”

“Water? I have a few types. Sparkling, spring, and flavored.”

“Sparkling is fine.”

Oliver went to a cabinet next to the bookcase and pushed it. It popped open to reveal a refrigerator. He removed two bottles of Perrier and opened them before he came back to the table. He lifted the cover of the tray to reveal two white plates: a turkey wrap and a roast beef sandwich on a soft roll with a side of au jus.

“That looks good,” I said.

A smile danced on his lips, “Would you like a bite?”

“No, thank you.”

I took a small bite of my turkey wrap. I was surprised that the turkey was fresh, not deli meat. It was subtly spiced and juicy. Oliver watched me as I chewed.

“What?”

“You take such small bites.”

“I’m nervous.”

“Don’t be.”

“How can I not?”

"You either want to have a relationship with me or not. I'm not asking anything of you other than to get to know me before you decide."

"But you're Oliver Fox."

He put his sandwich down and stared at me with his beautiful sapphire eyes.

"I'm just a man."

I sawed at my bottom lip with my teeth. "You say it just like you're an average Joe. You're not."

He laughed. "Get to know me before you judge. Are you dating anyone?"

"No. Not right now. I'm surprised you didn't know."

"I told you, I'm not a stalker. I know basic information about you."

I had only eaten half my wrap before my nerves got the best of me. I put it down on the plate and sipped my water.

"Finished?"

"I had a big breakfast," I lied.

He clasped his hands together. "I'd like to take you out to dinner this weekend."

"I have plans," I lied.

"Then lunch."

"I'm busy."

I was losing control with Oliver, and I couldn't. Once he found out about my nightmares, he would be done with me anyway.

He let out a frustrated breath. "Ryleigh, why are you making this difficult?"

"I'm not. It's not every day that a millionaire asks you on a date."

"I've had lots of millionaires ask me on a date."

He didn't correct me. I knew he was a lot more than a millionaire. Oliver Fox was well diversified and had several billion dollars in assets. He was the perfect catch but I didn't think he was for me.

My mouth suddenly felt dry, and I took a gulp of water. "I bet. I'm sure women throw themselves at you."

"They do, but I'm not that kind of man."

I snorted. "I saw many images of you with plenty of different women. It seems you don't want for dates."

Oliver leaned back in his chair and gripped the arms. "I thought you didn't check me out? How do you know I've dated plenty of women?"

I shrugged. "I saw pictures, that's all."

"I won't beg. Either you want to go on a date with me or not."

He reached into his pocket and withdrew a thick, cream-colored business card, sliding it toward me. It had Fox

Asset Corporation's logo in black and all Oliver's contact information, including his personal cell.

"I expect you'll keep these numbers confidential. If you change your mind, call me. I'd like very much to take you on a date."

"You're throwing me out of your office?"

"No, but if you check the time, your lunch hour is almost up."

I glanced at the clock on Oliver's wall and saw that it was nearing the top of the hour. I had four minutes to get back to my desk. I rose and so did Oliver.

"Thank you for lunch. It was delicious."

"I hope we can share another meal together soon. Don't break my heart by waiting too long."

"I'll let you know soon. Thank you."

He walked me to the elevators, not touching me and he made no moves to shake my hand or kiss my cheek. Oliver stood in front of the elevators as the doors closed and then he was gone as the car descended.

I was flustered when I got back to my desk. I sat down and held my hands together to stop them from shaking. I put Oliver's business card to my nose, smelling his citrusy cologne on the paper. Candice came into my cubicle to ask me to get Beatrice some coffee and I nearly jumped out of my skin.

"What's up with you? You're very pale. Are you okay?" she asked.

"I'm fine. Just tired."

"You know how Beatrice likes her coffee. Meet us in her office."

Candice walked out and I silently cursed. Two weeks and I was just an errand girl. What a waste of an Ivy League education.

~

I was still nervous when I left the office for the day. Sadie was waiting for me in front of my building so we could walk to the subway together. I dropped my purse when I got to her, spilling half the contents on the ground. She helped me recover everything and when she handed it to me, I dropped it again but this time it was zipped.

Sadie narrowed her eyes at me. "What happened at work?"

"I'll tell you when we get home," I said quietly.

"Now. Tell me now," she demanded.

"Home."

We started walking to cross the street and the black car that I'd seen Oliver slide into the week before pulled up to the curb. The back window opened, and Oliver's handsome face came into view.

"Ladies, can I give you a ride home?"

"Absolutely," Sadie said. She didn't hesitate and I had no choice but to join her. The driver got out, the same hulk of a man I saw before with slicked back black hair, a graphite gray suit and a thin mustache. He opened the back door and Oliver stepped out to let us into the car. Sadie glanced at me, and I gave her a weak smile. When we were on our way, Oliver turned to me.

"How was the rest of your day?"

"It was okay," I said in almost a whisper.

"Miss Fulbright, Ryleigh tells me she's too busy this weekend to have lunch or dinner with me. Is that true?"

I almost died right there on the back seat. I glanced at Sadie and pleaded with her to say I was busy.

"I know she has a couple of things going on."

"I was hoping she would join me for dinner tomorrow night."

"I told you, I have to check my schedule."

"And I told you I hoped I didn't have to wait too long."

"You only asked me a few hours ago."

"I can be impatient."

"I noticed," I mumbled.

Sadie sat there gaping as we continued our banter back and forth. Fifteen minutes later, we pulled up in front of our building. I had no idea how Oliver knew where I lived but an explanation would have to wait until we were in private.

Oliver stepped out and offered his hand so he could assist both Sadie and I from the car. He grasped my elbow as Sadie started to walk to the entrance, leaning into my ear and whispering.

“Don’t torture me too long. You have my number.”

His lips brushed against my ear, causing tingles to rush down to my core. He let me go and waited until the doorman opened the door and I was safely in the lobby. I watched the car pass by us before I turned around to join Sadie at the elevator.

She grinned. “You have some explaining to do.”

“Upstairs.”

She couldn’t ask me anything else because other residents had joined us. She started badgering me as we walked down the hall before we got inside our apartment. I kept silent until the door was closed.

“What the hell was that all about?” she demanded.

“I had lunch with Oliver today.”

I kicked off my shoes and padded to my room with Sadie hot on my heels.

“You had lunch with him? Where?”

I pulled out a tank top and shorts from my dresser. “His office. He took me up there and ordered food to be brought in.”

“Am I missing something? Why?”

“He wants to date me.”

I started unbuttoning my dark blue blouse and Sadie grabbed my hands.

“Did you just say he wants to date you?”

I nodded. “Yes. He made it perfectly clear what his intentions are for me.”

“And what did you tell him?”

“I said I need to think about it.”

She let my hands go and sat on the corner of my bed. “What do you need to think about? The man is a God in more ways than one. He’s fabulously rich, handsome and from what I can see, polite.”

“He’s also much older than me and more sophisticated. I’m afraid I would lag behind and... I don’t know, embarrass him?” I trailed off.

She chastised me. “Are you serious right now? You’re well read, Ivy League educated and smart. It’s not like you haven’t been places.”

Sadie was right about that. My parents had taken my brothers and me to many places. I’d been to several countries in Europe, Asia and South America besides

Canada, Australia and Mexico. I could speak three languages although my French was not the greatest, but I was fluent in Spanish.

“He’s older. Fourteen years older. In four years, he’ll be forty and I won’t even be out of my twenties.”

“You’re crazy. That man seems stuck on you. I saw how he was looking at you. What could it hurt to go on a few dates with him?”

The truth was that Oliver Fox scared me. I was afraid of the effect he had on my body when I was in his presence. I knew if I fell for him, it would be hard and fast. If we broke up, I would be devastated. I wasn’t sure if I wanted to deal with the aftermath.

“He can have his pick of women.”

I removed my blouse and Sadie scowled, “You wore that bra?”

It was a basic white cotton bra with matching panties. Usually, I wore the set to work out but today I didn’t feel like wearing lacy lingerie.

“What’s the problem?”

She groaned loudly when she saw my panties as I removed my skirt.

“You had lunch with Oliver Fox and wearing *that*?”

“Jesus Christ, Sadie, I wasn’t fucking him. It was lunch,” I huffed.

"But you never know. It could have escalated."

I shook my head. "I refuse to allow myself to fall that fast for him. If I decide to date him, we won't be having sex anytime soon."

She threw up her hands. "You're out of your mind. I could only imagine how hot he is in bed. I barely know the man, and if he offered, I would sleep with him right now."

"You have more confidence than I do."

"So? Are you having dinner with him this weekend?"

"I don't know."

I went to my closet and placed my clothing in the basket at the bottom before putting on the shirt and shorts I selected.

"Have dinner with him and see how it goes. You two might just hit it off."

"Maybe. I'll call him later."

Sadie rose and went to her room to change. I was taking a bottle of water from the refrigerator when the lobby phone rang.

"Hello?"

"Miss Stewart?"

"Yes?"

"We have a delivery for you."

I frowned because I wasn't expecting anything. "What is it?"

"It looks like flowers."

"I'll be right down."

Sadie came out of the bedroom in the same outfit as me except her tank top was yellow.

"What was the call for?"

"I have a delivery."

She smirked at me as I opened the door.

Chapter 6

Oliver had sent me a dozen roses. They were gorgeous in colors of peach, orange, red, yellow, pink and white. He wasn't making it easy to say no and I called him after I placed them in a vase to say thank you.

"Will you go to dinner with me?" he asked.

I twirled a lock of hair around my finger. "You're making it very hard to say no."

"Then don't. Have dinner with me tonight. I want to see you."

"I thought you said tomorrow," I said.

My stomach already had butterflies in it from our ride home, but now, with the prospect of seeing him, they turned to bats.

"Do you have plans?"

"I'm not in the mood to dress up."

"I could take you to a fast-food place."

I chuckled. "You really want to start with that impression?"

"You don't need to dress up. We can get something casual like pizza or pasta. I can have Vlad pick you up."

"Who's Vlad?"

"My chauffeur and bodyguard. You met him earlier."

I tapped my bare foot on the floor as my anxiety ramped up. "You mean that big wall that was driving us home?"

He laughed. "Yes, that's Vlad. He can be there in fifteen minutes."

"I'm not sure. This is moving so fast," I whined.

"If you say no, you've sentenced me to a sleepless night."

"How so?"

"I can't stop thinking about you."

"Oliver...," I cautioned.

"Just dinner. I'll have Vlad take you home right after."

I felt obligated, but I didn't want to be in this position.

"You want me to come to your place?"

"I live on Central Park West. You said your brother did, too."

"He does."

"You can't see me but I'm on my knees begging."

I giggled. "I doubt you've begged anyone in your entire life."

"If you believe that's true, then you're the first."

"You convinced me. Send Vlad. What should I wear?"

"Whatever you have on now. I'll speak to you soon. Thank you."

I hung up the phone and looked up to see Sadie watching me.

She smirked. "You're having dinner with him tonight?"

"Just pizza at his apartment."

"What are you wearing?"

"He said to come casual. I guess this is fine," I said, gesturing to my outfit.

"The fuck it is. Change your underwear."

"Sadie, I'm not having sex with him. He won't see my underwear."

"Don't be silly. Change it and change your shorts too."

"What's wrong with my shorts?"

"Just change them into something sexier."

I looked down at my white shorts. They were okay as far as I was concerned but before I could say anything,

Sadie was digging through my drawer to find a pair of light blue frayed jean shorts. The pockets hung out the bottom of the thighs because they were cut so high.

I rolled my eyes. “Those scream trashy.”

“They scream sexy.”

She dug around in my underwear drawer and came out with a pale-yellow lace bra and panty set.

“Put this on.”

I sighed. “Are you done playing dress up? I should change into a t-shirt.”

“What’s wrong with the tank?”

“I don’t feel comfortable.”

She left the room as I changed, coming back with her makeup bag.

“No. You are not making me up like I’m going to a club.”

“Why not?” she protested.

“Oliver has already seen me with my usual makeup.”

“Put on lip gloss at least.”

She handed me her strawberry lip gloss and started to leave the room as I applied it.

“Where are you going? Take this,” I said.

Sadie waved her hand. “Keep it. You might need to reapply it.”

“What’s that supposed to mean?”

“You do the math.”

I wanted to argue with her, but the lobby called and said Vlad was waiting in front of the building. I grabbed my purse and phone, called out a goodbye to Sadie and headed downstairs.

The car was waiting out front, and Vlad opened the back door for me. I thanked him and he nodded. He didn’t speak to me as we navigated to the Upper West Side. I was probably crazy for going to Oliver’s apartment when I barely knew him, but I must admit, I was intrigued.

We arrived at a large modern building and Vlad double parked to let me out. The lobby was more opulent than Matthew’s place. The walls were covered in rich dark wood and contrasting light marble floors. A man at the front desk asked my name then directed me up to the penthouse.

My stomach churned as I rode the elevator to the top floor. I was surprised it opened into a wide hallway decorated much the same as the lobby. I expected the doors to open right into Oliver’s home. I guess I’d seen too many movies. Oliver was waiting for me when I arrived at his door. His smile lit up his entire face. He was dressed in a pair of jeans and a form fitting black t-shirt that showed every cut and ridge of his torso.

He pressed a kiss to my cheek. “I’m so glad you came. You look lovely.”

“Thank you, but these shorts are old and so is the t-shirt.”

“Anything you wear is lovely. Come in.”

He took my hand and I again felt tingles at his touch. Once again, he was turning me on. I was in awe of his apartment, it was huge. As I walked through his marble foyer, I couldn’t stop looking at the artwork on the walls. I was sure the Picasso and Van Gogh was real. Oliver must have been reading my mind.

“They are real.”

“They’re beautiful.”

“What would you like to eat? Let me order before we talk.”

I was like a small child, looking at everything in Oliver’s apartment. The massive kitchen, the park through the thick tinted windows, the modern furniture and the dining table with seating for twelve.

“Ryleigh?”

“I’m sorry. This place is just so… gorgeous. My brother Matthew has a large apartment, but this is at least three times the size. How can you stand living alone?”

“I just do. I’m not here that often. I work many hours and travel a lot.”

I realized he was holding my hand still and when I tried to pull away, he lifted it to his mouth and kissed the back. His lips lingered on my skin before he let me go. I'm more than aroused now. I could feel my nipples tighten and my core flood. Oliver was so hot, and he wanted me. Why me?

"What would you like to eat?" he repeated.

"Anything really. It's your home, you decide."

He licked his lips. "If I had what I really want, you wouldn't be upright."

I raised my eyebrows and my heart started to pound. I knew he was referring to sex. I might want the same thing, but I barely knew this man. I wouldn't sleep with him this soon.

"Pizza is fine."

"Any toppings?"

I smirked and he cocked his head at me. "What's so funny?"

"This is so ordinary."

"Sweet Ryleigh, I'm an ordinary man. You mistake my level of sophistication. I enjoy drinking beer and downing nachos while watching baseball."

"I can't see it."

"Trust me."

He picked up his phone and ordered dinner. My eyes are all over this place as I gobbled up the beauty. He touched my arm as I looked out the window.

“Can I get you a drink? Some wine?”

Wine would dull my senses. I decided on sparkling water. Oliver seemed quite at home in the kitchen as he took out glasses and opened a large bottle of Pellegrino. He sat down next to me at the massive white granite counter and stroked my hand with his fingers. I want to pull away, but I like the feel of his flesh on mine.

“You have such soft skin.”

“Thank you. Why do you want me?”

He let out a frustrated breath. “You just keep pressing the issue.”

I smirked. “I have to, I’m naturally inquisitive. Remember?”

“I do. I’m very attracted to you.”

“I’m practically a child compared to you.”

He scowled. “Are you trying to talk me out of pursuing you?”

“I just want to know your motives.”

“I have no motives. You make it sound so sordid, but today, can’t I just want to get to know you better?” he asked.

"I guess. Haven't there been other women in your life you wanted to get to know better? Frankly, no. Those that run in my circles are jaded and spoiled."

"So you want an ordinary, boring girl?"

"Is that what you think you are?"

I turned to him and he ran the pad of his thumb down my jawline before he propped my chin with two of his fingers and leaned in for a kiss. And what a kiss it was. I thought I would burst into flame right where I sat. He didn't move his mouth, only applied soft pressure to mine. When he pulled away, he licked his lips and smiled.

"Strawberry."

I reached up to swipe my fingers over his lips to remove the gloss and he sucked one into his mouth, gently biting the pad. A look of desire crossed his face and I'm sure it was a match for the one I was giving him. He let my finger go as the blood rushed in my ears.

"You taste delicious," he said seductively.

"So do you," I squeaked.

"Come, dinner will be here soon, and I want to show you the rest of my home."

He took my hand and led me down a long hallway, showing me his bedroom, three other guest rooms, a full library, his office, a workout room and the patio that was accessed from his bedroom as well as the hallway.

"You could get lost in this place."

“I guess you could.”

He pushed open the slider and led me out to the patio. It was a large space with several small gardens in decorative planter boxes. Furniture was dotted around the large space in several different groupings. You could see the park and hear the traffic from below.

Oliver pulled me into his arms and kissed me again, harder and more insistent this time. He hugged me against his hard body and I melted into him. I was falling fast for this man, which was dangerous since I barely knew him. I came to my senses and gently pushed against him with my hands. He immediately let me go but I could see it on his face that he did it with reluctance.

His voice was husky. “Ryleigh, you’re making me break all the rules.”

“What rules?”

“My rules.”

I heard his phone buzz in his pocket, and he took it out then offered his arm to lead me back inside.

“Dinner is here.”

I softly moaned as Oliver latches onto my neck. Dinner had been over for more than an hour and we hadn’t been able to keep our lips off each other. After finishing a wonderful dinner of coal fired pizza and Caesar salad, he'd led me to his couch. We talked for a little while, but our attraction got the best of us and we were soon lip locked.

"Oliver, I have to go," I choked out.

"You can't. I need you here," he insisted.

I leaned back so he would stop kissing me. "And where will that lead? Into your bed? I don't sleep with men so soon after meeting them."

"I don't sleep with women so soon either. I have morals and standards."

I put my hand on his muscular chest. "I didn't mean to imply you didn't. I'm just saying that if I stay here, we will end up in bed together."

He caught my gaze. "Would that be such a horrible thing?"

"We don't know each other."

"What would you like to know that you haven't already read about me?"

"You never told me about your family."

He sat back against the couch and rubbed the back of his neck. "My parents died when I was nineteen. It was a plane crash. We had no relatives, so I was given guardianship of my brother, Jonah. I was in college at the time, and that took a toll on my duties as a parent. Jonah got into quite a bit of trouble. He was arrested several times and I finally washed my hands of him when I was twenty two and he was nineteen.

“Do you still see him?”

“Yes, but it’s limited. I don’t want Jonah to taint my business.”

“I’m sorry. You have no one else?” I asked.

“No. I started my company after I graduated from Yale. We were both given an inheritance in the will. It wasn’t big, but it was enough for me to start my own business. I got my real estate license and went from there.”

This beautiful man sounded like he had some rough bumps in life. My heart hurt for him that he lost his parents at a young age, but he persevered. I told him about myself.

“We have a lot of family and my brothers, Matthew and Finley live in the city. Matthew is a trader and Finley has a software start up. He just scored some big money from some investors.”

“I could’ve helped. I’ve invested in several startups, a few in the city.”

“Finley’s a computer nerd but he’s very smart. He’s twenty-seven and Matthew is twenty-five.”

“You’re the baby of the family?”

“Yes, and they treat me like it too. My parents wanted me to move back home after I graduated.”

We talked some more about our lives until the attraction was too much and we ended up lip locked again. Oliver moved on top of me and broke from my mouth to kiss my neck, moving down to my chest and gently biting my peaked nipples. It sent shockwaves to my core. I could just imagine how wet I was. I knew it was having an effect on him since his erection was pressed against my thigh. He groaned before he sat up and adjusted his jeans.

"I hate to say this, but you should go home."

I quirked an eyebrow. "You want me to leave?"

"If you don't, I'll want to take you to bed. That's not a gentlemanly thing to do. You said so yourself."

"Suppose I want to forget the rules? I've never slept with someone so soon."

"Go home, Ryleigh," he growled.

I sat up and smoothed out my wrinkled t-shirt, rising from the couch. I knew he wasn't trying to be mean. He was trying to be rational. Oliver didn't want me to have any regrets, but oh, how I wanted this man.

"I'll have Vlad take you home. Would you like me to accompany you?" he asked.

"Would you?"

He nodded. "Of course. Just say the word."

"I want you to."

"I will then. Let me call Vlad."

It happened again on the way home. Our lips locked together, and hands roamed the other's body. At one point, I felt bold enough to stroke Oliver through his jeans, but he stopped me.

"If I allowed that then you wouldn't be going home," he whispered.

I pretended to pout but I knew he was right. We needed to wait. He walked me inside my building and gave me a chaste kiss on the cheek.

"What about tomorrow?" I asked.

"What about it?"

"I thought we would see each other."

"I have some business to attend to at the office. I'll call you if I have a chance."

I frowned as I watched him walk out the door and slip into the car. I was confused by his behavior since his demeanor became frosty before he departed. Sadie was asleep on the couch with the television on when I walked in the door. It was only 11:30 and I went over to wake her up.

"I thought you would stay over," she said as she let out a loud yawn.

“No. I told you I wouldn’t sleep with Oliver so soon.”

“So, how was dinner?”

“It was nice,” I said as I frowned.

Her eyebrows slammed together. “What’s the matter?”

“Oliver was icy after he dropped me off. I asked him about getting together again, and he said he had work to do.”

Her face clouded. “What the fuck? He tells you he wants you and then acts like you don’t matter?”

I plopped down on the couch, feeling worn out. Oliver had ever-changing moods, and he was making me dizzy. “I don’t get it.”

“Did you do anything with him?”

I put my head on the back of the sofa and closed my eyes. “We kissed. He is such a good kisser.”

“Maybe he wanted more, and he figured if you didn’t put out, then he would move on.”

I opened my eyes and looked at her. “No, that’s not it. He said the same thing about waiting.”

“Men are fucking weird.”

I didn’t want to talk about Oliver because if I did, it would stir up two emotions, anger and sadness. He couldn’t trail after me like a salivating dog and then go cold. I changed the subject.

"Did you talk to Dan tonight?"

She smiled. "He was here for a little while."

"Just a little while?"

I was afraid she was getting into the same pattern she followed in college where she would latch onto a guy she thought could take care of her.

"We're seeing each other tomorrow. I might not be home. Will you be all right by yourself?"

"Seriously? I'm not a child."

"I was just asking." She yawned again and stood up, shutting off the television. "I'm heading to bed."

"This is early for you."

"I'm tired and I might not get much sleep tomorrow night."

"I think I'll go to bed too. Talk to you in the morning."

"Goodnight."

I went into my room and took off my clothes. My panties were damp, and I removed them before I slipped under the covers naked. My nightmares were replaced with one of the dirtiest dreams I ever had with Oliver as the star.

I woke up the next morning aroused enough to take an almost freezing cold shower, and when it didn't help, the shower head between my legs did. Oliver Fox was under my skin, and I wasn't sure how to push him out. I was still very much perplexed by his behavior just before we parted.

I didn't hear from Oliver all day Saturday, so I moped around our apartment in the morning while Sadie chattered on about her date with Dan. I was pretty sure I would be alone overnight. The weekends were usually our cleaning days, so I pulled on a pair of old shorts and a threadbare T-shirt to work on the bathroom.

Sadie vacuumed and dusted while I scrubbed the kitchen. By noon, we were finished and she went to take a shower. She was meeting Dan at 2 p.m. for some shopping.

I called Finley because I hadn't spoken to him in almost three weeks. Our communication was always limited after he started his company, but I wasn't offended because I knew how busy he was. We usually had brief exchanges through text, so I was surprised when he answered.

"Hey Ry, what's up?"

I heard him typing on his keyboard and figured he was working on a project.

"I just wanted to hear your voice. It's been a while."

His tone was apologetic. "I'm sorry. That's my fault. Work is crazy now that I have plenty of seed money. We have several projects going at once."

I sat down and yanked at a string on the hem of my shirt. "I'm glad to hear things are going well."

"What's the matter?" he asked with concern.

"Nothing. I miss you."

"Bullshit. Tell your big brother what's wrong."

I took a deep breath before I revealed my problem with Oliver, though I didn't plan on saying his name.

"It's about a guy."

"You're dating someone?"

"I don't think you can even say it's at the dating stage. Maybe we're just seeing each other."

"So it's not serious. What's the problem?"

I exhaled loudly. "I thought we had something, but then he went cold on me."

"That's the way young guys are. You should know that."

"You're young. Do you do that?"

"I don't have time for a relationship. I play the field when I can."

It wasn't a surprise. Finley was handsome and brilliant, I'll admit. The fact that there was a possibility that he would eventually be wildly rich and successful didn't hurt either.

I swallowed hard. "He's older."

I was waiting for my brother to go into protective mode. When we were younger, and he was home, he would interrogate my dates, sometimes scaring them away. I decided to only reveal enough so he could help me with my problem but not enough to reveal who it was with.

“Older? How much older?”

I bit my lip. “Older.”

“Older than me?”

“Yes.”

“Do you think that’s wise?”

Here it came; he was in full protective mode and would try to draw every detail out of me until he got the true story.

“Why? Do you think I can’t handle an older man?” I asked with annoyance.

He coughed. “I didn’t say that. Older men are in a different frame of life. They’re thinking about marriage and kids.”

A headache was starting to thud behind my eyes and I rubbed them as I put my head on one of the pillows.

“I doubt this man is. He’s married to his business.”

“Do I know him?”

“Maybe, but I don’t want to say his name.”

“Why?”

I could hear the suspicion in his voice. Finley might have been a little fish in a big city, but he knew all the big players.

"I just don't. I know you. You'll start doing research on him."

"Don't fault me because I want to protect you. Mom and Anders made us swear we would take care of you."

I ground my teeth. "So, the big city doesn't swallow me whole? You forget that I lived here for four years."

He hesitated while he spoke to someone in the background. "That was for school and not permanent."

"What should I do about this guy?"

"Don't get strapped down. You're young, beautiful and intelligent. You're a catch. I'm sure plenty of guys would want to date you."

"I like Oliver. He's different than anyone I've dated before."

Dammit. I didn't want to reveal my connection to Oliver this soon, and now I would have to explain.

"Oliver? Who is it, Ryleigh?"

I sighed. "It's Oliver Fox."

Finley whistled into the phone. "Shit, he's like thirty-five and a high-profile businessman."

"He's thirty-six."

"Where did you meet him?"

"He has offices in the building where I work. I met him in the elevator and the lobby. He was also the guest speaker at my graduation. You would know that if you attended," I chided.

"You know why I couldn't. I was there even if I wasn't."

"I know. I'm sorry."

"Oliver Fox dates a lot of women. He'll break your heart."

He already has.

"What should I do?"

"Date other people. Play the field and enjoy yourself. You've only lived in the city full-time for a month." I heard Finley talking to someone in the background again. "I have to go. Take my advice, and let's have lunch sometime soon."

"Can you tear yourself away?"

"I can for you. Text me with some dates. Love you, Ry."

He hung up before I could reply, and I sagged against the back of the couch as the line went silent. All answers were pointing toward staying away from Oliver. He wasn't for me, especially if he turned on and off like a faucet. I hated it when guys were so mercurial.

I picked up one of Sadie's magazines from the coffee table and paged through it. They did a spread on BattleAxe. The guitarist was hot as hell, and the article said he was twenty-nine. He would be a better choice than Oliver.

“How do I look?”

I glanced up and saw Sadie in a cute little sleeveless light blue dress. She had painted her toe and fingernails the same color.

I brightened for her sake even though I was miserable. “Very pretty. Dan will love it.”

“I heard you talking to Finley. What does he say?”

“He said Oliver is too old for me. I guess it wasn’t to be. Finley said I should play the field.”

She smoothed the skirt of her dress. “Dan has some friends.”

I looked down at my clothes. I was not in the mood to get changed, dress up, and put on a smile while I fended off some guy wanting to get lucky.

“No. I want to sit here and do nothing for the rest of the day. I hoped Finley could have dinner with me tonight, but he’s usually busy.”

“Where’s Matthew?”

I yawned. “He went to Long Island with some friends for the weekend.”

She went to the foyer mirror and removed some lip gloss from her purse. “He left Blackie alone?”

“He took him with him. That dog is so spoiled.”

“Will you be all right tonight?”

“You’re really spending the night with Dan?” I asked.

She shrugged. “We have chemistry. He might be the one.”

I rolled my eyes because Sadie said that about half a dozen guys in college.

“Only time will tell.”

She went to the foyer closet and pulled out a pair of white sandals, sitting on one of the kitchen chairs to slip them on. I watched her and wondered what I would do for the rest of the day and evening.

Chapter 7

By 6 p.m., I was bored out of my mind. I read on my Kindle for a few hours, watched television, and straightened my underwear drawer. Maybe I should've taken Sadie up on dating one of Dan's friends. Even if I went out for a drink, I would be out of here.

I made myself a turkey sandwich for dinner, and it reminded me of the fresh turkey wrap I enjoyed last week with Oliver. It seemed like months ago. I hadn't heard from him all day, and I wasn't about to contact him. I started flipping the channels on TV and settled on a nature show until I saw it was about poaching. I was dozing on the couch when I heard my phone chime with an incoming text.

Come downstairs, I'm out front.

. . .

My heart started to pound when I saw the message from Oliver. I was curt in my answer.

I'm busy tonight. My time is valuable.

Don't make me come up there.

Come up? How would he get up here since he would need the concierge to call me before he came upstairs? As much as I wanted to see him, I was hurt by his behavior the night before. I ignored his text and closed my eyes again.

My phone kept chiming, but I held strong. A few minutes later, someone knocked at my door.

"Go away. I'm busy."

"Ryleigh, open the door. Stop being childish."

That pissed me off because he acted like a jerk last night, not me. I stomped to the door and threw it open.

Oliver was standing there grinning and making me want to smack him. He looked delicious in a tight black t-shirt that framed his muscular chest and torso and a pair of light blue jeans.

“That didn’t take long.”

“I don’t want to see you anymore.”

I walked away, and he came inside, closing the door after him. He grabbed my arm and pinned me to the wall, giving me a bruising kiss. His tongue pressed against the seam of my mouth until I opened, and he thrust it inside. It took me seconds to bend to his will. What a weakling I was. I didn’t even fight him. He moved his lips down my neck and marked me with his teeth.

“I’m busy,” I mumbled, drunk with the scent of his cologne.

Oliver pulled away to look at me, staring down until I averted my eyes.

“You’re not busy. You’re upset with me,” he almost whispered.

“You hurt me.”

“I’m sorry. You’re throwing my balance off. I’ve never had this happen before.”

“You were cold to me, and I didn’t hear from you all day.”

He eased up his hold on me. “I had to think what my next move was. I think I’m falling for you. I didn’t want to admit it to myself, but I have no choice.”

“You don’t even know me.”

He was admitting to me the same thing I should be admitting to him.

“I don’t have to know you to know how I feel.”

“Either that, or you’re just saying it to get me into bed.”

Oliver looked like I just slapped him in the face, and his eyebrows knitted together.

“I would never do that. It’s not about sex, even though I will admit that I want to have it with you. It’s something deeper.”

I walked away from him because I didn’t know what else to say without telling him I had fallen for him. Behind me, I heard him chuckle.

“That’s quite an outfit.”

I never changed from my tiny shorts and threadbare white t-shirt. When I looked down, I realized he could see my red bra as clearly as day.

“Shit. Let me go change.”

“Does that mean I can stay?”

“Yes.”

I ran to my room, closing the door as I searched for a pair of shorts and a t-shirt to change into. Oliver was sitting on the couch flipping the channels when I came out. He looked at ease as if he lived here. His eyes traveled my body up and down.

“I much prefer the other outfit,” he said.

“Too bad. This is what you get.”

“I like your bra. Fiery red suits you.”

I felt my face heat, but I knew I shouldn’t be embarrassed. The way we were going, my underwear wouldn’t be the only thing Oliver would see. I sat down next to him, and he turned to kiss me again, but I pushed him away, straddling his hips. It was my turn to be the aggressor.

I pulled the remote from his hand, dropped it on the couch, and gently kissed his face and neck. His light stubble brushed against my skin as I moved along. I wanted to consume him and much more; I wanted him to make love to me. He stroked my back, slipping his hands under my t-shirt to touch the flesh on my stomach.

I could feel my core flooding and his erection against my center. He moved his hand further up until he was skimming the undersides of my breasts. I softly moaned against his neck. We were both breathing heavily when he pulled me hard against him, holding me tightly in his arms.

“We have to stop,” he said.

“No,” I groaned.

“Ryleigh, I’m not ready to have sex with you.”

I almost laughed. “Shouldn’t that be my line?”

"It works both ways."

I pushed off his chest and moved back on his knees to meet his gaze.

"I want you. I know you want me."

I went to reach for his hard-as-steel erection, but he grabbed my wrist.

"I can't help my reaction to you," he growled.

"Then why?"

"You said so yourself. We need to get to know each other better."

I sighed and slid off his lap, leaning back against the couch. Oliver put his arm around me, stroking my shoulder.

"You're driving me crazy," I said.

He chuckled. "You think you're the only one?"

It was nice to know that I could unravel this man as much as he could unravel me. Oliver always seemed so damn cool and put together while I was sweating my next move.

"So what do we do?" I asked.

Oliver stroked my hair. "Have patience. You don't want to just jump into bed with me."

I was honest. "But I do. I want you to fuck me."

"I don't just want to fuck you. I want to make love to you."

My stomach did flip-flops, and my heart picked up, pounding hard in my chest.

"I had a dream about you," I admitted.

Oliver smirked. "Did you? What was it about?"

"It was dirty, very dirty."

"I assure you that your dream is nothing like what I can provide."

I nudged him in the ribs with my elbow. "Shut up, Oliver. Don't tease me."

He turned my head to him and planted a soft kiss on my lips. I deepened it, licking the corners of his mouth and clenching his t-shirt, but he didn't let me go further like I wanted, pulling away.

"Did you eat?" he asked.

"I had a turkey sandwich. It was nothing like the one I had in your office."

He pursed his lips. "Too bad. I would like to take you out to dinner."

"Have you eaten?"

"No. I was hoping you would have dinner with me."

"I could make you something. What would you like?" I offered.

“If I told you what I wanted to eat, I would break my vow.”

I groaned. “Dammit, Oliver, stop it!” I yelled.

“I’ll take a sandwich and some water.”

“I have turkey and ham.”

“Both.”

I got up from the couch and went to the kitchen, taking out everything I needed to make a sandwich for Oliver. He picked up one of the magazines from the table and paged through it.

“You read this crap?”

I shrugged. “It’s Sadie’s. I’m not really interested. Why are you?”

“I just wanted to see if I was in here.”

“My, you are conceited. I’m sure you’re not the only eligible bachelor on the East Coast.”

“I don’t want to be eligible.”

I knew what he meant by his statement. He hoped we would start dating and he would be off the market. I wanted that, too.

~

“Stop, stop,” I panted.

Once again, we were bordering on sex. After Oliver ate his meal, we started to kiss, and I ended up underneath him. He teased me with his mouth, sucking my earlobes and nibbling on my neck. His large erection was pressed against my cleft, and with each shift of his hips, I was almost sure I would orgasm.

He sat up, sweeping his hand over my taut nipples as he backed away, adjusting his shaft in his khaki shorts.

“I should go home before we do something we shouldn’t.”

“I want to,” I said quietly.

He sighed. “We’re not ready.”

“When? Because I can’t take much more of this. Throw me a bone here.”

Oliver’s face clouded. “That’s not the right choice of words.”

“I’d like your bone, but you won’t oblige.”

“That’s a crude thing to say.”

“Does that bother you? I can be a bit brash at times,” I admitted.

He smirked. “I hope that brashness transfers into bed.”

“Do you want to find out?” I challenged.

“Not tonight.”

Oliver stood and once again adjusted his shorts. His erection had barely abated and was still as large as it had been a few minutes ago. I looked at it longingly, wanting to open his shorts.

“I need to use your bathroom,” Oliver stated, his tone urgent.

“I hope you aren’t going to do something that I could help with,” I replied, eyebrow raised in suspicion.

“I have to urinate,” he admitted, almost sheepishly.

I couldn’t help but chuckle. “I think in your state, it would end up on the ceiling.”

Oliver snorted. “Cute. Where is the bathroom?”

I pointed down the hall, my gaze lingering on him as he walked away. Minutes ticked by before he returned.

“Took you long enough,” I remarked.

“I needed to employ some breathing exercises to fix my issue,” he explained.

“I could’ve fixed your issue,” I teased.

“I need to leave. I’d like to see you tomorrow,” he said abruptly.

I bit my lip, feeling a sense of hesitation. “I guess.”

“What’s the matter?” Oliver asked, sensing my reluctance.

"I have the whole apartment to myself. Sadie isn't coming home tonight," I confessed.

"You want company?" he offered.

"Would you stay?" I asked, almost pleadingly.

"Can you keep your hands to yourself?" he challenged.

"I could try," I replied, though uncertainty laced my words.

"Not good enough. Give me your word, and I'll stay," he demanded.

I hesitated, unsure if I could keep such a promise. "I promise."

"Then I'll stay," he agreed.

As he took out his phone and tapped a text, I couldn't help but ask, "Who did you text?"

"Vlad. He's waiting for me," Oliver revealed casually.

"Waiting? Where?" I inquired, surprised.

"Somewhere in the area," he replied nonchalantly.

"You made that poor man wait?" I chided him lightly.

"He gets paid well to wait and do other things. If you wanted something to eat, I could have him bring it," he offered.

"No. I know how it feels to be an errand girl. It's all I seem to do at work," I declined.

Oliver sat down beside me, his touch gentle as he stroked my hair. "You don't like your job?"

"Not really. I told you this before," I confessed.

"Work for me," he suggested suddenly.

"Doing what?" I asked, surprised by his offer.

"We hire all the time. You have a degree, and I'm sure we can place you," he assured me.

"I think that would be too familiar. We should have some space," I reasoned.

"I doubt I would see you during the day. I'm in and out of the office most of the time," he pointed out.

It was so tempting. I really hated my job, and Beatrice had gotten worse as time wore on. She piled on all the shitty jobs no one else wanted to do, and she was nasty, not respecting those who worked for her. It was grating on my nerves.

"But still. You would know I was on the floor somewhere," Oliver remarked, his tone contemplative.

"And you think I would seek you out?" I countered, studying his expression for any hint of sincerity.

"Wouldn't you?" he prodded.

"I would try not to," I admitted, though a part of me knew it would be futile.

"And if you didn't succeed?" he pressed further.

"Then I would take you into the privacy of my office," he admitted, his voice dropping to a near-whisper.

"To do what?" I inquired, curiosity piqued.

"Ryleigh, where is this conversation going?" Oliver interjected, his eyes narrowing slightly.

"I'm simply trying to ascertain if you would try something during the day," I explained, trying to maintain a semblance of professionalism despite the escalating tension between us.

"Try something?" he repeated, a hint of amusement in his voice.

"Sex, Oliver. Sex in the office. Sex in your very large, very comfortable office," I stated bluntly, daring him to deny the possibility.

"Highly inappropriate," he retorted, though his gaze lingered on mine, betraying a flicker of interest.

"But not improbable. Face it, we're like gasoline to flame," I pointed out, unable to deny the magnetic pull between us.

"Gasoline doesn't catch fire; the fumes do," he countered, his lips quirking into a half-smile.

"You know what I mean," I shot back, feeling a flush creeping up my neck.

Oliver kept staring into my eyes, his gaze unwavering. “Yes, I do.”

“So, would you?” I pressed, the question hanging between us like a charged wire.

“Have sex with you in my office? Would it make or break your coming to work for me?” he countered, his voice low and measured.

“Make? Like it’s a perk? You might be horrible in bed,” I challenged, refusing to back down.

“I assure you, I’m not,” he replied confidently, a glint of mischief in his eyes.

“Then show me,” I dared him, my heart pounding in my chest.

“I won’t tonight. You’ll just have to trust me,” he murmured, his gaze intense.

“I hate you,” I muttered, though the words rang hollow even to my own ears.

“Now that I know is a lie,” he said softly, a knowing smile tugging at the corners of his lips.

~

I couldn’t sleep. I’d been tossing and turning for the past hour. Oliver was asleep next to me. I almost came in my panties when he got undressed and slipped into my bed. His body was sublime, and I wanted him in the worst way. I was highly aroused with him so close that it made me consider handling my business in the bathroom. The nagging throb between my legs was annoying, and I unsuccessfully willed it away.

Oliver was on his back with the covers around his waist. His chest and torso were in full silhouette, and I had to restrain myself from touching him. I gave up and gently ran my fingers over his smooth skin, circling his nipples. He grumbled in his sleep. I did it again, and he shifted, startling me by speaking.

"Ryleigh, you promised. Stop trying to seduce me."

He kept his eyes closed, but I could see a slight smile on his face even though I could barely see it.

"You're hard to resist. I'm not doing well," I confessed, feeling the weight of my desire pressing against the walls of restraint.

Oliver turned on his side, his eyes scanning my face with concern. "What's wrong?"

"I'm uncomfortable," I admitted, unable to meet his gaze.

"You hurt?" he asked, his voice laced with genuine concern.

"I'm heated," I confessed, my cheeks flushing with embarrassment.

"We're not having sex," he stated firmly, drawing a line in the sand.

“All sex or just penetration?” I pushed, my curiosity overriding my better judgment.

“What are you driving at?” he questioned, sensing the direction of my thoughts.

“What about oral sex?” I ventured, feeling the tension crackling in the air

between us.

“No. That is considered sex,” he replied, his brows furrowing in contemplation.

“What about if I jerk you off?” I pressed further, testing the boundaries of our conversation.

“Again, sex,” he stated definitively, his tone leaving no room for argument.

“I have to go to the bathroom,” I announced, moving to push the covers off.

Oliver grabbed my arm, his touch gentle yet firm. “If I do something for you, will you promise to be good?” he proposed, his eyes locking onto mine with a mixture of seriousness and underlying desire.

“What did you have in mind?”

“Lie on your back.”

He let my arm go as I returned to bed, lying on my back. My stomach churned with anticipation. I was dressed in panties and a long t-shirt. Oliver slipped his hand over my panties, searching for the waistband. He leaned in and claimed my mouth as he pushed his fingers down to my cleft.

"You're very wet."

"I told you I was," I choked out as he began to make slow circles around my swollen nub.

"Do you always get so wet?"

"I guess. It's been a while since I had sex."

He clamped his mouth on mine again and sped up his finger. I bucked my hips and within a minute I was coming. I tore my mouth from his and moaned loudly. Oliver kept rubbing me until my body went limp.

"There, now go to sleep," he said as he gave me a final peck on the cheek.

"What about you?"

"What about me? I have self-control."

"Is that to say that I don't?"

"Ryleigh, stop arguing with me and turn on your side so I can cuddle you."

I smiled in the dark and moved to my side. Oliver took me in his arms and tucked his chin against my shoulder. It was the last thing I remembered—besides his erection pressed into my back—as I fell asleep.

When I woke up the next morning, Oliver was still next to me. I see his gorgeous face in the light that's seeping in from around the curtains. During the night, I turned in his arms and was now facing his chest. I planted kisses on the muscled flesh and a rumble escaped from him.

As I blinked my eyes open to the soft light filtering through the curtains, Oliver's voice greeted me. "Good morning. I thought I was dreaming."

I couldn't help the smirk that tugged at my lips. "About what?" I inquired, teasingly.

"You in my arms. I like having you in my arms," he confessed, his tone warm and genuine.

"I like it. I like you," I responded, though the truth flickered behind my words. My heart belonged to Oliver, but admitting it felt like stepping into a whirlwind of uncertainty. I had fallen into this situation so quickly, it was hard to untangle myself.

His smile widened. "I'm glad to hear that. Can I interest you in some breakfast?"

I raised an eyebrow. "How do you know I have anything here to eat?"

"I'm not asking to eat breakfast here. Come to my apartment," he suggested, his eyes twinkling with mischief.

"You want me to go all the way to your apartment to eat brunch?" I quipped.

"Brunch. You won't be disappointed. You owe me," he reminded me, a playful glint in his eyes.

I leaned in, trailing a kiss along his chest. "I owe you for what?"

"Last night. It's your turn to please me," he murmured, his voice husky with desire.

"I wanted to, but you said no," I reminded him, feeling a pang of frustration mingled with longing.

"Not with sex. Come home with me. Let me feed you," he urged gently.

"Can we eat on the patio?" I asked, my mind already envisioning the warm sunlight dappling our skin as we dined al fresco.

"If that's your pleasure, we can," he acquiesced with a smile.

As Oliver sat up, I took a moment to admire the contours of his body, resisting the urge to trace kisses along his skin.

"Should I shower?" I asked, breaking the moment.

"You can, unless you want to do it at my place," he suggested, a hint of temptation lacing his words.

"That's tempting in more ways than one," I remarked, my eyes lingering on him suggestively.

"It would be a shower, nothing else," he clarified.

My heart raced at the thought of being so close to him.

"I'll take a quick one here," I decided, slipping out of bed and heading for the bathroom.

He watched me go, a soft smile playing on his lips. When I emerged from the shower, Oliver was already dressed and fussing with his hair in front of the mirror.

"Leave it messy, I like it that way," I suggested, stepping up beside him.

"I don't," he replied, his attention still on his reflection.

He continued to work on his hair while I moved around him and pulled out a pink bra and panty set. When he saw it, Oliver focused on me.

"Are you going to watch me get dressed?"

"I should sit in the living room. I'm giving up on my hair," he declared.

"You can stay if you want."

He smirked. "That's not a good idea and you know why."

"I'll be out in a minute."

He went to sit on the couch, and just to be a brat, I left the door open while I dressed. From his vantage point, he could partially see me, but when I looked at him, he was typing something into his phone.

"Typical," I muttered under my breath, sliding into my clothes with an air of defiance.

Vlad was waiting for us downstairs when we exited my building. Traffic was still light since it was before 9:00 AM on a Sunday morning. I snuggled up against Oliver's shoulder as we drove to his place, the city slowly waking up around us. He kissed the top of my head, his touch warm and comforting, and put his arm around me.

When we arrived at his building, he took me upstairs. A man was standing in the kitchen wearing chef's whites, and I detected the aroma of cinnamon wafting through the air. Oliver nodded at the man as he led me out to the patio, the anticipation of what awaited us stirring in my chest.

The rectangular teak table had two places set with China, silverware, and glasses, the morning sunlight casting a golden hue over everything. The oversized umbrella had been opened to shade us while we ate, creating an intimate oasis amidst the urban chaos. A large pitcher of blood orange juice sat in a silver platter with raised sides, glistening with condensation like dewdrops on a summer morning.

Oliver pulled out my seat for me, a gesture that felt both chivalrous and endearing. After I was comfortable, he sat down next to me, his eyes gleaming with a hint of excitement. A few seconds later, a woman wearing a black uniform came to the table, her demeanor poised and professional. She placed a bowl of fruit salad and a plate with cinnamon buns and danish on the table with a practiced flourish, adding to the allure of the scene before us.

"Cinnamon buns? You?" I teased, raising an eyebrow.

"You think I don't eat simply?" Oliver replied with a playful grin.

"Oliver, this is hardly simple. You have a chef and a waitress serving us," I pointed out, gesturing to the attentive staff.

"Would you rather I send them home and cook for you?" he quipped, a hint of challenge in his tone.

"If I asked, would you?" I countered, curiosity dancing in my eyes.

"Are you challenging me? I can cook," he declared, his competitive spirit coming to the surface.

"I'm sure you can, but since your chef is here, let him do his magic," I conceded, a smile tugging at my lips.

"Would you like some juice?" Oliver offered, changing the subject smoothly.

I smirked, unable to resist. "Is it fresh squeezed?"

"Absolutely, and I have the pulp strained because I dislike it," he assured me, a twinkle in his eyes.

"Can I have some ice? I like my drinks cold," I requested, playfully pushing the boundaries.

"I'm sure it can be arranged," he replied, his tone

indulgent as he signaled for the waitress to fulfill my request.

We had a leisurely breakfast. The coffee was an exotic blend, and the cinnamon buns were homemade as were the danish. The chef himself brought out a mushroom and cheese frittata and served us. It was delicious. I couldn’t stop myself from touching Oliver. Every so often, I stroked his arm or hand.

"Are you trying to seduce me again?" Oliver's asked, his voice smooth as silk.

"Not at all," I replied, a playful glint in my eyes as I met his gaze. "Your skin is so soft and so tan. You’re always in the office. How are you that tan?" I couldn't help but ask, my curiosity piqued.

"I have a boat and a house on Long Island. I spend time there on the weekends. I can work from anywhere, really," he explained, a hint of wanderlust in his tone.

"You know what they say about all work and no play?" I teased, a smile playing at the corners of my lips.

"I do play, but not as often as I would like. Now that I have a playmate, I might have to make changes," Oliver countered, his eyes dancing with mischief.

"Is that how you see me? As a playmate?" I questioned, my heart skipping a beat at the implications.

"No. You’re so much more than that," he assured me, his words sending a warm rush through me.

I returned his smile before taking another bite of my second cinnamon bun, savoring the decadent flavor. They were delicious, undoubtedly baked with plenty of butter. A pang of guilt crept in as I contemplated the potential impact on my waistline. I'd been lucky my freshman year, avoiding the dreaded freshman fifteen, but I knew I needed to be mindful.

"So what do you have on the agenda today? Should I go home now that you fed me?" I inquired, shifting the conversation.

"I would like you to stay, but only if I'm not keeping you from something," Oliver replied, his gaze soft with concern.

"I have nothing going on, but it's what I might be keeping you from," I confessed, my thoughts racing with possibilities.

"It's nothing that can't wait. I'd rather spend time with you," he insisted, his words washing over me like a soothing balm.

Oliver leaned in, his lips meeting mine in a coffee-laced kiss that ignited a spark between us. I eagerly deepened the kiss, losing myself in the sensation of his touch.

"You're making me crazy. I think it's time for me to take a cold shower," he murmured, his breath hot against my skin.

"Where should I wait for you?" I asked, anticipation coursing through me.

"My bedroom or the study. The choice is yours," he offered, his voice low and inviting.

My pulse quickened at the thought of being alone with Oliver, my mind racing with possibilities. As he helped me from my chair and escorted me to his bedroom, my stomach tightened with anticipation. Maybe today, I'd catch a glimpse of Oliver in his boxers.

A thrill ran through me as I allowed myself to hope. As we passed by the chef and waitress cleaning the kitchen, Oliver nodded at them, a silent acknowledgment of their presence before leading me into his private sanctuary.

I sat down on his bed while he showered, snuggling into his soft comforter. I almost fell asleep until Oliver came out of the bathroom with a thick white terry cloth towel wrapped around his waist. I opened my eyes and ogled him. I still couldn't believe how hot he was.

Oliver turned and I quickly closed my eyes, but he was wise to me. He sat down on the edge of the bed and stroked my hair.

"Were you watching me?"

I opened my eyes and smiled, "I can't help it. You're hot."

"You're the one that's hot."

I moved my hand to his thigh and began to rub. He put his over mine to stop me.

"Don't start."

"Why not?" I pouted.

"Because. The time isn't right."

"How do you know?"

"I just do. Now behave."

He got off the bed and went into the walk-in closet. I could see part of him, and when he removed his towel to slip on his boxers, I thought I'd died and gone to heaven. His taut ass was beautiful and muscular. My core tightened, thinking about digging my nails into it while Oliver fucked me. I couldn't take it and turned to face the window.

I could see out to the patio from his bed. The table we ate breakfast at was clean and the umbrella was now in the closed position. It was nice to be served once in a while. I could get used to this, but we were just starting our relationship. Maybe Oliver would find something out about me that he didn't like and end us.

I still hadn't revealed to him about my father. If he did any research on me, he would've known about the murder. I was sure once I had a nightmare, startling him out of a deep sleep, he wouldn't want to bother with me. I had already lost a boyfriend once before because I couldn't stop waking up screaming. It was only a matter of time.

"Ryleigh, what's the matter?"

I turned my head to see him dressed in a pair of pressed

gray shorts and white polo shirt. His sandy hair was neatly combed, thick on the top and short on the sides.

“Nothing. I was just thinking about....” I fumbled for a topic. “About how beautiful your patio is. I really enjoyed breakfast.”

“I’m glad. They say the way to a woman’s heart is food.”

“No, that’s a man. The way to a woman’s heart is diamonds.”

I was joking of course but Oliver gave me such a serious look that I wondered if I overstepped my bounds. He was a man of means and I’m sure there were plenty of women that viewed him as a meal ticket.

“I would buy you many if that would make you give me your heart,” Oliver confessed, his voice tinged with sincerity.

“You don’t have to buy me things. I don’t expect it, and I’m not asking,” I reassured him, my tone gentle yet firm.

“I hoped you would say that, but it still doesn’t mean I wouldn’t want to buy you gifts,” he admitted, a hint of vulnerability in his words.

“I don’t need gifts. Maybe we should talk,” I suggested, feeling a weight settle in the pit of my stomach.

“Are we about to have a deep conversation?” Oliver inquired, his brow furrowing slightly.

“You know about me, but not everything. I haven’t told

you all the details," I confessed, feeling a knot form in my throat.

I sat up and leaned against the headboard, my knees drawn up to my chest. Oliver mirrored my movement, sitting a couple of feet away from me on the bed and crossing his legs. I took a deep breath, steeling myself for the conversation that lay ahead.

"My father was murdered when I was six."

His face tightened, "Excuse me?"

"My father was murdered. I was with him when it happened."

He tried to hide his look of horror, but it was apparent. "I'm sorry. I thought you lived with your parents."

"Anders is my stepfather, but he adopted me and my brothers. He's been married to my mother for fourteen years. He's been my father longer than my biological father was. I don't remember him well and I remember almost nothing about the murder."

"Jesus Christ. You saw it happen?"

"I don't know. I only remember our car being hit and my father getting out to talk to the other driver. The next thing I remember is sitting by his bloody body. It was late and there were few cars on the street. I don't know how long I sat there with him before someone came by."

He reached out for me but I moved away. If he touched me while I told the story, I would burst into tears. I wanted Oliver to know that I was damaged and there was still time for him to walk away.

My voice cracked. “I stopped talking for a while. I missed a whole year of school and went to a therapist.”

“Did they find the killer?”

I shook my head. “No. It’s unsolved.”

“Someone shot your father just for a small fender bender?”

I shrugged. I didn’t know the motivation of my father’s killer. “I guess. I don’t know what it was about. My father told me to stay down. I think he knew the man.”

“Are you okay?”

I shifted uncomfortably under Oliver's intense gaze, feeling the weight of his concern as he reached out to me.

"No," I whispered, avoiding his eyes. "I have nightmares, especially when stress piles up. I scared Sadie half to death when we first shared a room. But she... she got it. She pushed her bed next to mine, stayed close until the terrors ebbed away. That's why she's so special to me. She understood when others might have just walked away."

"Come here," Oliver urged, his voice a gentle command.

I hesitated, uncertainty flickering in my eyes, but Oliver moved swiftly to envelop me in his arms, drawing me onto his lap, peppering my face with soft kisses.

"I won't leave you because of your nightmares," he murmured against my skin.

"Thank you," I whispered gratefully.

"You don't need to thank me," he replied, sincerity coloring his words. "I care about you."

My shoulders slumped, a sigh escaping my lips. "I have to work tomorrow. I can't keep being the coffee runner."

Sliding off Oliver's lap, I returned to my previous spot.

"Work for me," Oliver offered, his tone determined. "We can find a role for you. We're always expanding."

I shook my head, worry creasing my brow. "What would your staff think if I joined? They'd speculate about favoritism because of us being together."

"It's none of their concern," Oliver stated firmly. "I'm the boss. I can hire whomever I choose."

I sighed, frustration edging into my voice. "True, but that won't stop the gossip. I've seen it in my own workplace."

"Do you care what they say?" Oliver questioned, his gaze unwavering.

"It would bother me," I admitted reluctantly.

"Then we'll keep it discreet," Oliver decided. "Does that mean you want to be exclusive with me?"

"Do you?" I countered, my heart pounding in my chest.

Oliver's expression softened, his eyes reflecting his sincerity. “Don’t ask a question with a question. Do you?”

I played with a lock of my hair. "I still don't understand why you want me."

"You don't need to understand," I replied softly. "Just know that I do. You're everything I've ever wanted, and I've waited a lifetime to find you. I'm not letting you slip away."

Chapter 8

I've been dating Oliver officially for two weeks. I still hate my job and I've seriously been considering a position at Fox Asset Corporation. We haven't slept together yet, and it's killing me to be so near him without having sex. I've spent evenings in his bed and he in mine, but it's never gone farther than Oliver getting me off with his fingers. He has incredible control and, frankly, some set of blue balls.

We'll spend the Fourth of July holiday at Oliver's house in Southampton since Sadie is going away with Dan to Rhode Island. His home is huge, and I wonder why someone who has no family needs a house with seven bedrooms.

My boss gave us a reprieve, letting us leave at 2 p.m. I'm glad because any time I can escape her is a plus. She still treats me like I'm an idiot, and my biggest tasks are filing and entering data.

My plan is to go home, get changed, and take a nap before Oliver arrives with Chinese food for dinner. Since he hates driving in traffic, we won't leave until 11 p.m. By the time he arrived, looking delicious in khaki shorts and a blue polo shirt, I'm starving.

"I come bearing gifts, and I get no kiss," he said as he sat down at the table.

I put down the glass I'm washing and kiss him hard on the lips. Oliver pressed his body to mine, running his hand down my back to cup my ass. He caressed my tongue with his own, and my core started to flood. I'm getting sick of changing my wet panties and wiggled out of his grasp.

His expression is one of humor. "What's the matter?"

I rolled my eyes. "Don't get me started. Let's just eat and relax before we leave."

Oliver rose from the chair. "Let's go."

I raised my eyebrows. "Go where? I thought you didn't want to leave now."

"I don't want to leave right now. I want to make love to you."

I gasped. "Don't tease me."

Oliver took my hand, leading me into my bedroom.

I pulled back on his hand. "No. Seriously? Why now?"

He shook his head. "I can't win with you. You want sex, and now you don't?"

I bit my bottom lip. "It's just that you get me so heated sometimes. Why are we waiting?"

"We're not. I want to make love to you."

My stomach twisted with anxiety. This was so unexpected. "Suppose I'm not in the mood?"

He chuckled. "I don't believe it. I get you off almost every night."

I crossed my arms. "I want your cock, not your fingers."

Oliver smirked. He was so fucking smug that I wanted to slap him.

"How about my mouth?"

"Huh?"

He licked his lips for emphasis. "I'm going to use my mouth on you. I know you want me to."

I was speechless, which for me was rare.

"Oliver, I..."

"Stop giving me a hard time. I want to taste you."

I just stood there as he came to me, kneeled, and opened my shorts, pulling them down with my panties. I still hadn't said anything when he backed me to the bed, spread my legs, and got between them. This was the first time my most intimate part had been exposed to Oliver.

He bent my knees, pushing my heels against my ass so I was opened wide. I heard him suck in his breath.

"You have such a pretty pussy, pink and wet."

I was so aroused that I had a feeling the minute he touched me with his tongue, I would explode. Oliver bent down, and instead of going for the kill, he teased me by kissing my inner thighs, belly, and mound. He moved on top of me and kissed me hard, tweaking my budded nipples as he slid off.

"Are you ready for this?"

I groaned. "I've been ready for three weeks."

I closed my eyes and felt his fingers spread me wide before his tongue darted inside me. He lapped at me like I was an ice cream cone and joined in my moans as if he were enjoying a tasty treat. By the time he got to my clit, I was ready to come. He circled my swollen tissue three times, and I was falling apart as my orgasm tore through me while I screamed his name. My body quaked and shook as he sucked and lapped me until I stopped.

Olive moved alongside me, planting kisses on my face and neck. If this is what he could do with his tongue, I would probably pass out when he fucked me. If there was any doubt I was in love with him before, this sealed the deal. I had fallen so deep for him that I would need a ladder to get me out.

"How was that sweetheart?"

I kept my eyes closed when I answered. “I can’t move. I want to go to sleep.”

He pressed a kiss to my neck. “You need to have dinner, and then you can take a nap.”

“I don’t have the energy to get up,” I whispered.

He climbed off the bed and picked up my shorts and panties from the floor.

“Do you need help getting dressed?”

I opened my eyes and grinned at him. “I think I’ll just walk around bottomless.”

“You absolutely will not. Get dressed and I’ll set the table.”

I grumbled as he retreated into the kitchen. I felt weak but I willed myself to get up and dress. When I came out, Oliver had the table set and a small black velvet box sat on my dinner plate. My heart rate doubled. I knew we were moving fast but what was in the box worried me.

“What’s this?”

“A gift. Don’t hurt my feelings by saying no.”

Oliver’s dark blue eyes were shining as he watched me sit down and open the box. Inside was a pair of teardrop diamond earrings. They were beautiful and I bet expensive since the diamonds were at least a carat apiece.

“Thank you. These are gorgeous,” I said as I ran my finger over the stones.

“When we make love, I want you wearing nothing but these.”

“Oh? You’re finally giving in?”

He smirked, revealing his pearly whites. “I have several surprises this weekend.”

I regained my strength and ate a good amount of food. The only problem was that it made me sleepy, and I took a nap on the couch after we cleaned the kitchen. I woke up just before 10:45 p.m. to Oliver stroking my face. I give him a smile as I looked up.

“Almost time to go.”

I’m so ready to spend a quiet weekend with him. Even though it’s a holiday, I’m sure his office will contact him with some headache. I’ve gotten used to the interruptions. Oliver has so many things going on, and was very hands-on in his business. I’ve accepted it because it’s part of him and kept my opinions to myself.

“I want to brush my teeth before we go.”

He nuzzled my cheek with his nose before I headed to the bathroom. Ten minutes later, we were on our way. Vlad is following us, and I wonder if the man ever sleeps.

"Will we be alone for the weekend?" I ventured, a flicker of uncertainty dancing in my eyes.

Oliver's gaze met mine, a hint of amusement playing at the corners of his lips. "Yes. Why would you think otherwise?"

I swallowed, the nerves fluttering in my stomach. "Is Vlad staying in the house with us, or will he return to the city?"

Oliver reached for my hand, his touch grounding me in his presence. "Vlad's job is to protect me. He'll be in the guest house if he's needed."

My curiosity piqued. "You have a guest house?"

He nodded, a small smile gracing his features. "Yes. Three bedrooms."

"Lucky guests," I quipped, a hint of mischief in my tone.

Oliver chuckled softly. "There have been. I don't often have visitors at my home."

"Matthew is in Southampton this weekend. Maybe we can meet him for drinks," I suggested tentatively, the prospect of him meeting my brother adding another layer of excitement to our weekend.

Oliver's expression softened, his focus unwavering on me. "If you would like, though I'd prefer us to be alone."

A surge of warmth filled me at his words. "I want you to meet my family."

“I want you to meet my family.”

“There will be plenty of time for introductions. I have no plans to let you go.”

. . .

I smiled to myself, fingers tracing the delicate sparkle of the diamond earrings adorning my ears. Anticipation twisted in my stomach, a potent mix of nerves and desire as I replayed Oliver's earlier touch in my mind. His skillful tongue had left me reeling, a memory I couldn't shake.

Lost in thought, I watched the expressway lights blur past, casting fleeting shadows across the car's interior. Despite the light traffic, the journey to Oliver's home stretched ahead, a silent countdown to the moment I'd been yearning for.

We arrived just shy of 1 a.m., the night heavy with the scent of salt and anticipation. Oliver's strong arms guided me from the SUV, Vlad trailing behind with our luggage. Exhaustion weighed on me despite the nap I'd stolen earlier, my attention drifting as we approached Oliver's imposing mansion.

Before I could protest, Oliver scooped me up effortlessly, cradling me against his chest. I nestled into his warmth, clinging to him as we ascended the staircase to his sanctuary. The plush bed welcomed me, its softness a comforting embrace as Oliver tenderly removed my sneakers.

In the hazy blur of sleep, I drifted off quickly, cocooned in the tranquility of Oliver's presence.

Waking to darkness, the room enveloped in the silvery glow of moonlight, I reached out and found Oliver beside me, his chest rising and falling in steady rhythm. Fingertips trailed over his bare skin, drawing a soft sigh from him.

"Are you okay?" His voice, a gentle murmur, broke the silence.

"Yes, fine. Sorry, I fell asleep," I murmured, my words muffled against his chest.

"You were tired. Didn't you sleep last night?" His concern was palpable.

"Not much. I was excited," I admitted, shifting slightly.

"You should've woken me," he insisted.

"Oliver, you already get so little sleep. You didn't need to be up with me," I protested softly.

"I wanted to," he countered, his sincerity touching.

Uncomfortable in my shorts, I shifted to remove them, a sudden wave of self-consciousness washing over me.

"What are you doing?" His voice held a hint of surprise.

"Taking off my shorts. Why didn't you?" I questioned, unsure.

"I didn't want you to think I was taking advantage," he confessed, his vulnerability echoing my own.

“You had your mouth on me a few hours ago, and you were worried about taking advantage?”

“That was consensual. I wouldn’t touch you without your say so.”

I giggled. “What about now?”

“Do you want me to touch you now?” he said, his voice thick with seduction.

“I want you to fuck me. I had an arousing dream.”

He chuckled. “Oh? Tell me about it.”

“I’d rather show you.”

“Now I’m intrigued.” His voice was full of mischief.

I slipped from the bed and removed all my clothing. I wanted Oliver.

“Should I show you with your boxers on?”

“You want them off?”

In the moonlight, I saw him staring at me, and when I moved to the bed, he told me to stop.

“Why?”

“You look so beautiful in the moonlight. You’re gorgeous, Ryleigh,” he said.

A hot flush heated my face. “Don’t be ridiculous.”

“I’m not.”

He pushed the covers off, lifted his hips, and stripped off his boxers. I noticed his cock was sticking straight up, and I smiled.

"That didn't take long."

"You have my mind going. Now show me."

I crawled onto the bed and straddled his hips, moving his penis so that it was flat against his belly. He gasped when I positioned it between the soaked lips of my pussy and began to slide back and forth. My dream had me wet and wanting.

"Oh fuck," he growled.

"I want you inside."

"Then stop what you're doing before you make me come."

I leaned forward, placing my hands on Oliver's shoulders. My long mahogany hair brushed his face as I moved back and forth. With each stroke, cock tip hit my clit in just the right way. I wanted to come, and I was reaching the point of no return.

"Stop, Ryleigh," Oliver panted.

I didn't, and he moaned, placing his hands on my thighs. He murmured for me to stop again, but I ignored him. I sped up my hips, and he dug his nails into my skin as I started to come. I didn't stop moving, wanting him to climax. A few seconds later, jets of cum spurted up his stomach and chest as he grunted. I continued to move until we both finished, and then I folded my body onto his. Oliver held me tightly with his arms around my back.

“I thought you wanted me to make love to you,” he whispered.

“You’ve been giving me pleasure for weeks and ask nothing in return. I wanted to give you this.”

“We made a mess.”

“I don’t care.”

His cum was sticky and warm against my belly and chest, but I didn’t care. It was part of Oliver, and I loved him. He held me for a few minutes, planting kisses on my cheek.

“We should shower.”

“I agree.”

He let me go, and I rose off him. The scent of sex was thick in the air as I moved from the bed. Oliver followed, taking my hand to lead me into the bathroom. He flicked the light on, and I squinted. The room was huge and white. The shower stall was the size of a small bedroom with two large white tiled benches and three shower heads.

He reached into the glass enclosure to turn on all three shower heads, and when he turned back, I got a good look at his body. His dick was still semi-erect, glistening in the bright lights with my juices. He had come a lot, and our bodies were coated.

“We never discussed birth control,” he said quietly.

I searched his face for traces of anger, but there were none.

“I take birth control, and you know we’ve both been tested.”

“I just wanted to be sure.”

"I wouldn't trap you with a baby," I blurted out, the words tinged with a hint of desperation.

"That was the furthest from my mind. I want children," Oliver responded, his tone soft but resolute.

My heart skipped a beat. "That's not the point. The point is that we barely know each other."

"Don't you want children?" he pressed, his gaze searching mine.

I wondered if I answered differently if it would be a game changer in our relationship.

"Yes, but not this soon. I'm only twenty-two," I confessed, the weight of our conversation settling heavily between us.

“Our children would be beautiful. The water is warm; let’s shower.”

He held the thick glass door open for me, and I stepped into the stall. Oliver lovingly washed me with his hands and vanilla-scented body wash. I let him because I wanted him to touch me. He paid particularly close attention to my breasts, taking each of my nipples in his mouth to suck.

I, in turn, washed him while he watched as my fingers stroked over his body. We spent over twenty minutes in the shower, and by the time he wrapped me in a thick white terry towel, I was ready for sex. I reached for him, stroking his shaft, which was thick with arousal from our shower. Even at thirty-six, he had a low refractory rate, and he got hard quickly.

Oliver pulled the towel from my body and turned me to face the large white granite vanity.

“Spread your legs,” he growled.

I did and his hand slipped between my folds as he inserted a finger inside me.

“You’re soaked.”

He removed his finger just as fast as he stuck it in and replaced it with his cock, pressing his wide head against my opening.

“Are you ready for me?” he asked, his voice choked with emotion.

“I’ve been ready for three weeks.”

“Put your hands on the counter.”

I wasn’t fast enough with his request, and he gently bit my shoulder then licked the spot where he sank his teeth. He roughly pulled me back and then thrust into me. It was so much all at once that I gasped loudly.

“Shit, I’m sorry,” Oliver said.

“Just give me a few seconds before you move.”

He wrapped his arm around my waist and kissed the back of my neck as he waited for me to acclimate to his size. I was sure I would be sore when we woke up later this morning. He pulsed inside me, and I tightened my slick walls against him.

“No fair,” he growled.

I did it again and heard him hiss. “Behave. I’m giving you what you want.”

“You wanted this too, or we wouldn’t be here.”

“Duly noted.”

He was gentle when he started to move his hips until he got into a methodical rhythm. His hand moved his hand to my cleft and began to rub my clit. I didn’t need the extra stimulation because after only a few strokes, I was at the cusp of my second orgasm.

“Oh God, Oliver, you’re going to make me come.”

He thrust harder, and I exploded, squeezing his shaft as I cycled through one of the most powerful orgasm I’d ever had. He continued to gently rub my clit, and I clawed at his hand so he would stop. My sensitivity was making me shudder with each touch, and my legs were so weak I braced my hands on the counter to hold me up.

"It will go away in a few seconds. You know how good that felt when you came? I want you to do it again."

"I don't think I can," I whined.

"Shh, you can. I know you can."

I leaned forward on the smooth counter and tried to steady my shaky legs as Oliver continued. He pumped inside me and applied more pressure to my swollen tissue with his finger. Within two minutes, I could feel another orgasm building. I rippled against him as his dick massaged my walls, and he pounded harder into me, pushing my hips against the counter and sandwiching his hand.

"Oliver," I moaned as I started to come again. This time, he joined me, and I felt a hot spurt after hot spurt of semen deep inside me as he continued to thrust through our orgasms. When we finished, I was numb and weak. Oliver leaned over my back to support me before he pulled out and scooped me into his arms.

He took me back into the shower and sat down on one of the tiled benches while he held me.

"I don't want to scare you," he whispered.

"Scare me how?" I mumbled as I rested in his arms with my eyes closed.

"I love you, Ryleigh. I can't help it, and I don't want to hold it in anymore."

“So soon?” I wasn’t surprised because I had been in love with him since the first few days we spent together. I’m glad he said it first.

“You’re who I want.”

“How long, Oliver?” I asked.

I raised my head and opened my eyes to look into his.

“Since graduation. I saw you in line, and this feeling came over me.”

God, it was like a fucking fairytale. He fell in love with me at first sight. I always thought it was so stupid when people talked about that kind of love, but he was proof it could happen. And I had to admit I wasn’t far behind when it came to loving him.

“Suppose I didn’t work in the same building as you? Would you have looked for me?” I asked.

"I had your name, and that’s all I needed," he declared, my voice edged with determination.

"So you would have stalked me?"

Oliver's eyebrows shot up in surprise.

"Of course not. I would’ve had Vlad do it," he replied casually as if it were the most natural thing in the world.

I narrowed my eyes. "That sounds creepy."

"Tell me you don’t feel the same," he challenged, daring me to deny the undeniable connection between us.

My gaze softened. "I don't yet."

"I think you're lying. I know when a woman is in love with me," he countered, his confidence unwavering.

"I thought you said you didn't have girlfriends?" My tone was laced with skepticism.

"I don't, but that doesn't mean women don't fall in love with me," he shrugged.

"That sounds pretty arrogant," I remarked, a smirk playing at the corners of my lips.

"It's true. I can't help if women fall in love with what they see in front of them. It's not real because they don't know me. You know me," he admitted, a flicker of vulnerability beneath his confident exterior.

"I do know you and love you," I confessed.

A smirk tugged at Oliver's lips. "See, I knew it."

“Ass.”

I eased off him, feeling a twinge of reluctance as he rose to turn on the shower. The warm water cascaded over us once again, cleansing away the remnants of our passion. Side by side, we lathered and rinsed, the intimacy of the moment wrapping around us like a comforting embrace.

As we stepped out, Oliver took the towel, his touch gentle as he dried my body, each stroke igniting a trail of warmth. Returning to bed, we cocooned ourselves in the sheets just as dawn's soft light filtered through the window, painting the room in hues of gold.

Hours slipped by unnoticed as we slept, lost in the tranquility of each other's arms. When the sun reached its zenith, its rays streaming through the French doors with unrelenting intensity, I buried my face into the pillow, seeking refuge from its brightness.

A gentle kiss on my forehead stirred me from my drowsiness, and I turned to meet Oliver's gaze, his eyes soft with affection. At that moment, bathed in the warmth of the morning sun and the tenderness of his touch, I knew that this was where I belonged.

“I love you,” he murmured.

“I know,” I know, I mumbled.

Oliver snorted. “Now who’s being arrogant?”

I elbowed his ribs. “Hey, I said I loved you. Give me a break.”

“I said it first.”

“You win.”

I circled the tip of my tongue over his nipple and heard him suck in his breath.

“Don’t do that because right now I’m ready for round two.”

I kissed his neck, running my tongue down the thick column of muscle. “Don’t you mean round three?”

“Whatever. Don’t tease.”

I gently sank my teeth into his nipple this time, sawing my teeth over it. Oliver sprang up and was on top of me with his erection trapped in between us.

"You want to play?" he growled.

I leveled my gaze at him. "I want you to fuck me, if that's what you mean."

"Oh, I definitely will, but you'll have to wait for it."

"This place is magnificent," I said as I gazed out to the ocean view beyond the pool. Oliver had taken his time with me this morning, deliberate in his actions as he made love to me. I was soaked and begging for him to fuck me when he finally did. We made it out to the pool just before noon.

I lounged back on the cushioned lounger, the sun kissing my skin, as I surveyed the sprawling estate around me. Dressed in a silver bikini that left little to the imagination, I felt a surge of confidence wash over me. Oliver, sporting nothing but a pair of sleek black swim trunks, reclined beside me, the epitome of casual elegance.

Despite the opulence surrounding us, I couldn't help but feel a pang of curiosity about the rest of Oliver's home. From what little I had seen; it was clear that luxury was the name of the game.

The kitchen alone could rival that of a five-star restaurant, with its gleaming stainless steel appliances, pristine white cabinets, and an island of white granite that practically begged to be danced upon. It seemed Oliver had a penchant for white, evident even in the modern contemporary living room with its panoramic views of the rolling green lawn and ocean beyond.

As I soaked in the sights, Oliver rose from his lounger with easy grace, tossing his sunglasses aside before striding purposefully toward the pool. With a practiced ease, he bounced lightly on the diving board before executing a flawless swan dive, slicing through the water with effortless grace. My eyes followed him as he swam leisurely laps, each stroke a testament to his strength and athleticism.

When he finally emerged from the water, droplets cascading down his sculpted physique, I found myself captivated by the sight. His sandy hair tousled, and his skin glistened in the sunlight, he was a vision of raw masculinity. A primal desire stirred within me, an urge to reach out and pull him close, to taste the salt of his skin and lose myself in the heat of the moment.

"See something you like?" Oliver's playful voice cut through the air.

I shook my head, a smirk playing on my lips. "No."

His brow furrowed in mock offense. "You don't?"

A smile tugged at the corners of my mouth. "I see something I love. You're beautiful, Oliver."

"You're the one that's beautiful. Swim with me," he suggested, extending his hand towards me.

"I want to work on my tan," I protested, settling back onto the lounger.

But Oliver had other plans. Before I could react, he scooped me up effortlessly, tossing me over his shoulder like a sack of potatoes. I pounded on his back as he strode purposefully towards the edge of the pool.

"NO! Don't you dare," I warned, my voice tinged with laughter and alarm.

With a mischievous glint in his eye, Oliver leaned forward and plunged into the pool, taking me with him. I resurfaced with a sputter, splashing him playfully despite the distance between us.

"I can't believe you just did that," I exclaimed, a mixture of amusement and indignation in my tone.

"You're sexy when you're angry. I should do it more often," Oliver teased.

"Upset me?" I challenged, raising an eyebrow.

"Yes. I love the look on your face," he admitted.

"You wouldn't like me when I'm angry," I warned, though the threat lacked any real conviction.

. . .

"I would, because we have makeup sex to look forward to," he countered, his voice husky with desire.

"You don't need to make me angry to have sex," I murmured, swimming towards him and pressing my body against his, my hand trailing teasingly to his crotch. I leaned in, capturing his lips in a passionate kiss, my fingers dancing over his growing arousal.

"You're making me hard," Oliver groaned, his desire evident in his voice.

“Get used to it because I plan to do that a lot.”

We were interrupted when Vlad came across the lawn from the large guest house on the other side of the property. Oliver let me go to swim to the stairs. This was the first time I'd seen Vlad in casual attire. He was wearing a red polo shirt and gray slacks. I couldn't hear their conversation, but it seemed serious. Oliver nodded, and Vlad went back toward the guest house.

"Everything all right?" I inquired, concern lacing my tone as I watched Oliver retreat to make a call.

"Yes, fine. I have to make a call," he replied briskly, the weight of his words hanging in the air.

"We were interrupted," I pointed out, a hint of disappointment coloring my voice.

"I'm sorry. I'll make it up to you after I get off the phone. We should make a decision on lunch," Oliver deflected, his tone apologetic yet distracted.

"I guess," I murmured, unable to shake off the feeling of being brushed aside.

"Ryleigh, don't be upset. You know this is my business," Oliver reassured me, his words tinged with genuine concern.

"It's a holiday weekend. I thought they would leave you alone," I countered, my frustration bubbling to the surface.

"It's never a holiday for me. I'll try to limit my time away from you," Oliver promised, though his tone lacked conviction.

With a sigh, he grabbed a towel and disappeared inside to make his call. Left alone by the pool, I swam to the stairs and emerged from the water, feeling a chill as the cool air conditioning hit my damp skin.

As I dried myself off, I couldn't shake the sense of unease that lingered in the air. Oliver's absence gnawed at me, and I couldn't resist the urge to tease him. With a mischievous grin, I untied the bottom of my bikini top, flashing him a playful glance as I did so. His reaction was fleeting, his gaze flickering away, but I knew I had succeeded in distracting him, if only for a moment.

Tying my top back in place, I glanced around but found Oliver gone. With a shrug, I dried myself off and headed inside, the enticing aroma of food drawing me to the kitchen. The sight of the fully stocked refrigerator lifted my spirits, and I quickly set about fixing myself a meal, hungry after our earlier exertions.

His huge refrigerator was stocked with everything. I hunted around until I found some grapes and a container of crab salad. I loved crab and opened the container then hunted for a fork. By the time Oliver came back, I was enjoying my lunch.

"Eating without me?" Oliver's voice, rich with amusement, interrupted my meal.

"We haven't had anything since dinner last night," I defended, fork poised mid-air.

"I did," he countered with a playful smirk.

"When?" I challenged, curiosity piqued.

"I feasted on you this morning," he replied, his tone low and suggestive.

I felt a shiver run down my spine as Oliver brushed my wet hair away from my neck, planting a trail of soft kisses along my skin. My body responded eagerly to his touch, a familiar heat building within me. Oliver had a way of igniting a fire that I couldn't resist.

"Was I filling?" I teased, though the truth was far from a joke.

"More than filling. I'd like another meal of you later," he murmured, his words sending a delicious thrill through me.

"I'll see what I can do," I replied, unable to hide the anticipation in my voice.

He leaned forward as I lifted a forkful of crab to my lips, and I held it out for him to take, relishing the intimacy of the gesture.

"How did your refrigerator get stocked?" I asked, changing the subject.

"Henri. He always takes care of my more personal errands," Oliver explained, his gaze never leaving mine.

"Did he buy me the earrings?" I questioned, a hint of curiosity in my tone.

"No. That was all me. I don't need my assistants to find gifts for you," he replied, sincerity shining in his eyes.

"I love them. Thank you so much," I said, genuine gratitude coloring my words.

"I want to give you more, so much more," Oliver confessed, his voice soft with emotion.

"You said you had surprises for me," I reminded him, anticipation bubbling within me.

"One of them was sex. Surprise," Oliver quipped, a mischievous glint in his eye.

"What else do you have planned?" I pressed, curiosity lacing my voice.

"I thought you wanted to stay here alone all weekend?"

Oliver countered, a hint of amusement tugging at the corners of his lips.

"I do, but if you keep getting interrupted by phone calls..." I trailed off, a note of frustration creeping into my tone.

I didn't want to start an argument, but I was possessive of Oliver. I wanted to spend as much time with him as possible, and constant interruptions took his limited time away from me.

"I told my attorney to put it on hold until Tuesday," Oliver reassured me, his gaze softening.

"Put what on hold?" I prodded.

"I'm purchasing another business. We're negotiating right now. It can wait," he explained, his voice tinged with determination.

"I don't want to take you away from anything important," I admitted, a pang of guilt tugging at my heart.

"Right now, you're the most important thing in my life. Nothing else can divert my attention like you can," Oliver confessed, sincerity shining in his eyes.

Setting aside the crab salad and fork, I wrapped my arms around him, pressing a kiss to his chest. I reached up to brush his hair off his forehead.

"I like your hair like this," I murmured, a fond smile gracing my lips.

"I don't. I can't work with my hair in my eyes," he grumbled, though a hint of amusement danced in his eyes.

"It makes you look young," I teased gently.

"Excuse me, I am young. Thirty-six is hardly old," Oliver retorted, a playful glint in his eye.

"To me, it is," I admitted with a smirk.

"Would you like to see how old I am? I bet you'll tire before me," Oliver challenged, a devilish grin spreading across his face.

Before I could respond, he scooped me up into his arms and carried me upstairs, the promise of passion hanging between us like a shimmering veil.

Chapter 9

A week later, I found myself sandwiched between Finley and Matthew at a table, an achievement considering their hectic schedules. As we settled in and placed our orders, Finley launched into interrogation mode.

"What's the deal with Oliver Fox? Are you two an item now?" Finley's sharp gaze bore into me.

I took a sip of my drink, stalling for a moment before responding. "Yeah, we are."

Matthew, usually the quieter of the two, chimed in, "Have you mentioned him to Mom and Anders?"

I shook my head. "Not yet. And I'd prefer if neither of you spilled the beans."

Finley leaned back, crossing his arms. "It's your life. But I still think he's too old for you."

I raised an eyebrow. "Is it really his age that bothers you, or is there something else?"

Finley, always immersed in his business world, hesitated before replying. "No, it's not that. I just worry he might hurt you."

I frowned. "Why would he be any different from any other guy?"

"Because he's been around the block a few more times than you," Finley retorted. "He's got experience."

"So, you're saying I'm naïve? A foolish girl who's going to fall for the wrong man?" My voice held a hint of frustration.

Finley shook his head, exasperated. "That's not what I meant. Matthew, help me out here."

Matthew raised his hands in surrender. "I'm staying out of this one. You're the one with the words."

Finley sighed. "Look, I just want what's best for you. You seem to be stuck to this guy like glue."

"Because I love him," I declared, my heart swelling at the thought of Oliver.

My brothers exchanged surprised glances, their mouths agape. It had only been a month, but my feelings for Oliver were undeniable and deep.

"Does Oliver know that?" Matthew interjected, his brow furrowing with concern.

I nodded, a small smile playing on my lips. "Yeah, he was the one who said it first."

"You two are diving in headfirst," Matthew remarked.

I shrugged. "Why is that a problem?"

"It's not, but it's happening pretty fast. How long have you been together, two or three weeks?" Matthew inquired.

"A month," I replied, trying to gauge their reactions.

Our conversation was momentarily interrupted by the arrival of our drinks. I had initially ordered an iced tea, but feeling the tension rise, I changed my mind and asked for a vodka cranberry. I needed something to take the edge off.

"I'm not thirteen anymore," I muttered as I accepted the drink.

"We know that," Finley said, his tone softening. "But this isn't some high school fling. He's older."

"I'm aware," I replied, a hint of frustration creeping into my voice. "I don't give you grief about your random hookups."

"They're not random," Finley protested. "I know those women, and I'm not looking for anything serious. But what makes you think a catch like Oliver wants a committed relationship?"

"Because he told me he does, and I believe him," I stated firmly.

. . .

My brothers exchanged skeptical glances, but before they could retort, Matthew shifted the conversation to a lighter topic, sharing details about a new client of his. I silently thanked him for the reprieve.

"Have you seen Ty lately?" Finley suddenly asked, changing the subject.

I hesitated, masking my unease. "Not in a couple of weeks. He's been swamped. The last time we met for lunch, he could barely keep his eyes open."

"I should give him a call," Finley mused.

"He could call you," I pointed out.

"He's busy," Finley insisted.

I had been avoiding Ty because I feared he would press me about our father's murder investigation again. I hadn't divulged to my brothers that Ty was looking into it, and I didn't plan to. They had moved on, but for me, it was still a raw wound, especially since they weren't there when it happened.

As we savored our meal, the tension that had gripped us earlier gradually dissipated. We laughed, shared stories, and for a moment, it felt like old times. Just as we were wrapping up, Finley's phone rang, pulling him back into the fast-paced world of his work.

With a resigned eye-roll, Finley hastily threw some bills on the table, planting a quick kiss on my cheek and clapping Matthew on the shoulder before darting off to address the urgent issue. Watching him go, I couldn't help but notice the similarities between Finley and Oliver - both driven, focused, and always ready to leap into action when duty called.

~

"No more," I panted, pushing Oliver's head from between my legs. He had been more than generous tonight, giving me several orgasms. I didn't want his tongue but he couldn't seem to get enough of me.

"One more. You taste so good."

"No more," I repeated. "I need to sleep."

Earlier that evening was the first time I sucked Oliver off. He was reluctant to let me do it but I insisted. I liked giving blowjobs. He felt he needed to repay me for what I did when I told him it wasn't necessary. If we were keeping score, he gave me far more orgasms than I gave him.

"Are you sure?" Oliver's voice was husky against my ear.

"You're a wicked man," I murmured, trying to catch my breath. "Now stop before I pass out."

He chuckled, a sound that sent shivers down my spine, before he climbed over my body, trailing kisses along my skin. I sighed contentedly as he suckled on my nipples before settling beside me, his head resting on my shoulder. I ran my fingers through his hair, tracing the stubble on his jaw.

"I had lunch with my brothers today," I said, breaking the comfortable silence.

"Is that where you disappeared to while I was at the office?" Oliver teased.

I nodded. "Sadie's been spending a lot of time with Dan. They argue constantly, and I'm worried it might not be just a phase."

"Maybe they're just not compatible," Oliver suggested.

"Sadie wants it to work," I explained. "She didn't have an easy upbringing like me. Money means a lot to her."

"She shouldn't settle for someone just because they have money," Oliver remarked firmly.

"I agree, but I've given up on arguing with her about it. I don't want to strain our relationship."

"What did your brothers have to say?" Oliver inquired, his tone shifting.

"They're worried you'll break my heart," I confessed, a hint of vulnerability creeping into my voice.

Oliver's gaze softened as he reached for my hand. "I would never. You mean too much to me."

"We fell so far, so fast," I admitted. "Doesn't it worry you that we'll burn out?"

He lifted his head to meet my gaze. "Do you think that?"

"I worry sometimes," I admitted.

"Don't," Oliver said firmly. "It won't happen. I love you. You're the first woman I've ever thought about a future with."

I swallowed, deeply touched by his words. "Wasn't there anyone before me that you considered marrying?"

"My life was consumed by my business," Oliver confessed. "Sure, I had dates, but none as captivating as you."

"So I'm interesting now?" I teased, a smile playing on my lips.

"Very," Oliver replied with a smirk. "You keep me entertained in more ways than one."

He nipped at my shoulder playfully, leaving his mark, before the conversation shifted again.

"I need to start working out again," Oliver remarked casually. "You make me lazy."

"Your body looks great," I assured him. "Maybe I should borrow your trainer," I mused.

Oliver's firm declaration sliced through the air like a knife. "Absolutely not."

"Why?" I countered, my voice laced with frustration.

"Bronson is a smooth talker. He'd try to charm you out of

your panties, and he's good-looking enough to pull it off," Oliver explained, his tone tinged with concern.

"Do you honestly think I'd fall for that with my legs in the air? You don't give me much credit," I shot back, feeling a surge of annoyance.

"I'm pretty sure it wouldn't happen, but just in case, you stay away from him," Oliver insisted, his words hanging in the air.

I flung my legs over the edge of the bed, seething at Oliver's implication that I was so easily swayed. When his hand touched my back, I recoiled, a surge of anger coursing through me.

"You're an asshole," I spat out, rising abruptly and fleeing to the bathroom, slamming the door shut before Oliver could follow.

Inside the bathroom, I turned on the faucet in the tub, the sound of running water offering a fleeting sense of solace. I dumped in some lime basil bath beads, hoping the soothing scent would calm my frayed nerves.

As I waited for the tub to fill, Oliver's persistent knocks on the door grated on my nerves.

"Come on, Ryleigh. I'm sorry," his voice pleaded from the other side.

"You're a dick. Just leave me alone. I need a bath," I retorted, my anger still burning bright.

Finally, the knocking ceased, and I sank into the warm water, trying to find some semblance of peace. But even as I closed my eyes, the memory of Oliver's lack of trust gnawed at me.

The bathroom door creaked open, and I tensed; my anger reignited at the sight of a naked Oliver standing there.

"Get out. I'm so pissed at you right now," I snapped, turning my face away from him, unwilling to meet his gaze.

But despite my protest, Oliver approached and sat on the edge of the tub, his presence unwelcome yet strangely comforting.

"Let me sit behind you," he pleaded softly, his tone laced with remorse.

"Do you understand that I want to be alone?" I demanded, my voice tinged with venom.

"I want to talk about this. I made a mistake," Oliver admitted, his words hanging heavy in the air.

“You act like I’m some dummy. Why is it that you men think I can’t make a rational moral decision?”

"I don't think that. I don't trust any other men around you, now move forward," Oliver urged gently.

Reluctantly, I shuffled forward, allowing Oliver to settle behind me in the tub. He eased himself into the water and pulled me back between his legs. I leaned back against his chest, his arms encircling me as he began to massage my shoulders. Despite my lingering anger, I couldn't deny the comfort his touch brought me.

He bent down to kiss my neck, his lips trailing to my ear as he whispered, "I'm sorry."

"Oliver, you need to trust me. I love you, and I would never jeopardize our relationship," I asserted, my voice soft but firm.

"I know. It was a lapse in judgment. I never should've said it," he admitted, his fingers moving from my shoulders to my breasts, where he began to knead and caress, sending shivers down my spine.

"Don't think sex is getting you out of the doghouse," I warned teasingly, though a part of me was tempted to give in to his advances.

"I'll do anything. I don't like when we're at odds. Can I buy you something?" he offered, his voice earnest.

"So if there was a time to get anything I want, it's now?" I teased, a smile tugging at the corners of my lips.

"Anything, just pick," he replied without hesitation.

"I only want your love," I responded, sincerity coloring my words.

"You have it," he assured me, his tone filled with warmth.

"On second thought, I've decided what I want," I declared, a mischievous glint in my eyes.

"What?" he asked, curiosity piqued.

"Breakfast in bed," I announced.

"What time? I can set it up tonight," Oliver offered eagerly.

"No, I mean I want you to cook for me," I clarified, a playful smirk dancing on my lips.

"You know it's not a problem. I can cook, but I prefer to order so we can spend time together," he countered.

"We will, after you cook me breakfast," I insisted, a hint of challenge in my voice.

He sighed in resignation. "Very well."

I turned to face him, straddling him in the water and reaching for his semi-erect cock. But he pushed my hand away, a teasing glint in his eyes.

“No. I want to give you pleasure.”

“You will if you let me ride you.”

We didn’t have penetrative sex this evening, instead opting for oral sex. I needed to feel Oliver inside me, and I held him steady as I sank down to his root. I rode him as we shared deep, soulful kisses that were full of meaning. I knew he loved me hard, and I loved him just as much.

After our lovemaking, Oliver slipped out of the tub and turned on the shower to rinse off the bubbles clinging to our skin. We took our time, washing each other tenderly before wrapping ourselves in fluffy towels and heading to the kitchen for a late-night snack. My stomach rumbled in anticipation as I stood in front of the open refrigerator, surveying the contents.

As I rummaged through the containers, searching for my favorite crab salad, Oliver came up behind me, his hands wandering to cup my ass. I chuckled as I found what I was looking for, feeling his warm touch.

"Big surprise," he murmured teasingly.

"Can you unhand my posterior, please?" I replied, a playful glint in my eyes.

"Suppose I say no?" he teased back, his grip tightening slightly.

"Then I'll have to dole out some punishment," I retorted with a smirk.

His grin widened as he released me. "I like your punishments."

"I bet you do. Now, about breakfast tomorrow," I said, shifting the conversation.

"What would you like?" he asked, his tone attentive.

I described my craving for silver dollar pancakes and Canadian bacon, accompanied by a toasted cinnamon raisin bagel with jelly and butter.

"Is that all? Perhaps I should squeeze you some fresh orange juice," he suggested, his lips curling into a playful smile.

"That sounds lovely, but I prefer it without pulp," I replied, unable to resist the opportunity to tease him back.

"You're really making me pay for what I said, aren't you?" Oliver chuckled, shaking his head in mock exasperation.

"Yes. Maybe you'll choose your words more carefully next time," I replied, flashing him a mischievous smile as I grabbed a fork from the silverware drawer.

I shared the salad with Oliver; only one fork was needed since I fed him. He held me when we went to bed, stroking my hair until I fell asleep.

~

I was roused from my sleep the next morning by the sound of Oliver banging the edge of a tray against the bedroom door. Blinking away the remnants of sleep, I watched as he approached the bed, a mischievous glint in his eyes.

"Yummy, I'm starved," I mumbled, sitting up as he placed the large wooden tray beside me. On it were two plates piled with everything I had requested, along with a carafe of freshly squeezed blood orange juice and a steaming mug of coffee. Oliver settled next to me, and I narrowed my eyes suspiciously.

"You didn't make this," I accused, eyeing him skeptically.

"I certainly did. I got up an hour ago," he insisted, his grin widening.

I knew he was lying. "So, if I go in the kitchen, I'll find all the utensils and pans you used?"

"No, I cooked, washed, and dried everything already. It's in the cabinet," he countered smoothly.

"You're such a bad liar," I teased, though I couldn't help but admire his effort.

"I was busy this morning. I had a phone call with Hong Kong," he defended himself.

"So you ordered in?" I pressed, raising an eyebrow.

"You said breakfast, and I provided it," he replied with a shrug.

Despite my slight annoyance, I couldn't resist the temptation of the delicious spread before me. I cut into one of the pancakes, savoring the warm syrup that I dipped it in. Forgiveness came easily with each bite.

"I'll do my penance some other way," Oliver offered, his eyes sparkling with mischief.

"How?" I inquired, curious despite myself.

Oliver took a sip of his juice before responding, "How about I buy you something? I saw a beautiful ruby tennis bracelet at a jeweler in midtown."

"I told you I don't need you to buy me things," I reminded him firmly.

"Your birthday is at the end of the month; call it an early birthday present," he suggested.

"Then buy it for my birthday or not at all," I said.

"I want to buy you something," Oliver insisted, his gaze unwavering.

"Take me to the park and buy me an ice cream," I proposed, a smile tugging at the corners of my lips.

"Is that what you want to do for today?" Oliver asked, leaning in to plant a kiss on my lips, his touch lingering.

"That sounds like fun. It's where I saw you when I was walking Blackie. I thought you looked so good in your running attire," I admitted, a blush creeping onto my cheeks.

He chuckled softly, his breath warm against my skin. "Don't."

"Why not?" I protested weakly, feeling myself succumbing to his charm.

"Because we won't get to the park if you continue," he teased, his eyes twinkling with amusement. "Spending a Sunday in bed with you sounds perfect. I vote for choice two," his tone suggestive.

"Tough. We're going to the park, and I expect you to show me a good time," I replied, determined.

I chuckled as I took a bite of my bagel.

We strolled through the park, Vlad trailing a few steps behind us, his presence casting a slight shadow over our otherwise idyllic day. I couldn't shake the feeling of unease, wondering why Oliver felt the need for security in such a peaceful setting. He garnered plenty of looks, mostly from women, but it seemed like few recognized him despite his appearances in magazines and television interviews.

"Why does Vlad have to be with us?" I finally voiced my curiosity.

"He's my security. You never know who might be around," Oliver replied casually.

"Do you deal with terrorists or something?" I teased, unable to resist a smirk.

"Of course not, but I'm worth quite a bit. Security is necessary," he explained, his tone serious.

"You sound arrogant again," I teased, though I couldn't hide the affection in my voice.

Oliver pulled me closer, planting a kiss on the top of my head before indulging me with a chocolate éclair ice cream bar and a leisurely stroll to Central Park Lake. In that moment, happiness enveloped me, and I knew Oliver was the reason for it all.

By the time we returned to his apartment, the fatigue of the day settled in, and I began to pack my belongings into my small duffel bag. It was time to head home and prepare for work the next day.

"You know you can leave things here. I have plenty of room in my closet," Oliver offered, his voice soft with sincerity.

"Do I get a drawer too?" I teased lightly.

"You can have several. The dresser on the right side of the closet is empty. Bring whatever you want. In fact, maybe we should talk about more permanent arrangements," he suggested, his words catching me off guard.

"What are you talking about?" I asked, my stomach twisting with anxiety.

"I want you to move in with me," Oliver declared, his gaze unwavering.

The weight of his words hung heavy in the air, and I struggled to find the right response. Our relationship was moving at lightning speed, and the thought of such a significant commitment made my head spin.

"No, Oliver. You're moving too fast," I finally managed to voice my hesitation.

"I'm moving fast because you're my future," he insisted, his tone earnest.

"It's too much for me. Maybe we should spend time apart at night," I suggested, trying to alleviate the pressure building inside me.

His frown deepened, and he raised his voice slightly. "That's not what I want. I do everything a hundred times better when we're together."

"Oliver, relax. We're not breaking up. I just need time to myself," I reassured him, hoping to ease his concerns.

"It sounds like you want to break up," he accused, his voice tinged with hurt.

"I don't. I love you, but moving in so soon is crazy. You haven't even met my family. My parents don't even know I'm dating you," I confessed, the weight of my words heavy on my heart.

"Why? Why haven't you told them?" Oliver pressed, his frustration evident.

"I just haven't. They would say the same thing if I told them how intense we are together. It's too much," I admitted, feeling the weight of uncertainty pressing down on me.

“So you want space? Is that what you’re saying?” Oliver’s voice was laced with concern as he sought clarification.

“I think so. I feel pressured to make you happy,” I admitted, my words heavy with uncertainty.

“Ryleigh, I want you to know that I want no one else but you,” Oliver assured me, his sincerity evident.

“I feel the same, but you’re pushing me too soon,” I confessed, feeling the weight of my words settle between us.

I hastily shoved the rest of my belongings into my bag and zipped it up, avoiding Oliver's gaze. He sat on the corner of his bed, chewing on his bottom lip in silence, his turmoil evident.

“You’re not staying with me tonight?” he asked, his voice tinged with disappointment.

“No. I haven’t been home since Friday. I have some things to do, and I need to spend time with Sadie,” I explained, trying to keep my tone firm.

“I’ll have Vlad take you home,” Oliver insisted, his concern palpable.

“I think I can manage on my own,” I replied, feeling the need for independence.

“I insist. In fact, I’d like to see you home,” he pressed, his tone becoming more insistent.

“No. Stop smothering me,” I snapped.

“Jesus Christ, I’m not smothering. I care about you,” Oliver protested, frustration creeping into his voice.

“If you do, then give me some space to think,” I pleaded, hoping he would understand.

“I don’t want to lose you,” Oliver confessed, his vulnerability laid bare.

“You’re not. I just need some time to sort my head out,” I assured him, my heart aching at the thought of hurting him.

I picked up my bag, and he followed me out to the foyer. Pushing me against the door, he kissed me fiercely, his desperation evident. Despite my attempts to resist, I found myself giving in to him, his touch stirring up a tumult of conflicting emotions within me.

"I love you," he whispered as he broke the kiss.

"I know," I whispered back, my voice barely audible as I walked out the door, leaving Oliver behind. Tears stung my eyes as I pressed the elevator button, feeling the weight of my decision settling over me. Oliver watched me until I disappeared into the car, leaving me alone with my thoughts.

As Vlad drove me to my apartment, I tried to hold back the tears that threatened to spill over. But as soon as I was safely inside, the floodgates opened, and I sobbed uncontrollably, grappling with the turmoil of emotions raging inside me. I was torn between wanting to accept everything Oliver offered and the desire to maintain my independence. It was a conflict I couldn't seem to resolve, and for now, space seemed like the only answer.

Chapter 10

As much as I resisted it, I found myself keeping my distance from Oliver. I prayed I wouldn't run into him at work. He had pleaded with me all Sunday night to change my mind and come back over, but I remained firm in my decision.

Three days later, I couldn't shake the sinking feeling that maybe it wasn't the right choice. He had gone silent on me, and I feared it spelled the end of our relationship. What I had thought would give us both space seemed to have backfired, leaving me longing for him more than ever.

I missed him terribly. After work on Wednesday evening, I rode the elevator up to his office floor. Oliver typically worked late into the evening, and we often met afterward to share a meal and spend the night together. I hoped fervently that he wasn't in a meeting or, worse, out of town.

The receptionist had already left for the night, and most of the office staff had cleared out. A few executives remained in their offices, and I prayed Oliver was among them. I passed Henri in the hall, and he stopped to talk to me.

“Can I help you with something, Miss Stewart?” he inquired politely.

“I’d like to see Oliver if he isn’t busy,” I replied, trying to keep my voice steady despite the nerves churning in my stomach.

“Mr. Fox hasn’t been in the office for the past few days. He’s been working from home,” Henri informed me.

“I didn’t know that. We haven’t...I haven’t seen him,” I admitted, feeling a pang of guilt.

“I’m sure he would welcome your call,” Henri offered kindly before nodding and continuing on his way.

I sighed heavily, my heart aching once again. Oliver seemed to be taking our separation harder than I had anticipated. Shouldn’t I be the one paralyzed with sadness, considering my age? With a heavy heart, I made my way back downstairs. A light drizzle had just begun to fall, and I hurried down the sidewalk, eager to escape the melancholy that threatened to consume me.

“Miss Stewart?” a familiar voice called out.

I looked up to see Vlad standing at the curb, holding the door open for me. His presence was unexpected, and I couldn’t help but wonder if Henri had sent him to fetch me or if Oliver himself had made the request. In the month since I had started dating Oliver, I had never addressed Vlad personally, but now I felt compelled to seek answers.

“Vlad?” I said tentatively.

“Yes, Miss Stewart?” he replied, his tone formal as ever.

“Ryleigh, please,” I corrected him, hoping for a more personal exchange.

“I prefer to address you as Miss Stewart,” he insisted stoically.

I sighed inwardly, pressing on. “Is Oliver all right?”

“Mr. Fox is under the weather,” Vlad informed me cryptically.

“He’s sick?” I asked, concern flooding through me.

“He’s unhappy,” Vlad clarified, his words heavy with meaning.

“I guess that’s my fault,” I murmured, feeling a pang of guilt.

“I’m taking you to him,” Vlad announced abruptly.

“Thank you,” I replied softly, grateful for the opportunity to see Oliver, even if it meant facing the consequences of my actions.

Behind my eyes, a stinging sensation threatened tears, but I held them back. I didn’t deserve Oliver. Fifteen minutes later, Vlad pulled up in front of Oliver’s building.

He offered me a tight smile as he opened the back door, and I stepped out, walking into the lobby where the concierge directed me to go right up to the penthouse.

Oliver was waiting for me, looking worn and haggard. Dark circles shadowed his blue eyes, and wrinkles I hadn't noticed before marred his usually smooth face. Dressed casually in black shorts and a light blue t-shirt, he stood barefoot, his expression stoic as I entered the room.

"Oliver..." I began tentatively.

"Shut up, Ryleigh," he growled, cutting me off.

"I'm sorry," I whispered, feeling the weight of my actions.

"I said, shut up," he repeated sharply.

I fell silent as he approached me, forcefully taking my purse from my hand and dropping it to the floor. He pressed his lips to mine with such intensity that I was sure they would bruise, gripping my hair so tightly it hurt. I remained silent until I felt wetness on my cheeks. Opening my eyes, I saw tears streaming down Oliver's face. I pulled away gently.

"No, Oliver, don't cry," I pleaded softly.

"I thought you were gone for good," he confessed, his voice strained with emotion.

“I just needed space. We should talk about everything,” I suggested, trying to ease the tension between us.

“I’m sorry I pushed you,” he admitted, his tone filled with regret.

“I’m sorry I didn’t handle it better. I’ve been miserable without you,” I confessed, reaching up to wipe away his tears, a small smile playing on his lips.

“I’m glad I wasn’t the only one. Why didn’t you call me?” he asked, his voice laced with concern.

“I wanted to see you in person. Why haven’t you gone to the office?” I inquired, trying to redirect the conversation.

“Working here is just as good. I’ve been in such a foul mood that my negotiation skills are better. I shaved a quarter of a million for a building I wanted to purchase,” he explained, a hint of pride in his voice.

“I thought you had people to do that?” I questioned, surprised by his hands-on approach.

“Sometimes, I like to take the helm. Congratulate your boyfriend on a job well done,” he replied, his smile widening.

“Let’s talk,” I suggested, taking his hand and leading him to the leather couch in his living room. Oliver remained close, as if he couldn’t bear to let me go.

“I’ll do anything you want. Don’t leave me again,” he pleaded, desperation evident in his voice.

“I didn’t leave you. I just needed space,” I reassured him, feeling a surge of affection.

“I know. I pressed too hard,” he admitted, his grip on my hand tightening.

“We should set some rules so this doesn’t happen again,” I proposed, hoping to find a solution.

“Like what?” he asked, willing to compromise.

“Maybe we could have a day or night apart each week,” I suggested tentatively.

“Day. I sleep better with you next to me,” he countered, his voice softening.

“I don’t want to neglect my friends and my brothers. I haven’t seen my parents since we got together. I should visit them,” I explained, wanting to maintain my connections.

“I can go with you,” Oliver offered, surprising me with his willingness.

“You want to meet my parents? You haven’t even met my brothers,” I pointed out, surprised by his sudden enthusiasm.

“I want to meet all your family,” Oliver insisted, his tone determined.

“I think you should meet my brothers first,” I suggested cautiously.

“Arrange it,” he commanded.

"Finley doesn't have a lot of time. He's busy with his business. Maybe we can have drinks or dinner with Matthew," I proposed, trying to find a compromise.

"I'd like that. I want to know all about you," he replied, his expression softening.

"Do you want me to sleep over tonight?" I asked, hoping for closeness after our recent rift.

"I would. I haven't slept in three nights," he admitted, his exhaustion evident.

"What are you going to do when you travel?" I questioned, concerned about our time apart.

"Pack you in my suitcase and take you with me," he joked.

"Very funny. I have a job," I retorted.

"If you work for Fox, then you can come with me. How is work going? Any better?" he inquired, shifting the conversation.

The truth was that my job hadn't improved much. I was considering a change.

"I think I want to look for another job. Sadie said her company is hiring," I admitted.

"Connect?" Oliver guessed.

"Yes," I confirmed.

"Then you would be working for me," he revealed, surprising me.

"Excuse me?" I exclaimed, caught off guard.

"Because Connect is a subsidiary of Fox Asset," he explained calmly.

"Why didn't you tell me this before?" I questioned, feeling a mix of emotions.

"Does it matter?" he deflected.

"I guess not. I wanted to get into PR, but not like this. My degree is being wasted," I lamented.

"Consider working for me. Speaking of traveling, I have a trip scheduled the first week of August," Oliver revealed, changing the subject.

"You're leaving me for a few days?" I asked, feeling a pang of loneliness already.

"Four. I have several meetings in Vancouver," he confirmed.

"I guess I'll be lonely," I admitted sadly.

After the past few days, I didn't want to be separated from Oliver. I was miserable without him around and I now knew, so was he.

"Not if you work for me. You can be one of my assistants," he suggested, trying to reassure me.

"Oliver, you have three. What the hell would I do?" I protested.

“I would find work for you to do. You could be my personal assistant,” he proposed.

“Does that include sex?” I teased, trying to lighten the mood.

“It could,” he admitted.

“Then I would be a high-paid prostitute,” I joked further.

He looked at me horrified, “Jesus Christ, don’t say that.”

“It’s true. You would be paying me to work, and if we had sex, then I would be a prostitute,” I reasoned, feeling a mix of amusement and discomfort.

“Then we won’t have sex until you’re off for the day,” he decided.

“You told me your assistants are always working, so we would never have sex,” I countered, teasing him playfully.

“The hell we wouldn’t. I would fire your ass,” Oliver retorted, his tone half-joking, half-serious.

“You would terminate me to get your rocks off?” I teased back, a smirk playing on my lips.

“Why don’t you just become my wife and then you can work for me for free,” he suggested, his tone suddenly more serious.

“Oliver,” I cautioned, feeling a rush of emotions at his unexpected proposal. We had just discussed living together, and now he was talking about marriage.

"I'm sorry, but I won't lie to you. I want you to be my wife in the future," he confessed, his eyes sincere.

"That's a while away. We're several months from that. How is it that you lived thirty-six years without being caught?" I asked, trying to lighten the mood with a touch of humor.

"Because I didn't find the right girl until now. You're the right girl," he replied, his gaze unwavering.

"What am I going to do with you?" I sighed, feeling both overwhelmed and deeply touched by his words.

"Kiss me," he requested, his voice soft but filled with longing.

~

I stayed over Oliver's without going home to get clothing. He made slow, sensual love to me. It was filled with passion and need. I loved him with all my heart and even more so because he showed me that he could be vulnerable. I was tired in the morning when he woke me. I had to leave to get ready for work at my apartment. Vlad took me home. I wasn't sure if he ever slept.

I called Matthew that afternoon to ask if he wanted to meet up for dinner or lunch on the weekend. We made a date for Saturday afternoon. I hoped that Oliver could tear himself away from work to join me. I really wanted my brother to meet him.

“We’re having lunch with Matthew on Saturday. Can you make it?” I asked eagerly.

Vlad was driving to my apartment. I was picking up some clothing for the next day so I could spend the night at his place.

“What time?” he asked.

“I have several calls on Saturday.”

"1 p.m.,” I said.

“I think I can swing it, but I’ll have to meet you there," Oliver responded, his voice laced with determination despite his busy schedule.

"I really want you to meet my brother," I emphasized, hoping to convey the significance of the occasion.

"What about Finley?" Oliver inquired, displaying genuine interest in meeting every member of my family.

"He has a deadline and can’t spare the time. You’ll meet him soon enough," I assured him, already picturing the moment when my siblings and Oliver would finally cross paths.

"I hope so. I want to meet your entire family," Oliver confessed, his sincerity warming my heart.

As I debated whether to invite him upstairs or let him stay in the car, Oliver interjected, "I have a phone call to make. Do you mind if I stay here?"

"No. I should be down in a few minutes," I replied, grateful for his understanding as I prepared to head upstairs to pack. Stepping out of the car, he escorted me to the lobby of my building, a gesture of his unwavering consideration.

Once upstairs, I began gathering my things when Sadie, perspiring from the oppressive July heat, breezed into the room. "You're home?" she remarked, her voice tinged with surprise.

"Yeah, but I'm leaving," I responded, though my attention was immediately drawn to the tear-streaked anguish etched across her face.

Concern flooding my senses, I dropped the panties I had been holding and rushed to her side. "What's the matter?" I inquired, the worry evident in my tone.

Through choked sobs, Sadie revealed, "Dan wants to be friends. He said we don't have chemistry."

My heart sank as I processed her words. She had invested herself in their relationship, only to be met with rejection and heartache. Despite my own reservations about Dan, I couldn't help but empathize with Sadie's pain.

"I'm sorry. I knew you really liked him," I offered, extending a comforting embrace.

"Now I have to work across from him every day when I

don't want to see him at all," Sadie lamented, her voice heavy with frustration and disappointment.

I listened empathetically, knowing the sting of heartbreak all too well. "Ignore him. You didn't do anything wrong," I reassured her, hoping to provide some comfort in her distress.

"To top it off, he's been flirty with Megan, who sits a few cubicles down from me. You think he was just using me?" Sadie's voice cracked with a mix of anger and hurt.

"He sounds like a jerk. I think you dodged a bullet. Suppose he did that when you were dating for six months? It would've been worse," I reasoned, trying to offer a perspective that might ease her pain.

"I just can't seem to find a decent guy. What am I doing wrong?" Sadie's voice wavered with self-doubt, her vulnerability laid bare.

"Maybe you're trying too hard?" I suggested gently, hoping to provide insight without causing further distress.

"Are you leaving?" Sadie interrupted, wiping her nose and gesturing toward my bag, her need for companionship evident in her plea.

"I was. Do you want me to stay?" I asked, willing to set aside my plans to support my friend in her time of need.

"I need you. I did it for you," Sadie confessed, her words revealing the depth of our bond and her unwavering loyalty.

"Let me call Oliver. He's waiting," I offered, recognizing that Sadie's need for solace shouldn't come at the expense of my relationship. She left my room to wash her face and blow her nose in the bathroom, leaving me to dial Oliver's number.

He answered right away, his voice a comforting presence on the other end of the line.

After Sadie excused herself to freshen up, I dialed Oliver's number. He picked up almost immediately.

"What's taking so long?" His voice was tinged with curiosity.

"I can't go. Sadie needs me," I replied, feeling torn between my friend's distress and the longing to be with Oliver.

"I'm not sleeping alone tonight," he declared firmly, his words soothing my worry.

The line clicked off abruptly, leaving me with a frown. I tried calling Oliver back, but it went straight to voicemail. Before I could attempt another call, a knock echoed through the apartment.

Opening the door, I found Oliver standing there, a determined look on his face. "We're not sleeping apart. I'll stay here tonight," he announced, his voice leaving no room for debate.

"Thanks for hanging up on me," I muttered, a mixture of amusement and exasperation in my tone.

"I wanted to get up here as fast as possible," Oliver confessed, his eyes reflecting urgency.

"You didn't have to hang up," I chided gently, though a smile tugged at the corners of my lips.

Leaning in, he kissed me softly and whispered in my ear, "I'll make it up to you later."

As Sadie emerged from the bathroom, she was surprised to see Oliver. "How are you?" he asked, his concern evident in his voice.

"Shitty. Men are pigs," Sadie replied with a sigh, her frustration palpable.

"Oink," Oliver quipped, eliciting a weak smile from Sadie before she retreated to her bedroom to change.

Oliver followed me into my room, closing the door behind him. As I began to undress, he approached me, his touch gentle yet possessive as he cupped my breasts when I removed my blouse.

“No,” I whispered. “Sadie does not need to hear us having sex.”

For the past few weeks, Sadie had been spending time at Dan's apartment, which meant when we were here, we could make noise.

“Does that mean we aren't having sex tonight?” Oliver teased, his voice laced with a hint of disappointment.

“Oliver, you're like a sex-starved teenager,” I chuckled, playfully swatting his arm.

“It has nothing to do with being sex-starved. I love having sex with you,” he admitted, his eyes filled with desire.

“We can wait until tomorrow night when we’re at your apartment,” I suggested, trying to stifle a giggle.

“I’m sure we can find other things to do instead,” Oliver countered, a mischievous glint in his eyes.

“Such as?” I raised an eyebrow, feigning innocence.

“Other things,” he replied with a smirk. “What about dinner?”

“We could order in,” I proposed, considering our options.

“What do you feel like having?” Oliver inquired, his tone suggesting he had something particular in mind.

“You,” I teased, unable to resist a flirtatious remark.

“Besides me, sex fiend,” Oliver chuckled. “I feel like a steak.”

“I don’t think any of the restaurants will deliver steak,” I mused, pondering our culinary choices.

“I don’t,” Oliver declared confidently, his eyes lighting up with excitement.

I rolled my eyes at his confidence because I was sure he was right. With just one phone call, we could be enjoying a five-star meal in less than an hour.

“Then get steak. Ask Sadie what she wants,” I

suggested, knowing Oliver would handle the arrangements.

Oliver stepped outside to find Sadie sitting on the couch, wiping her eyes with a tissue. As I finished changing, I observed how tender he was with her, putting his arm around her shoulders for comfort. When I emerged from the room, he released Sadie and went into the foyer to make the phone call for food.

~

"That was nice of you to comfort Sadie. She appreciated it," I murmured, snuggling closer to Oliver's chest as we settled into bed.

"Why is she so worried about finding a rich guy?" Oliver inquired, his voice tinged with curiosity.

"I told you that she didn't have much when she was a child. She wants her adult life to be different," I explained, tracing circles on his chest.

"I could ask Connect to promote her. She doesn't need to find a guy to make her own money," Oliver suggested, his concern for Sadie evident.

"Don't do that. You can't demand your companies promote people," I cautioned gently, understanding the complexities of corporate dynamics.

"I'm sure she's quite capable at her job," Oliver persisted.

"She's also only been there for five weeks. It would look strange. Even stranger if people found out we're friends and I'm dating you," I pointed out, recognizing the potential complications.

I playfully stuck my tongue out and licked his nipple, eliciting a surprised hiss from Oliver.

"Don't do that unless you want to wake Sadie," Oliver warned with a grin.

"Is that a challenge?" I teased, raising an eyebrow suggestively.

"I'd bet that you can't keep quiet," Oliver challenged, his eyes dancing with amusement.

"You act like I'm the only one that makes noise during sex. You're pretty loud yourself," I countered playfully.

"I can be quiet," Oliver retorted confidently.

"Go for it. I want to see who cracks first," I dared, a mischievous glint in my eyes.

Oliver reached down, lifting his hips to remove his boxers with a determined grin.

"Come on, get undressed. I'm taking you up on your bet," he urged, his tone laced with anticipation.

I bit my lip nervously, unsure if I could keep quiet. Sometimes Oliver made me want to scream when we made love. As I hesitated, he grew impatient and clawed at my panties, tearing them off with a swift motion.

"Those were expensive," I protested weakly.

"I'll buy you several pairs if you like. Now off with the t-shirt. I take great pleasure in your breasts," Oliver said, his voice low and husky.

I sat up and shucked off my t-shirt, tossing it to the floor. My panties were somewhere under the covers which Oliver pushed off us. He crawled between my legs and started to tease me with his tongue, eliciting a suppressed moan from me. The things he could do with his mouth.

I practically tore the bottom sheet off the mattress with my fists as he brought me to climax. It felt exquisite. He gently cleansed me with his tongue before moving up to kiss and suck my breasts, finally capturing my mouth in a hungry kiss. He positioned himself at my entrance, slowly sliding inside, and we lost ourselves in the intimacy of the moment.

"You feel so delicious," Oliver murmured, his voice low and husky.

"Shouldn't that be 'taste'?" I teased, a playful smile tugging at my lips.

"That too. Have I ever told you I could eat you all night?" Oliver whispered, his breath hot against my skin.

"Several times. Are you going to move or sit inside me all night?" I quipped, a hint of impatience in my voice.

"I like being inside you," Oliver admitted, his tone filled with desire.

“I want you to fuck me, not park your penis,” I insisted, a surge of need coursing through me.

“It’s the perfect parking spot,” Oliver countered, his voice laced with amusement.

“Fuck me, Oliver,” I whispered, my voice thick with desire.

He began to move his hips, starting slow before gradually picking up the pace. It was a rhythm I found myself enjoying, his attentiveness in bed unlike anything I had experienced before. I reached out, gripping his taut ass, my nails digging into his muscles as waves of pleasure washed over me.

“I need to stop,” Oliver suddenly said, his voice strained.

“What? No. It feels so good,” I protested, disappointment coloring my tone.

“Too good. I’m going to come,” he explained, a hint of urgency in his voice.

“Then come,” I urged, my own desire driving me to encourage him.

“You haven’t yet,” Oliver pointed out, his breath coming in ragged gasps.

“Do you want to argue or come?” I challenged, a mix of frustration and desire in my voice.

He responded by thrusting into me harder, his movements becoming more erratic until he spilled inside me. I gripped him tightly, my own orgasm crashing over me in waves. Oliver trailed kisses down my throat as I arched into the pillow, his teeth marking my shoulder in a possessive gesture.

"Do you always have to do that?" I whispered, a hint of annoyance in my voice.

"I'm marking my territory," Oliver replied, his tone teasing.

I scowled at him playfully, but he remained on top of me, lavishing attention on my breasts and nipples. I could feel him still partially erect inside me, a promising sign of his desire for more.

I shifted my hips. "Are you getting hard?"

Oliver groaned. "As a matter of fact, I am."

I raised my eyebrows. "I didn't know you could do that."

"I have a low refractory period."

I wasn't sated. It seemed whenever I was with Oliver, I couldn't get enough. I could be sore and muscles aching but I still wanted him.

"Do you want to have sex again?"

He nuzzled my cheek. "That's my plan. If we were at my apartment, I would make love to you all night."

"I have to work in the morning."

“So do I. If you worked for me, we could play sick and stay home.”

I feathered my lips across his. “My boss wouldn’t like that. He’s a workaholic.”

“He would if you promised to stay in bed with him.”

“You’re rock hard.”

“And I’m making good use of it,” he said as he began to thrust inside me.

The next morning, my alarm disrupted the haze of sleep, reminding me of my obligations. Despite being groggy, I couldn't help but marvel at Oliver's stamina, considering how he kept me awake for most of the night. His embrace was comforting, yet tinged with desire, evident from the hardness pressing against me.

"How can you be hard after last night?" I teased, feeling the soreness from our passionate night.

"You turn me on," he replied, planting kisses along my shoulder and arm.

"I'm sore, so you should take a cold shower," I suggested, half-jokingly.

"Want to join me?" he countered, his tone suggestive.

"If I join you, the cold shower won’t be needed," I quipped, the playful banter between us continuing.

As the sound of running water filled the room, signaling Sadie's early rise, Oliver proposed, "Want to play? You can make noise now that she's showering."

"I'm not in the mood," I admitted, feeling the fatigue seeping into my bones.

"I can get you in the mood," he assured, his hand finding its way to my breast, eliciting a response from my body as I arched my back, pressing my chest into his palm.

"Still not working," I chuckled, appreciating his efforts but knowing that rest was more pressing than another round of passion.

“Liar. I bet your soaked.”

“Not really. I’m just not into it this morning.”

Oliver pushed off the covers and rolled me onto my stomach, sliding his hard body over mine. He slipped his hand between my legs and found out I was lying.

“Spread your legs.”

“Like this?”

“You’ve never made love in this position?”

The few partners I had were limited to two or three positions and this was not one of them. Oliver and I hadn’t explored many others yet.

“No.”

“You’ll like it. It’s very intimate.”

He moved his hips so his cock was poised at my opening and in one fluid thrust, he was inside me. Oliver was the first man to give me a vaginal orgasm. Before him, I needed my clit stimulated to come. He pounded his pelvis against my ass, pushing my body into the mattress with each thrust. I moaned into my pillow and he bent down to kiss my back.

It didn't take long before I had another explosive orgasm, probably because my swollen clit was rubbing against the sheets. He followed, filling me up with his hot semen. I was exhausted and ready to call into work when I heard the water turn off.

"Time for a shower."

"I can't move," I mumbled.

"Do you need me to carry you?"

"You're naked and so am I. I don't think Sadie would appreciate it."

The bathroom door squeaked as Sadie came out. I heard her footsteps as she padded down the hall and closed the door to her bedroom. Oliver scooped me up and popped open the door, hightailing it to the bathroom. I wanted to yell at him because Sadie could open the door at any minute, but I held back.

"You're crazy," I said as he turned on the water.

"That's what they tell me."

I grinned. "Who are they?"

“Business associates,” he said as he perused my naked body.

“Maybe it’s true.”

“You just said it was.”

We washed each other tenderly, the warmth of the water soothing our bodies. Wrapped in towels, we emerged from the bathroom, relieved to find Sadie absent from the living room or kitchen. I knew that once she got over Dan, I'd seize every opportunity to spend time at Oliver’s. Keeping quiet during sex was a challenge; I was naturally vocal, and suppressing my expressions of pleasure, especially with Oliver, felt stifling.

Chapter 11

As we sat in The Tea Garden, waiting for Oliver, I couldn't shake the feeling that something was wrong. The atmosphere was elegant, the chatter of other diners intermingling with the soft clinking of cutlery against plates. But Oliver's absence weighed heavily on me, exacerbated by his tardiness.

"Where is he?" Matthew asked, voicing my own concern.

"He'll be here. He had a bunch of conference calls today," I reassured, though my own worry betrayed my words.

"On a Saturday?"

I shot my brother a pointed look. "Are you kidding? You work Saturdays."

"Not all the time. I've been taking it easy this summer."

I scanned the room, sipping my coffee nervously, and breathed a sigh of relief when Oliver finally entered. But any sense of relief evaporated when I noticed the slight disarray of his hair and the smear of blood on his cheek. Concern tightened my chest.

"There he is," I announced, trying to mask my apprehension.

I introduced Oliver to Matthew, who greeted him with a handshake before taking his leave to head to the buffet tables. As Oliver started to rise, I caught his arm, determined to address the unsettling sight.

“Not now, Ryleigh,” he hissed, his discomfort palpable.

Ignoring his protest, I reached for my cloth napkin and dipped it into my water glass, dabbing at the blood on his cheek. The attention drew stares from nearby diners, but I paid them no mind. Oliver brushed my hand away and excused himself from the table, leaving me with a knot of worry in my stomach.

Throughout brunch, Oliver's demeanor remained strained, his appetite all but nonexistent. Despite his efforts to engage Matthew in conversation, I could sense the underlying tension. I knew the importance of making a good impression on my brother, especially considering he would likely be the one to relay details of Oliver to our family.

Despite the lavish spread before us, I found it difficult to eat, my own anxiety mirroring Oliver's. His repeated orders for scotch only added to my unease, his usual restraint abandoned in favor of seeking solace in alcohol.

Once brunch was over, Oliver settled the bill and bid farewell to Matthew, offering to give him a ride, which Matthew declined. Alone in the car with Vlad at the wheel, I turned to Oliver, my concern mounting.

“What happened?” I asked.

“Nothing you should worry about,” he growled, his tone clipped.

“Vlad, please drop me off at my apartment,” I interjected, my patience wearing thin.

“You’re going home?” Oliver questioned.

“You don’t want to talk, so why should I go to your place?” I retorted, my frustration mounting.

“It doesn’t concern you,” Oliver insisted, his jaw clenched.

“It happened to you, so of course it does. Now are you going to tell me or should I spend the evening with Sadie?” I asked, unwilling to back down.

Oliver sighed heavily, his reluctance evident. “When we get home.”

He leaned in, his breath laced with the scent of scotch, and pressed a kiss to my lips, lingering for a moment before pulling away. As he looked into my eyes, I saw the worry etched in his gaze, sending a wave of apprehension through me. What had transpired before he arrived at the restaurant? The unanswered question lingered heavily between us.

~

Once we were inside Oliver's penthouse, I pressed him for details about the morning's events.

"Get changed, and I'll tell you," he responded, his voice tight with tension.

"What could be so bad?" I asked, my concern growing.

"Jonah," he replied simply.

"Your brother?" I clarified, feeling a knot of worry form in my stomach.

Oliver walked to the bedroom, shedding his clothes as he went. I noticed blood on his shirt, concealed by his jacket.

"Oh my God. Where did the blood come from?" I gasped, my eyes widening in alarm.

"I had a physical altercation with Jonah. He wanted money, and I refused. I won't support his bad choices anymore," Oliver explained, his tone firm.

"So he hit you?" I inquired, my heart sinking.

"He sucker-punched me. We were talking, and the next thing I knew, my nose was bleeding," he recounted, his jaw clenched.

"What did you do?" I pressed, my worry escalating.

"I hit him hard in the chest. He couldn't breathe, and I called security to escort him out. Fortunately, they got there before he recovered," Oliver explained, his gaze steely.

I approached him, intending to help him undress, but he stopped me, taking my hands in his and pressing a kiss to my palms.

"I love you and I want to protect you," he confessed softly.

"Why would you have to protect me?" I questioned, furrowing my brow in confusion.

"Because your profile goes up now that you're with me," he explained, his expression grave.

"Should I be concerned?" I asked, feeling a twinge of apprehension.

"I don't think so. Would you like to take a bath?" he offered, changing the subject.

"Yes, a bath sounds nice," I agreed.

We finished getting undressed, and Oliver ran a bath, adding my favorite lime and basil bath beads. As we lounged in the tub, we discussed plans for my upcoming birthday.

"I'd like to plan the whole day," Oliver suggested.

“I have to work. My birthday is next Friday,” I reminded him.

“I meant Saturday, but we can still celebrate on Friday evening,” he proposed.

“My parents asked me to dinner at home,” I informed him.

“I could go with you. You said you wanted them to meet me. Vlad could drive us,” Oliver suggested, his tone hopeful.

“Sadie would be coming,” I mentioned, considering the logistics.

“She can come with us,” Oliver suggested easily.

“You would be okay with that?” I asked, a bit surprised.

He wrapped his arms around me, locking his hands underneath my breasts. I snuggled against him, planting a kiss on the underside of his chin. I liked this very much.

“Of course, I would. She’s your friend,” he reassured me.

“You usually don’t want to share me,” I pointed out.

“I won’t keep you from friends and family. I’ll have to get used to sharing you,” he admitted.

“I share you,” I countered.

“With who?” he challenged.

"Your business. In case you haven't noticed, you work a lot," I teased.

"Do you want me to slow down?" he offered sincerely.

I did want him to slow down. I worried he was burning the candle at both ends. There were nights we stayed up half the night and I spent my day yawning from exhaustion. Oliver was almost always up before me and would work late or in his office at the penthouse after dinner.

"Just like you, I have to get used to sharing you. I know how important work is to you," I replied honestly.

"Not as important as you. In case you haven't noticed, I've built quite an empire," he said, a hint of pride in his voice.

"Arrogant ass," I muttered playfully as I rubbed my back against his chest.

"Excuse me? Did you just call me arrogant?" He feigned offense.

I giggled. "If the shoe fits."

"I would end it all if that's what makes you happy," he declared dramatically.

"And do what? Move to an island, surf and sun all day and live in a hut?" I teased.

"You forgot make love all night. I could do it. Just say the word," he suggested with a smirk.

"Nope. You love working," I teased back.

He cupped one of my breasts, thumbing the nipple. "I do but I love you more," he countered sweetly.

"Knowing you love me makes me happy. It's enough," I admitted.

"You have my love. Now, about your birthday gift," he changed the subject.

"Nothing extravagant," I insisted.

I looked up at him and he was frowning. He spoiled me far too much and I didn't want him to think I was taking advantage.

"Why?" he questioned.

"I'm not with you for what you can buy me," I asserted.

"You forget that I pursued you," he reminded me.

I nudged his ribs. "I know that, but now that I have you wrapped around my little finger, I can get whatever I want," I teased.

Oliver took my hand and put my pinkie in his mouth, sucking on it teasingly.

"This finger?" he asked with a mischievous grin after I pulled it away.

"Yes," I confirmed with a playful smile.

knew it was true. All I needed to do was mention that I wanted something and Oliver would have it, but that's not how I wanted my relationship to go. I didn't care about what he could buy me. I had money to buy whatever I wanted.

"So I can ask for a house in the country and you would do it?" I teased.

"Just point it out and it's yours," he replied confidently.

"Suppose someone lives there?" I challenged.

"Anything can be bought for a price," he stated matter-of-factly.

"You think you can just walk up to someone's house, knock on the door and make them say yes?" I pressed.

"I've done it before," he admitted casually.

I turned to look at him, intrigued. "With what?"

"The house in Southampton. I was looking for a home and I saw what I wanted from my boat. I made them an offer that very afternoon and it was accepted," Oliver revealed.

"It must have been some offer because that house is beautiful," I remarked, impressed.

He grinned at the compliment. "It was, quite a bit over the value. The owners were easy to convince, and I found out why later," he explained.

Nothing surprised me with Oliver. He was a monster when it came to negotiations.

“Why?” I inquired.

“They were planning to put the house up for sale at the end of the summer,” he disclosed.

“So you paid over asking when you could have gotten it cheaper,” I noted.

“Yes, but with the way the market was, it was worth it. My agent told me they probably would have received multiple bids on the property, and it would have been over what I offered. I won,” he explained confidently.

“It’s too large for one person,” I observed.

“That’s why I need a wife to fill it up with children,” he said with a hint of longing.

“How many?” I asked curiously.

“Several, four if possible. I miss having a family. Jonah breezes in and out of my life, and when he does, it’s usually because he’s in trouble,” Oliver said.

Curiosity got the best of me and though I didn’t want to stir up trouble or force him to tell me more than he was willing to reveal, I asked.

“What did he need the money for?”

“He didn’t say, but he’s been involved in shady deals before. I’m not financing his illegal activities,” Oliver stated firmly.

“I’m sorry. I would be upset if I had a bad relationship with my brothers,” I sympathized.

"Matthew seems very protective of you," he observed.

"He is, as is Finley. I was always the baby," I reminisced.

"They don't have to worry about you now; you're my baby," he declared with affection.

I moved my head to the side and kissed his chin. "The water is cooling, want to get out?"

"I think so. What do you want to do after this?" he asked.

"I'd like to sit on the patio. We don't do that often enough."

"It's very hot out today," he pointed out.

"Why don't you have a pool?" I inquired.

"Would you like me to put one in? The roof can support the weight," he offered.

"I've seen them enclosed by glass so you can swim all year around," I mused.

"Ryleigh, just say the word, and I can have a team up here to start construction by next week," he assured me.

"You would do that for me if I asked?" I confirmed.

"I told you... anything," he reaffirmed with sincerity.

~

I cried out as Oliver pounded me to another mind-numbing orgasm. We never made it out to the patio. The minute I removed my towel to dress, Oliver scooped me up and carried me to the bed. We'd been making love all afternoon and I was spent. He pulled out of me and moved to my side, cradling me against his body.

"I love you," he whispered into my ear.

"Thank you."

He quirked an eyebrow. "Thank you?"

"For loving me. I've never had anything like this."

"I've never found anyone to love like I do you."

"I'm hungry."

"You didn't eat much at brunch."

"Neither did you. I was worried."

Oliver sat up as if to assure me he was fine. "Don't worry about me. Jonah will get over his tantrum."

"Will you talk to him again?"

I couldn't imagine being at such odds with my brothers. We always got along and though they were protective, I knew it was out of love.

He sighed. "As long as he behaves. He is highly volatile and always has been, even when my parents were alive. I could barely keep him in control when I became his guardian. I finally gave up when he turned eighteen."

"Do you miss having a close relationship with him?" I asked, my voice barely above a whisper.

Oliver's eyes darkened, a flicker of regret passing through them. "I wish it could be different, but he'll never change," he said, his tone heavy with resignation.

"Is that why you have security?" I pressed, not letting the topic drop.

"No," Oliver replied firmly, shaking his head. "I don't worry about Jonah."

"But he attacked you," I insisted, my concern palpable.

A bitter smile tugged at the corner of Oliver's mouth. "I'm used to it. You think this was the first time?" He looked away, as if the memories were too painful to confront.

"He sounds dangerous," I murmured, feeling a shiver run down my spine.

"He isn't," Oliver said, his voice softening. "I can handle him. Now stop worrying your pretty little head about my brother. What would you like to eat?"

I hesitated, then decided to shift the conversation. "Do you have any crab salad?"

He raised an eyebrow, a playful glint returning to his eyes. "What do you think?"

"I'd say yes," I guessed, smiling despite myself.

Oliver's grip on me loosened, and I sat up in bed, reaching for his t-shirt draped over the chair. I slipped it on, the fabric soft against my skin. Oliver watched me, his gaze intense.

A smirk played on his lips. "No panties?"

"Your shirt is long enough to cover my ass," I retorted, feeling a blush creep up my neck.

"But I know you have none on," he teased, his eyes gleaming with mischief.

I chuckled. I knew what I was doing. Maybe I would tease him, accidentally on purpose dropping something on the floor I would need to bend over to pick up.

I met his gaze, a challenge in my eyes. "What are you going to do about it?"

Oliver's smirk widened into a grin. "You'll see."

"Would telling you I'm sore be a deterrent?" Oliver's voice, husky and laced with desire, filled the room.

"Maybe for a little while," I replied, a smirk playing on my lips.

"Get up so we can eat," I urged, glancing over at him.

"Go ahead. I'll be there in a minute. I just remembered I need to make a call," Oliver said, his eyes flicking to his phone.

"For business?" I raised an eyebrow.

"Yes," he confirmed with a nod, already dialing.

"It's 4:30 on a Saturday. Are all your associates as bad as you?" I teased, folding my arms.

"No, I'm the baddest," he shot back with a grin, his confidence palpable.

"Get over yourself," I retorted, shaking my head with a chuckle as I headed towards the door.

As I made my way to the kitchen, the faint sound of Oliver's voice on the phone followed me down the hall. I made myself at home, grabbing a fork from the drawer and opening the container of crab salad.

A few minutes later, Oliver emerged, dressed only in a pair of form-fitting gray boxers. The way they hugged his thighs and accentuated his ass sent a shiver down my spine, reminding me of what drew me to him in the first place.

My eyes traveled his body, fixing on his legs. “Those look good on you. You look good.”

His eye lit up with mischief. “Good enough to eat?”

I jutted my chin out. “If you want me to, I will.”

“Tempting but let’s eat first.”

I didn’t get to pleasure Oliver as much as I wanted to. He was all about my satisfaction, but sometimes I needed to return the favor.

"I’ll put it on hold for now," I said, a hint of reluctance in my voice.

He kissed me, his tongue teasing my bottom lip before he pulled away. "You taste yummy."

"My lips or something else?" I asked, raising an eyebrow.

"Everything," he replied, his eyes dark with desire.

I giggled, a blush spreading across my cheeks. "Sounds about right."

"Now who's the one acting arrogant?" he teased, a playful smirk on his lips.

"Maybe just a little," I admitted, my smile widening.

We spent the rest of the day relaxing on the patio, the late afternoon sun casting a warm glow over us. I sunned myself while Oliver read beside me, occasionally reaching over to trace patterns on my skin. As the sun began to set, we watched the sky transform into a tapestry of oranges before heading inside for dinner.

That night, I slept in Oliver's arms, feeling safe and content. In the early hours of the morning, he gently woke me, his touch igniting a familiar desire. We made love, our movements slow and tender, savoring every moment until the first light of dawn began to creep through the curtains.

As my birthday drew near, I couldn't contain my excitement. Oliver had been acting mysteriously all week, and by Friday, I was practically buzzing with anticipation.

Our plan was to drive up to Hudson Brook after work, but Oliver surprised me by swapping our usual sedan for a sleek black limo. I welcomed the change, relishing the added privacy it afforded us.

During lunch, Candice and a few coworkers treated me to a birthday celebration. Beatrice, always aloof, managed a polite birthday wish, though her detachment only added to my growing disillusionment with my job. While I was slowly learning the ins and outs of the PR business, too much of my time was still spent on mundane errands.

Outside the office building, Oliver and Sadie awaited me, with Vlad standing by the limousine. Vlad, ever stoic, greeted me with a nod and a subtle smile. Once inside, Oliver pulled me close, his arm secure around my waist. Had Sadie not been seated opposite us, I was certain I'd be in Oliver's embrace the moment the privacy glass rose. A bouquet of mixed roses adorned the seat beside Sadie, a thoughtful gesture from Oliver.

"Did you have a nice day?" Oliver asked, his voice warm against my ear.

"Yes, my coworkers took me to lunch at Filipos," I replied.

"That Mexican place? I've heard they make great tacos," he remarked.

"They do. You should try it sometime."

While Sadie fiddled with the radio, seemingly oblivious to our conversation, Oliver whispered in my ear, his lips teasing and igniting a familiar fire within me. "I can't wait to get you home," he murmured, eliciting a smile from me, though I willed myself not to dwell on our intimate moments.

"What's your mom serving?" Sadie interrupted.

"Take a guess," I replied with a grin.

She knew me too well and it wouldn't be hard for her to figure out what was on the menu.

"Chicken Cordon Bleu?" Sadie asked.

I pointed at her. "Bingo. It's my favorite," I confirmed.

"Are Matthew and Finley coming?" She inquired.

"Yes, Matthew left work early, and Finley should be arriving by 6:30. He's taking the train," I explained.

"He could've come with us," Oliver interjected.

"Finley had some work to finish. He's worse than you," I teased, rolling my eyes.

"He knows the importance of running a business," Oliver defended, punctuating his point with a firm kiss that left me breathless.

I rolled my eyes and Sadie looked away as Oliver pressed a hard kiss to my mouth. Traffic was a bit heavy and we rolled into Hudson Brook just before 6 p.m. I couldn't wait to see my parents since I hadn't since my graduation two and half months before.

My mother was waiting at the door. She looked great with her wavy auburn hair curled around her face. Some said we looked like twins except her eyes were blue, not hazel. She stepped out as we approached, offering her hand to Oliver before I even introduced them.

“I’m Livia.”

“Oliver Fox. Thank you for inviting me.”

Oliver handed the bouquet of flowers to my mother, who accepted them with a radiant smile. I could tell she was charmed by his gesture. At the door, my stepfather awaited us, and I introduced Oliver to him. Watching them interact, I couldn't help but notice the uncanny similarity in their ages despite Anders being only twelve years older than Oliver.

Anders, with his dark brown hair sprinkled with little gray and his handsome face almost devoid of wrinkles, greeted us warmly. Hugs were exchanged all around before we were ushered out to the screened-in patio off the kitchen, where Matthew was already seated.

Mylar "Happy Birthday" balloons danced in the breeze from the overhead fan, adding to the festive atmosphere. My mother had laid out a spread of appetizers, including mini quiches, another favorite of mine. As we settled in, the inquisition commenced, with my parents bombarding Oliver with question after question, to which he graciously responded.

Finley arrived just before seven, his gaze assessing Oliver with suspicion. I hoped he wouldn't be hostile, but within minutes, they were engrossed in conversation, bonding over discussions about software. Oliver's expertise in the field, stemming from his ownership of a small company specializing in educational software, seemed to impress Finley.

Meanwhile, Sadie hung on Finley's every word, though she likely had little understanding of the technical jargon. As they conversed, their interaction took on an intimate tone, sparking a curiosity within me. Was there something more between them? I pondered the question silently, resisting the urge to voice my thoughts.

Dinner was served by my parents, featuring chicken cordon bleu accompanied by sautéed green beans and lemon pasta. Despite the heaviness of the meal for such a hot night, I savored every bite. Leaning back in my chair, a sense of contentment washed over me as I basked in the warmth of family and love on my special day.

"I'm stuffed," I declared, leaning back in my chair.

"No room for dessert?" Oliver teased.

"There's always room for dessert," I replied with a grin.

"Good. I'm glad to hear," he said cryptically, leaving me curious about his sudden interest in sweets. My suspicions were soon answered when my favorite seven-layer chocolate cake, adorned with twenty-three candles, was brought to the table, one extra candle for good luck. I blew out the candles, silently grateful for Oliver's thoughtfulness.

As my mother and Anders presented an array of pastries from white bakery boxes, I couldn't help but feel overwhelmed.

"Wow, I feel special," I remarked.

"Oliver had them sent up," my mother revealed.

You sent these up when?" I asked in surprise.

"This morning. I ordered them from a place on Mulberry Street," Oliver explained.

"I can see I'll have to starve myself this week after all these calories," I joked, though secretly touched by his gesture.

"You look beautiful," Oliver whispered, kissing me softly on the cheek.

After indulging in dessert, fatigue washed over me, and I longed for sleep. My thoughts about Finley and Sadie were confirmed when I stumbled upon them kissing in the hallway. Retreating upstairs to the familiar comfort of my old bedroom, I couldn't help but feel a mix of emotions. While I was happy for them, I couldn't shake the uncertainty surrounding the origin of their relationship.

Returning downstairs, I found Finley and Sadie seated at the table, their smiles betraying their secret rendezvous. Resolving to address the matter later, I accepted the thoughtful gifts from my family and friends. Sadie's baby blue v-neck sweater, a symbol of her affection despite her tight budget, warmed my heart.

We left my parent's home shortly before 10 p.m. We were exhausted since we worked all day. Everyone hitched a ride in Oliver's limo since we were all heading back to Manhattan. I insisted on feeding Vlad during my party. He quietly ate his meal even though I offered for him to join us on the patio.

Matthew fell asleep on the ride while Finley and Sadie spoke in hushed tones on the bench seat to our left. Oliver whispered to me about them.

"When did that happen?"

"I have no idea. I think it's cute. They make a nice couple."

"Are you sure it doesn't have anything to do with your brother's money?"

"I hope not. Finley might seem hard on the outside but he's a mush inside. I know he would be hurt if Sadie used him. I'll get to the bottom of their relationship next time I'm home."

"And when will that be," Oliver said with a smirk.

"I need a night to myself. We discussed this."

He nuzzled my ear. "Ryleigh, I'm kidding. I'm well aware of your need for space. I don't like it but I'm giving it to you."

I laced my fingers with his. "That doesn't mean I don't miss you."

"I know. I don't sleep well without you next to me. In fact, I hate it," he grumbled.

"What do you have planned tomorrow?" I asked.

He smiled widely. "I can't tell you. You'll just have to be patient."

"My mother loved the roses. She said you're very polite."

"What else did she say?" He asked with curiosity.

"She's worried about our age difference."

"I won't hurt you. It would hurt me more."

"I know. I told her that, but she can still worry. I'm her baby."

"You're my baby too."

I reached up to run my finger through his lush hair. He smiled and planted a soft kiss on my mouth. Fatigue finally took me. I leaned against him and he cuddled me against his body, fading off to sleep. The next thing I knew, I was being carried into his bedroom.

"What happened?" I mumbled.

"You fell asleep and wouldn't wake up. In fact, you growled at me to leave you alone."

I chuckled. "I did?"

"You did. No playtime tonight. You need to sleep. Tomorrow is a big day."

"I want to play tonight. I want to ride you."

Oliver shook his head. “As much as I would love that, it’s not gonna happen. You’re tired.”

I protested as he helped me undress. He placed me in bed in just my panties. I curled up on my side with my back toward him as he undressed, not feeling him slip in next to me.

Chapter 12

I thought I was dreaming when I felt my panties shred. I woke up to Oliver's tongue on my clit and I shuddered. Dawn was just starting to leak in the windows and I could see silhouettes of the patio furniture out the sliding glass door in Oliver's bedroom.

"What are you doing?" I asked.

"Giving you a happy birthday wake up."

I wasn't going to protest because my climax was hurtling so fast that I knew it would be less than a minute before I was shredding apart like my panties. I moaned, grabbing a handful of Oliver's thick hair. I kept him against my cleft, making sure he wouldn't bring me to the edge and back away. He kept circling my swollen bundle of nerves until I slipped under the surface, floated for half a minute and popped back up.

"Fuck," I sighed, "that was so good that it hurt."

“I’m glad I could be of service,” Oliver said as he wiped his face and moved alongside me.

He kissed me, his tongue thrusting in my mouth. I sucked it with the urge to suck something else. My hand wandered down his taut stomach to the waistband of his boxers, sliding in and encircling his rigid penis. I stroked him, getting more excited at the prospect of having him in my mouth.

“Easy,” he hissed.

“I want to suck you,” I demanded.

“It’s not my birthday,” he protested.

“You said I could do anything. Why does it surprise you that I like to suck you?”

“I’ve never been with many women that did.”

I couldn’t imagine why not. It wasn’t a turn off to me. It made me feel powerful to see him unraveling as I sucked him off.

“Oliver, I like to give you pleasure and I’m not turned off by anything that’s part of you.”

“You want me to submit?”

“Only if you want to.”

He rolled to his back, and I pushed the sheet off, throwing my shredded panties onto the floor. I let his shaft go and tugged at his boxers until he lifted his hips, removing them. I loved seeing him naked and when he was hard, it excited me to no end. I still couldn't believe we were together.

He kept his mouth shut as I climbed in between his legs, caressing his balls with my fingers. He moaned and fixed his pillow, so his upper body was partially propped up. His stare was intense as I place my lips on his wide head and sucked the pooled bubble of precum into my mouth.

I fisted him, squeezing his base while still massaging his balls. He hissed when I took him deeper, gently thrusting his hips upward as I bobbed on him.

"I'm close," he groaned.

I was shocked since Oliver had staying power. I hollowed my cheeks as I moved as low as I could go without choking. He was almost to the back of my throat when he made a feral moan, and I felt the first splash of ejaculate hit my tongue. I kept moving as he fuck my mouth, swallowing all he had to give. After he finished, I licked him clean and moved to his side.

"Christ, that was wonderful."

"I wish you would let me do it more."

"You amaze me. I'm never letting you go."

He cuddled me in his arms and pulled the sheet over us. We fell back to sleep, waking to the vibrating of Oliver's phone on the bedside table. He yawned and reached over to look at the screen.

“Your first surprise is in two hours.”

I smirked. “I thought your first surprise was sunrise oral.”

"Okay, your second surprise," Oliver announced, a mischievous glint in his eyes.

"What is it?" I asked eagerly, already brimming with anticipation.

"We have to get a move on. Vlad will be here in an hour and a half," Oliver replied, evading my question.

"Tell me what we're doing, or I don't move," I insisted, crossing my arms defiantly.

"I can make you move," Oliver teased, a smirk playing on his lips.

"I want to know," I persisted, my curiosity getting the best of me.

"Do you know the meaning of a surprise?" Oliver countered, raising an eyebrow.

"I'm curious. Indulge me," I pleaded, unable to contain my excitement.

"No. Now get in the shower," Oliver commanded, his tone playful yet firm.

"I refuse unless you tell me," I declared, digging my heels in.

. . .

Without further ado, Oliver swiftly climbed out of bed, effortlessly pulling the sheet off me. Scooping me up in his arms, he carried me into the bathroom, my protests fading into playful laughter.

Setting me down on the bench in the shower stall, he turned on the water, the warm cascade enveloping us both. Though I pouted for show, deep down, I was bubbling with excitement for the surprises that lay ahead. Today was shaping up to be an unforgettable adventure.

“Can I soap you?” He asked.

“Only if you fuck me first.”

“Demanding little vixen, aren’t you?”

“I’m the birthday girl. I should get what I want.”

He came to me, stood me up and pushed me against the steamed glass of the shower, gently biting my neck.

“Vampire,” I whispered.

“I love sucking things on you.”

Oliver spread my legs with his hands and pressed his cock through my slick folds. This was another position we hadn’t tried.

“Are you okay?” Oliver asked.

“Fuck me,” I whispered.

He wrapped his hand around my throat as we fucked, trailing kisses along my shoulder and the back of my neck. My hands were pressed against the thick glass. I was sandwiched between hot and cool. I reached back and dug my nails into his hip, wanting him to make me come.

He pulsed inside me as he backed away from the glass, taking me with him. Once he sat down on the long tiled bench, it was my time to do the work. I rode him, pressing my back to his chest until we had simultaneous orgasms.

“Marry me,” he whispered as he held me.

“Don’t ruin this,” I hissed.

“How am I ruining this?” He questioned.

I ground my teeth. “You’re pushing again.”

“I love you. I want you to be my wife. Is that such a bad thing?”

“No, but it’s too early. I’m committed to you.”

“But I want you to wear my name.”

As I contemplated the idea of being Mrs. Ryleigh Fox, I couldn't help but wonder if I'd ever grow accustomed to Oliver's wealth and the lifestyle it entailed. Would his long hours and frequent travel become too much for me to handle? Next week's trip, the first time we'd be apart in weeks, loomed ahead as a test for our relationship.

"And I will. You have my promise," I assured Oliver, trying to ignore the twinge of uncertainty in his voice.

"Why not soon?" Oliver pressed, his gaze searching mine.

"Why the rush? I've told you; things could fall apart if you find out something you don't like about me," I explained, hoping he'd understand.

"Like what?" he prodded, his brow furrowing with concern.

"I don't know. Just...something," I shrugged, unable to articulate my fears.

"I love everything about you, even the bad stuff," he declared, his words stirring a warmth in my heart.

"What bad stuff?" I asked, genuinely curious.

"You whimper in your sleep," he confessed, watching my reaction carefully.

"I do? Why didn't you tell me?" My surprise was evident, prompting him to reassure me.

"It's never led to anything serious, so I didn't think it was a big deal," he explained, feeling a pang of guilt for not discussing it sooner.

"Were you expecting it to?" I inquired.

"You mentioned screaming during nightmares," he reminded me, taking my hand in his.

"I do. I don't want to, but sometimes it happens," I admitted, vulnerability seeping into my tone.

"I don't care. I love every part of you," he reassured me,

guiding me towards the shower as we prepared for the day ahead.

As we washed and dried each other, the mystery of Oliver's plans for the day lingered in the air. Opting for casual attire—a pair of jean shorts and a short blue t-shirt—I couldn't help but feel a mixture of excitement and apprehension about what lay ahead.

"Is this all right?" I asked tentatively, seeking his approval.

"Fine," Oliver replied, his tone betraying none of his hidden plans.

"Still no clue?" I inquired, a hint of frustration creeping into my voice.

"Nope. All I can say is you'll love it," Oliver teased, a twinkle of excitement dancing in his eyes.

"Says you," I muttered under my breath, feeling a mix of anticipation and skepticism.

As I sat on the bed, watching the news, Oliver dressed in pressed olive-colored shorts and a tan polo shirt—making me feel somewhat underdressed in comparison.

"Should I change?" I asked self-consciously, suddenly aware of the disparity in our appearances.

"Wear whatever you want. This is a relaxed day," Oliver reassured me, his easy confidence helping to quell my rising nerves.

"But you look nice—better than me," I confessed, feeling a pang of insecurity.

"Nothing you wear could make you look bad," Oliver insisted, planting a tender kiss on my forehead.

"We have a half hour. Want some coffee?" he suggested, diverting my attention.

"I'm hungry. I want breakfast," I protested, my stomach grumbling impatiently.

"Be patient," Oliver chided gently, though the twinkle in his eye betrayed his amusement.

"Oliver, where are you taking me?" I whined, unable to contain my curiosity any longer.

"You're impossible. Let's have coffee," he deflected, leading the way to the kitchen where a small light blue gift bag and a stunning bouquet of red roses awaited me.

“For me?”

Oliver rolled his eyes and chuckled, “Of course. It’s not my birthday.”

I pulled the card out from the bag and read it. It was simple but to the point and contained a love poem by Lord Byron.

“It’s lovely. Thank you.”

He watched me as I removed the dark blue tissue paper. Inside the bag were two black velvet boxes, one larger than the other. I removed them and my heart began to pound because one was the size of a ring box. Oliver must have realized what I was thinking.

“No, one is not a ring.”

I inwardly breathed a sigh of relief that I wouldn’t have to ruin this day by saying no to his official marriage proposal. I know I already had in the shower, but I considered that a discussion rather than a proposal. I opened the larger box, finding a beautiful ruby tennis bracelet. In the smaller one were ruby earrings.

“These are gorgeous,” I gushed.

“Put them on.”

I took the teardrop diamond earrings out of my ears and put the ruby studs in. Oliver secured the bracelet on my wrist. His phone buzzed and he checked the screen.

“Vlad is downstairs. Time to go.”

“I didn’t have coffee,” I complained.

“Too late.”

He took me by the hand and led me to the door.

~

As we drove, I couldn't contain my curiosity any longer, begging Oliver to reveal our destination. He pretended to ignore me until I dug my nails into the palm of his hand, eliciting a playful yet firm response.

"Be nice or I'll give you a spanking," he teased, his eyes dancing with mischief.

"That's something we haven't tried," I quipped, a hint of excitement coloring my tone.

"This one will be for punishment," Oliver warned, though I couldn't help but tease back.

"I might like it," I countered, a playful smirk tugging at my lips.

Oliver raised an eyebrow and chuckled before pulling me onto his lap, distracting me until we reached our destination. The orgasm he gifted me with his skilled fingers lightened my mood, leaving me breathless and eager for what lay ahead.

"Where are we?" I asked, taking in our surroundings as we arrived at the marina.

"The marina," Oliver replied with a grin.

"Your boat?" I guessed, excitement bubbling within me.

"Yes. I told you I had one," Oliver confirmed, his eyes gleaming with anticipation.

"Where are we going?" I pressed, unable to contain my curiosity.

"For a little excursion," Oliver replied cryptically, helping me out of the car as Vlad joined us.

I hoped Vlad wouldn't intrude on our intimate time together. I longed to be alone with Oliver. What Oliver called a boat turned out to be a luxurious yacht, a breathtaking sight with its gleaming white exterior and sparkling windows.

"This is yours?" I asked in awe, unable to tear my eyes away from the magnificent vessel.

"It could be yours too if you would stop being stubborn," Oliver teased, his words hinting at marriage again.

Ignoring his reference, I focused on the yacht's beauty. Oliver led me onto the gangplank, where seven white-uniformed staff awaited us. Oliver introduced me to the captain, Jeffrey Conway, before leading me inside the yacht's main salon.

The room exuded elegance with its polished wood, plush carpets, and light-colored furnishings. Oliver dismissed the stewardess, opting to give me a personal tour of the yacht. We explored the stainless-steel kitchen, the crew's sleeping quarters, and the stunning dining area with its mahogany table.

Speechless at the yacht's opulence, I followed Oliver outside to the deck, where a picturesque scene awaited us. A small eating area with a hot tub and dining table overlooked the ocean, inviting us to soak in the breathtaking views.

"Would you like to sit down? We'll be eating soon," Oliver offered, his eyes sparkling with excitement.

"We're having breakfast here?" I marveled, unable to contain my delight.

"We're having it in the middle of the ocean," Oliver revealed, his words filling me with joy.

As Oliver sent a text and the engines roared to life, I couldn't help but squeal with excitement. His thoughtful gesture filled me with happiness, and I couldn't resist expressing my gratitude.

"You're wonderful," I whispered, my heart overflowing with love for the man who had orchestrated this unforgettable surprise.

“You’re happy?” Oliver asked, his gaze softening as he took in my expression.

“You’re wonderful,” I replied, my heart swelling with gratitude.

“Let’s sit. Breakfast is coming right up,” Oliver suggested, guiding me to the dining area as two white-uniformed stewardesses emerged with an array of breakfast delights.

As the stewardesses offered us coffee and took our breakfast orders, I couldn't help but marvel at the luxurious setting.

“This is nice,” I murmured, a dreamy smile playing on my lips.

The yacht began to move, gliding gracefully out of the marina and into the vast expanse of the Atlantic Ocean. The sun beamed down, warming my skin as I reveled in the sensation of the ocean breeze tousling my hair.

Glancing at Oliver, I caught him watching me with a softness in his eyes.

“What?” I asked, turning to face him.

“You’re like a kid,” Oliver chuckled, his affectionate tone warming my heart.

“How so?” I inquired, curious about his observation.

“Full of wonder,” he explained, his gaze lingering on me.

“I’ve been on boats before but never one so large,” I admitted, a sense of awe washing over me.

“I rarely use it because I’m busy,” Oliver confessed, a hint of regret coloring his words.

“How many staterooms are on this boat?” I asked, my curiosity piqued.

“Five besides the crew’s,” Oliver replied, his tone thoughtful.

“Do you have guests often?” I probed, sensing there was more to his story.

“I have, but it’s been a while,” Oliver admitted, his gaze drifting towards the horizon.

“Oliver, why do you bother having things with so many bedrooms if you never seem to use them?” I questioned.

“I might have a reason to use them now. Suppose we took a trip somewhere down the eastern seaboard? We could take some of your family with us. Finley and Sadie seem to be very cozy," Oliver suggested, his eyes sparkling with possibility.

The idea of embarking on an adventure with Oliver and my loved ones filled me with excitement, and I couldn't help but smile at the thought.

"I need to talk to them about that. I was totally unaware they were seeing each other. You would think they would've said something," I mused, my thoughts drifting to Finley and Sadie.

"They make a nice couple," Oliver remarked.

"I just hope she isn't with him for his money. I would have to take his side and lose a best friend," I confessed, my worries bubbling to the surface.

Our conversation was interrupted as the staff brought out our meal. I ordered a vegetable omelet with cheddar cheese, while Oliver opted for sunny side up eggs. Platters of crispy bacon and petite bagels, accompanied by an array of jellies, were placed before us, igniting my appetite. I requested some orange juice, watching as one stewardess went to fetch it while the other refilled Oliver's coffee cup.

We savored our breakfast in leisure, basking in the tranquility of the ocean. Once we had finished, I retreated to the couch to enjoy the refreshing sea breeze, Oliver joining me with a tender nuzzle.

"This is the life. I could get used to it," I sighed contentedly, reveling in the moment.

"You can have it anytime you want if you grant me my request," Oliver suggested, his gaze lingering on me expectantly.

"Oliver, I love you. Can't I enjoy these things without the ring on my finger?" I countered, a flicker of resistance in my tone.

"You can, but you would make me very happy if you would wear it," Oliver persisted, his eyes pleading.

"Suppose I said yes right now?" I teased.

"Then I would have the good captain turn this boat around and take you to my jeweler to pick out your engagement ring," Oliver replied, his smile widening at the thought.

"I really do have you wrapped around my little finger," I chuckled, feeling a surge of affection for him.

He smirked, his expression playful. "From the world congratulations."

"Congratulations?" I echoed, confusion flickering across my features.

"When I handed you your diploma. I saw you in line but when I shook your hand, that was it. I wanted you," Oliver confessed, his words filling me with warmth.

“Kiss me,” I whispered, unable to contain the rush of love that flooded my heart.

Oliver pressed his lips to mine, not moving them. He cradled my head and stroked the side of my breast with his fingers. I was growing heated by the time he pushed my mouth open with his tongue, softly moaning as he licked mine.

“You’re teasing me, Mr. Fox,” I chided playfully, a hint of anticipation in my voice.

“I can deliver. I haven’t shown you the staterooms yet. Would you like to see them?” Oliver suggested, his eyes twinkling.

“I’m afraid if I do, I won’t be able to enjoy this glorious day,” I confessed.

“How so?” Oliver inquired.

“You have a way of exhausting me,” I admitted with a playful grin.

“You’re all of twenty-three,” Oliver pointed out, his tone teasing.

“But you’re that good—and don’t give me that arrogant look,” I countered, feeling a blush creeping onto my cheeks.

Oliver smirked before he thumbed my nipple. I felt my face heat when I noticed one of the stewardesses was at the bar wiping the counter until I realized Oliver’s body hid what he was doing.

“Stop trying to seduce me,” I whispered, trying to maintain a semblance of composure.

“Just an hour,” Oliver pleaded, his eyes sparkling with desire.

“Ha, an hour turns into three and then the day is over for me because I want to sleep,” I teased, shaking my head.

“You lead. I promise to obey,” Oliver suggested, his voice laced with amusement.

“Since when has that ever worked? I get started, and you finish it,” I retorted, unable to suppress a giggle.

“It’s your fault for being so irresistible,” Oliver said, his grin widening.

“That’s right, blame me,” I quipped, unable to resist a playful jab.

He placed a wet kiss on my cheek before leaning back against the couch, closing his eyes as the breeze ruffled his hair. I reached over and traced his nose with my finger, feeling a rush of affection for this man who knew just how to make me smile. He sucked my finger into his mouth, gently biting the tip, and I couldn’t help but laugh at his playful antics.

"Do you have more to show me?" I asked, my curiosity piqued.

"You want the rest of the tour?" Oliver replied.

"As long as you don't get me into a compromising position," I muttered.

"Like what?" Oliver inquired, his tone suggestive.

"Like on my back with my legs spread," I quipped, unable to resist poking him.

"Fuck," he hissed, his reaction catching me off guard.

"What?" I asked, puzzled by his sudden shift in demeanor.

"That got me hard. Stop talking about sex," Oliver confessed, his cheeks flushing slightly.

I chuckled as he stood up and took my hand, leading me to explore the rest of the yacht. He showed me all the staterooms on the upper floor, each one more luxurious than the last. The master stateroom, in particular, caught my eye with its king-sized bed and plush gray carpet.

I couldn't resist bouncing on the corner of the bed, earning a bemused look from Oliver.

"Let's get out of here before we get into trouble," Oliver suggested, a hint of playfulness in his voice.

"It's your boat. How could we get in trouble?" I countered.

"You know what I mean. You want to enjoy the sunshine, then let's go," Oliver insisted, tugging gently on my hand to lead me back outside.

With a laugh, I followed him, feeling grateful for this carefree day on the ocean with the man I loved.

We spent all morning and early afternoon on the yacht, soaking in the sun and sea breeze until it docked back at the marina. Oliver behaved surprisingly well, leaving me wondering what other surprises he had in store for the rest of the day.

Vlad chauffeured us back to the penthouse where Oliver had lunch served on the patio. Despite the tempting spread, I didn't have much of an appetite, still feeling full from breakfast.

"Are you serving me dinner too?" I asked, glancing at Oliver as I pushed my food around my plate.

"Do you want me to serve you dinner?" he countered.

"I'd rather have something light. I'm not very hungry," I admitted, feeling a pang of guilt for not fully indulging in the birthday festivities.

"Light? Like what?" Oliver inquired, raising an eyebrow.

"A sandwich," I replied, shrugging nonchalantly.

"That's what you want for your birthday dinner?" Oliver seemed surprised.

"It's fine. I don't need anything special," I reassured him, not wanting to make a fuss.

"I thought we would relax this evening," Oliver suggested, his tone softening.

"What you did for me today was wonderful. I don’t need anything else," I insisted, smiling gratefully at him.

"Want to take a nap?" Oliver suggested.

"How did you know?" I chuckled, feeling a yawn escape me.

"You look sleepy," Oliver replied with a grin.

"I am a little," I admitted, feeling the fatigue settling in.

Oliver scooped me up in his arms and carried me to his bedroom. As he opened the door, I let out a surprised squeal and jumped out of his arms. The entire room was filled with blue balloons of all shades, reminiscent of the balloon-filled surprises my parents had arranged for my eleventh birthday.

"Oh my God, this is awesome," I exclaimed, my heart swelling with joy at the unexpected gesture.

There were so many balloons that they obscured the furniture in the room, creating a whimsical atmosphere that filled me with nostalgia. I hadn't anticipated Oliver repeating such a cherished childhood memory, and I couldn't help but feel overwhelmed with gratitude for his thoughtfulness.

“Do you like it?” he called.

“I love it.”

I pushed my way through the balloons, looking for him. This might have been a childish gesture, but it meant the world to me because Oliver was listening when I talked. I bumped into him at the center of the room and pressed a kiss to his cheek.

“Thank you for this. Who did it?” I asked, admiring the sea of balloons that filled the room.

“My assistants,” Oliver replied with a grin.

“You owe them a bonus,” I teased.

“I’ll take it under advisement,” Oliver replied.

I hit balloons into the air, attempting to clear a path through the room. Opening the door, I let several balloons spill out into the hallway, and Oliver followed me as I kicked a few along the way.

“This is fun,” I remarked, feeling a surge of childlike excitement.

“I have a question,” Oliver said, his tone turning more serious.

“What?” I asked, turning to face him.

“How exactly did you dispose of all these?” he inquired, a hint of curiosity in his voice.

“We popped them. It was just as much fun as playing in them,” I admitted with a laugh.

We were like two little kids as we kicked and filled the hallway with balloons. Eventually, Oliver got me on the floor and covered my body with his own amid the rubber chaos. He made love to me passionately while we were surrounded by the blue latex, and I held onto him tightly as waves of pleasure washed over us.

“Don’t fall asleep,” Oliver whispered as we lay tangled together on the thick wool carpet.

“I’m tired,” I confessed, a yawn escaping me.

“We have to clean this up,” Oliver reminded me gently.

“Later,” I murmured, already feeling sleep beckoning me.

Ryleigh?” Oliver called out softly, but I was already drifting off into a peaceful slumber.

When I woke up, I found myself in Oliver’s bed. The room was no longer filled with balloons, and I was naked under the sheet. Calling out for Oliver, I waited as he appeared at the door a few seconds later, his presence comforting and familiar.

“Sleeping beauty awakens,” Oliver greeted me with a smile as I stirred from my slumber.

“Where did all the balloons go?” I asked, rubbing the sleep from my eyes and taking in the now-empty room.

“I cleaned them up,” Oliver replied, his voice carrying a hint of mischief.

“How? I didn’t hear any pops?” I questioned, puzzled by his method.

“You were passed out,” he chuckled.

“I'm sure I would've woken up if I heard popping,” I retorted with a smirk.

“I used scissors,” Oliver explained matter-of-factly.

“Wait, you cleaned everything up yourself?” I asked.

He crossed his arms. “You sound surprised. I'm self-sufficient when I need to be,” he replied, his tone laced with amusement.

“Lay with me,” I requested, feeling a sudden urge to snuggle up to him.

“I have something to finish up. Are you hungry?” Oliver inquired, changing the subject smoothly.

I shook my head. “No more.”

“Not even for cake?” he teased.

“You got me a cake?” I exclaimed, feeling a surge of excitement.

“Of course. You can't have a birthday without cake,” Oliver replied with a grin.

“Maybe later. I need a shower,” I said, feeling the need to freshen up after my nap.

“Can I watch?” Oliver asked, waggling his eyebrows.

“Why don't you join me?” I asked.

“I already took one,” Oliver said as a smile tugged at his lips.

"What exactly do you do when I'm sleeping? You cleaned up about two hundred balloons, did some work, and took a shower? How long was I asleep?" I questioned, curious about his activities in my absence.

"About three hours," Oliver answered, his gaze softening as he looked at me.

"My birthday is almost over," I remarked, feeling a twinge of sadness at the thought.

"Yes, it is. Did you enjoy it?" Oliver asked.

He sat down at the edge of the bed and I held my hand out for his, squeezing it as a silent gesture of gratitude. This man had changed my life in so many ways.

"It's number one on the list of birthdays," I replied with a smile, feeling truly grateful for the wonderful day Oliver had planned for me.

"I guess I have all year to figure out something to beat it," Oliver mused, his mind already racing with ideas.

"I hope it will be more subdued," I teased, though secretly intrigued by the prospect of another extravagant celebration.

"Nope. More extravagant. Maybe I'll take you to Europe for the weekend," Oliver proposed, his eyes gleaming with excitement.

"That would be a lot of traveling," I remarked, feeling a mixture of thrill and apprehension at the thought.

“I have two company jets, so we don’t need to worry about commercial flights. We could fly out Friday night and Sunday night to come home. One has a full bedroom. You could sleep on the plane and be into work on Monday morning as fresh as a daisy,” Oliver explained, his confidence in his plan evident.

“Don’t remind me about work,” I groaned, the thought of Monday morning already dampening my spirits.

“Still hating it?” Oliver asked, concern etched in his features.

“It’s not what I expected, and it’s only gotten slightly better,” I admitted, feeling the weight of dissatisfaction settle in my chest.

“You know the solution,” Oliver stated simply, his gaze steady on mine.

“I’m not sure if I want to work for you,” I confessed, my hesitation clear in my voice.

“Why?” Oliver asked.

“Because familiarity breeds contempt. We’re together almost every night and you want to be together all day too?” I explained, my concerns bubbling to the surface.

“I could never dislike you. I love you too much,” Oliver declared, his sincerity melting my resolve.

“I’ll think about it,” I relented, surprising both him and myself with my admission.

Oliver raised his eyebrows, clearly taken aback. “Really?”

“Yes. I’m getting close to the end of my rope. If things don’t change, I think I’ll look for a new job,” I affirmed, feeling a sense of liberation in my decision.

“You already have one if you want out,” Oliver reminded me, his offer still open.

“I heard the boss is a really pain in the ass at Fox,” I joked, trying to lighten the mood.

“He is but not if you do him special favors,” Oliver said.

I raised my eyebrows. “I can’t believe you just said that. You know you can be sued for sexual harassment making those types of statements,” I scolded him, though unable to suppress my laughter.

“Then become my fiancée so I don’t end up scandalized,” Oliver suggested, his grin widening.

“All in due time Mr. Fox,” I replied, feeling a rush of warmth at the thought of our future together.

He grinned and pulled me close, wrapping his arms around me. In his embrace, I found solace, knowing that no matter what challenges lay ahead, we would face them together.

Chapter 13

"Ryleigh, are you almost finished?" Sadie asked.

I was in a horrible mood. I had to sleep alone the night before and for the next few nights because Oliver was in Vancouver for meetings.

"Give me a fucking minute," I growled.

I heard her retreating and the door to her room slam. Last night she didn't come home until late after I was in bed. I wanted to have a talk with her about Finley. Neither one had mentioned their relationship to me, and I was annoyed even though it was obvious.

I stormed out of the bathroom, the slamming of the door echoing my frustration. Sadie's shower started soon after, but I couldn't shake the feeling of discontent. My fingers flew over my phone, texting Oliver despite knowing it was the middle of the night where he was. My head wasn't right today. And with Beatrice's constant berating for my mistakes yesterday, I'm sure I was in for more today.

In my room, I pulled out a simple royal blue dress from my closet, opting for comfort over anything flashy. After slipping on a pair of white cotton underwear and a bra, I felt somewhat more put together. I didn't bother with anything sexy; there would be no seeing Oliver for another three days.

As I entered the kitchen, Sadie was already seated at the breakfast bar, nursing a steaming mug of coffee. Her blunt words cut through the tension like a knife.

"You're a real bitch today. What's your problem?" she snapped.

"I'm sorry. I miss Oliver," I admitted, the frustration still evident in my voice.

"That's no excuse," she retorted sharply.

"Well, maybe my excuse should be why my best friend and brother didn't tell me they were together," I shot back, feeling the anger bubbling up inside me.

Her expression shifted, a mixture of guilt and defensiveness. "We wanted to tell you. We were going to tell you."

"You had a chance at my birthday party. How long has this been going on?" I demanded, feeling the sting of betrayal.

She stared into her coffee cup. “A couple of weeks. And in my defense, you’re never home. You’ve been spending your nights with Oliver. I barely see you,” she explained, her tone softer now.

“What about my night off?” I challenged.

“One crappy night to hang out? You’re too wound up in him,” she accused, her frustration mirroring my own.

I pursed my lips. “Newsflash, I love him, and we’re not talking about me. How did you two get together?” I pressed, needing to understand.

She exhaled loudly. “Finley stopped by here to see if you wanted to get dinner. He was in the neighborhood. When I told him you weren’t home, he asked me to go. We hit it off,” Sadie explained, her tone more subdued.

“Did you sleep with him yet?” The words were out before I could stop them, a mix of curiosity and resentment driving my question.

Her reaction was instant, her eyes flashing with anger. “You really are a bitch. Why would you ask that?” she shot back, hurt evident in her voice.

I wanted her to feel as bad as I did, to share in my misery. “Because that’s your MO,” I retorted, my own frustration boiling over.

The tension in the room was palpable as Sadie slammed her coffee mug down, hot liquid splashing everywhere.

Without a word, she stormed off to her room, the force of her departure reverberating through the walls as she banged her door shut.

I sighed heavily, the weight of the situation settling heavily on my shoulders. Cleaning up the mess, I couldn't bring myself to face Sadie again. With a heavy heart, I left the apartment, hoping to escape the tension that hung thick in the air.

“What the hell is with you today, Ryleigh?” Candice whispered.

I appreciated Candice's concern as she whispered to me, sensing something was off. "Nothing, I'm fine," I replied, trying to brush off the mounting frustration and disappointment.

But inside, I was seething. I had messed up a few tasks assigned by Beatrice, and she had swiftly relegated me to mind-numbing data entry. It felt like a slap in the face after all the effort I had put in.

Candice saw through my facade. "You're not fine," she insisted, her voice laced with worry.

"I'm sick and tired of doing shit work," I confessed, the frustration bubbling to the surface.

“I told you that it takes time to earn Beatrice's trust," Candice reminded me, her tone gentle but firm.

. . .

“On second thought, I feel ill. My stomach hurts,” I lied, needing an excuse to escape the suffocating confines of the office.

“Go home. I’ll tell Beatrice you weren’t feeling well,” Candice offered, concern evident in her voice.

“Thanks,” I muttered gratefully, gathering my things and leaving before Beatrice could question my sudden departure.

As I walked away from the office, the weight of frustration and disappointment lingered in my mind. I seriously contemplated not returning. The day had been terrible from the moment I woke up, and work only added to the misery. But I knew I had to face Sadie and apologize for my harsh words that morning.

Usually, Vlad would give me a ride home, but today I opted for the subway. I needed the solitude to sort through my thoughts. He had no idea I was leaving early, and I didn't bother to inform him.

Just as I stepped out of the station a few blocks from my house, my phone buzzed. The screen displayed Oliver's face, and I answered quickly.

"Hi, baby," he greeted.

"Hi," I responded, relief washing over me at the sound of his voice.

"What's wrong?" Oliver asked, sensing my distress.

"Everything is falling apart," I admitted, my voice betraying the turmoil within me.

"Falling apart how?" he inquired, concern evident in his tone.

I recounted the events of the past two days and what transpired that morning with Sadie.

"Two days away and you're already a mess?" Oliver remarked, his voice tinged with amusement.

"I miss you, Oliver. I miss you so much," I confessed, longing evident in my words.

"Enough to accept my proposal?" he asked, his voice full of hope.

"Suppose I say no? Will you stay away until I do?" I teased lightly.

"That's a good idea, but I wouldn't be only punishing you," he replied with a hint of playfulness.

"I hate my job. I don't want to go back," I confessed, feeling a sense of relief at opening up to him.

"Does that mean I gain a new employee?" Oliver asked.

"You might gain a new roommate because Sadie hates me right now," I admitted, feeling a pang of guilt for my earlier behavior.

"She doesn't hate you, but you were rough on her this morning," Oliver pointed out gently.

"I know. I'm miserable without you," I said, the truth of my words weighing heavily on my heart.

Oliver chuckled, his voice warm and reassuring. "I'll be home on Thursday night."

"What do I do about work?" I asked, feeling uncertain about my job situation.

"I don't think you should just walk out of your job. Give your notice, and I'll get you squared away at Fox when I come home," he advised, his tone practical.

"What will I be doing?" I inquired, curious about my potential role.

"Personal assistant to me," he responded.

"Personal?" I repeated, feeling a mix of excitement and apprehension.

"Yes. You'll handle any and all personal requests by me," he explained, his words teasing.

"Such as?" I prompted, trying to gauge the extent of his jest.

"Ordering and eating meals with me, sharing afternoon orgasms, doing strip teases in my office while I'm on boring conference calls," he joked, his tone playful.

"I hope you don't mind parting with your money because I think I have a clear-cut case of sexual harassment on my hands," I retorted, trying to keep up with his banter.

"You can have it all in exchange for your love," he countered, his words tender.

"What a bargain," I replied, unable to suppress a smile at his charm.

"Not really since your love is priceless. We can discuss where you should be placed when I get back," he assured me, his voice filled with affection.

"I won't be working for you directly?" I asked, feeling a twinge of disappointment at the thought.

"Do you want to work for me directly? You were worried about familiarity breeding contempt," he pointed out, his words thoughtful.

"I don't know what I want right now except you," I confessed, feeling a surge of emotion.

I heard shuffling in the background, and Oliver's voice became muffled as he attended to something momentarily.

"I have my next meeting. Where are you anyway? I thought I would leave a message," Oliver inquired.

"I left work early. I just got off the train," I explained.

"Why didn't you text Vlad?" he asked, concern evident in his voice.

"I just wanted to get away from there," I admitted, feeling drained from the day's events.

"Go home, relax, and think about your apology to Sadie," he advised, his voice gentle.

"I love you," I said softly, longing for his comforting presence.

"Love you too," Oliver replied before ending the call.

As the line went silent, I felt a heavy weight in my chest. Slowly, I made my way back to my apartment. Collapsing onto the couch, I gazed up at the ceiling, contemplating how I would begin to mend the rift I had caused with Sadie.

After I changed out of my dress, I fell asleep on the couch with the television on. Sadie woke me up.

"I'm sorry for what I said this morning," I blurted out as soon as I regained consciousness.

She had a sour look on her face. "You were having a nightmare."

I sat up, feeling a pang of guilt. "Fuck. I don't even remember."

"You were whimpering and calling for your father," Sadie explained.

Feeling a surge of embarrassment, I rose from the couch and followed her, grabbing her arm.

She stopped walking and turned. “You were a major bitch this morning. Why would you say something like you did?”

I hung my head. “I don’t know. I was hurt you didn’t tell me about dating Finley,” I admitted, feeling remorseful.

“I really like him,” Sadie confessed.

“How does he even have time to date? He’s always so busy,” I questioned.

“He’s made time for me, and to answer your question, we haven’t had sex,” Sadie disclosed.

I was surprised by her revelation. Sadie wasn’t one to wait for an emotional connection before getting intimate with a man.

“Are you two dating exclusively?” I inquired, concerned about their relationship dynamics.

“We’re seeing each other,” she responded, her tone indicating uncertainty.

Her words sparked worry within me. Finley wasn’t known for maintaining close relationships with women due to his focus on his business. I didn’t want either of them to end up hurt.

“We’re seeing each other.”

Her statement worried me because Finley didn’t have close relationships with women because he was afraid it would take time away from his growing business. I didn’t want either of them to get hurt.

“I'm happy for you. I hope it works out,” I said sincerely.

“I wanted to tell you, but Finley said we should wait,” she said.

I leaned on the kitchen counter. “I'm sorry I haven't been around much. Maybe we can have a girl's night?” I suggested.

She smiled. “That sounds like fun. Let's ditch the men and go out,” Sadie agreed.

“What about tonight?” I proposed.

She hesitated, then replied, “Finley is meeting me for dinner at 7:30 near his office.”

I gave her a side hug. “Sadie, Finley is so involved in his business. I don't want you to get hurt if he cancels on you last minute for anything.”

“I'm well aware. We discussed it. You deal with Oliver and his weird schedules. I can take care of Finley,” Sadie assured me.

“I really hope it works out for you two. You both deserve someone nice,” I said sincerely.

She hugged me back, and I went to the refrigerator to get something to eat. I hadn't eaten breakfast or lunch and was starved. Sadie stayed in her room until 7 p.m. when she came out wearing a pair of black Capri pants and a gold halter top.

"Going out to dinner?" I asked, a hint of curiosity in my tone.

"Yes," Mom replied, her voice tinged with anticipation. "Finley is running a little late but he said he'd meet me there."

"Have fun," I said, offering a small smile. "I'll see you later."

I finished my sandwich and called my mother, feeling a sense of boredom creeping in. The anticipation of her reaction to my news about Oliver's proposal made me hesitate, but I dialed her number anyway. I decided not to tell her unless she brought it up.

"Ryleigh, how are you?" Mom's voice sounded warm, but there was an underlying curiosity in her tone. "I'm surprised you called since we saw you on Friday."

I settled on the couch, stretching out my legs. "I just wanted to say hello."

"How was the boat?" Mom's question was gentle yet filled with interest.

"Oliver told you?" I raised an eyebrow, intrigued by her knowledge.

"Yes. He invited us to join him sometime." Mom's voice held a note of excitement.

"It was beautiful," I said, a smile tugging at the corners of my lips. "We sailed on the ocean for part of the day. I had a good birthday."

"Your relationship is serious?" Mom's question hung in the air, filled with concern.

"Are you asking me or telling me?" I replied, a touch of defensiveness creeping into my voice.

"Oliver asked us for your hand in marriage," Mom revealed, her tone cautious. "He said he wants to marry you. Don't you think it's a little premature?"

"He's asked and I said no," I admitted, feeling a weight lift off my shoulders. "It's too soon. We've barely been dating three months."

"I worry because he's so much older than you," Mom confessed, her concern evident.

"I don't care what they say," I asserted, determination coloring my voice. "It's my relationship. How can I be a gold digger when I have my own money?"

"People don't know that," Mom pointed out, her tone soft but firm. "They might say you're some young woman latching onto an older man for security."

"Oliver pursued me, not the other way around," I insisted, my voice growing stronger.

"Again, that won't be broadcast to the world," she said, her words filled with conviction.

"I'm sick of pleasing other people," I confessed, frustration seeping into my tone. "It's my relationship."

“Don't say I didn't warn you,” she quickly changed the subject. “Have you seen Ty lately?”

I started to play the fringe on the blanket we kept on the

back of the couch. “No. He didn’t even call me on my birthday which is unlike him.”

“His mother was very sick.”

I felt alarm because I really liked Ty’s mother. “When?”

“Her heart is not doing well. She has pneumonia and was in the hospital.”

“Why the hell didn’t anyone tell me this on Friday?”

“We didn’t want to worry you on your special day.”

“But I love Mrs. Barnes. I don’t care if it was my special day. I need to call Ty. He must feel horrible.”

“She’s doing much better.”

“I haven’t spoken to him for weeks because I’ve been with Oliver. I’m a horrible friend.”

“You have your own life. Ty wouldn’t fault you for that.”

But couldn’t help feeling I should’ve known. I should’ve called him. I’d been avoiding Tyler because I didn’t want him to question me about my father. It was grating on me and whenever he did, I had nightmares after, but I would never tell my mother or anyone else in my family.

“I feel guilty.”

“I’m sure he’ll understand.”

“I’ll talk to you later. I love you, Mom. Tell Anders I said hello.”

“I will. Love you, Ryleigh.”

I was upset. Ty's mother was sick and I didn't even know. I dialed his number and waited. He was probably on duty but who knew since I hadn't talked to him in a while. He wasn't angry and wished me a happy birthday which I was thankful for.

"I got so busy with my mother, work and your father's case."

I was silent for a few seconds. "You're still working on it?"

It was what I didn't want to hear. Suppose he solved the case? I thought of how I would feel, how we all would feel when the assailant was caught.

"I told you I want justice. Your father deserves it."

"I hope you haven't told my brothers or mother you're investigating."

"I wouldn't do that until I have credible evidence."

"Then why did you tell me?" my voice cracked.

"Because you're the only witness. I had to."

"But I don't know anything," I protested.

"You said that."

"You doubt me?"

"No but I still think you should see a hypnotist. Maybe they can help you remember."

"Ty, even if I did see the killer's face, what good would it do? You can't put a face to a person you don't know."

"I was just asking. Don't get upset. So lunch?"

"Where?"

"The Iron Horse."

"What time?"

"1:00."

"You won't fall asleep on my couch after, will you?"

"I promise I won't. I miss you. It's been a while."

We chatted for a few more minutes and Ty had to go. After I said goodbye, I got ready for bed and slipped under the covers. Exhaustion took me until Sadie woke me. I squinted at the light on my bedside table.

"Again?"

She nodded. I looked at the bedside clock and it read 12:42 AM.

"Fuck."

"Do you want me to sleep here?"

"Would you do that for me?"

"Don't be ridiculous."

She clicked out the light and slipped into bed on the other side. Having two nightmares in such a short span of time was not good. It meant that I was stressed. I hoped Sadie next to me would curtail them.

~

I called in sick the next day. I just didn't have the energy to put up with Beatrice and her stupid demands. I spent the morning watching game shows and eating cereal from the box by the handful. It was just a lazy day for me.

I finally moved myself and went to take a shower at noon, standing under the water and wishing I was in Oliver's bathroom instead of mine. He called me at three when I was back on the couch flipping through one of Sadie's magazines.

Oliver called me full of concern because I had told Vlad I was staying home. I knew he would worry. I finally conceded, telling him I couldn't work for Beatrice any longer. Each day was a struggle for me to go to work and I didn't want to feel miserable when I woke up each morning. He laughed as we discussed what my role would be at Fox Asset.

"I'm sure we can fit you somewhere into a department."

"What would I do without you?"

"Fall apart apparently."

"Shut up. I just needed a mental health day."

I didn't tell him that I wished I could take a mental

health day for my two weeks notice so I never had to see Beatrice's pointy mouse face ever again.

"You have two weeks to deal with your job and you're done. Can you handle it?"

"I think so. Knowing that the end is near will help make the pill easier to swallow. I'm sure Beatrice is not going to be happy. She's constantly telling me she chose me over many applicants."

"Then she should be using your skills and intelligence properly. I'm sure they won't have a problem finding someone to take your place."

"I'm sure," I said dryly.

Oliver changed the subject. "What did you do today?"

I smiled to myself. "Absolutely nothing. I've been watching television all day. What have you been doing today?"

"I had three meetings and a tour of a potential piece of property I'm interested in purchasing."

"Busy man."

Our conversation was kept light though I wanted to tell him how much I missed him, and I wish he was here with me. I needed his support, but I didn't want him to feel guilty about being away.

After I hung up with Oliver, I got my laptop and turned it on. Sure enough, an email from the Fox Asset Corporation HR department was sitting in my inbox. I opened it and printed out the pages. I hated filling out paperwork. The offer letter was in a separate email, and I was astonished to find the salary was just under six figures even though a position hadn't been decided.

I would have to talk to Oliver when he got back because I didn't want any special favors because I was his girlfriend. I filled out all the paperwork and was scanning it when Sadie walked through the door.

"Did you have a good day?" she asked.

"I needed it. I'm leaving my job, I decided."

She raised her eyebrows. "You're quitting?"

"I can't deal with the bullshit anymore. Oliver offered me a position."

"At least you'll still be in the same building. What will you be doing?"

I shrugged. "I haven't the slightest idea, but I asked Oliver if I could work in the PR department."

She snorted. "You hate PR."

"No, I hate my boss. I was nothing more than an errand girl. I've been there for almost three months and all I do is get coffee or make copies. It's ridiculous. Beatrice is a major bitch and I have to adjust to her moods."

"What do you think they'll say?"

I smirked. "I have no idea and what's more, I don't care."

Chapter 14

"What do you mean you're giving your two weeks notice?" Beatrice said.

I shifted in the uncomfortable hard gray plastic chair in front of her glass desk.

"This isn't working out for me. I've been here three months and I do is run errands."

Beatrice leaned back in her chair and stared at me with her beady black eyes. I had to will myself not to look away.

She ground her teeth. "You can't just start working with clients. You need to learn the business."

I was flippant. I could be since I already had another job. I didn't need a reference from her and I had a feeling that if I asked for one, she would decline my request.

"I'm not learning anything as far as I'm concerned."

She raised her voice an octave. "We picked you because you had promise out of a sea of applicants. Now you're telling me we made the wrong choice?"

I jutted my chin out in defiance. "You made the wrong choice by making me a gopher. I could have more than been up to speed by now."

She waved at the air. "No PR firm will put you directly in contact with clients without experience."

"No firm or just you?"

I knew I shouldn't challenge Beatrice, but I felt bold because I already had a job with Fox Asset Corporation.

"Maybe it's better we part ways. You've made a lot of mistakes lately and I don't think you're cut out for this type of work. Today will be your last day."

"Why doesn't right now be my last hour?"

I rose from my chair before she could say anything and yanked open the door. I didn't care. I could take the next couple of weeks off and enjoy the waning days of summer while I waited for my job to start with Fox.

My desk didn't have many personal items that I had brought, just a picture of my family and the card I was given by some of my coworkers for my birthday. I shoved them into my purse and when I looked up, security was standing at my cubicle. Two gray uniformed officers waited for me to grab the sweater I kept when it got too cold in the office and escorted me out to the elevators.

It was embarrassing since several of my former coworkers were gaping as I was led out of the office. I wished Oliver was back so I could go upstairs. It was barely eleven in the morning, and I had the whole day to myself. I didn't bother with Vlad, taking the subway home instead. I texted Oliver to let him know I was free and could start sooner than expected. He called me a few minutes later.

"They let you go?"

"They had security escort me out like I was a common criminal. I wish you were here; it was embarrassing," I said, remembering how my cheeks flushed as they led me to the lobby.

Oliver chuckled. "Do you want me to buy Blaze and fire your boss?"

"That sounds like a nice idea but I wouldn't bother. It's not worth it."

"You want to start early?"

I wasn't sure if I did. The prospect of enjoying the next two weeks relaxing and enjoying what was left of the summer was tempting but I would be bored. I addressed the salary portion of my offer.

"Maybe. Why is my salary so high?"

“Because you’re worth it. You’re Ivy League educated.”

“With little experience.”

“You have your internship.”

“But no other experience,” I protested.

“Are you trying to talk me out of paying you what you’re worth?” he asked.

“I just want it to be fair. Do you pay your other new hires that same?”

“You’re a horrible negotiator.”

He changed the subject. “Will you be at my apartment when I come home?”

“I have to pack a few things.”

“Be naked when I arrive.”

My belly clenched at the prospect of Oliver making love to me. I missed his scent and his body next to me in bed.

“I’ll see.”

He chuckled. “I hope you’re ready for me tonight. I haven’t been in a very good mood the past few days.”

“Why?”

“I’m backed up.”

“You can always jerk off,” I offered.

He groaned. “Nope. The only place I want to come is inside you. That’s my plan for tonight.”

My nipples hardened as we got deeper into sex talk.

“I’m hanging up because you’re getting me hot.”

“Hold on until I get there.”

“I mean it. Hold on.”

“How would you know if I did or not?”

“I’ll know. Just wait for me.”

I grumbled, “Fine. I’ll see you at your apartment.”

We hung up and I went to my room to pack a duffel bag with some casual clothing. I wouldn’t need to dress up for the next couple of weeks. I didn’t want to bother Vlad and took a cab over to Oliver’s. One of the concierges handed me keys to Oliver’s and I went upstairs by myself.

His penthouse was quiet, and my shoes echoed as I walked inside. I was trying to resist snooping, but I had an urge to know him more intimately. I put my duffel bag in the master bedroom, kicked off my shoes and opened the bottom drawer of the island in the closet. I had seen several photo albums there and I pulled one out to page through it.

I saw Oliver in happy times with his parents. They lived in a medium sized white colonial with black shutters. Oliver looked like his father with the same colored hair and deep blue eyes. His mother had been very pretty with long blonde hair to her waist and light brown eyes.

I looked for pictures of his brother Jonah, but I couldn't find one in the entire album. I wondered if Oliver discarded them. His relationship with his brother was rocky and maybe there had been a time where they didn't communicate at all. I felt for him because I would miss my brothers if I couldn't see them.

There were several other photo albums but I put the one I looked at back and closed the drawer. I got up and buried my nose against one of Oliver's suits. It smelled like him and made me miss him even more. I know I shouldn't have but I opened the drawers on top of his dresser in the closet. He had two velvet lined ones that held watches, jewelry and rings. I slipped on one of his chunky Rolexes. It was huge on my wrist, but I kept it on as I looked at the rest of his stuff.

Inside one of the drawers was a white velvet box which I removed and opened, inside was at least a five-carat oval ring set into a platinum band. My heart began to pound as I removed it from the box, slipping it on my finger. It was the right size and fit me perfectly. I wondered if this was the ring Oliver planned on giving me when he asked me to marry him.

I quickly took it off and put everything back in the drawer. It was a beautiful August day and I went out on the patio to sun myself. I stayed there until the sun dipped in the sky then scrounged around in Oliver's refrigerator for something to eat. It hadn't been stocked because he was out of town. I was in the mood for crab salad but there wasn't any. Instead, I sliced some sharp cheddar cheese and paired it with water crackers I found in the pantry.

The rest of the night I spent naked in Oliver's bed, watching television and dozing. He never told me what time he would be home and by eleven, I shut out the light and snuggled into Oliver's pillow.

"Mmm, that feels nice," I mumbled.

Oliver woke me with his kisses on my bare shoulder. He stroked my hair and pressed his lips against my cheek.

"You smell good," he said.

"No different than usual."

"It must be because I've been away. Thank you for granting my request."

I knew he was talking about my nakedness. He got up and I turned over on my back to watch him get undressed. He was wearing a navy-blue suit, white shirt and light pink tie. Oliver disrobed and shoved his boxers down his hips, leaving everything in a heap on the floor before he slipped into bed with me.

His body was warm and hard. I molded myself against him, kissing under his stubbly chin.

"You need a shave."

"Should I do it now?"

"Absolutely not. I don't care if your face is full of stubble. It makes you look rugged."

"Like a cowboy?"

"Or a smuggler."

I hugged him, slipping my hands around his stomach and pressing my face into his chest as I kneaded his muscles.

He hummed. "I like that. Today was stressful."

"Did you get your property?" I asked.

Oliver nuzzled my forehead. "Yes. It took some negotiation, but I got it done."

I quirked an eyebrow. "Don't you have people for that?"

"I do but I prefer to be involved in the mix."

"Is this it for traveling for a while?" I asked with hope.

I hated it when he was gone for several days. I needed my space but that was usually one night. More than one night made me miss him too much.

"Unfortunately, not. I have a meeting in Los Angeles at the end of September. You could come with me."

"I could but my new boss might not let me go."

"Your new boss definitely will let you go. I'd like to make love to you at thirty thousand feet," he said, his voice husky with desire.

“The mile high club?”

“The six mile high club,” he said with a chuckle.

“That might be fun.”

“You wouldn’t even know you’re in the air.”

“Where are you putting me?”

“Errands I told you.”

I smacked his arm. “I just left a job because all I did was errands.”

“These are of a more personal nature.”

I began to protest again until Oliver pressed his lips against mine, aggressively forcing my mouth open with his tongue. He fucked me with it and my body bloomed with heat. I moaned loudly, digging my fingers into his arms. Oliver turned me so I was on top of his body. I positioned his cock beneath me and slid my slick lips back and forth.

He groaned. “Fuck, that feels so good. You better take it easy or you’re going to make me come.”

“Isn’t the point?”

“I want to do it inside you.”

Oliver reached up to cup my breasts, thumbing the nipples as I continued moving over him.

“Please, Ryleigh. I want to be inside you,” he begged.

I smiled because he was at my mercy. "How about you let me decide?"

He stroked my thighs with his hands, rubbing his palms across my smooth flesh. Oliver wasn't the only one who was nearing orgasm. With each stroke, the head of his penis was rubbing against my swollen clit. I couldn't stop and I sped up my motion until I threw my head back as my orgasm took hold.

"That's it, baby, come."

It felt wonderful to let go. I'd been holding back for the past few days. I stopped moving and pressed my chest against Oliver's. I felt him pulsing between my lips and began to move my hips again.

"Stop," he whispered.

"You need to come."

He gently rolled me onto my back, positioning his cock at my soaked entrance before he thrust inside. Oliver went deep and he worked at a steady pace until a few minutes later he was coming with a loud moan of my name. He filled me with his hot semen before he collapsed on top of me.

"It was worth the wait."

He latched onto my mouth and kissed me hard, stroking his tongue against mine.

"I love you, Oliver."

"I love you more."

"Debatable," I said.

"You want to fight about it?"

He stifled a yawn and for the first time I noticed how sleepy he looked.

"Let's take a quick shower and go to bed," I said.

Oliver hugged me, tangling his legs with mine.

"I'd like a repeat of what we just did."

"Later. I don't have to work tomorrow," I said smugly.

"It's 1:30. It is tomorrow," Oliver stated.

"We can sleep in."

"We? I have to work."

"You're the boss. You can take a day off."

"Maybe. Let's shower."

Oliver woke me several times throughout the night, and I enjoyed every bit of attention he paid to me. I mulled over telling him I found the ring but then I would have to admit I was snooping through his things.

In the morning, I found him sleeping next to me, curled around my body. A glance at the clock told me it was after nine. I tipped my face up and kissed his chin. Oliver stirred but didn't wake up. I tried to escape his grasp but he held me tighter.

"Oliver, I need to get up to pee."

"Hold it," he mumbled.

"I will not. Let me go."

"I'm quite comfortable."

Next, I bit his chin, stroking my tongue against his rough stubble. He didn't open his eyes. Stubborn bastard.

He held me tighter. "That just makes me want you to stay here even more."

"Can we bargain?" I asked.

No matter what I did, I would lose. Oliver was a master at negotiation and unless it was completely out of the ordinary, he would outmaneuver me.

"What do you have to offer?" he asked, in total business mode.

"Anything."

"Leaving the negotiation open like that could be dangerous."

I tried to wiggle out of his arms, but he wrapped his leg around my hip, holding me in place. "How so?"

"Because I have so many wicked things going through my head."

"Can we discuss it after I go to the bathroom?" I whined.

"Fine, but I expect you to be agreeable to my terms."

He let me go and I slipped out of bed. When I came back, Oliver was in the same position I left him. His eyes were still closed when I got into bed, reaching down to stroke the erection I felt pressed against my back when I got up. A rumble came from his chest as I squeezed his steely length.

"Is this part of the negotiation?" I asked.

"It might be."

"What do you want?" I whispered.

"You know what I want but it's the position."

"Just say the word."

Oliver gently pushed my hand away and opened his eyes, grinning as he propped his back against the padded headboard. His beautiful organ was sticking straight up, beckoning me to climb on.

"This way?"

"It's very intimate. I want you in my arms when we have sex."

He held open his arms and I crawled up the mattress and his legs. I positioned myself over him and sank. His thick length stretched me and when he was fully inside me, he bent his knees and wrapped his arms around my back. We rocked back and forth as I smoothed the hair from his forehead. I loved him so much.

“I like this.”

“Just like?”

“Okay, I love it,” I panted. It made me want to say yes and as we made love, it was at the tip of my tongue. I wondered if Oliver could read my thoughts.

“Marry me, Ryleigh,” he groaned.

“Yes,” I whispered.

He froze and raised his head to look in my eyes.

“Did you say yes?”

“I did. I have a confession to make.”

“Am I going to be upset?”

“Maybe.”

“Tell me.”

I could feel embarrassment creeping into my face. “I found the engagement ring.”

He nuzzled my cheek. “That would mean you were in my jewelry and watch drawer.”

“I’m sorry for snooping. I was just curious.”

“If you don’t like the ring, I’ll buy you a new one.”

Right now, I didn’t care about the ring. He felt so good

inside me and as I shifted my hips, he hit the perfect spot inside me.

“Shut up and make me come.”

“Hold on.”

I clung to him while he thrust upward. I came a few seconds later and Oliver followed with a loud howl. We held each other as the pounding of our hearts slowed and breathing returned to normal.

"Now you have to be my personal assistant," Oliver declared, his tone laced with determination.

I arched an eyebrow. "Why?"

"Because I want you working with me now that we’re engaged," he explained, his gaze unwavering.

"We have to tell everyone," I pointed out, shifting the conversation to our impending announcement.

Oliver considered my suggestion for a moment. "How about we invite them to our home in Southampton?"

My lips twitched with amusement. "Don’t you mean your home?"

A smile tugged at Oliver's lips. "No. We’re getting married, so it’s our home."

I was touched by his sentiment. "So, it won’t be included in the prenuptial?"

Oliver's demeanor turned serious. "There won’t be a prenuptial."

I furrowed my brow in confusion. "That makes no sense. I'm sure your lawyers will insist."

"I don't care what they say," Oliver asserted, his voice unwavering. "If you leave me, you can take it all. Nothing will make me happy if I don't have you."

My breath caught in my throat, my heart swelling with emotion. "I don't need your money. I have my own."

"I'm aware," Oliver replied. "I spoke to Anders. You won't need your money. You have mine."

I was touched by his gesture. "When do I start work?"

"Anytime," Oliver replied smoothly. "You want to this upcoming week?"

My lips quirked into a smirk. "I should familiarize myself with my fiancé's business in case I decide to take it over after we divorce."

Oliver chuckled. "You have us divorced before we're even married?"

I met his gaze with a knowing smirk. "You have nothing to worry about as long as you satisfy me."

As our conversation took a heated turn, our bodies moved in sync, igniting a passion that consumed us both. Afterward, as we lay entwined, Oliver's reminder of his conference call brought us back to reality.

"Let's get up. I have a conference call at eleven," Oliver said, reluctantly pulling away.

I nodded, feeling a hint of disappointment "Does that mean you're going into work?"

Oliver shook his head with a smirk. "Nope. I can conduct business from my home office. I have incentive to stay home today."

My lips curled into a satisfied smile. "I'm glad."

Together, we headed for the shower, our bond stronger than ever. Later, as Oliver took his call, I basked in the warmth of the sun on the patio, a sense of contentment settling over me. I was engaged and it made me giddy with happiness. He came out after his call.

"I meant to tell you that I had my contractor look over this space to build a pool."

I squinted as I looked up at him. "And?"

"He said it's possible, but it won't be a large pool."

"I'd settle for a lap pool. Just something we can take a dip in and cool off. This is a lovely space. Have you ever had a party out here?"

He shook his head. "No. I'm not much for entertaining."

"I think we'll have to change that. You should entertain."

"I'm not a very good host."

I snorted. "Are you kidding? You've been a wonderful host to me."

He reached into the pocket of his gray shorts and produced the ring I found in his jewelry drawer.

"I think you should be wearing this now."

Oliver got down on one knee and asked me to marry him. I giggled before I said yes, holding out my finger so he could slip it on. It was huge on my small hand and the diamond glinted in the bright sunlight.

"This is so big."

"Nothing but the best for my fiancée. Should we call your family?"

"That would be a good idea. Sadie and Ty too. I'm having lunch with him tomorrow."

He pursed his lips. "I know."

Oliver's tone was flat. I had a feeling he didn't like Ty very much. It could be possible he was aware of Ty's crush on me or the fact that he was digging into my father's murder investigation, whatever it was, Oliver wasn't impressed with him.

"Are you okay with that?" I asked.

He shrugged. "Fine. I can't stop you from having friends."

"Does it bother you that I'm friends with Ty?"

"Not at all. I know you're committed to me so why should it bother me?"

"Just checking."

He fingered the string around my neck. "I like this bikini on you. You're very sexy."

I giggled. "Ever the charmer."

"Shall we call everyone to let them know we're engaged?"

"Not yet. Let it be our little secret for a day."

Oliver sat down on the lounge chair and kissed me, caressing my breast with his fingers. I looked up at the buildings around us and felt my face heat. The building across from us had a direct line to the patio.

"What's the matter?"

"People can see us," I whispered.

"You're not naked for heaven's sake."

"But your hand is on my breast."

Oliver gave me a wicked smile. "Should I take you inside and do this?"

"I thought you had work to do?"

"I do but you come first. Are you declining sex?"

"I never said that, but I am a little sore."

"I have the cure for that," he said as he licked his lips.

"Later."

He looked at me shocked. “I get it. I put a ring on your finger and now you’re freezing me out.”

“That isn’t what I’m doing.”

His phone rang before he could answer me. He rose from the chair and walked away as he talked to the person on the other end. I wondered what he was up to.

Chapter 15

"Were you really working this morning?"

"Yes. I had a bunch of things to take care of. Why?"

"Because this meal is unbelievable."

At five, Oliver had a dress delivered to the penthouse. He corralled me in the bedroom, closing the drapes that looked out on the patio. I knew he had something planned but I played along as my excitement grew. I took my time in the shower and hoped he would join me, but he didn't. When I came out, he was dressed in a light gray suit, lavender shirt and purple tie. A handkerchief the same color as his tie was neatly folded and sticking out of his pocket.

"Are we going out?"

"Maybe."

"Tell me where," I demanded.

Oliver held his hand up. “It’s a surprise. Get dressed,” he ordered.

“What’s going on outside?”

“Nothing you should concern yourself with.”

“I’m beginning to hate surprises.”

“Why?”

“Because you always do them for me, and I don’t do them for you.”

“You can.”

“Not to the extravagance you do.”

Oliver eyed me as I removed my towel and went into the closet naked. I dug through my duffel bag, finding a burgundy bra and thong set. I slipped the body-hugging black dress Oliver got me over my head and adjusted the hem. It was short and accentuated my breasts.

When I came out, Oliver couldn’t take his gaze off me. I saw him in the mirror while I applied a light layer of makeup, finishing with some bubble gum lip gloss. I put my hair in a ponytail and wound it into a loose bun, so it was off my neck.

“How do I look?”

“Good enough to eat.”

“What do you have going on outside?” I asked again.

He gave me a mischievous smile. “Wait and see.”

"Now?"

"Now."

He rose from the bed and opened the drapes. I could see a table set with a white linen cloth and two place settings. A waiter in a black uniform stood next to a raised bucket holding a bottle of champagne.

"For me?"

"Well for us. I'll be eating too."

I went to him claiming his lips in a hard kiss. He licked his after I pulled away. "Mmm, bubble gum."

Oliver pulled open the slider and led me out. I had neglected to put on shoes

but it didn't matter. The patio was warm from the summer sun.

After a meal of arugula salad, filet mignon with asparagus and Dutchess potatoes, I was stuffed. Oliver had the meal cooked and catered by the same chef who made us breakfast. I leaned back in my chair as Oliver sipped champagne.

"Full?" he asked.

"Yes. That was so good," I said, rubbing my tummy.

"Anything for my bride."

"I could get used to this. You're spoiling me."

"Don't fault me for wanting to make you happy."

“I’m happy without the spoiling. I have you.”

“For the rest of your life,” he added.

I reached over and stroked his hand. I loved Oliver’s hands. They were perfect, soft and he got his nails manicured once a week. What’s more, I loved when he put them on me.

“I hope so.”

“Do you want dessert?” he asked.

“Dessert too?”

“Do you?”

“No. Not now anyway.”

“Excuse me for a moment.”

Oliver rose and strode to the slider next to the kitchen. I saw him talking to the chef and a couple of minutes later, he came back.

“We can have dessert later. Come, let’s sit on the terrace so they can clean up.”

He poured me and himself another glass of champagne and we headed to the terrace which faced Central Park. I settled into one of the soft beige cushioned chairs and sipped from my glass.

“How do you feel?” Oliver asked.

I grinned. “Still getting used to being engaged.”

“I want you to be aware that there will be reports in the paper.”

I quirked an eyebrow. “Reports?”

"I’m an eligible bachelor," Oliver declared with a hint of pride.

"No, you’re not. You’re now off the market," I teased.

"Exactly—I was an eligible bachelor and now I’m not. There will be reports about it."

"You could nip it in the bud and do a PR release so they get the facts straight," I suggested.

"Smart girl. Why didn’t they utilize your skills better at Blaze?" Oliver mused, impressed.

"I have no idea. You’ll have to ask them that," I shrugged, a touch of frustration in my voice.

"Fools. Too late, you’re mine now," Oliver stated possessively, his gaze locking with mine.

"Maybe I should work in the PR department," I said, considering her options.

"You have time for that. I want you with me," Oliver insisted, his voice firm.

"Do I get an office or a cubicle?" I inquired, raising an eyebrow.

"Office. I have one being prepared right next to mine," Oliver revealed, a hint of excitement in his tone.

"The one with the windows that looks out onto the city? I'm not an executive," I pointed out, a touch of disbelief in my voice.

"You're an executive's fiancée," Oliver countered, a smirk playing on his lips.

"People will talk," I said.

"Who cares? You shouldn't. They'll talk even more when you're Mrs. Oliver Fox," Oliver reassured me, his gaze unwavering.

"Mrs. Oliver Fox? You mean Mrs. Ryleigh Fox?" I challenged.

He put a hand to his chest. "Excuse me, how male chauvinist of me," Oliver chuckled, admitting his oversight.

I snorted. "Not even engaged for twenty-four hours and already trying to clip my wings," I joked.

Under the soft glow of the evening sun, amidst the faint scent of fresh paint, Oliver and I stood in the midst of our future office space, the canvas of a new beginning.

"I would never. You will always be your own woman," Oliver reassured me, his voice carrying a depth of sincerity.

"Can I pick my own office furniture?" I inquired, a spark of excitement in my voice.

"Anything you want. I'm just having the walls painted," Oliver replied, his gaze fixed on me.

"But I wanted to choose the color," I pouted, the desire for personalization evident in my tone.

"I think you'll like it very much," Oliver said with a confident smile, his hand reaching out to gently caress my cheek.

"How can you be sure?" I questioned.

"Because we've been together for three months. I think I know what you like," Oliver replied, his eyes reflecting the depth of our connection.

As I took another sip of champagne, a thought crossed my mind. "Oliver, do you have any pictures of Jonah?" I inquired, curiosity lacing my words.

"Jonah? Why?" Oliver's brow furrowed with confusion, a hint of suspicion in his tone.

"I was just wondering," I replied casually, attempting to mask my true intentions.

"You looked at my photo albums, didn't you?" Oliver's accusation hung in the air, his eyes searching mine for answers.

"Only one. Your parents were very good-looking. You look like your father," I admitted, a sheepish smile playing on my lips.

"I can't believe they've been gone so long," Oliver sighed, a hint of sadness coloring his tone.

"Was Jonah always hard to deal with?" I probed gently, my heart aching for his past struggles.

“Why do you care so much about Jonah?” Oliver's gaze bore into mine, searching for the truth behind my questions.

"Because it pains me that you have no family besides him. Don’t you want a relationship with your brother?" I voiced my concern, hoping to bridge the gap between them.

"I tried. Jonah can’t stay away from illegal activities. I can’t be enveloped in scandal because my brother can’t avoid trouble," Oliver confessed, his tone tinged with resignation.

"I'm sorry," I murmured, sympathy coloring my words.

“There’s nothing to be sorry for. It’s not your fault. Besides, I have family, yours. Your brothers will become mine and your parents will be grandparents to our babies," Oliver reassured me, his voice filled with conviction.

"I’m glad," I replied, a warmth spreading through my heart at his words.

"Then we’re on the same page," Oliver said, a smile gracing his lips as he pulled me into his embrace.

"Yes, we are," I affirmed, feeling a sense of completeness wash over me.

. . .

As the evening unfolded, we found ourselves lost in each other's company, the late August heat enveloping us as we basked in the promise of our future. Oliver swept me into his arms, our champagne glasses forgotten on the table as we embraced the passion of the moment.

With each tender touch, I felt a surge of love and contentment fill me, knowing that together, we could weather any storm. And as we indulged in seven-layer chocolate cake and an old movie, I couldn't help but feel giddy with happiness, grateful for the love that bound us together.

As the clock struck 12:45, I stepped into The Iron Horse, my heart racing with anticipation. There, amidst the dimly lit ambiance, I spotted Ty, his presence commanding attention. His hair was shorter now, a change that accentuated his features.

He wore navy-blue cargo shorts paired with a vibrant red t-shirt, a casual yet striking ensemble. With a gentle kiss on my cheek, he greeted me, and I found myself enveloped in his embrace as I returned the gesture, savoring the familiar warmth of his touch.

"I missed you. You look great. I like the dress," Ty remarked, his eyes tracing the contours of my attire.

I was wearing a short pale yellow sundress with a button front and I decided to wear my engagement ring. I spent the morning calling my family to let them know I had accepted Oliver's proposal. I didn't need to call Sadie since she was with Finley. Their relationship seemed to be advancing as fast as mine and Oliver's had. When we sat down at the table, Ty immediately spied my engagement ring and grabbed my hand.

"You're engaged?" His voice carried a hint of disbelief, mingled with regret.

"Yesterday," I confirmed.

"Isn't it a little early for engagements?" Ty's inquiry hung in the air, his expression betraying a mix of disappointment and sorrow.

"We've been together for three months," I explained, the weight of our whirlwind romance evident in my tone.

In Ty's eyes, I detected a longing, a desire unspoken yet palpable, and I knew that beneath his facade of familiarity lay a heart yearning for something more.

"Does he know how lucky he is?" Ty's words echoed with a sincerity that touched my soul.

"I think he does," I replied.

"I wish it was me," Ty confessed.

"Ty, you know we could never be," I stated softly, the truth hanging heavy between us.

"Why, because we've known each other forever?" Ty's question lingered in the air, a poignant reminder of the intricacies of our shared history.

I reached out to clasp his hand. “Yes. I’m sorry if that hurts you.”

"I guess I can understand," he conceded, his tone laced with a hint of resignation.

"Haven’t you been dating?" My question hung in the air, laden with curiosity.

"I have no time for dating. I’ve been busy, and your father’s case is taking most of my free time," he explained, a sense of weariness creeping into his voice.

"You've been working on it for weeks," I observed, my brows furrowing with concern.

I was afraid of what he might unearth. I wanted my father’s murder to be solved, but Ty had no idea he was dredging up long buried emotions in me. I wanted to tell him to stop.

"I have a few clues. If you remember anything, now would be the time to tell me," he said.

"What do you have?" I asked.

Before he could respond, we were interrupted by the arrival of the waitress, her presence a temporary reprieve from the weighty conversation. If Ty wanted to delve into the murky waters of my father's murder, I knew I'd need something stronger than a glass of water. With a decisive nod, I ordered a martini with extra olives, while Ty opted for soda.

"Are you okay?" Ty's concern was palpable, his eyes searching mine for reassurance.

I just need something to take the edge off if you want to discuss this," I confessed, a sense of vulnerability seeping into my words.

"We don't have to," Ty offered, his voice gentle.

"I know you want to, so just tell me," I urged, my voice steady despite the unease gnawing at me.

"Years ago, we couldn't get a good enough picture even with the digital equipment. Things have improved, and we're working on enhancing the pictures," Ty explained.

"So why do you need me to identify the person?" I questioned, a flicker of doubt clouding my thoughts.

"Because we need corroboration," Ty clarified, his gaze unwavering.

"Ty, I don't know. This is crazy," I admitted, uncertainty coloring my words.

As the waitress brought our drinks, I wasted no time in downing half my martini in two swift gulps, the liquid burning a trail down my throat as I sought solace in its numbing embrace.

"We're so close. Would you consider the hypnotist?" Ty's question hung in the air, a subtle yet persistent reminder of the lengths we were willing to go to seek justice.

"I don't know. I'm not going to remember," I protested

weakly, the thought of unlocking buried memories sending a shiver down my spine.

"You don't know or you're not going to remember? Which is it?" Ty pressed, his tone edged with determination.

"Maybe I don't want to remember. Why do you always bring this up when we have lunch together?" I countered, frustration seeping into my words.

"Because I never see you unless it's for lunch," Ty confessed, his voice tinged with a hint of sadness.

"Can we just eat lunch and talk about it after we're finished?" I pleaded, a sense of exhaustion washing over me.

"We don't have to talk about it at all. I made my request, and you can think about it," Ty relented, his gaze softening.

As we lapsed into a companionable silence, I signaled for another martini, the clinking of glasses punctuating the moments between bites of food. Ty respected my request for respite from the weight of the past, and we filled the void with mundane chatter, discussing the small details of our lives. I shared with him my decision to quit my job and start anew at Fox Asset Corporation.

"Are you sure you want to work with your husband?" Ty's question cut through the air, his tone laced with skepticism.

"He's not my husband yet," I reminded him, a hint of defiance in my voice.

"Boyfriend, fiancé, same thing. Eventually, he'll be your husband," Ty said.

"I couldn't stay at Blaze. All I did was run errands and get coffee," I explained, a trace of frustration tainting my words.

"What a waste of your degree," Ty remarked, sympathy coloring his tone.

"Exactly," I agreed, the weight of unfulfilled potential weighing heavy on my shoulders.

"Ready to go?" Ty's voice broke through the tension, a welcome distraction from the weighty conversation.

"Yeah," I replied, grateful for the change in subject.

After settling the bill, Ty guided me out of the restaurant, as the effects of the three martinis I had consumed began to take hold. Without his support, I knew I would've stumbled on the uneven pavement, my steps unsteady with each passing moment. His arms encircled my waist, holding me closer than I felt comfortable, yet I welcomed the stability his touch provided.

"Thank you," I murmured, the gratitude evident in my voice.

"You drank too much," Ty observed, concern etched into his features.

"I think so," I admitted, the alcohol-induced haze clouding my thoughts.

"Do you need me to escort you home?" Ty offered.

"No. I'll be fine," I assured him, summoning what remained of my resolve.

"Are you sure?" Ty pressed, his gaze searching mine.

"Yes. Vlad will take me," I replied, gesturing towards the sleek black sedan parked nearby.

Ty raised an eyebrow. "Your driver?"

"And bodyguard. Oliver worries," I said.

Ty chuckled, shaking his head in amusement. "I'm a fucking police officer."

"I know, but still," I countered, unwilling to risk my safety despite Ty's profession.

Vlad extended his arm towardsme, and I pressed a kiss to Ty's cheek before allowing him to lead me towards the waiting car.

"Talk to you soon," Ty called out as Vlad helped me into the sedan, his voice carrying a note of warmth.

I settled into the plush seat, the exhaustion of our lunch settling over me like a heavy blanket. As the car glided through the streets, I succumbed to the pull of sleep, my eyelids growing heavy with each passing moment. And when we arrived at Oliver's building, I stirred from my slumber to find him lifting me gently from the car.

"I can walk," I protested weakly, the remnants of alcohol still clouding my senses.

"You had too much to drink," Oliver chided softly.

I put my head against his chest while he carried me into the elevator.

“Should I undress you and put you to bed?” Oliver said as we entered his apartment.

“No. Put me down.”

“Take off your heels before you fall down.”

He steadied me as he put me on the marble floor, holding my shoulders while I removed my heels. The air in the apartment was cooler than the restaurant and I started to wake up.

“Why did you drink so much? You had three martinis.”

I narrowed my eyes. “Who told you that? Vlad?”

Oliver clenched his jaw. “His job is to keep an eye on you.”

I sighed. “Ty asked me something that upset me.”

“What?” he asked.

"Ty found video, and the digital department is working on making the photo clearer. He wants me to see a hypnotist," I informed Oliver, the weight of the conversation settling heavily between us.

"So, he thinks you’ll be able to identify the murderer from a memory that’s years old?" Oliver's concern mirrored my own doubts.

"Yes. He wants to solve the case," I confirmed, a note of uncertainty tainting my words.

"Does anyone else in the family know Ty is working on it?" Oliver inquired, his brow furrowing with worry.

I shook my head. "No. I don't want to upset my mother. She was a mess after my father died. I didn't speak after it happened, and I took a year off from school because of it. You know this," I explained, a pang of guilt gnawing at me.

"I understand he wants to solve the case, but I don't like him upsetting you," Oliver admitted, his protective instincts kicking in.

"Ty means well. He loved my father. When we were kids, we all used to play ball in the backyard. My father was always the pitcher. Ty took it hard when he was killed," I reminisced, a bittersweet smile tugging at the corners of my lips.

"I don't want you seeing a hypnotist," Oliver declared, his tone firm.

"I don't want to see one either," I agreed, relieved to find common ground.

"It's your choice," Oliver said.

"I don't feel so good," I admitted, a wave of dizziness washing over me.

As I started to sway, Oliver swiftly swept me up in his arms, carrying me to the bedroom with ease.

"Do you have to throw up?" Oliver's concern was palpable, his voice gentle.

"No, just a little dizzy," I assured him, grateful for his steady presence.

He settled me on the bed, his hands deftly assisting me as I shed my dress and bra, the weight of exhaustion pressing down on me like a heavy blanket. Nestling under the covers, I succumbed to the warmth of sleep, the comfort of Oliver's presence lulling me into a peaceful slumber within moments of my head hitting the pillow.

My mind is a whirlwind of panic, every nerve screaming in terror. Daddy's voice echoed in my head, urging me to hide, but I couldn't move. I'm frozen in place as I watched the figure approach, the sound of gunshots ringing in my ears as my father stepped out of our SUV. His silhouette crumpled to the ground, a grotesque dance of violence unfolding before my eyes. "Daddy!" I screamed, but he didn't answer, and the world narrowed to the sight of his lifeless form.

The acrid scent of gunpowder filled the air, suffocating me like a vise. With trembling hands, I clawed at the car seat strap, finally wrenching it open. Desperation fueled my actions as I stumbled out of the car, my gaze fixed on my father's prone figure. Blood stains his chest, a stark contrast against the fabric of his shirt. "Daddy!" I cry out again, my voice breaking with raw anguish as I scrambled towards him.

His hazel eyes, once warm with love, now stare blankly into the void, and my heart shattered at the emptiness within them. Tears blurred my vision as I reached out to shake him, to wake him from this nightmare. But there's no response, no comforting embrace to chase away the terror.

I screamed, a primal sound of agony tearing through the silence, reverberating off the walls of my shattered reality. My body trembled with each gut-wrenching wail, my mind consumed by a maelstrom of grief and disbelief. I kneel beside him, my fingers stained with his blood, and I don't know what to do. All I can do is scream, to release the torrent of anguish that threatens to consume me whole.

"Ryleigh!"

I blinked back the remnants of my nightmare to find Oliver sitting beside me, his expression etched with concern. This was the first time I'd experienced such vivid dreams with him by my side.

"Oh God, I'm sorry," I stammered, my voice thick with residual fear.

"It's not your fault. Damn Ty. He shouldn't have upset you," Oliver reassured me, his frustration evident.

"I'm stressed. Lots of changes. New job, quitting my old one, and our engagement. It was bound to happen sooner or later," I rationalized, attempting to downplay the impact of my turmoil.

His brow furrowed. "You were screaming so loud it sounded like you were right next to me. I was in my office," Oliver recounted, a trace of worry lingering in his voice.

I bit my lip, my doubts resurfacing. "You sure you want to marry me?"

"I don't care about the nightmares. I care about you. Maybe you should see a doctor," Oliver suggested gently, his concern unwavering.

"A shrink? I saw one when I was a child. It wasn't a pleasant experience," I admitted, memories of past traumas flashing through my mind.

"You're not a frightened child anymore. You're an adult. Maybe it would help you get over these things," Oliver reasoned, his voice soothing.

"Would you hold me?" I requested, needing his embrace.

"Of course," Oliver replied, slipping under the sheet and pulling me close. His warmth enveloped me, a comforting presence amidst the turmoil of my thoughts.

"Better?" he asked softly, his fingers tracing soothing circles on my back.

"Much. I hate this. I want to stop," I confessed.

"That's why I suggested you talk to a therapist," Oliver reminded me, his tone gentle yet firm.

"I'll think about it. I might have a few more," I conceded, my reluctance still palpable.

"I hope not. That one was so bad I thought you were being killed," Oliver confessed, his admission sending a shiver down my spine.

"Don't say that," I whispered, the memory of my nightmare still haunting me.

He tightened his hold on me. "Shit. I'm an ass. I'm sorry," Oliver apologized, his remorse genuine.

I changed the subject, eager to shift away from the darkness that lingered in the air. "I told my family about going to your house next weekend."

"Do they want to come?" Oliver inquired, a hint of excitement coloring his tone.

"Yes. My mother is excited. She and Anders usually rent a house in Southampton but not this year. They went to Rhode Island instead," I explained, a smile tugging at the corners of my lips.

"They don't have to rent anymore. They're welcome to use my house anytime they like," Oliver offered generously.

"You're spoiling all of us," I teased, grateful for his generosity.

"It sits vacant most of the time except for the cleaning people. Someone might as well enjoy it," Oliver reasoned.

"Do you have homes anywhere else?" I asked.

“No. New York is my home, and that’s where my residences are. We can buy something elsewhere if you like,” Oliver replied, his tone thoughtful.

“I was thinking somewhere warmer so we can visit in the winter,” I suggested, my mind already drifting to sunnier climes.

“Like where?” Oliver’s curiosity piqued, his gaze meeting mine.

“Orlando. I like Disneyworld,” I confessed, a hint of excitement coloring my voice.

“You want me to walk around a theme park?” Oliver chuckled, amusement dancing in his eyes.

“It would be fun. Maybe Vlad would crack a smile,” I teased, imagining our stoic bodyguard amidst the whimsical charm of the park.

“There would be more than Vlad with us. It’s a big park,” Oliver pointed out, a note of practicality in his voice.

“Have you ever been there?” I asked, eager to learn more about his past.

“Many years ago. Jonah disappeared, and we spent two hours looking for him. My mother was livid when she found him enjoying an ice cream sundae without a care in the world," Oliver recounted, a fond smile tugging at his lips.

"How old was he then?" I inquired, intrigued by the glimpse into Oliver's family dynamics.

"I was twelve," Oliver calculated, his brow furrowing in concentration, "so he was about nine."

"He was a troublemaker from the beginning, wasn't he?" I mused, the pieces of Oliver's past coming together in my mind.

"He was a handful. My father kept him in control," Oliver admitted.

"But he went off the rails when he died?" I ventured, sensing the weight of Oliver's unspoken words.

"Yes. He was into some pretty bad shit. I caught him with drugs. He stole a car and got arrested a few months after my parents died. By the time he was eighteen, I washed my hands of him. I couldn't stop my life to try to get him to straighten out," Oliver said, shaking his head.

"That must have been hard," I sympathized.

"I tried to be supportive over the years. I've given him money and used my pull to get him out of trouble. I can't do it anymore," Oliver admitted, a sense of resignation creeping into his voice.

"I'm sorry. I wish things were different for you," I murmured, my heart aching for the burdens he carried.

“They are different now that I found you. My life was empty until I found you. You make me whole,” Oliver confessed, his gaze tender as he met my eyes.

“I think your life was pretty busy with your business,” I countered, a smile tugging at the corners of my lips.

“But I had no personal relationships,” Oliver admitted, his vulnerability shining through.

“Why? I saw plenty of pictures of you with women,” I pointed out, curiosity getting the better of me.

“They were, are, acquaintances. They merely escorted me to events,” Oliver explained, a hint of weariness in his voice.

“That reminds me, why haven’t we attended any events?” I questioned, the thought occurring to me for the first time.

“We will. I prefer to keep you to myself for the time being. There will be plenty of publicity surrounding our engagement,” Oliver reassured me, his hand reaching out to brush a strand of hair from my face.

“Should I be worried?” I asked.

“Not at all. Vlad will be with you, and now that you’re working for Fox, you’ll have security during the day,” Oliver assured me.

I yawned, exhaustion settling over me like a heavy blanket. “I don’t want it to be disruptive.”

“It won’t. You won’t get disrupted by Vlad, do you?” Oliver teased, a playful glint in his eyes.

“Not really, though he is pretty intimidating,” I admitted, recalling Vlad's imposing presence.

“Vlad intimidates you?” Oliver's surprise was evident, his eyebrows arching in disbelief.

“Not me. I have a feeling he’s a big pussy cat,” I confessed, a smile playing at the corners of my lips.

“I assure you, he’s not. You haven’t seen him in action,” Oliver insisted.

“I hope never to,” I replied with a shudder, the image of Vlad's formidable demeanor sending a chill down my spine.

“Me either,” Oliver agreed with a chuckle, pulling me closer into his embrace as we settled in for the night.

Oliver moved his hand to my breast, kneading it while he bent down to kiss my neck. I could feel him starting to grow in his sweatpants. I turned so I was facing him, and he pushed me to my back, sliding under the sheet so I couldn’t see him.

“Where are you going?”

“You’ll see.”

He tugged at my panties. I wasn’t fast enough lifting my hips and they ended up in shreds. Oliver didn’t waste any time, stroking his tongue over my clit. I whimpered as he brought me to a fast orgasm. In no time, he was crawling up my body, pressing his hips to mine as he latched his mouth onto my nipple.

"You're aggressive tonight," I panted.

"I know what I want," he growled.

I shifted my hips. "Fuck me, Oliver. I want you inside me."

"Now who's being aggressive?"

I tugged his pants and he slid them down with me until his dick was free. Our lovemaking was fast and hard. He pounded me, grinding his base against my already sensitive bundle of nerves. I exploded around him, flexing and squeezing his cock until he filled me with his semen.

After, we lay in each other's arms, breathing heavily and I pressed my face against his strong chest, inhaling his masculine scent. Oliver smelled clean, like soap and his citrusy cologne. I kissed his pec, flicking my tongue over his nipple making him hiss.

"You want more? You know I can go again," Oliver murmured, his voice laced with a hint of desire as he trailed a finger along my skin.

"I do, but I'm a little hungry," I said, my stomach rumbling faintly.

"What would you like?" Oliver inquired, his tone indulgent.

“Cake,” I declared, a sudden craving for something sweet overtaking me.

“Excuse me?” Oliver chuckled, amusement dancing in his eyes.

“Cake. I’m in the mood for sweets,” I reiterated, undeterred by his skepticism.

“For dinner?” Oliver raised an eyebrow, a playful smirk tugging at the corners of his lips.

“Does it matter what I eat for dinner?” I countered.

“I guess not. Except I don’t think I have cake,” Oliver admitted, his tone tinged with regret.

“But you can get some. I have faith in you,” I teased, a playful smile gracing my lips.

“How do you know?” Oliver asked.

“One phone call and my favorite chocolate layer cake will be up here in fifteen minutes. Am I wrong?” I challenged, confidence oozing from every word.

“You aren’t. I think I’m spoiling you too much.”

“Why marry you if I can’t take advantage of your influence?” I asked, a playful twinkle in my eyes.

“I’m not sure I should be flattered by that,” Oliver teased, though his eyes sparkled with affection.

"That's besides the fact that I'm head over heels in love with you," I said, my heart swelling with warmth.

"I'm glad to hear that," Oliver replied.

"So can I have cake?" I pressed, eager to indulge in my craving.

Oliver grinned at me, reaching over my head to grab his cell from the nightstand. He kept me in his arms while he made his call, his touch sending shivers down my spine as I dozed against his chest.

"Your cake will be here in twenty minutes. Would you like to shower?" Oliver suggested, his voice warm against my ear.

"We probably should. I'm sticky," I admitted, feeling a flush creep into my cheeks.

"You should be used to it by now."

"I am, but that doesn't mean I don't want to shower," I retorted.

Oliver released me from his embrace, and I slipped out of bed to take a quick shower. He joined me as I washed my hair, his presence comforting me amidst the steam and warmth of the bathroom. We shared a few stolen kisses, but we both knew that if he stayed any longer, we wouldn't be eating anytime soon.

~

"Oh God, this is the best," I exclaimed, savoring each decadent bite of cake as if it were a delicacy.

"It is good, but we should eat something more substantial for dinner," Oliver suggested.

"This is substantial. It has some of the food groups mixed in," I protested, gesturing with my fork towards the cake.

"No protein though," Oliver pointed out, his brow furrowing slightly.

"Eggs are protein," I countered, taking another forkful of cake.

Oliver leaned forward, swiping a bit of chocolate frosting from my lips and sucking it off his fingers, his gaze smoldering.

"Don't do that," I chided, feeling a flush rise to my cheeks.

"Why? Am I turning you on?" Oliver teased.

"You know you are," I admitted, unable to suppress a small smile.

"Are you naked under that robe?" Oliver's voice was low, a hint of desire creeping into his tone.

"You saw me put it on in the bedroom," I replied, my pulse quickening at the suggestive undertone of his words.

"Perfect," Oliver murmured, his eyes darkening with desire.

He rose from the table and headed to the refrigerator, retrieving bread, cold cuts, and mustard.

"Perfect what?" I demanded.

"Just perfect. Less for me to take off you," Oliver replied cryptically, his gaze lingering on me suggestively.

"Who says we're having sex again?" I joked.

"Don't challenge me. You know I love challenges," Oliver retorted, a smirk playing at the corners of his lips.

I chuckled softly as I took another forkful of cake, savoring the rich flavors before deciding I had indulged enough. Setting the fork down, I carefully placed the remainder of the cake back in the box, a sense of satisfaction washing over me. I rose to put the box in the refrigerator.

"Can you get me a bottle of water?" Oliver requested.

"Sure. Sparkling or spring?" I asked.

"Spring is fine," he replied.

I returned to the table with his water after I washed my fork, taking a seat next to Oliver.

"Are you sure you don't want a sandwich?"

I shook my head. "No. I think I ate too much cake," I confessed, as I settled back into my seat, content in the warmth of Oliver's presence.

He ran his hand over my arm causing goosebumps to pepper my skin. “I wanted to indulge you.”

“Is this how it’s going to be? You’ll indulge me?”

He pressed a soft kiss to my cheek. “I’ll do whatever I need to so you’re happy.”

“I am happy. Sometimes I need to pinch myself.”

Oliver reached over and gently pinched me which made me giggle.

“I’m real. I promise.”

He took the hand with my engagement ring and sucked on my index finger. My nipples beaded as his tongue stroked over the pad and I pulled back as my belly clenched.

“Don’t,” I said softly.

“Why not?”

I met his gaze and licked my lips, tasting remnants of sugar from the cake.

“Because I want you and I’m sore.”

He flicked his tongue out of his mouth. “I can do other things besides be inside you.”

“I know you can. You have a very talented tongue.”

"Thank you. I aim to please. What would you like to do the rest of the night?"

"Snuggle in bed with you. I like doing the simple things."

"So do I if you haven't noticed."

"I have."

Oliver got up to take his plate to the sink and we retired to the bedroom, snuggling in bed while we spent the rest of the night in bed watching reruns of shows from the eighties.

Chapter 16

I decided not to be lazy and start work at Fox the following Monday. I spent a lovely weekend with Oliver, and now it was time to learn all about his business. He took me home Sunday to get some clothing for the next day. Our apartment was empty, and I assumed Sadie was with my brother.

Oliver gave me the other side of his closet, which was almost empty. I brought a few dresses and skirts because I had a feeling I would be sleeping here more often than not. I chose a gray business suit and short-sleeved white blouse. Oliver dressed in a black suit and white shirt with a silver tie. We sort of looked like twins.

"You look very businesslike today," Oliver remarked as he adjusted his tie in the mirror.

"Thank you. So do you," I replied, smoothing down the lapels of my jacket.

"Do you want coffee?" Oliver offered, his gaze meeting mine in the reflection of the mirror.

I shook my head, declining the offer. "No, thank you."

"Don't be nervous. You're working with me," Oliver reassured me, his voice gentle.

"I can still be nervous. I heard my boss can be a hardass sometimes," I joked.

"He can, but he melts around his beautiful fiancée," Oliver said, stepping closer and wrapping his arms around me from behind.

I smiled at his words, leaning back into his embrace. "And the sexual harassment starts. You should be ashamed of yourself."

"I don't feel ashamed. I love you. I love everything about you," Oliver whispered, pressing a kiss to my neck.

"You'll need to learn to keep your hands to yourself at the office," I teased, gently pushing his hands away.

He chuckled, the sound rumbling deep in his chest. "We'll see."

Oliver left the room to fill his travel mug with coffee, giving me a moment to put the finishing touches on my outfit. I applied a light layer of makeup and tied my mahogany hair back into a sleek ponytail. It was getting long, and I toyed with the idea of cutting it short.

He returned a few minutes later to inform me that Vlad was downstairs. I slipped on my black heels and followed Oliver out to the foyer, feeling a mix of excitement and nerves as I prepared to embark on this new chapter in my life."

When we got to the lobby, my stomach started to churn, and I felt my nerves go into overdrive. They got worse as we got closer to midtown. I hoped I wouldn't see any of my old coworkers, at least not so soon after my departure. I started wringing my hands and Oliver reached over to stop me.

"You'll be fine. No one will give you a hard time," Oliver reassured me, his voice steady and comforting.

"It's not that. I don't want to see any of my old coworkers," I said.

"What if you do? You have a better job now. Blaze should've taken care of you better," Oliver remarked, his expression reflecting a hint of annoyance.

"Yes, they should've," I agreed, a touch of bitterness coloring my words.

Vlad pulled up to the curb, and Oliver exited the car first, extending his hand to help me out. I straightened my skirt and glanced up at the imposing building before us. Oliver offered his arm, and I gratefully accepted as he led me inside.

I breathed a sigh of relief when I didn't spot any of my former coworkers in the lobby. However, my heart sank when Candice appeared while we were waiting for the elevator. Oliver was engrossed in conversation with an associate, leaving me to face Candice alone.

"Ryleigh, you work in this building?" she said with surprise as she approached us.

"Yes. I have a job with Fox," I confirmed, trying to maintain a composed demeanor despite my discomfort.

"And I see you got engaged. Congratulations," Candice remarked, a forced smile plastered on her face.

"Thank you. This past weekend," I replied, forcing a smile of my own.

"Who's the lucky man?" she inquired, her curiosity evident.

"Oliver Fox," I answered, my voice steady as I met her gaze.

Her eyes widened in astonishment, especially when Oliver turned and extended his hand for her to shake.

"Mr. Fox, congratulations."

"Thank you," Oliver replied politely, shaking her hand before turning his attention back to me.

Our conversation came to an abrupt halt when the elevator doors opened, and we stepped inside. Oliver squeezed my hand reassuringly as we moved to the back of the car. His office was on the top floor, so we would be the last to exit anyway.

"Who was that?" Oliver inquired softly after Candice had departed on her floor, his expression curious.

"Candice. I worked with her. I'm sure the gossip will be going around the Blaze once she tells everyone. Beatrice will probably justify my leaving because I'm dating you."

"You're not dating me. You're engaged to me."

When the elevator arrived on the floor for Fox Asset Corporation, Oliver led me to our offices. Mine was right next to his and empty of furniture except for a desk and a large black leather office chair. I would need to select a few items to fill up the space. I saw the walls were painted a very light blue and I smiled. Though we had only been together for a short time, Oliver knew what I liked.

"Thanks. I love the color."

He smiled. "I thought you would."

Oliver walked into my office and led me to one of the corners, pressing one of the panels in the wall. It popped open and I saw I had a full bathroom with a small closet.

I felt sheepish. "This office isn't for me. This is an executive's office. I should work in a cubicle."

"Eventually, you will be an executive. Mrs. Ryleigh Fox will have her own staff and take care of a percentage of my business," Oliver declared with unwavering confidence.

"You would trust me?" I asked.

"Of course. You're smart and talented. Once you learn the business, you can do anything," Oliver affirmed, his voice brimming with certainty.

“Thank you for having faith in me,” I replied gratefully, feeling a surge of determination coursing through me.

“Always,” Oliver murmured softly, pressing a gentle kiss to my forehead before excusing himself. “Now if you’ll excuse me, I have a conference call in five minutes. Join me when you get settled.”

I watched him depart, feeling a sense of excitement bubbling within me. It was my first day, and already I had a spacious office with its own bathroom. I imagined my coworkers whispering about the new girl working for Oliver, especially once they discovered our engagement.

Taking a few moments to compose myself, I settled into my new surroundings. I stowed my purse in the desk drawer and discovered a furniture catalog waiting for me. Flipping through its pages, I selected a few pieces to personalize my office. Before long, Henri knocked on my door, startling me from my thoughts.

“Yes?” I answered, slightly taken aback by his sudden appearance.

“I see you found the catalog. I can take your choices and create a requisition for whatever you desire,” Henri offered, his tone professional yet friendly.

“Uh, thank you,” I replied, feeling a pang of guilt as I considered the disparity between his role and mine.

Henri efficiently took note of my selections before swiftly departing. As I prepared to head to Oliver’s office, I couldn’t shake the feeling that Henri deserved my office more than I did.

Quietly entering Oliver's office, I found him pacing as voices emanated from his desk phone. His gestures were confident and decisive, and he looked entirely at ease with his sleeves rolled up.

Taking a seat on the couch, I observed him conduct his meeting with a mixture of admiration and intrigue. When the call finally concluded, Oliver joined me on the couch, his expression expectant.

"Did you gain anything from my meeting?" he inquired, his gaze fixed on me.

"I did. It seems like you have a problem with your distributor," I responded, drawing on what I had gleaned from the conversation.

Oliver nodded thoughtfully. "What do you propose I do about it?"

"Find another distributor," I suggested, my mind racing with possibilities.

"I've looked. They're more expensive," Oliver admitted, a hint of frustration evident in his voice.

"Are your circuit boards getting made without parts?" I pressed, seeking to understand the root of the issue.

"No. The line is at a standstill," Oliver confirmed, his brow furrowing with concern.

"Doesn't it make more sense to pay the higher prices and take a smaller profit than letting the line sit? Do you have orders to fill?" I reasoned, offering a solution to the dilemma.

"Yes. We're backlogged," Oliver conceded, his expression softening as he considered my suggestion.

Our conversation continued, with each exchange reinforcing my belief that I could make a valuable contribution to Oliver's business. As we brainstormed solutions together, I felt a sense of purpose blossoming within me, eager to prove myself in my new role alongside Oliver.

Oliver stroked his chin then went to his desk and typed a few things on his laptop. He looked at me and smiled then picked up the phone. He was talking to his production manager, Stanley. I listened closely. Oliver was taking my advice.

"You were right," he said as he hung up the phone.

"You needed me to tell you that? You should fire your other people," I teased, a playful smirk tugging at my lips.

"It wasn't their choice. I tried to negotiate with the other distributors," Oliver explained, his tone filled with exasperation.

"And how did that work out?" I quipped, unable to resist needling him a bit.

"Smartass," he retorted with a chuckle.

"But you love me. So, what is the end result?"

"We're offsetting the increase in parts price by passing half the cost onto the consumer. It's only a few dollars and shouldn't be a problem," Oliver revealed, his expression softening as he shared the resolution.

"See, it wasn't so bad," I remarked, feeling a sense of satisfaction at our successful brainstorming session.

"I decided I don't want you to be my personal assistant. I want you to be my trainee. I'll teach you everything so you can handle things in my absence," he announced, his eyes full of determination.

"Are you planning on going somewhere?" I inquired, a hint of concern creeping into my voice.

"I have meetings planned and might need you to handle a negotiation," Oliver explained, his gaze steady as he assessed my reaction.

"I can't do that. I'm nowhere near ready," I protested, feeling a surge of apprehension at the thought of such responsibility.

"Did I say tomorrow?" Oliver countered, a faint smile playing on his lips. "Your education started ten minutes ago and so far, you get an A."

"Do I get a reward?" I asked, unable to resist a playful remark.

"When we get home," Oliver replied with a suggestive grin.

“My home or yours?” I asked, feeling a flutter of excitement at the prospect of spending more time together.

He settled into his chair. “I wanted to talk to you about that. You should move in with me.”

I gasped. “Move in?” I echoed, feeling a mixture of surprise and anticipation at his proposal.

“You’re there a lot anyway,” Oliver pointed out, his voice gentle as he voiced his reasoning.

“But Sadie can’t afford the apartment on her own,” I objected, feeling a pang of guilt at the thought of leaving my best friend in a difficult situation.

“You can pay until the lease is up or I’ll give her a check,” Oliver offered, his tone reassuring.

“I’m not sure how much she’s there anyway. I think she’s been at Finley’s apartment,” I admitted, feeling a twinge of concern for my best friend’s budding romance.

“They’re getting hot and heavy?” he asked.

I shrugged. “I guess. I need to spend some time with her,” I mused, making a mental note to catch up with Sadie soon.

“This weekend. We’re heading to Southampton,” Oliver said.

“I can’t wait. Should we go there early?” I suggested, eager to start our weekend getaway.

"You just started and you're asking for a day off already?" Oliver teased, a playful smirk gracing his features.

"No. I wouldn't take advantage," I replied, shaking my head with a laugh.

"I know you wouldn't. It's all taken care of. My staff will clean and stock my home with food and drinks. We'll have a chef there all weekend so we can relax without cooking," he said.

I clasped my hands together. "I can't wait. I want to swim in the ocean," I said, already envisioning the blissful weekend ahead.

"Do you know when everyone will arrive?" He inquired, shifting the conversation back to our plans.

"Probably late. My parents and Matthew are taking the Jitney," I replied.

"They don't need to. We can all travel in my limo," Oliver suggested, his practicality shining through.

"You always want to leave late," I pointed out, teasing him gently.

"Because I hate the traffic," Oliver countered with a grin.

"I don't think everyone wants to leave at eleven," I remarked, considering our family's preferences.

"What time will they get there on the Jitney?" Oliver questioned, his brow furrowing with concern.

“Probably eleven,” I said.

“So four hours from the city to sit in a bus?” Oliver mused, his expression reflecting a mixture of amusement and disbelief.

“Yep. What do we do in the meantime?”

Oliver gestured to the chair. “You learn. Sit and I’ll go over a few things with you.”

~

My head is spinning. Oliver kept me busy all day and I’m exhausted. When Vlad picked us up, I leaned against my fiancé and promptly fell asleep. He woke me when we arrived at his building.

“Time to go upstairs.”

“I’m quite comfortable here.”

“Should I ask Vlad to drive around the city?”

“Like I’m a baby?”

“You are a baby, my baby.”

“I’ll go upstairs. Your bed is much more comfortable than this seat.”

I yawned as I opened my eyes. Oliver held my hand as we walked to the elevator. In the penthouse, he pressed me against the wall of the foyer and gave me a bruising kiss.

"What was that for?"

"It's from all the sexual tension. Working with you is harder than I thought."

He moved his hand to my breast, cupping it and pinching my nipple. All the exhaustion I felt slipped away as my arousal took over. We were like two dogs in heat, tearing at each other's clothing. Oliver lifted me against the wall and lowered me down on his hot shaft. He wasn't gentle and I didn't want him to be, fucking me harder than he ever had before.

"Yes, yes, fuck me," I screamed.

"You like that? I love being inside you," he panted.

Our union was short as I detonated and my orgasm tore through me. He gave me a few more punishing thrusts before he spilled into me with a loud grunt.

"Jesus Christ, that was good," he murmured into my ear.

"Yes, it was," I muttered, boneless and sated.

Oliver carried me to the bedroom, leaving our discarded clothing on the floor of the foyer. We stripped off the rest and took a long hot shower together where we couldn't stop touching each other. After we dried ourselves, we went to the kitchen to find something to eat.

"I have crab salad," Oliver said as he peered into the refrigerator.

I rubbed my hands together. "That's fine. Who exactly does your shopping?"

"The building supplies grocery service."

He removed the container of crab salad and some cold cuts for sandwiches. If people thought wealthy people always ate filet mignon and caviar, they should see us.

I took silverware from the drawer. "Wow, this place is awesome. Maybe I should move in here."

Oliver chuckled. "You really are getting spoiled."

"I have to agree. Maid, grocery, dry cleaning and restaurant service. I would have a field day."

He pressed a kiss to my temple. "You can have it all if you move in with me."

I sighed. "Can we discuss it later?"

"If you granted me one wish for my birthday, it would be to have you here all the time."

I raised my eyebrows. "Your birthday? Is it coming up? You never told me when it was."

"First week of October."

I sucked in a breath. "I'm glad you said something. I would look like an ass if I didn't get you a gift."

It was just another reason why I didn't want to move in. There was so much we didn't know about each other. Shit, I didn't even know when his birthday was and that was serious.

"You are my gift. My most favorite gift ever."

“I feel the same way,” I said, catching his gaze.

We sat at the dining table, the clink of silverware punctuating the comfortable silence. I savored the delicate flavors of the crab salad, watching Oliver as he meticulously rolled ham slices around Swiss cheese. He was a man who found joy in the simplest pleasures, a trait I cherished, especially given the wealth that could have easily made him pretentious.

"I'll need to plan something special for your birthday," I thought aloud, a smile playing on my lips. "You went all out for mine."

Oliver glanced up, his eyes full of warmth. "Don't worry about it too much. Just having you there will be enough."

I finished my salad and leaned over to kiss him on the cheek, a soft, affectionate gesture. As I got up to put the bowl away, I noticed the sky through the window. The sun was beginning to set, painting the clouds in hues of orange and pink.

"I want to sit out on the patio," I said, drawn to the beauty outside.

"Do you want a glass of wine? I have white," Oliver offered, already moving to get up.

"That sounds good," I replied, my heart warming at his thoughtfulness.

"Go on," he insisted, waving me off with a smile. "I'll get it for you."

• • •

As I stepped toward the patio door, I paused and turned back to him, my voice soft and earnest. "I love you."

Oliver looked at me, his expression tender. "I love you too," he said, his words a promise that filled the space between us with a profound sense of belonging.

"Not more than me," Oliver called out as I opened the slider. The warm pavers greeted my bare feet as I made my way to the conversation area, a cozy space adorned with brown wicker furniture and light blue cushions. Settling into the chaise lounge, I stretched out, the evening air wrapping around me as I waited for Oliver to bring my wine.

Fifteen minutes passed, and a sudden, frantic yell from inside startled me. My heart pounded as I leaped up and rushed back into the house, only to skid to a halt in the kitchen. There, facing off with Oliver, was a man who looked eerily similar to him. I stumbled against a bar stool, drawing both their gazes.

"This doesn't concern you," Oliver growled, his voice hard and unyielding.

I frowned, planting my feet defiantly. The other man's eyes lingered on me, making my skin crawl with a feeling of unwanted exposure.

"Who's this?" the man slurred, his speech thick with alcohol.

"No one," Oliver snapped.

The words sliced through me, and I felt tears prick at the corners of my eyes. Overwhelmed, I turned and fled to the bedroom, closing the door firmly behind me. Moments later, the front door slammed. I curled up on the bed, hearing Oliver's footsteps approach. He entered quietly and sat down next to me, but when he touched my shoulder, I recoiled.

"I'm sorry," he murmured, his voice soft with regret.

"You said I was no one," I sniffled, my heart aching.

"It's none of his business who you are to me," Oliver explained, his tone urgent. "I don't want to expose you to his toxicity."

"Who was that?" I asked, wiping my eyes.

"Jonah. He wanted money."

"How did he get upstairs?" I asked.

"I let him up. He said he had something important to tell me about our parents."

"Did he?" I pressed, needing to understand.

"No. It was a lie to get up here. Jonah is a manipulator. I don't want him to stain your innocence," Oliver said, his voice laced with frustration as he sat beside me on the bed.

"I'm not innocent," I retorted, pulling away slightly, my eyes meeting his with defiance.

"You're innocent of his misdeeds, and I want to keep it that way. I don't want you around him," he insisted, his hand reaching out to touch my shoulder, but I shrugged it off.

"He's your brother," I argued, the words hanging heavy in the air between us.

"He's done awful things. He'll never change, and I can't risk his presence," Oliver responded, his tone resolute, a shadow of pain crossing his features.

"What about when we get married? You won't invite him?" I asked, my voice filled with disbelief.

"No. I want to enjoy my day, and I won't if I have to worry about him causing trouble or getting drunk and insulting our guests," he said firmly, his jaw tightening.

"I can't understand it," I said, shaking my head in bewilderment.

"Because your brothers are good. Matthew and Finley would never hurt you the way Jonah has hurt me. He disgraces the Fox name. My parents would be ashamed if they found out how he turned out," Oliver explained, his eyes darkening with a mixture of sorrow and anger.

"He looks like you," I observed quietly, my heart aching for the man beside me.

"Yes, he does," Oliver agreed, a bitter smile touching his lips.

"Aren't you afraid he'll go public?" I asked, the thought of scandal adding to my anxiety.

"With what? If he does, the reporters can dig out a rap sheet as long as your arm. The only reason why it's not as long as your leg is because I've stuck my neck out to save his ass. I can't do that anymore. I have you to think about and eventually, our children," Oliver replied, his eyes locking onto mine with determination.

"He spoiled a good day," I whispered, the weight of the evening's events pressing down on me.

"Don't let him. You were brilliant today. I expect great things from you," Oliver said, his voice softening as he tried to comfort me.

"Are you finished for the evening?" I asked, the exhaustion evident in my voice.

"I thought you wanted to sit outside with a glass of wine?" he reminded me, his eyes searching mine.

"Not anymore. I had a busy day," I sighed, feeling the fatigue settle in.

"Are you sure?" Oliver asked, concern evident in his tone.

"Positive. My boss worked me like a pack mule," I replied, managing a small smile despite the heaviness in my heart.

"I should have a talk with him," Oliver said, a playful glint returning to his eyes, trying to lift the mood.

"Maybe I'll let you," I said, my smile growing a bit, appreciating his attempt to make me feel better.

"Can you tell him I love him and I would like him to hold me?" I murmured, my voice barely above a whisper.

"Let me empty out the wine glasses and lock the slider. I'll be back in a few minutes," Oliver replied, his tone gentle and reassuring.

I nodded and snuggled into my pillow, exhaustion overtaking me. It wasn't long before I drifted into a restless sleep. My dreams were troubling, not my usual nightmares, but unsettling, nonetheless.

Jonah's face haunted me, even though I had never seen pictures of him. His resemblance to Oliver made him disturbingly familiar. I woke with a jolt, my heart racing.

Oliver looked up from the paperwork he was paging through beside me. "Are you okay?" he asked, concern etching his features.

"Yes. Just a bad dream," I replied, trying to steady my breathing.

"Another one?" he asked, his brow furrowing.

"This was different, but not as bad as my usual," I said, hoping to downplay it.

"About what?" Oliver pressed gently.

. . .

I hesitated, unwilling to admit that Jonah had been the central figure. "I felt like I was falling," I lied.

"Don't be nervous about working. You're with me," Oliver said, trying to comfort me.

"I know. It's a lot to take in. I don't want to disappoint you," I admitted, my voice small.

"You? Never. You're doing a wonderful job. Keep it up. I think I want to take you to Los Angeles with me in September," he said, his eyes lighting up.

"Really? I haven't been there in a long time," I replied, feeling a spark of excitement.

"Then I definitely want you to come with me," he said, a smile playing on his lips.

"Is this because you want to teach me something or because you can't go without sex for a few days?" I teased, trying to lighten the mood.

"Both. I need you and I sleep better when you're with me," he confessed, his voice softening.

"I think I want to move in here," I said, the words surprising even me as they left my mouth.

"You do? What changed your mind?" Oliver asked, his eyes widening with a mixture of hope and surprise.

"I love you. Of course, I would still have to pay rent. Sadie can't afford it on her own," I explained, the practicalities of my life creeping in.

"I said I would write her a check," he reminded me, his tone patient.

"The only thing is this place is big and I'm not sure I want to be alone when you're not here," I admitted, my fears bubbling to the surface.

"Then come with me for every trip. We can even take a few extra days to enjoy whatever city we visit," Oliver suggested, his eyes shining with excitement at the prospect.

I smiled, feeling a sense of relief and anticipation. "I like that idea," I said, reaching out to take his hand.

"Good," he replied, squeezing my hand gently. "We're going to make this work. I promise."

"That would be lovely. You really are scoring points," I said, smiling as Oliver nuzzled my cheek and stroked my hair with his fingers.

"We should probably talk about the wedding. What do you want?" Oliver asked, his voice soft and thoughtful.

"I haven't thought about it yet. We've only been engaged a few days," I admitted, feeling a bit overwhelmed by the sudden shift in conversation.

"You can have whatever you desire," he assured me, his eyes full of promise.

"Suppose I want to get married on the great lawn of Central Park?" I suggested, testing the waters.

"I'm sure it can be arranged. I have a few friends in government," Oliver replied with a confident smile.

"Who would be your best man?" I asked, genuinely curious.

"I have a few friends from college. They're scattered across the country, but you'll meet them," he said, a hint of nostalgia in his voice.

In the entire time we were dating, I hadn't seen Oliver hang out with any friends in Manhattan. I wasn't sure if he had any.

"Do you have any in the city?" I probed.

"Of course, I do," he replied, almost defensively.

"Why haven't I met them?" I pressed, raising an eyebrow.

"It's the summer and most of them are busy just like I am. Besides, I've been wrapped up in my gorgeous fiancée," Oliver said, smirking playfully.

"I want to meet them," I insisted, not letting the subject drop.

"The summer is almost over. You will," he promised.

"What are their names?" I asked, wanting to know more about the people who were important to him.

"Ivan, Dax, and Wilmer. They've spent most of the summer overseas," Oliver said, relaxing back into the conversation.

"Conducting business?" I asked, curious about their lives.

Oliver started to laugh. "Enjoying the European sun. All three are trust fund babies."

"So how do you know them?" I asked, intrigued.

"From college," he replied simply.

"You're the only one of the four of you that works?" I asked, feeling a mix of admiration and curiosity.

"No. They work but sparingly. Dax and Wilmer buy and sell art and Ivan is a retired hockey player," Oliver explained.

"Hockey?" I echoed, surprised.

"He's Russian. He played in the league for a few years until he got his brains scrambled one too many times. He had to call it quits," Oliver said.

"Are they all your age?" I asked, picturing the eclectic group of friends.

"More or less. We all met in college, so we're around the same age," Oliver said, smiling as he reminisced.

"I'm looking forward to meeting them," I said, feeling a sense of anticipation.

“Yes. I'll have to keep you close so the wolves will stay away,” Oliver teased, his eyes twinkling with mischief.

My eyes grew wide. "They wouldn't hit on me, would they?"

"No, of course not," he reassured me, chuckling. "But I'm sure they will be quite taken with you. You're beautiful. They thought I would never get married."

Oliver picked up the remote and flipped through the channels a few times, stopping abruptly on a gossip show called *"On the Six"* when he heard his name mentioned. I sat up, alert, when the word "engagement" caught my ear. The show was reporting on our engagement, and the screen displayed a picture of us walking out of work that evening, followed by a close-up of my ring.

I leaned closer, my heart racing. "How did they even get that picture?"

"Fuck. I'm sorry," Oliver muttered, running a hand through his hair.

"What are you sorry for?" I asked, my brows knitting in confusion.

"I thought we would have more time before it got into the news cycle. I was having the PR department write a press release. It was supposed to be sent out tomorrow," he explained, his frustration evident.

"It's not your fault. Stop apologizing. You didn't tell me you were having a press release prepared," I said, trying to soothe him.

"I would have once I approved it," he replied, sighing.

"I love you. I don't give a shit if people know," I declared, taking his hand in mine.

"It's not a matter of caring; it's a matter of security," Oliver corrected, his eyes serious.

"We have security," I pointed out.

"But now that it's out, you'll need it when you're not with me," he said, a protective edge in his voice.

"Who? Vlad?" I asked, thinking of the stoic bodyguard.

"Would you like Vlad?" Oliver asked, raising an eyebrow.

"He doesn't talk much," I said with a small smile.

"His job isn't to talk; it's to make sure you're protected," Oliver replied, his tone firm.

"Is there anyone else I can choose?" I inquired, hoping for options.

"Who do you have in mind?" Oliver asked, his curiosity piqued.

"A woman?" I suggested tentatively.

"I don't have any on staff, but I could get you a couple," he said, considering it.

"Two?" I asked, surprised.

"I'm high profile and now you are too," he explained.

"What about before? I only had Vlad driving me. He didn't follow me around," I reminded him.

"People didn't know you before. Now they do," he said, his voice heavy with the new reality.

"This sucks. I think you should buy a house on some private island in the Caribbean," I joked, trying to lighten the mood.

Oliver smirked. "I own a few."

"I thought you said you didn't have any other residences?" I asked, confused.

"I don't, but I do own a few islands. I can build a house if I like," he said casually.

"That would be a perfect honeymoon. No cameras and totally private," I mused.

"Would you like that?" he asked, his eyes sparkling with the idea.

"Maybe," I said, smiling at the thought.

"I can start building right away. It might take a few months," Oliver said, already planning.

"Jesus Oliver, I was only kidding," I laughed.

"I'm not. Perhaps it could be a new tradition. We could take vacations there," he said, his tone serious.

"What about your businesses?" I asked, practical concerns surfacing.

"I can still be reached by satellite phone if anything arises," he assured me.

"So, no internet or anything? Just a phone?" I asked, feeling a bit skeptical.

"You sound disappointed. Aren't I enough entertainment for you?" he teased, his eyes twinkling.

I rolled my eyes. "Yes, you are, but I might get bored. You might get bored of me," I said, voicing my insecurities.

"Highly unlikely. You constantly turn me on. Sometimes I'm in awe of you, like this morning. You amaze me," he said earnestly, his eyes filled with admiration.

I could feel my face heating with embarrassment. How could this business tycoon be in awe of me?

"Stop teasing," I murmured, feeling shy.

"I'm not. It's true. You're everything I always wanted," he said, pulling me close.

I smiled, feeling a surge of love and gratitude. "And you're everything I always wanted, too."

Oliver pushed me onto my back, his touch igniting a fire within me. His lips found my neck, and a shiver ran down my spine as he trailed kisses along my skin. In moments like this, I couldn't get enough of him. I wanted to lose myself in the intensity of our passion, to consume every moment with him.

Chapter 17

Working with Oliver was exhausting. Each night, I returned home feeling drained, ready to collapse into bed. We often had dinner in his office while he sifted through reports, the glow of his monitors casting a soft light across the room. Financial news played silently in the background, a constant presence in our evenings.

As I sat with him, I couldn't stifle a yawn. It was nearing 8 p.m., and fatigue weighed heavily on me. The previous night, despite multiple orgasms, sleep had eluded me. It seemed like Oliver was trying to make up for lost time, admitting that he hadn't been with many women over the past year and a half, despite numerous opportunities. If only they knew what they had missed.

"Am I boring you?" Oliver asked, breaking the silence.

"I'm ready to drop. Are you ready to leave?" I replied, longing for the comfort of my own bed.

"I have a couple of things to check, and then we can go," he said, his focus returning to his work.

"I want to pack when we get home," I mentioned, feeling a sense of excitement at the thought of moving in with him.

"I love when you say that," Oliver said, a smile tugging at his lips.

"Home?" I echoed, feeling a flutter of anticipation.

"Yes. I want you to live with me," he confirmed, his voice soft and sincere.

"Soon. I'll talk to Sadie this weekend," I promised, already imagining our life together.

"Is your entire family traveling with us to Southampton?" Oliver asked, shifting the conversation.

"I think so, though I haven't heard from Matthew. He has to find a babysitter for Blackie since I'm unavailable," I explained, thinking of my brother's beloved pet.

"Tell him to bring him," Oliver suggested, surprising me.

I raised my eyebrows in disbelief. "You with a dog?"

Oliver furrowed his brow. "Why do you say it like that? I like dogs."

"I know you do, but I didn't think you would want one running around your house," I admitted, intrigued by this new revelation.

"I had one when I was a boy, a German shepherd," Oliver revealed, a hint of nostalgia in his voice.

"What happened to her?" I asked, curious about his childhood pet.

"Like all dogs, she died. Daisy lived until she was twelve," he said, a touch of sadness coloring his words.

"Do you have any pictures?" I inquired, eager to see this side of him.

"Somewhere in my drawer. I'll show you sometime," he promised, his eyes softening.

I yawned again, feeling the exhaustion wash over me, and absently lifted my skirt to scratch my thigh. Oliver's gaze followed the movement, and I could sense his admiration.

"Don't even think about it," I warned playfully.

"About what? I can look at your legs," he said innocently, his eyes twinkling with mischief.

"I have no problem with you looking at my legs, but I'm sure it's not the only thing you're thinking about," I teased, feeling a surge of desire.

"Just your sexy legs," he replied, his voice low and husky, sending a shiver down my spine.

Oliver straightened the stack of papers he was looking through and stuck them into a folder, signaling the end of his work for the night.

"You're done?" I asked, a sense of relief washing over me.

"Yes. Let's go home. Vlad is waiting for us outside," Oliver replied, a hint of anticipation in his voice.

"Thank God," I mumbled under my breath as I stood up, feeling the exhaustion of the day weighing heavily on me.

"I heard that," Oliver said with a playful smile.

"Taskmaster," I teased, though a part of me was grateful for all that I was learning.

"You're learning a lot, are you not?" he remarked, his tone proud.

"Yes," I admitted, feeling a sense of accomplishment.

I watched as Oliver slipped on his graphite gray jacket and straightened his tie with practiced ease. He grabbed his briefcase, and I retrieved my purse before we headed for the elevator. Most of the offices were dark, the hum of the empty workspace echoing around us.

Vlad was waiting for us with the limo when we stepped outside. He held the door open, and Oliver gestured for me to slide inside first.

"Why does he have the limo? We don't need it until tomorrow," I asked, curious.

"Because I'm planning to fuck you on the way home. I can't do that in the sedan," Oliver replied, his voice low and seductive.

I was speechless at his boldness, but a surge of desire ignited within me at his words. Within moments, I was wet with anticipation, craving his touch.

He pulled me onto his lap as soon as we were settled inside the limo, and I could feel his erection pressing against me.

“You make it hard for me to concentrate,” he confessed, his fingers sliding under the panel of my panties. “You’re soaked.”

“I want you,” I admitted, my voice breathless with desire.

“And you shall have me,” he promised, his words sending a jolt of electricity through me.

I leaned in and pressed my lips against his, feeling the rough stubble of his chin against my skin. Straddling him, I let out a soft moan as he fingered me to a fast orgasm, my pleasure mingling with the taste of his lips.

Once I came down from my orgasm, he held my limp body in his arms, whispering sweet nothings into my ear.

“I love you so much, Ryleigh,” he murmured, his words sending a surge of warmth through me.

As soon as I had the strength, I moved back onto his knees and opened his belt. Oliver leaned back against the bench seat, his cock hard and ready as I stroked him with eager hands, lost in the intimacy of the moment.

“Not too much or I’ll come.”

“I want to ride you.”

He didn't move, letting me do all the work as I pulled my panties aside and sank down on him. His shaft stretched me in the most delicious way. I moved over Oliver as he leaned back and watched me, his eyes glazed with ecstasy. Only when he grew close did he participate, shoving his hips upward as he began to spurt into me. I didn't worry about my own orgasm because I knew he would take care of me.

Once he finished, I put my head against his shoulder while he rubbed my clit. I came with a loud cry against his neck. He gently lifted me off him and put me on the seat, removing a white handkerchief from the inside pocket of his jacket to wipe between my legs. It didn't help much since my panties were soaked with his semen and my juices.

"We'll shower together when we get upstairs."

He tucked himself in and zipped up his pants as Vlad pulled up to Oliver's building.

"Are you all right?" he asked.

"Fine."

I felt as I always did after we made love, lazy and boneless. I recovered as Oliver got ready to open the door.

"I much prefer baths," I confessed, sinking deeper into the oversized tub with Oliver's arms wrapped around me.

"I think I do too," he agreed, his touch sending tingles down my spine as he caressed my breasts.

I let out a contented sigh, feeling utterly relaxed in his embrace. But as the clock neared 9:30 p.m., the pang of hunger interrupted our tranquility.

"I think I'll go to bed without dinner. I'm not hungry," I murmured, feeling the exhaustion of the day settling in.

"You should eat something. You expended a lot of energy," Oliver insisted, concern lacing his voice.

"I know. You're hard to resist," I admitted with a smile, leaning back against his chest.

"Wait until you're trapped in a plane with me for hours," Oliver teased, his fingers tracing patterns on my skin.

"The mile-high club?" I joked, trying to lighten the mood.

"No, the six-mile-high club. We can sleep in bed the entire trip," he suggested, his tone playful.

"I'm not sure I want to do that," I replied, hesitating.

"The bed is very comfortable. You'll like it," he reassured me, his lips brushing against my ear.

"It's not that. I don't want to be groggy when we arrive," I explained, voicing my concern.

"Then I'll make sure you don't sleep," Oliver said, his voice laced with determination.

“You’re insatiable. Aren’t men your age supposed to be on the decline sexually?” I teased, unable to resist poking fun at him.

“Maybe some men, but not me—I’m in my prime,” he retorted confidently, a smirk playing on his lips.

“I’m glad,” I replied sincerely, feeling a surge of affection for him.

“I bet you are,” he said, his tone suggestive, a twinkle in his eye as he looked at me.

Oliver moved my long hair to the side and kissed my neck, gently biting my shoulder.

“You want to get out? My fingers are getting pruny,” Oliver chuckled, breaking the tranquil silence of the bath.

“Yes, I want to go to bed,” I replied, feeling the exhaustion of the day creeping in.

“Are you sure you don’t want to eat?” he asked, concern etched in his voice.

“No,” I responded simply, my hunger forgotten in my desire for sleep.

“Do you mind if I have something? I’m starved,” he inquired, his stomach rumbling audibly.

“Go ahead. I’ll meet you in bed,” I assured him, already anticipating the warmth of the sheets.

“Naked, I hope,” he teased.

“I'll be naked, but I doubt I'll have the energy to do anything,” I admitted with a weary smile.

“I just want your warm body against mine,” he murmured.

With Oliver's gentle prodding, I reluctantly got out of the bath, the warmth of the water replaced by the enveloping embrace of a thick white towel. He helped me dry my hair with the blow dryer before we both slipped under the sheets, exhaustion pulling us into its embrace.

I drifted in and out of consciousness, unaware of when Oliver joined me in bed. But when a bad dream jolted me awake, I found him curled around me, his presence a comforting anchor in the darkness. It's what I remembered as I drifted back to sleep.

“Sweetheart, wake up,” Oliver's voice cut through the haze of sleep.

My eyelids fluttered open to see him standing over me, his shirt clinging to his sweat-drenched body.

Was it morning already?

“Where did you go?” I asked, confused by his sudden disappearance.

“To work out on my treadmill. I was hoping you wouldn't hear it,” he explained, a sheepish smile playing on his lips.

"I didn't. I slept like a rock," I admitted, feeling grateful for the uninterrupted rest.

"You need to get up and pack. We're leaving at lunchtime," Oliver informed me, his tone businesslike.

I frowned, surprised by the change in plans. "I thought we were leaving tonight."

"We were, but I just got Finley's confirmation. He's leaving the office early," Oliver explained.

"What about everyone else?" I asked, feeling a pang of anxiety.

"All confirmed, even Sadie. She'll meet us at the limo," he reassured me, his efficiency calming my nerves.

"You called everyone and set this up?" I asked, amazed by his organizational skills.

"It's what I do," he replied simply, shrugging off the praise.

With a swift movement, Oliver peeled off his sweat-soaked shirt, revealing his glistening, toned physique in the morning sunlight filtering through the windows. I couldn't help but marvel at his beauty, feeling a surge of gratitude for having him in my life.

He leaned down to kiss me softly before disappearing into the bathroom for a shower, leaving me to drift back to sleep in the warmth of our bed.

"Ryleigh, you have to get up if you want to shower."

. . .

I opened my eyes to find a droplet of water falling onto my forehead from Oliver's shoulder.

"You like me dirty, so I won't shower," I remarked playfully.

"I do like you dirty, and that's your choice," he replied with a teasing smile.

"I took one last night anyway," I said.

I watched him as he dropped his towel, unable to tear my eyes away from his sculpted behind. The memory of the pleasure I felt when I dug my nails into it flashed through my mind. Oliver emerged from the closet a few minutes later, dressed in tan slacks and a light blue oxford shirt without a tie.

"Casual? Are you feeling all right?" I teased, raising an eyebrow.

"I don't have any meetings today, and we're leaving at noon," he explained, his tone relaxed.

"What will the other employees say?" I chided, unable to resist poking fun at his departure from the usual formal attire.

"I don't really care," he shrugged, dismissing the concern.

"Can I wear jeans?" I asked, seizing the opportunity to dress down.

"If you want," he replied, his gaze lingering on me appreciatively.

“You should have casual Fridays. Did you ever consider it?” I asked.

“No. We have too many clients in and out of the building,” he explained, his practicality winning over my suggestion.

“So that’s a no?” I clarified, a hint of disappointment in my voice.

“It’s a no,” he confirmed, his tone final.

“I guess I’ll have to wait to make changes when I become Mrs. Fox,” I said.

“You’re going to be a pain in my ass, aren’t you?” he joked, a playful glint in his eyes.

“Yes. I’m warning you right now,” I replied with a grin, enjoying the banter.

“Maybe I should reconsider and make you my personal assistant,” he teased back, his tone light.

“That would be wasted talent. Who would take over for you when you’re indisposed?” I countered.

“If I’m indisposed, it’s more than likely because of you,” he quipped, his smirk widening.

I giggled at his response, feeling the warmth of his gaze as his eyes traveled over my naked body. He approached me, pressing his body against mine and cupping my ass in his hands.

“We’ll be late. It will have to wait until later,” he murmured, his voice husky with desire.

“Later will be around nighttime. I’m not sure I can wait that long,” I teased, my own desire matching his.

“Patience, Mr. Fox,” I reminded him.

I left Oliver salivating like a dog and closed the bathroom door on him while I got ready for work. With a mischievous grin, I passed on showering, opting instead to tie my hair back in a ponytail, wash my face, and brush my teeth. Just to tease him a little more, I emerged from the bathroom still naked, sauntering into the closet with deliberate nonchalance. The look of pleading on his face was priceless.

"Two can play this little game," I declared.

"I’m not sure I know what you mean," I replied innocently, pretending to focus on selecting a bra and panty set from the drawer.

"Don’t you? You’re teasing me," Oliver insisted, leaning against the closet door with a smirk.

"I don’t think that’s what I’m doing," I retorted, my own smirk matching his.

"Payback is a bitch," he joked, his eyes twinkling.

I shivered at the memory of his teasing touches, the way he would bring me to the edge and make me beg for more. Those moments when I felt like I would combust from the intensity of my desire.

We quickly packed our suitcases in fifteen minutes flat before Vlad arrived to pick us up and transport us to the office. The playful banter and teasing glances continued throughout the morning, setting the tone for the day ahead.

~

I felt lazy as I worked on a few things in my office. Oliver had some phone calls to make before he left, and it wasn't necessary for me to sit in his office for them. He came to get me just before noon. Vlad would be waiting for us with the limo. This morning, he transported us in the black sedan so the limo could be cleaned and stocked with ice and drinks for the ride to Southampton.

"Sweetheart, let's go," Oliver said as he poked his head into my office.

"Why did you call me sweetheart? You never did before," I remarked, curious about the sudden endearment.

"Because that's what you are. Do you prefer something else?"

"No, I like it," I admitted with a smile.

He grinned. "Then stop giving me a hard time and let's go."

Vlad greeted us, opening the door so we could enter the limo. The dark interior smelled clean with a hint of coconut. I shuddered as I looked at the bench seat where we had made love the evening before.

“Are you chilly?” Oliver asked, noticing my reaction.

“No, just thinking,” I replied vaguely.

“About?” he prodded gently.

“Last night,” I admitted, feeling a flush creep up my cheeks.

I reached over and cupped his crotch. He quickly covered my hand with his own to stop me.

“We’re picking up your parents, Finley, and Sadie in fifteen minutes,” he reminded me.

“Then let me suck you. It won’t take that long,” I whispered, my tone suggestive.

“Ryleigh, stop talking like that,” he chided, though desire lingered in his voice.

“I’m just telling you what I want to do. Why is that so wrong?” I protested, pouting slightly.

“Because you’re making me hard,” he confessed, his breath catching slightly.

“Then let me suck you,” I persisted, my voice husky with desire.

“No. Behave,” he admonished, gently pulling my hand away.

I crossed my arms, pouting as I looked out the window. Oliver didn’t let me give him many blowjobs, even though I told him I enjoyed doing it. He preferred to give me pleasure.

"Don't be angry. You can do what you want with me tonight," he reassured me, sensing my disappointment.

"I'm not angry," I muttered, relenting slightly.

"Then stop pouting. I want to enjoy the weekend with your family. This is a celebration. Now come here," he urged, pulling me close.

I slid over to him, leaning into his embrace as he kissed the top of my head. Traffic wasn't bad at this hour, and I hoped we could navigate the highway to Southampton with just as much ease. As we drove off, the anticipation of spending time with our loved ones filled me with warmth and excitement.

I was delighted to see everyone was ready and waiting when we arrived at Finley's. Matthew would be picked up last with Blackie. Oliver and I got out of the car and exchanged greetings before Vlad began packing the trunk with suitcases. I left Oliver's side to sit with Sadie while my parents and Finley engaged Oliver in conversation.

"How do you feel now that you're engaged?" Sadie asked, her eyes sparkling with curiosity.

"Wonderful. I didn't think this would happen so soon in my life," I replied, feeling a rush of happiness.

"Well, when it's right, it's right," she said with a warm smile.

“What’s going on with you and Finley?” I whispered, eager for some gossip.

“I really like him a lot. I wish we’d gotten together sooner,” Sadie confessed, her cheeks flushing slightly.

“So, it’s official?” I inquired, leaning in closer.

“Yes. We’re officially dating,” she confirmed, her voice filled with excitement.

“I have something to discuss with you,” I said, changing the subject.

“Uh oh. I’m not going to like it, am I?” Sadie teased, raising an eyebrow.

“Oliver asked me to move in with him,” I revealed, feeling a mix of nerves and anticipation.

She frowned. “I can’t afford the rent on my own.”

“I would still pay my rent, and you would have the entire apartment to yourself,” I said.

“I’m not there that much. I’ve been spending time with Finley,” Sadie explained, a hint of excitement in her voice.

“Our poor apartment is abandoned,” I chuckled.

We chattered on until we stopped to pick up Matthew. He had Blackie in a brown soft sided carrier.

“Bring him here. I want to see my little chubby boy,” I exclaimed eagerly.

Matthew handed me the carrier, and I opened the top, taking Blackie into my arms. The Frenchie went wild, showering me with kisses and whines of joy. I cuddled him close, feeling a rush of affection for the adorable dog. Oliver smiled at me, and I couldn’t help but wonder if I could persuade him to get a dog of our own. After all, I had always dreamed of having one as a kid.

“Spoiling him already,” Matthew remarked with a grin as he watched me dote on Blackie.

“I love this baby. I want to take care of him for a weekend,” I replied, my heart melting at the sight of the adorable French Bulldog in my arms.

“I always take him with me. Everyone loves him,” Matthew shared proudly, his affection for Blackie evident in his voice.

“That’s because he’s such a sweet boy,” I cooed, scratching behind Blackie’s ears as he wagged his stumpy tail happily.

Blackie licked my hand affectionately, and I couldn’t help but shower him with kisses on his head.

“I’ve been replaced already?” Oliver’s playful voice interrupted, drawing my attention.

“No one could replace you,” I assured him, smiling warmly at Oliver.

"I hope not," Oliver replied with a chuckle, his eyes twinkling with affection.

"Are you getting up? Snacks are being served on the patio," Oliver called out, interrupting my lounging on the bed in the master bedroom. The trip to Southampton had been smooth, thankfully devoid of much traffic that might have soured Oliver's mood.

"I'm not sleeping," I replied, stretching lazily across the king-size bed.

"Maybe I should take this opportunity while everyone is downstairs," Oliver suggested, a mischievous glint in his eyes.

"You have guests," I reminded him.

"No, we have guests. This is your house too," he countered, his tone leaving no room for argument. "Not yet."

"As long as you wear any ring of mine on your finger, you own this house too," he added. "Now get up before I strip you naked and fuck you senseless."

"Promises, promises," I teased back, though my heart raced at the thought.

Oliver took a step toward the bed, and I quickly

scrambled off it. If he touched me now, we wouldn't be joining my family for at least an hour.

"Hmm, I'm not sure if your actions are flattering," Oliver mused.

"We have guests," I repeated, trying to quell the electricity between us.

He took my hand, and we headed downstairs, both changed into our bathing suits. I wore my black bikini under a pair of pink shorts and a dark blue t-shirt. My family was already seated on the patio, enjoying the sunny weather under the large umbrella while waitstaff served drinks and snacks. I was relieved that Oliver had arranged for a caterer for the weekend—I was looking forward to some relaxation.

"About time," Finley greeted us.

"We had to change," I replied with a grin.

"I'll bet," he muttered under his breath, his eyes dancing with amusement.

I settled down next to Sadie and helped myself to some guacamole and homemade tortilla chips. Meanwhile, Oliver engaged in a conversation with Matthew about the financial markets, and I rolled my eyes at their typical banter.

"Want to go to the beach?" I asked Sadie, sensing her restlessness.

"Yes. Is it private?" she inquired eagerly.

"Yes, we won't have to share with anyone," I assured her, already eager to escape the chatter.

We wiped our mouths and pushed our chairs back in unison. Oliver paused his conversation to shoot me a questioning look.

"Where are you going?" he asked.

"The beach," I replied nonchalantly.

"Wait a few minutes. We can go together," he said.

I chuckled, knowing how long his conversations could last. "You'll be here talking for an hour."

"Want to take Blackie?" Matthew asked. The dog, who'd been sitting at his feet, jumped up at his name.

"Does he like the water?"

My brother nodded. "Loves it. Get his leash. I left it on the counter inside."

"Sweetheart, I'll be there in a few minutes," Oliver said.

I bent down to kiss Oliver's cheek before I went inside to get Blackie's leash. Snapping it on before Sadie and I headed down the long expanse of perfectly manicured lawn to the sand.

"This is the life," she said as she stepped onto the warm sand.

I shivered. "I know. I can't believe it's mine."

"You're lucky."

"It will happen for you, and you always can enjoy what we have. I plan on having some parties here when we marry."

She sighed. "I want it permanently."

I placed the towels I brought with me on the sand under an oversized blue umbrella Oliver had set up. Blackie sat next to me and put his face on his paws. We had to be careful with him because Frenchies didn't handle the heat well.

"It will happen," I said.

"I want it to happen with Finley."

"You've only been dating a short time."

"But we've been with each other before."

I looked at Sadie as she tucked her long blonde hair behind her ears. What was she saying?

I frowned. "Huh?"

"I slept with Finley before," she said sheepishly.

I was shocked that I was just finding this out now. "When?"

"Junior year and a few times after that."

"I don't understand."

Sadie shrugged. "It just happened. Remember we met him in that bar with one of his friends? You didn't feel well that night and went home early. One thing led to another, and I ended up in his bed."

I clawed at my memory, trying to think of the time she was talking about. It came to me, and I remembered Sadie had walked in the door close to dawn.

"It was just sex?" I asked, hoping she would tell me it wasn't.

She shook her head. "No. We saw each other for a few weeks."

"Why the fuck didn't you say anything?" I demanded.

"Finley wanted it that way and I promised not to say anything."

"Why didn't it work out?"

"Finley didn't want to hurt me. He was working on his business and had so little time. He already canceled a couple of dinners with me. We mutually agreed to end it."

"And now?"

She smiled dreamily. "When we went out to dinner together, it just clicked, and he has more time now to cultivate a relationship."

"So, this isn't new?"

"It's a renewal. Come on, Ryleigh, your brother is fucking hot. He's handsome and built."

"And rich."

She frowned. “Money is not my motivation. I really like Finley. I think I love him. I had a crush on him from the time we met during your freshman year. But I figured, what would a guy like him want with a silly little teenager. He used to flirt with me when he came to see you. I’m surprised you didn’t notice.”

Was I that blind and unaware that my brother and best friend had a thing for each other? I guess I was.

“I didn’t. Shit, what does that say about me?” I asked, feeling stupid.

“It says you were busy. Don’t sweat it.”

Blackie whimpered at my side, eager for a walk. I secured his leash and together with Sadie, we strolled towards the water. As soon as we arrived, I released him, and he dashed gleefully into the waves lapping at the shore. By the time the others caught up with us, Blackie was already drenched, his fur glistening in the sunlight.

Oliver shed his shirt, revealing the toned muscles underneath, and I couldn't help but admire my stunning fiancé.

"I think I should take Blackie back to the house," Matthew suggested.

"Probably. He's been out in the heat long enough." I handed Matthew the leash, and he took it, getting a bit wet as Blackie shook off his coat.

"You're lucky I love your dog," Matthew joked, earning a round of laughter as he carried Blackie back home.

My mother and Anders wasted no time stripping down to their bathing suits. Mom, at forty-seven, could easily pass for twenty-something with her toned body, elegantly filling out her green bikini. Anders, too, showed off his fit physique as he peeled off his white t-shirt.

They raced towards the water, my mother pausing for a moment before Anders dove in. He accused her of cheating, prompting her to laugh as he pulled her into his arms. It was heartwarming to see their bond still strong. Sadie and Finley joined them, while Oliver settled beside me on one of the colorful towels.

"What were you and Sadie chatting about?" Oliver inquired.

"Oh, nothing much. Just some girl time."

"Well, I need some Ryleigh time," he grinned, pulling me closer.

"Later, sex fiend. You act like we never have sex," I teased.

"I should have let you suck me," he retorted.

"I'm glad you're suffering," I replied with a smirk.

"You're so cruel to me," Oliver pretended to pout.

"Wait and see how cruel I can be tonight," I countered playfully.

"I can hardly wait. Come swimming with me," Oliver suggested, extending his hand.

"I'm not really in the mood," I hesitated.

"Oh, come on. Let's swim together," he insisted.

I took his hand and stood up, letting him watch as I stripped off my clothes and adjusted my bikini bottoms.

"You look beautiful," he complimented.

"Yeah, yeah. Flattery will get you everywhere," I teased back.

"Even in your panties?" he asked with a mischievous grin.

"You know it will," I replied, chuckling.

Our banter was interrupted by Anders and my mother emerging from the water. They claimed our spots on the towels, prompting Oliver and me to head towards the water. I dipped my feet in the surf, but Oliver urged me further in.

"I need to get used to the water. It's cold," I protested.

"Just hop in. Sadie and Finley are doing fine," Oliver encouraged.

My brother was holding Sadie in his arms, spinning around with her. They looked happy together, and I silently hoped it was genuine. They both deserved happiness.

"No, I want to go in slowly," I insisted.

Ignoring my protest, Oliver hoisted me over his shoulder and charged into the water until it was too deep, then dropped me in. I spluttered as I went under, then resurfaced, glaring at Oliver before swimming hard to catch up with him.

“I can’t believe you did that,” I yelled.

“Aww, baby got her hair wet,” he said as he splashed me.

“You idiot!” I screamed as my brother and Sadie watched us.

“But I’m your idiot.”

I snorted. “Unfortunately.”

“Take that back,” he growled.

I swam toward shore, but Oliver was faster, grabbing my ankle and pulling me against him.

“Take it back Ryleigh.” He sounded and looked so serious.

I scowled. “I was kidding. I love you, Oliver.”

Sometimes this powerful, successful man showed his vulnerable side, like now. I wondered what would happen if we ever broke up. Oliver needed me.

"I hope so. You mean the world to me. You are my world," Oliver whispered tenderly.

"You have so much more than me," I replied softly.

"But it would mean nothing without you. You have me wrapped around your finger," Oliver insisted.

"I know. You already said that before," I teased lightly.

"It's true," he affirmed, sealing his words with a deep kiss.

As Finley and Sadie swam towards the shore, we found ourselves in deeper waters, hidden from view. Oliver slipped his hand into my bottoms, skillfully finding my clit with his index finger and gently rubbing.

"You can't do this here," I whispered, trying to maintain some sense of propriety.

"I can, and I will. Just enjoy it. I love getting you off," Oliver murmured, his breath hot against my skin.

"Why should I? You wouldn't let me suck you when I wanted to," I retorted.

"Shut up, Ryleigh," he interrupted, silencing me with another kiss before redoubling his efforts to pleasure me.

I gasped, my body responding to his touch, and as I reached my peak, I moaned his name. When I opened my eyes, Oliver was grinning like a fool.

"Bastard," I muttered, though there was a hint of affection in my tone.

"It was my pleasure," he replied.

"Let me go," I demanded, pushing him away playfully.

Just for good measure, I reached down and stroked his semi erection, causing him to hiss and swam away. He let me go this time and I walked out of the water with wobbly legs, plopping down on the towel next to my mother. Oliver stayed in the ocean, slicing his powerful arms through the waves as he swam the length of the jetty and back.

"Have you made any decisions about your wedding?" my mother inquired.

"No, we've only briefly discussed it," I replied.

"Only briefly? I remember you used to dress up your dolls and plan their weddings when you were a girl. I would've thought you'd have a whole folder of ideas by now," she teased.

"I just haven't had much time. Oliver has been keeping me busy at work. We've been getting home late most nights this week," I explained.

"Are you enjoying it more than your previous job at Blaze?" Anders asked.

"Yes, very much," I confirmed.

As Anders continued the conversation with my mother, I grabbed a towel to dry my hair. A few minutes later, Oliver emerged from the water, looking every bit like a Greek god with droplets of water tracing the contours of his muscular body. He took the towel from me, drying himself off before planting a kiss on my lips.

• • •

When everyone else decided to head back to the house, Oliver leaned in close to whisper in my ear.

"It would be my pleasure to make love to you out here tonight," he murmured.

"Are you crazy? What if someone from my family comes down here?" I whispered back.

"I was thinking of a midnight rendezvous. We could bring a bottle of wine," he suggested.

"Maybe," I replied cautiously.

"Are you suddenly shy? This coming from the woman who let me give her an orgasm in front of her family?" he joked.

I slapped his arm. "That was different. They couldn't see me in the water," I defended.

"You were still in front of them," he countered.

"I'll think about it," I conceded.

I tried to stifle a yawn but failed.

"Want to head back to the house? We can shower and take a nap before dinner. I asked them to serve at six."

"Sounds good to me," I agreed.

We gathered up the wet towels, closed the umbrella, and made our way up the sand towards the lawn.

Chapter 18

Oliver stirred me awake by nuzzling my cheek with his nose. I mumbled something incoherent, and he repeated the gesture.

"Do you want to go down to the beach?" he whispered.

"Now?" I groggily responded.

"Yes, now. Everyone went to bed," he urged.

"I think I ate too much at dinner," I admitted, feeling the weight of the meal still lingering in my stomach.

I had expected Oliver to have the chef prepare something extravagant, but instead, we had enjoyed a simple yet satisfying spread of chicken kabobs, T-bone steaks, Swordfish steaks, and several side salads. I had indulged in too many marinated chicken kabobs and a hefty portion of spring dill potato salad. Even hours later, I still felt stuffed.

"Then come to the beach, and we can work it off," Oliver suggested.

"You can do the same thing here," I countered, not quite ready to leave the comfort of our bed.

I heard him sigh audibly, and the bed shifted as he got up. Opening the French doors leading to the terrace, he let in the soothing sound of the waves. A gentle breeze wafted into the air-conditioned room, bringing with it the scent of the ocean. Oliver returned to bed and nudged me onto my back, his hand slipping under my t-shirt as I kept my eyes closed, relishing the sensation.

“Get undressed,” he growled.

“Oliver, I don’t have the energy,” I whined.

“I’m not asking you to do anything. I’ll do it all.”

“You want me comatose?” I asked.

“You won’t be after I get done with you.”

I whimpered as I sat up and removed my t-shirt. Oliver tugged at my panties, and I quickly lifted my hips before they ended up in shreds as so many pairs had before. The moonlight lit the room and I saw him in partial silhouette as he removed his boxers. Now I was wide awake.

He got between my legs, spreading them with his hands. I shivered in anticipation. He held my lips open and stroked his tongue through them and I couldn’t help myself and moaned loudly.

"You taste incredible. Must be the salt water."

I groaned my approval as Oliver spread me wide and tongue fucked me. After a few minutes, he slipped two fingers inside me and sucked my clit. I was so close and clenched the sheets with my fists before I exploded. Oliver didn't let up after I came, he stopped sucking me but kept his fingers inside, plunging them in and out until I felt another orgasm building.

I gritted my teeth and tightened my core as he continued, coaxing another mind-numbing explosion until my body went limp.

"That's my girl. Do you energy now?" he chuckled.

"I doubt it. I feel weak."

Oliver climbed up my body, planting kisses along my heated skin. His flesh was damp, and he left a wet trail as he ascended to my lips.

"I love you, Ryleigh."

"I know," I murmured.

"Wow, that's mighty arrogant of you."

"It's not arrogance. It's security. I know you love me."

He latched on to my ear, while he positioned his cock at my entrance and sank into me. I was wide awake now, loving how he stretched me with his penis. I wrapped my legs around his back as he rocked into me. We came together and I was done for the night as I went limp under him. I was fading off to sleep when I heard the familiar jingle of his phone.

I woke to a refreshing ocean breeze gently blowing through the open terrace doors. Oliver was nowhere to be found, and I found myself entangled in the sheets. I pushed them aside and reached for my shirt from the floor, the sound of voices drifting in from outside. The patio was directly below us, shared with three other bedrooms on each side.

As I stood up and closed the doors, I caught a glimpse of my mother, Anders, Sadie, and Finley gathered around the table outside. Matthew was likely out walking Blackie, and I had no clue where Oliver had disappeared to. After a quick shower, I made a feeble attempt to straighten the covers on the bed before slipping into gray terry shorts and a navy polo shirt.

Downstairs, the kitchen was bustling with activity as the chef and two waitstaff members prepared breakfast, arranging silver trays with covers. Despite having overindulged at dinner the night before, I found myself feeling hungry once again. I joined my family outside.

"There she is," Anders greeted me.

“He’s in his office working.”

I frowned but said nothing as the food was placed on the serving table. I lost my appetite and went inside to find Oliver. He said he wouldn't work this weekend. He was pacing his office dressed in a pair of pressed olive shorts and a black polo shirt. A small earpiece was in his ear as he talked. I didn't make my presence known as I peered in the partially opened door.

"We need more security. I don't want Ryleigh to worry."

My stomach tightened as he mentioned my name. Were we in danger? I waited by the door, listening to his conversation which ended less than a minute later. When Oliver hung up, I pushed into the room.

"You heard?"

"Are we in some kind of trouble?"

He thought for a few seconds before he answered, "Not particularly. We're out there because of our engagement. I've set up a security detail for you when we're not together or I'm out of the office. You're to follow their instructions."

I bit my lip. "I'm not sure I'm happy with this arrangement."

"Sweetheart, I've been accommodating with many things, but I'm not backing down on this one. I want to keep you safe," Oliver insisted.

"I understand, but it's... intrusive," I countered, feeling conflicted.

"Is Vlad intrusive?" Oliver questioned.

"Vlad is intimidating," I admitted.

"That's his job," Oliver affirmed, pulling me into a comforting embrace.

I knew he was only trying to protect me, but I couldn't help feeling a sense of frustration. He released me and led me out to the patio where everyone was enjoying breakfast. Despite waking up hungry, worry now dampened my appetite. I mechanically filled my plate with scrambled eggs, bacon, and fruit salad, but barely touched any of it.

As conversation buzzed around me, I couldn't shake the heightened awareness of the security detail surrounding the house. They blended in effortlessly, dressed casually like the rest of us. Vlad maintained a watchful eye from his position near the patio, while two other men, one tall with brown hair and the other short and stocky with a shaved head, stood further down the property. The lone female security agent patrolled near the beach. I wondered if they had been there all along, and I simply hadn't noticed.

"You didn't eat much," Oliver remarked as he finished his conversation with Anders.

"Not hungry. Can I go to the beach?" I asked, feeling the need for some space.

"You can do whatever you want," Oliver replied, his tone firm.

"But you said...," I started to protest.

"You can do whatever you want," he repeated, his tone leaving no room for argument.

I pushed my chair back, drawing everyone's attention as I announced, "I'm going to the beach."

"I could go with you," Sadie offered.

"Finish breakfast. I want to go for a walk," I replied, already making my way down the wide expanse of lawn.

As I passed the female security agent, she nodded in acknowledgment. I reached the water's edge, the cold surf lapping at my feet as I walked along the beach, kicking at the sand and pausing to examine shells attached to the jetty rocks.

"Ryleigh," Oliver's voice broke through my thoughts, and I turned to see him standing a few feet away.

"What?" I replied, feeling a mix of emotions swirling inside me.

"You're upset," he observed gently.

"I'm unnerved," I admitted, feeling the weight of our newfound fame bearing down on me.

"It won't always be like this. Our engagement news will die down, and they'll find something else to report on," Oliver reassured me.

"I wish we had our island," I murmured wistfully.

"We have our island. We just need a house. I've spoken with a few contractors. I think we can have our home together by next year," Oliver said optimistically.

"How? It usually takes a year or two to build a house here, and we have bridges to transport supplies," I questioned.

"Money talks. I have contacts that will bring in supplies and extra men to build our home," Oliver explained confidently.

"I want to be alone with you without interruption. I don't want to be the focus of a news story," I confessed, feeling vulnerable.

"This is my fault. I should've prepared you. I'm sorry," Oliver apologized, his sincerity evident.

I approached him, gently stroking the light stubble on his jawline. He always tried to make things right.

"You would never be able to prepare me as I step from anonymity," I admitted.

"You weren't anonymous. That's impossible," Oliver countered.

"I was Oliver until you came along. Now I'm the girl who captured the heart of one of the most eligible bachelors in the country," I protested, feeling the weight of my newfound identity.

"You're right, you did capture my heart. I'll do anything to make you happy," Oliver vowed.

"Just love me," I whispered.

"I do love you. Please don't be upset. I hate when you're upset," Oliver pleaded.

"I'm not," I assured him, taking his hand as he led me back up the lawn.

Today wasn't a beach day; it was a pool day. Later, we sat around the pool with my family, enjoying each other's company as Blackie chased a ball into the water. The sky grew dark, and we could see bolts of lightning in the distance.

As the rain began to sprinkle down, we quickly packed up everything and sought shelter indoors. Vlad called his staff inside, and we shut the French doors just as the rain turned torrential. Inside, the chef had set out a delicious spread for lunch.

I filled my plate with leftover spring dill potato salad, cold poached salmon and endive salad. For dessert, I ate many fresh strawberries with a dollop of whipped cream. We sat around the large dining table in the kitchen while Blackie went around begging for food. It warmed my heart to see my family accepting Oliver like he was one of us.

~

I moaned loudly as Oliver sank into me in our bedroom. Sadie, Anders, Finley and Matthew were playing a rousing game of Monopoly in the sitting room while my mother sat near them reading a book from Oliver's extensive library. I was in no mood to play a game and when I yawned a few times, Oliver asked if I wanted to take a nap. I already knew we would be doing anything but.

He quickly undressed me, then himself, getting me on all fours at the edge of the bed before he thrust his thick penis inside me. Sometimes it made me scared of how much I craved this man.

"You're so wet. I barely touched you and you're soaked," he grunted.

"You don't need to touch me," I panted.

Oliver grabbed my hips, curling his fingers into my skin as he pounded me. The room was filled with the slapping of flesh and our moans along with the sound of the rain pounding the house. He pushed my hand away when I reached under to rub my clit.

"You know you can come without that."

It was true. Oliver was the only man that had ever given me a vaginal orgasm. With my other boyfriends, I needed my clit stimulated. My fiancé was very skilled in bed and knew just how to move to hit that sensitive bundle of nerves inside me. He rolled his pelvis, stroking my tissue until I was on edge. I rippled against him and he immediately stopped.

"No," I whimpered.

"Shh, it will be so much better if we come together. I'm not ready to stop."

"I need to come," I mewled.

"And you will."

He once again started to move, slowly at first then sped up, bringing me to the edge time and time again until I was practically crying for him to make me come.

"I'm close sweetheart. So close."

He gave me three more powerful thrusts and I fell apart as he filled me with his liquid heat. I moaned his name before my body grew weak and I collapsed on the bed. Oliver lay alongside me, planting kisses on my back.

He ran his hand over my damp back. "My wife."

"Fiancée," I mumbled into the pillow.

"Indulge me, please."

"It could be months, even years," I said.

"Months I can deal with, but not years. I want you to be Mrs. Fox."

I turned to my side to look at him, stroking the damp hair on his forehead.

"We don't need a piece of paper for me to be Mrs. Fox. I'm committed."

"I need it. I want to know you're mine," he said.

I cupped his cheek, meeting his gaze. "I *am* yours."

Oliver pressed his lips to mine, holding them in place until I thrust my tongue into his mouth, stroking along his.

"You taste good," Oliver whispered, his lips brushing against mine.

"What do I taste like?" I asked, curiosity piqued.

"Strawberries," he replied.

"From lunch," I clarified, chuckling softly.

"Everything on you tastes good, especially certain things," he murmured suggestively.

"Are you sure you're thirty-six? You act like you're sixteen sometimes," I teased affectionately.

"You bring out the youth in me," Oliver confessed, his eyes sparkling with adoration.

"You are young. You think thirty-six is old?" I challenged playfully.

"No, but compared to you it is," he countered.

"It's not. Promise me you'll live until you're one hundred," I requested, half-jokingly.

"I promise, and in the interim, I want to give you the world," Oliver vowed sincerely.

"I think I'd like to get married at Hotel SW," I declared, suddenly feeling a surge of excitement.

Oliver's face lit up with enthusiasm. "You would? I can arrange it very quickly. I've dealt with Sebastian Wyatt before."

"The singer?" I questioned, recalling the name from somewhere.

"No, the father of the singer," Oliver clarified. "He's amassed quite an empire outside of the Wyatt brand. I've worked with him on a couple of real estate projects. I'm sure he could get us into one of his rooms at the hotel in midtown."

"I don't want just any room. I want the garden room," I insisted firmly.

"Why?" Oliver inquired, curious about my choice.

"Because I love the windows and the ceiling," I explained, my mind already envisioning the beauty of the garden room at Hotel SW. With its stained glass windows and partial glass roof, it was a truly stunning setting that overlooked the Hudson River.

"I'd have to pull some favors to get in there," Oliver admitted, his expression thoughtful.

"Please?" I pleaded, my heart set on the idea.

I had always dreamed of having my wedding in The Garden Room ever since we attended a function there several years ago. The size of the room and the breathtaking views had left a lasting impression on me.

"I'll call Sebastian on Monday," Oliver relented.

"Thank you," I said gratefully.

"What date would you like?" Oliver inquired.

"Late spring or early summer. I love that time of year," I replied, envisioning a romantic outdoor ceremony.

Oliver's face tightened slightly. "But that's so far away."

"It's not. It's less than a year, and I'll need time to figure everything out," I explained, hoping he would understand.

"Hire a wedding planner. You have carte blanche to do whatever you want. I don't care about the expense," Oliver offered generously.

"What about our honeymoon?" I asked, excitement bubbling up inside me.

"If you want to wait that long, maybe our island home will be finished by then," Oliver said, a hint of anticipation in his voice.

"A whole week on a private island? That sounds wonderful," I exclaimed, imagining the bliss of being away from it all.

"Not just a week. At least two weeks," Oliver corrected with a smirk.

"Two weeks away from civilization. That sounds delicious," I mused, feeling a wave of contentment wash over me.

Oliver pressed his lips to my shoulder, murmuring, "You're delicious."

I rolled my eyes and couldn't help but giggle. "You're so sappy sometimes."

"It's because I'm in love with you. You'll never see this side of me in the office," Oliver admitted, his tone softening.

"I'm sure. You're all business when you're there," I agreed, knowing firsthand how driven he was.

"I have to be. There's plenty of competition," he said.

"Like who?" I asked, wondering about his rivals in the business world.

“Several around the city, Jordan Grayson, Jonathan Lawson, Sebastian Wyatt just to name a few.”

I wrinkled my nose. “Sebastian Wyatt is from Boston.”

He smoothed my hair. “But he holds many interests in New York and the surrounding area. They are friends personally but foes in business.”

“You know them all? Who else do you know?”

“Zane Butler and Katherine Argento in the software space.”

My eyes widened. “I love Katherine Argento. Did you know she sold her share of One on One for half a billion dollars?”

“It wasn’t by choice, but it gave her the ability to start another company.”

“By choice?”

“She was forced out regardless of what you read in the papers. It reminds us all to keep our eyes open. I have another business acquaintance that didn’t and he lost it all. He owns another company that sells collapsible sporting goods like packable kayaks and paddles.”

“Who?”

“Killian O’Rourke. Do you know him?” Oliver asked.

I shrugged. “Not really.

“You might know his wife Victoria better. She built a large business consulting firm.”

“I vaguely remember reading an article about her a couple of years back.”

“Killian took his eyes off his business and his vice president torpedoed the whole thing. It’s why I work so hard. It’s why I want you to be my second pair of eyes. My company is growing, and I can’t keep my eyes on everything. If I have my wife with me, she can help,” he said with conviction.

“I plan on it. “

Oliver pushed me to my back and took my right nipple in his mouth. I hoped it would always be this way between us.

When Sunday rolled around, I felt a pang of sadness at the thought of leaving. Oliver reassured me that we would invite everyone to Southampton again and that the house would always be available for my family to use.

We departed shortly before three, leaving the staff to tidy up the house for the next guests. I leaned against Oliver's shoulder in the car, attempting to nap and make up for the sleep I had missed the night before. Upon arriving home, I felt utterly lazy and watched as Oliver unpacked my suitcase despite my protests.

"How do you have so much energy?" I marveled.

"I'm used to little sleep," Oliver replied casually.

"Even before me?" I asked, surprised.

"Absolutely. My schedule has been somewhat disrupted by you, but I can still function quite well," he explained.

I scowled playfully. "Disrupted?"

"Distracted, upset, whatever word you want to insert," he clarified with a grin.

I couldn't help but giggle at his choice of words. "Insert?"

"Ryleigh, you like to act so innocent sometimes, but I know otherwise," Oliver teased.

"Why don't you come and see just how innocent I am?" I suggested flirtatiously.

"I have work to do," Oliver replied, trying to sound serious despite the twinkle in his eyes.

"Will this convince you?" I asked, removing my t-shirt and opening my bra.

"You're such a tease," Oliver chuckled.

"I'll lie here like this until you make a move," I teased, enjoying the banter.

With a grin, Oliver dove onto the bed, and unpacking our suitcases was quickly forgotten as we surrendered to each other's embrace.

Chapter 19

I'm nervous as hell. Oliver's friends are meeting us at a steakhouse in midtown. I've never met them before, and I wondered what they'll think of me. I worry they'll question our age difference or think I'm a gold digger trying to get my hands on Oliver's millions.

I glanced at myself in the mirror, smoothing down the fabric of my royal blue dress with the modest scoop neck. I had opted for a somewhat conservative look compared to my usual style. As I applied mascara, Oliver emerged from the closet, impeccably dressed in a navy-blue suit, complemented by a blue shirt and a light yellow tie. He looked stunning, as always.

"You're beautiful," Oliver said, his gaze lingering on me in the mirror.

"I hope your friends will like me," I confessed, feeling a flutter of nerves.

“What's not to like? They'll love you. If they don't, I'm kicking them out of the wedding party," Oliver reassured me with a grin.

"You're asking them to be in the wedding party?" I asked, surprised.

"Of course. They're my closest friends," Oliver explained. "You never told me who your bridesmaids would be."

"Sadie will be my maid of honor. Most of my friends are scattered around the country, but I have some from Westchester that you haven't met," I replied, recalling the limited number of close friends I had.

"I'd like to meet them. You never talk about them," Oliver noted, genuine curiosity in his voice.

"We grew apart during college. Isn't that what always happens? I think people felt sorry for me because of my father. I didn't have a lot of friends in middle school because I was the weird quiet kid," I admitted, reflecting on my past.

"If they could see you now," Oliver murmured, standing behind me and straightening his tie in the mirror.

Before I knew it, his hands were sliding up to cup my breasts, and I gently pushed him away.

"Not now," I protested with a laugh.

"Party pooper," Oliver teased, pouting playfully.

"We have to leave in fifteen minutes. If you get me

started, you know we'll be late—very late," I warned, trying to maintain a sense of urgency.

Oliver was making up for lost time since we returned from our trip. Despite having some work to catch up on, he devoted plenty of time to me, and I was grateful for his attention considering how busy he was.

"I should have started earlier," Oliver complained.

"You were working in your office until an hour ago. What's got you so busy? I thought you caught up on everything this week," I asked, glancing at him in the mirror as I fluffed my hair and applied lip gloss.

"The house we're building. All the electrical, plumbing, and other utilities need to be figured out before we can build anything. It takes time and planning," Oliver said.

"You never said where your island is in the Caribbean," I remarked, curious about the location of our future home.

"The US Virgin Islands. It's beautiful with almost seven hundred acres of land," Oliver replied, a hint of excitement in his voice.

"Does it have any waterfalls?" I inquired, picturing idyllic scenes in my mind.

"A few. You'll love it," Oliver assured me with a smile.

As Oliver's phone vibrated in his pocket, he excused himself to take the call. I overheard snippets of his conversation about security, and I couldn't help but feel a twinge of unease. Despite trying to make themselves as inconspicuous as possible, having four security agents around still felt unnerving.

"Ready to go?" Oliver called from the doorway.

"One minute," I replied, adding the final touches to my makeup.

"Stop fussing. You're gorgeous, and they will be jealous when they see you," Oliver reassured me, his voice filled with admiration.

"Oh, so that's all I am to you? A pretty face?" I teased, pretending to be offended.

"Not at all. You're my love, my partner, and my future wife," Oliver replied earnestly, his eyes softening with affection.

With a smile, I finished touching up my lip gloss and followed Oliver to the foyer, where he helped me into my long black coat. The evening air had turned unseasonably cool for the end of September, prompting me to button up the front before grabbing my black clutch.

Vlad was waiting for us downstairs with the black sedan, and as we drove to the restaurant, Oliver nuzzled my neck, inhaling my perfume. I couldn't help but blush, knowing that he was already priming me for the evening ahead.

"Stop it," I laughed, swatting his arm playfully.

I put the finishing touches with some lip gloss and followed Oliver out to the foyer where he helped me put on my long black coat. The evenings had grown unseasonably cool for the end of September. I buttoned up the front, grabbed my black clutch and we walked out the door.

Vlad was waiting for us downstairs with the black sedan. Oliver nuzzled my neck, inhaling my perfume as we drove to the restaurant. He was getting me primed for later this evening.

“Stop it,” I demanded.

“What?” he asked.

I snorted. “You know what. Why do you do this when we have no opportunity?”

“I’m showing my love. I can’t help it if it gets you hot,” he replied huskily.

“I bet you don’t.”

“Brat.”

“Keep your hands and lips to yourself until we’re on our way home.”

“Hmm, maybe I should’ve asked Vlad to bring the limo,” he whispered.

I felt my face grow hot from embarrassment. We did

some very naughty things in the limo over the past few weeks.

“You’re killing me here.”

Oliver gave me one last kiss on the cheek before he fired up his phone to check some work emails. I looked out the window as we passed through the city streets. We arrived at Kimo Steakhouse in midtown just before six. My stomach started to churn with anticipation.

“Don’t be nervous.”

“I’m fine.”

Vlad pulled up in front of the restaurant and stepped out to open the door for us. Oliver exchanged a few words with him before assisting me out of the car. As we entered the restaurant, a raven-haired waitress in five-inch heels and a form-fitting black dress greeted us and led us to a table at the back. Three men were already seated there, and they stood up as we approached.

"Gentlemen, may I present my fiancée, Ryleigh Stewart," Oliver introduced me with pride.

The first to offer his hand was Ivan Persky, his slight Russian accent adding intrigue to his rugged appearance. He had a scar under his left dark brown eye and short-cropped black hair, neatly styled. I noticed his slightly crooked front teeth and was surprised that a hockey player like him had any teeth left.

Next was Dax Adderly, a tall, almost lanky man with a charming smile and twinkling blue eyes. Instead of shaking my hand, he pulled me into a tight hug, earning a disapproving look from Oliver which made him quickly release me.

Finally, there was Wilmer Hermann, broad-shouldered and bald as a cue ball, with piercing ice-blue eyes. He shook my hand firmly, placing his other hand over mine in a friendly gesture. I instantly warmed to all three men, who were dressed more casually than Oliver in sport jackets, jeans, and dress shirts.

"Wow, you really scored with this one," Dax commented, causing my cheeks to flush with embarrassment.

"Seriously, Dax? Don't be a jerk," Ivan chided him.

"What? She's beautiful," Dax defended himself.

I felt Oliver's reassuring squeeze as he pulled out a chair for me to sit down. Once I was seated, all four men took their places as the waitress arrived to take our drink orders.

"I'll have a glass of red wine, please," I requested.

"Which one?" the waitress inquired.

Feeling a bit unsure, I looked to Oliver for guidance.

"Please bring a bottle of Merlot for the table," Oliver instructed, indicating his choice.

"Thank you," I said gratefully as the waitress left. Oliver's hand found mine under the table, giving it a gentle squeeze, and I smiled appreciatively at him.

“Thank you,” I said after the waitress left. Oliver reached under the table to squeeze my knee.

Dinner was pleasant and my stomach loosened as I was engaged in conversation by all four men. After a meal of filet mignon, sautéed asparagus and fingerling potatoes, a delicious chocolate soufflé was served for dessert. I was full as I sipped my third glass of wine.

We said our goodbyes at the curb, and I felt like I had gained three new friends in Dax, Wilmer and Ivan. On the way home, Oliver turned to me.

“You were a hit,” Oliver said.

I nodded. “They seemed to like me.”

He smiled. “They loved you. Wilmer said you’re perfect for me.”

“Am I?” I asked.

“I think so. No, I know so. Don’t be so hard on yourself.”

I grasped his hand. “I wanted to make a good impression.”

“You did. They all said you were intelligent and classy.”

I furrowed my eyebrows. “When? I didn’t hear them say that.”

“They weren’t going to embarrass you by saying it in your presence. They told me when you went to the restroom. Now stop doubting yourself.”

He kissed me hard on the lips, sliding his hand up my leg and under the hem of my dress. He pressed his fingers against the panel of my black lace panties, stroking my clit.

“Vlad,” I mumbled.

“Then be quiet,” he whispered.

I shook my head, trying to pull his hand away but he already had me heated with just a few pets.

“Shh.”

I clung to his forearm with both hands, afraid that he would pull away at the pivotal moment when my orgasm was balancing on the edge, he didn’t. I softly moaned then cleared my throat to hide my impending orgasm. When it hit, sending waves of delicious pleasure coursing through my body, I bit my lip to keep quiet.

Oliver pulled his hand away and I could see him smiling as we passed by streetlights that illuminated his face. I leaned back against the seat to catch my breath a few minutes before we pulled up to his building.

“Can you walk,” he said with a smirk.

“Yes, I can walk.”

“Well usually....”

“Shut up,” I growled.

Upstairs, I quickly changed into my pajamas, washed my face, brushed my teeth, and then snuggled under the covers, eagerly awaiting Oliver's arrival. He slipped into bed beside me a few minutes later, and I immediately buried my face against his smooth, bare chest.

"That wasn't very nice what you did in the car," I chided.

"But you liked it, didn't you?" he teased in response.

"I made noise. What would Vlad think?" I retorted, half-serious.

"He wouldn't think anything. It's not his job to question what I do with my fiancée," Oliver reassured me.

"Well, in the future, if you want to seduce me in the car, please take the limo so we can have privacy," I said.

"I'll keep that in mind," Oliver replied, his tone suggestive.

Feeling mischievous, I gently bit into his nipple, swirling my tongue around the peaked flesh. His response was immediate.

"Are you interested in some extracurricular activities tonight?" he asked, his voice thick with desire.

"You know I am," I replied eagerly.

"Good, because that dessert wasn't as sweet as you," he whispered huskily.

I groaned in anticipation, knowing full well that Oliver planned to pleasure me with his tongue. He seemed to enjoy it even more than intercourse itself. As he slipped under the covers, I prepared myself for the intense sensations to come.

The rain continued its steady rhythm outside as I awoke to the dim light filtering through the window. Oliver was nowhere to be seen beside me, likely already immersed in his morning routine of work or exercise. I slipped into the blue dress shirt he had worn the night before and set out to find him.

Down the hall, I discovered Oliver engrossed in a phone call, his voice filled with intensity as he discussed security matters. I hesitated in the doorway, eavesdropping on his conversation. He mentioned my name several times, sparking a gnawing worry within me. As he finished the call and emerged from his office, I quickly retreated, hoping he hadn't noticed my presence.

"You're up?" Oliver greeted me as I stepped back into the hallway.

"I just woke up," I replied, trying to appear nonchalant.

"Nice outfit. I like when you wear my clothes," he remarked, his tone warm.

"This shirt smells good," I commented, attempting to divert his attention.

"Does it?" he chuckled softly. "I like anything that smells like you."

"And I love anything that smells like you," I returned, seeking solace in his embrace.

As Oliver enveloped me in his arms, showering me with affectionate kisses, I felt a surge of determination to address the lingering unease.

"My friends from home are coming to the city next weekend. I want to go out with them," I broached the topic tentatively.

"Why don't you invite them here?" Oliver suggested, ever the pragmatic one.

"They don't come to the city often. I want to do a pub crawl or maybe hit a dance club," I explained.

"Why don't I go with you?" he proposed, his protective instincts kicking in.

"I can't go by myself?" I countered, a flicker of independence surfacing.

"Sure you can, but you take security," he insisted, his tone firm.

"Vlad?" I inquired, already anticipating his answer.

"And Brenda. Maybe Trevor too," Oliver confirmed, leaving no room for negotiation.

"Why so much security? Do you know something?" I probed, feeling a knot tighten in my stomach.

Oliver drew in a deep breath, his expression grave. "Yes. There's been a threat."

My heart skipped a beat. "To me?" I squeaked, barely able to comprehend the gravity of his words.

"Yes. We're trying to figure out if it's credible," he admitted, his voice tinged with concern.

I stared at him in shock, the implications sinking in. "What kind of threat?" I whispered, my voice trembling with apprehension.

"Bodily harm. And I won't take the chance of losing you by letting you gallivant around without security," he declared resolutely, his unwavering commitment to my safety evident in his words.

Oliver held me close as tears streamed down my cheeks, his comforting embrace offering solace in the midst of my fear.

"Don't cry. You're safe with me," he reassured me, his voice a soothing balm to my troubled mind.

"I don't feel safe. Am I going to be trapped in here or at work because I might be injured?" I choked out between sobs, the weight of uncertainty bearing down on me.

"Look, threats like this happen all the time to people in the public eye. You think I worry every time my security team finds something? I can't afford to waste time. I pay them to handle it and they do. I don't want you to stifle your activities because of an unsubstantiated threat," Oliver said, his tone firm yet understanding.

"We're going to California next week. Will we be safe?" I pressed, seeking reassurance amid the tumult of emotions.

"Very. The entire team will be with us, and we're flying on the Fox jet," he assured me, his words instilling a glimmer of hope.

"I don't like this," I admitted, my voice trembling with vulnerability.

"I'll be with you the entire trip," Oliver promised, his unwavering commitment to my well-being shining through.

With a tender kiss to the top of my head, he guided me into the bathroom, where we shared a shower, the warm water washing away both our fears and uncertainties, if only for a fleeting moment.

~

"Are you comfortable?" Oliver asked as we settled into our seats aboard the luxurious Fox Asset Corporation jet.

"Yes, this plane is beautiful," I replied, taking in the opulent surroundings.

We were strapped into wide tan leather seats, the larger of the two jets owned by Fox Asset Corporation, awaiting takeoff. It was just before 8 am, and our flight to Los Angeles was expected to arrive by 11 am. However, I had spent most of the night tossing and turning from anxiety.

My conversation with Oliver had left me feeling uneasy, and I couldn't shake the nervous energy that had consumed me. I had barely slept, and the thought of facing a day full of meetings and responsibilities made my stomach churn.

Henri startled me when he knocked on my office door to inform me that Oliver had requested my presence on a conference call. The apprehension only intensified as the day progressed, leaving me restless and unable to focus on anything but my mounting worries.

"It's only two years old. I had it built to my specifications. Once we get off the ground, you can go to sleep in the bedroom," he said, attempting to ease my discomfort.

"Why would I want to go to sleep? I just woke up a few hours ago," I protested, though the fatigue was beginning to weigh heavily on me.

"Come on, Ryleigh. I know you didn't sleep the past two nights," Oliver insisted, his concern evident in his voice.

"One was your fault," I retorted, unable to hide the frustration that simmered beneath the surface.

"And the other was because you're worried. Don't be," Oliver reassured me, his words offering a small measure of comfort.

"You were awake?" I asked, surprised by his admission.

"A few times. You settled down, so I went back to sleep. If you keep this up, you're going to have a nightmare.

You know how you get when you're stressed," his tone gentle yet firm.

I nodded, feeling a pang of guilt for burdening him with my anxieties. As the plane began to taxi down the runway, Oliver rose from his seat and held out his hand.

"Come, let's get you settled in bed," his concern evident in his eyes.

"I'm fine," I insisted stubbornly, though the fatigue threatened to overwhelm me.

"You're not fine. Let's go," Oliver persisted, his hand outstretched.

Reluctantly, I placed my hand in his, allowing him to lead me to the back of the plane where a small bedroom awaited. Our security detail nodded in acknowledgment as we passed, their presence offering a sense of reassurance in the midst of my unease.

Once inside the bedroom, Oliver gently guided me onto the king-sized bed, his touch comforting as exhaustion washed over me. Despite my protests, I found myself succumbing to sleep, the soft mattress cradling me as Oliver lay beside me, his presence a source of comfort in the darkness.

Hours later, I awoke to the sensation of soft kisses against my neck and face, Oliver's warm embrace chasing away the remnants of my troubled dreams.

“Are you comfortable?”

“What time is it?” I asked, glancing around the cabin.

“New York or Los Angeles time?” Oliver responded with a raised eyebrow.

“Where are we closer?” I inquired, still a bit disoriented.

“Los Angeles. We should be landing in twenty minutes. Would you like to freshen up before you buckle yourself into your seat?” he suggested kindly.

“Yes. Thank you,” I replied, feeling grateful.

“For what?” Oliver asked.

“Making me take a nap,” I said with a smile.

Oliver chuckled. “You took an almost six-hour nap. You were tired.”

“I have to admit, I was,” I conceded.

“How do you feel now?” he asked, his concern evident.

“Good, I slept well. Did you stay with me the whole time?” I questioned, feeling a surge of affection.

He nodded. “Yes. After you fell asleep, I did some work on my laptop,” he said.

“So you didn’t sleep at all?” I asked, feeling a bit guilty.

“I didn’t need to. Now freshen up and I’ll meet you up front,” Oliver replied with a reassuring smile.

He kissed my forehead before giving me a gentle push toward the bathroom.

“It’s very nice out here. Maybe we can go swimming at the pool?” I asked, looking out from our suite’s private terrace.

We had just arrived at Hotel SW Los Angeles. Oliver had booked a large suite with a full bedroom and a private terrace. Below, I could see the large swimming pool, which looked incredibly inviting.

“We’re not here to vacation; we’re here to work,” Oliver reminded me, his tone firm but not unkind.

“We won’t have any leisure time?” I asked, feeling a bit disappointed.

“We might have a little, but I have several meetings scheduled,” he explained.

“Okay. Any chance to learn,” I said, trying to stay positive.

“You’ll learn plenty. I have meetings with a few real estate developers. We might be partnering with them for some projects,” he informed me.

“What kind of projects?” I asked, genuinely curious.

“Upscale residences paired with office buildings. They’ll have plenty of amenities and a large park in the middle,” he said.

“Sounds nice,” I remarked, imagining the plans.

"We're at the planning stages. On Thursday, I have a meeting in Big Bear about the possible purchase of a ski resort," Oliver added.

I raised an eyebrow. "Skiing?"

"Have you ever been?" he asked.

I shook my head. "Not my thing. I tried and I sucked," I admitted.

"I can teach you," he offered with a smile.

"You never told me you could ski," I said, surprised.

"I can also snowboard and ice skate," Oliver revealed casually.

"What else can you do? Do you surf or climb mountains?" I teased.

"I've never tried either. I do hike and canoe," he replied.

"A real outdoorsman," I remarked, impressed.

"I enjoy outdoor activities," he said with a shrug.

"Camping?" I asked.

"When I was young. I used to hang out with Wilmer and Dax during vacations. We would hike and camp for several days," he reminisced.

"Before you owned your empire?" I asked, imagining him in a different life.

“I was building my empire at the time. It was nice to get away for a break,” he said.

“I’m not much for camping. The last time I went, I burned my mouth on a s'more and fell into a pricker bush,” I confessed, laughing at the memory.

“How did you manage that?” Oliver asked, laughing with me.

“Peeing in the dark.”

Oliver raised his eyebrows. “Are you saying a certain part of you got prickers in it?”

I chuckled. “No. I stumbled after I pulled my pants up. My tender parts were protected by my jeans.”

“I can get you in shape for the wilderness?” he asked.

I grinned. “My hero. What are we doing for the afternoon?”

“I’d like to go over the proposals I prepared for the development meeting. I want you to be familiarized with the project.”

“Fine. Can I change first?” I asked.

“Be my guest.”

I unzipped the suitcase the bellhop had stacked on the bench at the end of the bed, pulling out my favorite pair of frayed jean shorts and a light blue tank top. Oliver watched me from the corner of his eye as I removed my dress. He stopped reading over his report when I was down to my lavender bra and panties.

He sighed loudly. “I love that color on you.”

I quirked an eyebrow. “Don’t you have work to do?”

“I can take a break.”

“Aren’t you getting changed?”

Oliver wore a full suit, dress shirt and tie on the plane but had only removed his jacket.

He leaned back in his chair. “In a minute. I rather like the view.”

I laughed. “You’re hopeless.”

“Hopelessly in love,” he murmured.

I dressed and when I was finished, Oliver changed. Just for good measure, I gazed at him as he stripped down to his boxers. The muscles in his back and arms rippled as he dug through his suitcase to select a pair of shorts and a polo shirt. A few minutes later, he was back at the dining table, and I was beside him.

Chapter 20

We worked all day, and by the time we took a break for dinner, my head was spinning with information. We had skipped lunch but munched on the complimentary fruit and snack basket provided by the hotel.

"I need to take a shower," I announced, feeling the grime of the day.

"Now? I thought we would eat dinner first," Oliver said, looking a bit surprised.

"I feel yucky," I admitted.

Oliver smirked. "What exactly does yucky feel like?"

"If you must know, I got my period this morning," I replied bluntly.

"Oh," he responded, caught off guard.

"Is that all you can say?" I asked, raising an eyebrow.

"No, this isn't my first time dealing with your period," he said with a reassuring smile.

"So, I want to take a shower," I insisted.

"Pick something for dinner and I'll call it in while you're taking one. We can eat when you come out," he offered, handing me the tablet with the menu.

I searched through it, craving everything salty, fatty, and sugary thanks to my period. "I'll have a cheeseburger, fries, and chocolate-covered strawberries," I decided.

"Is that it?" he asked.

"And a chocolate milkshake," I added.

"Wow, you really are piling on the chocolate," Oliver noted, amused.

"I have my period. Just wait until I'm pregnant," I joked.

"Go shower, I'll call it in," he said, laughing.

I went to the bathroom, which was pristine and full of glass and white tiles. The shower stall was as big as a small bedroom, with three shower heads and two large, tiled benches. Complimentary bath products were provided. I turned on the water, examining the shampoo while I waited for it to warm up.

Just as I began lathering my hair, Oliver came in. He came up behind me and cupped my breasts. They were slightly sore from my hormones, but I loved when he rubbed them at this time of the month.

"What about dinner?" I asked huskily.

"Already ordered. It won't be here for forty-five minutes," Oliver replied with a sly smile.

"And you thought you would come in here to cause some trouble?" I teased.

"I can't have you in our bed, so I want you here," he said, his voice deep with desire.

Oliver helped me rinse the shampoo out of my hair, then pushed my back against the wall, pressing his body against mine as he claimed my mouth. I felt his hardness and reached down to stroke him.

"I want to fuck you," he whispered, his voice full of urgency.

"Yes," I murmured, my body already responding to his touch.

Oliver easily lifted me against the wall, positioning his cock at my entrance before letting gravity do the work. I let out a soft moan as he entered me. This was my most sensitive time of the month, and I loved getting fucked. He hammered at me, tucking his head into the crook of my neck. A scream was poised at my throat as he drove me to a quick orgasm.

Once he felt me squeeze him, he sped up his pace until he spilled into me with several grunts of my name. When we finished, he held me in his arms, planting kisses on my neck and face.

“You’re incredible,” he whispered, his breath warm against my skin.

“Are you just saying that because we just had sex?” I asked, smiling.

“I’ll say it anytime you want,” he replied, his eyes full of genuine affection.

A half-hour later, we were sitting at the rectangular dining table. Oliver's folders and laptop were neatly stacked at one end while we ate at the other. We were both dressed in the complimentary white terry robes provided by the hotel, with "Hotel SW Los Angeles" embroidered in black script over the left breast.

I dipped a French fry in my chocolate shake and stuck it into my mouth. It was a habit I picked up as a child and never grew out of.

“You’re really enjoying that shake, aren’t you?” Oliver asked, amused.

“I am. Let me enjoy all the fat, salt, and sugar I want for the next few days,” I replied, savoring the indulgence.

“I wish you would work out with me,” he said, eyeing my fry-shake combo.

"You said you didn't want me near Bronson," I reminded him.

"Not with Bronson. We can work out in my building's gym. Have you thought about moving in with me?" he asked casually.

"I'm considering it. Sadie has been spending so much time with Finley, I think we should end our lease. No one is there," I admitted.

"Do you think it's for real between them?" Oliver asked, sounding genuinely curious.

"Maybe," I replied thoughtfully.

"You haven't mentioned Ty for a couple of weeks. How is he?" he inquired, his tone gentle.

"I called him, but he never got back to me. Frankly, I'm afraid of what he has to say about my father's case," I confessed, feeling a knot of anxiety tighten.

"Do you want me to talk to him?" Oliver offered.

I shrugged. "And what would you say?" I asked, raising an eyebrow.

"I'd tell him to leave you alone," he said, a protective edge in his voice.

"That won't help solve my father's murder," I pointed out.

"I know, but every time you talk to him, you have nightmares," he said softly.

"Ty is my friend," I reminded him.

"I'm only looking out for your best interest," Oliver said, reaching across the table to take my hand.

"I know," I replied, squeezing his hand gently.

I took a big bite of my burger, and juice dribbled down my chin. Oliver reached over with his napkin to wipe it off.

"Thank you," I said, smiling.

"I like you messy. Maybe we can play with some body paints when we get home," he suggested with a mischievous grin.

"Body paints?" I asked, intrigued.

"Edible paints. We can draw and lick them off each other," he explained.

"Sounds like fun," I admitted, laughing.

"Anything I lick off you would be fun," he said with a wink.

"Is sex all you think about?" I teased.

"That's not sex, it's art," Oliver defended with a smirk.

"Painting me is art?" I asked, rolling my eyes.

"You're already a work of art. Paint would just enhance your beauty," he said, his eyes full of admiration.

I rolled my eyes again and took another bite of my burger while Oliver finished his grilled cheese and onion rings. We spent the rest of the night going over more reports, watching television, and snuggling. I fell asleep in my bathrobe and felt Oliver lift me to slip me under the covers.

It was still dark when I woke, the bedside clock illuminating the time of 1:08 am in soft blue numerals. I heard Oliver talking in another room. When I tried to concentrate on what he was saying, I fell back asleep.

Oliver

"I don't care about your bullshit. If you threaten my fiancée again, I'll kill you with my bare hands," I seethed into the phone.

"I'm trying to help you, Oliver. I have no control over this situation," Jonah insisted.

"You're trying to extort money from me," I accused him.

"I'm trying to protect you," he pleaded.

"Who is this man?" I demanded.

"Someone from Ryleigh's past," Jonah admitted reluctantly.

"Who?" I pressed.

"I can't tell you that. If I reveal who it is, we're all dead," he warned.

"Does this have anything to do with her father's death?" I questioned, my voice trembling with anger and fear.

"Yes, and that's as much as I can say. I just need enough money to hide. You have security and can protect her, but me they'll kill," Jonah explained urgently.

"Why should I believe anything you have to say?" I spat out.

"Because I'm your brother," he reminded me.

I ran a hand through my hair, nauseated by the fact that someone was after my fiancée.

"You're a fuck up. I tried to help you, tried to tear you away from the illegal life you lead. Now you want to come and destroy my happiness?" I accused him bitterly.

"Without me around, he won't have a link to you," Jonah reasoned.

"I want to know who it is," I demanded.

"I can't tell you, and it's better you don't know," he insisted.

"She's all I care about," I confessed, feeling helpless.

"Oliver, I wish things were different," Jonah said sadly.

"But they're not. Where can I reach you?" I asked, resigned.

"I'll call you soon. How much time do you need?" Jonah inquired.

“Give me a few days to consider your request,” I replied before hanging up.

I sank onto the sofa, the weight of Jonah’s revelation settling heavily on my shoulders. Ryleigh’s past was coming back to haunt her, and I couldn’t bear the thought of losing her. I grabbed a pad and pen from the dining table, preferring the comfort of the written word over electronic devices.

As I scribbled out a plan to protect Ryleigh and apprehend her father’s killer, my stomach churned with anxiety. Keeping the truth from her would be difficult, but I had to do whatever it took to keep her safe. I didn’t know if my plan would work, but I had to try. The alternative was too terrifying to contemplate—losing the love of my life.

To Be Continued - Check out an excerpt from When He Was Mine - Book 2 of The Sly Fox Series and click here to purchase

I was involved in our act of love but movement by the now slightly opened door caught my eye. I looked and saw Lara watching us, her face was stoic and I smiled just before I closed my eyes as I came. When I looked again, she was gone and the door was once again closed.

After I came, Oliver moved me onto my knees and pounded me until he came with a loud grunt. He gently moved for a couple of minutes until he grew semi hard and pulled out, joining me on the bed where I collapsed. He stroked my hair as we heard horns blowing and people cheering. I checked his watch to see it was a few seconds after midnight.

"Happy New Year," I said.

"Happy New Year," Oliver echoed before he placed a firm kiss on my lips.

We went downstairs fifteen minutes later and the party was still in full swing. Oliver kept his arm around me as we floated from one group of people to the next. Everyone was polite and even engaged me in conversation. I was in a great mood, my body full of champagne and endorphins. I didn't think anything could ruin my high, until I once again encountered Lara on the way to the bathroom. There were few people in the hallway since Wilmer had the caterers place out trays of hot food.

"That's the only way you might keep him."

I whirled around with my hand poised on the door handle.

"Excuse me?"

"To fuck him. Oliver likes sex and as long as you give it to him, he'll keep sniffing around. Once you cut him off, it's over."

"What the hell do you know about our relationship?"

"I've known Oliver for years. He's like a dog in heat. You should think about what will happen when you get pregnant. He'll lose interest. I know."

My stomach started to roil, "How do you know?"

"Why don't you ask him?"

"Why don't you tell me yourself?"

"I'm not helping you."

She turned and walked away. I watched her round the corner and sagged against the door. I no longer wanted to spend any more time here. I forgot the bathroom and went to find Oliver. When I did, he was engaged in a conversation with Ivan and another man with a shaved head and long platinum dyed goatee.

"I'd like to go home, I'm tired."

"Sure. Give me a few minutes."

"Now Oliver."

I turned before he could answer and walked toward the foyer where our coats were. Oliver followed and gently grabbed my elbow.

"What happened in the last fifteen minutes?"

"I don't want to discuss this here," I hissed.

"Ryleigh, talk to me."

I looked around for a room to duck into, noticing a pair of French doors. I grabbed Oliver's hand and pulled him inside. I felt around for a light switch and found one near the door. The room was furnished with dark leather couches and walls of bookcases, some of them empty.

"What happened?"

"Lara."

He gritted his teeth, "What did that vapid bitch say to you?"

"She said as long as we kept having sex, you would stay interested in me. And that once I got pregnant, it was over. Why would she say that?"

Oliver's face tightened and he began chewing on the corner of his lip, "I have no idea."

"What occurred between you two?"

"We had sex and that was it. Even with it I lost interest. We weren't dating, just fucking. I told you this before."

"Then how would she know you would lose interest if I got pregnant? Did you get her pregnant?"

"No, of course not. You know how careful I am."

"Then why?"

"I have no idea why she would say that. She's trying to get under your skin and it's working."

I pinched the bridge of my nose and closed my eyes. It was the start of a new year and I was already fucking up. But Lara had me curious. What did she know about my soon to be husband that I did not?

"I'm sorry. Can we just go home?"

"Yes. I'd like to spend some time alone with you."

Oliver led me to get our coats, handing the attendant the ticket he was given at the beginning of the night.

"Aren't you saying goodbye to your friends?"

"It's not necessary. Wilmer is surrounded by a few ladies and I'm sure he won't miss us."

Vlad came to pick up a few minutes later which made me wonder where he was. It seemed that he never had time off.